THE TAVISTOCK PLOT

TRACY GRANT

The Tavistock Plot

Ebook ISBN: 9781641971416
KDP POD ISBN: 9798645374266

NYLA Publishing
121 W 27th St., Suite 1201, New York, NY 10001
http://www.nyliterary.com

For Robert Sicular, a wonderful actor and friend, with thanks for inspiration onstage and off

ACKNOWLEDGMENTS

This book was finished during the shelter-in-place for the COVID-19 pandemic. As we all cope with this unprecedented situation, I am more grateful than ever for all the people who support my writing and the Rannochs' world in so many ways. As always, huge thanks to my wonderful agent, Nancy Yost, for her support and insights. Thanks to Natanya Wheeler for once again working her magic to create a truly amazing cover that captures Mélanie Rannoch and the world of the Tavistock, and for shepherding the book expertly through the publication process, to Sarah Younger for superlative social media support and for helping the book along through production and publication, and to the entire team at Nancy Yost Literary Agency for their fabulous work. Malcolm, Mélanie, and I are all very fortunate to have their support.

Thanks to Eve Lynch for the meticulous and thoughtful copyediting, and to Jayne Davis for answering extra grammar questions.

Thank you to Kristen Loken for a magical author photo taken in one of my favorite places, San Francisco's War Memorial Opera House, on one of my favorite occasions of the year, the Merola Grand Finale. Your brilliance never fails to amaze me, Kristen!

I am very fortunate to have a wonderful group of writer friends near and far who make being a writer less solitary. Thanks to Veronica Wolff and Lauren Willig, who both understand the challenges of being a writer and a mom. To Penelope Williamson, for sharing adventures, analyzing plots from Shakespeare to *Scandal*, and being a wonderful honorary aunt to my daughter. To Jami Alden, Tasha Alexander, Bella Andre, Allison Brennan, Josie Brown, Isobel Carr, Catherine Coulter, Deborah Coonts, Deborah Crombie, Carol Culver/Grace, Catherine Duthie, Alexandra Elliott, J.T. Ellison, Barbara Freethy, C.S. Harris, Candice Hern, Anne Mallory, Monica McCarty, Brenda Novak, Poppy Reifiin, Deanna Raybourn, and Jacqueline Yau.

Thank you to the readers who support Malcolm and Mélanie and their friends and provide wonderful insights on my Web site and social media.

Thanks to Gregory Paris and jim saliba for creating and updating a fabulous Web site that chronicles Malcolm and Mélanie Suzanne's adventures. To Suzi Shoemake and Betty Strohecker for managing a wonderful Goodreads Discussion Group for readers of the series. Thanks to my colleagues at the Merola Opera Program who help me keep my life in balance. Thanks to Peet's Coffee & Tea at The Village, Corte Madera, for welcoming me and my daughter Mélanie and giving me some of my best writing time. And thanks to Mélanie herself, for inspiring my writing, being patient with Mummy's "work time", and offering her own insights at the keyboard. This is her contribution to this story – The world is like a big story that's always being written and never ends, the pages keep turning and writing nonstop and the book doesn't overflow. As long as we exist, the story is still writing. The animals are also part of the story, especially any type of cat.

DRAMATIS PERSONAE

*INDICATES REAL HISTORICAL FIGURES

The Rannoch Family & Household

Malcolm Rannoch, MP and former British intelligence agent
Mélanie Suzanne Rannoch, his wife, playwright and former French intelligence agent
Colin Rannoch, their son
Jessica Rannoch, their daughter
Berowne, their cat

Laura O'Roarke, Colin and Jessica's former governess
Raoul O'Roarke, her husband, Mélanie's former spymaster, and Malcolm's father
Lady Emily Fitzwalter, Laura's daughter from her first marriage
Clara O'Roarke, Laura and Raoul's daughter

Miles Addison, Malcolm's valet
Blanca Mendoza Addison, his wife, Mélanie's companion
Pedro Addison, their son

Valentin, footman

Mrs. Erskine, cook

The Davenport Family

Lady Cordelia Davenport, classicist
Colonel Harry Davenport, her husband, classicist, and former British intelligence agent
Livia Davenport, their daughter
Drusilla Davenport, their daughter

Archibald (Archie) Davenport, Harry's uncle, MP, and former French intelligence agent
Lady Frances Davenport, his wife, Malcolm's aunt
Chloe Dacre-Hammond, Frances's daughter from her first marriage
Francesca Davenport, Frances and Archie's daughter
Philip Davenport, Frances and Archie's son

Aline Blackwell, Frances's daughter from her first marriage
Dr. Geoffrey Blackwell, Aline's husband
Claudia Blackwell, their daughter

At the Tavistock Theatre

Letty Blanchard, actress
Lewis Thornsby, Letty's beau
Cranley, Lewis's valet

William (Will) Carmarthen, actor and Leveller
Brandon Ford, actor and Leveller
Bessie, seamstress
Tim Scott stagehand and Leveller
Donald McDevitt, Leveller

Jennifer Mansfield, actress
Sir Horace Smytheton, her husband, patron of the Tavistock
Their daughters

Manon Caret Harleton, actress
Crispin, Lord Harleton, her husband
Roderick, their son
Roxane, Manon's daughter
Clarisse, Manon's daughter

Simon Tanner, playwright, part owner of the Tavistock, and Leveller
David Mallinson, Viscount Worsley, his lover
Teddy Craven, David's nephew
George Craven, David's nephew
Amy Craven, David's niece
Jamie Craven, David's nephew

Others in London

Thomas Thornsby, classicist, Lewis's elder brother
Edith Simmons, classicist and governess, Thomas's friend

Lady Shroppington, Lewis and Thomas's aunt

Bertrand Laclos, French émigré and former British intelligence agent
Rupert, Viscount Caruthers, his lover, MP and former British intelligence agent
Gabrielle, Viscountess Caruthers, Rupert's wife and Bertrand's cousin
Stephen, Rupert and Gabrielle's son
Nick Gordon, Gabrielle's lover

Sofia Vincenzo
Kit Montagu, her fiancé, Leveller
Lady Thurston, Kit's mother
Selena, Kit's sister

Hubert Mallinson, Earl Carfax, Malcolm's former spymaster and David's father
Amelia, Countess Carfax, his wife
Lady Lucinda Mallinson, their youngest daughter

Billy Hopkins, agent for Carfax

Lord Beverston
Benedict Smythe, his younger son
Nerezza Russo, Benedict's beloved
Roger Smythe, Beverston's elder son, MP and Leveller
Dorinda Smythe, Roger's wife

Julien St. Juste, former agent for hire
Katelina (Kitty) Velasquez Ashford, former British and Spanish intelligence agent, his mistress
Leo Ashford, her son
Timothy Ashford, her son
Guenevere (Genny) Ashford, her daughter

Juliette Dubretton, novelist
Paul St. Gilles, painter, her husband
Marguerite, their daughter
Pierre, their son
Rose, their daughter
Gavin, their manservant

George Bartlett, barrister
Hetty Bartlett, novelist, his wife

Mr. Hapgood, bookseller

Toby Wilton, diplomat
Sally Wilton, his daughter
Winston Wilton, his son

Jeremy Roth, Bow Street runner
*Sir Nathaniel Conant, chief magistrate of Bow Street
*Lord Sidmouth, British home secretary

*Emily, Countess Cowper, patroness of Almack's
*Harry, Lord Palmerston, Secretary at War, her lover
*William Lamb, her brother
*Lady Caroline Lamb, his wife

*George, Prince Regent of the United Kingdom of Great Britain and Ireland

All the world's a stage,
And all the men and women merely players
—Shakespeare, *As You Like It,* Act II, scene vii

PROLOGUE

Saint-Maurice-en-Valais
September, 1811

Mélanie Lescaut sat on the riverbank, arms linked about her muslin-covered knees, sketchbook and pencil abandoned beside her. She closed her eyes and pushed the plaited straw brim of her bonnet back from her forehead. The sun beat down warm on her face and the Rhône river rushed by clean and cool below her. Difficult on a day like this to believe that winter was not far off. And that a little boy would spend his first Christmas without either of his parents present.

"Seeking solace in nature? How Wordsworthian. Though there are other ways we could have found solace on this journey. I have quite agreeable memories of two years ago."

She opened her eyes and bit back a curse. She should have heard him long before he spoke. "Two years ago was work."

Julien St. Juste dropped down beside her, arms hooked round one knee, his other leg dangling over the bank. "Meaning you don't indulge outside of business?"

"Meaning I'm rather fastidious about whom I indulge with."

"Fair enough." He pulled a silver flask from his coat. "Thought perhaps you could do with this."

"Am I so obvious?"

"The press of emotions in the inn was a bit thick, even for me."

Mélanie accepted the flask and took a swallow. The brandy was warm and rich and tasted of apples, but it seared her throat. "How was she when you left?"

"Quiet. Flahaut was the one who looked as if he was going to be sick."

"It's his baby too."

"And unlike some men, he seems to be aware of that. Hortense will pull through. She's got more of her mother in her than one would think."

Mélanie was fond of the Empress Josephine, but she had met her at times when Josephine was in trouble and desperate for assistance. For a moment the memory of the day the divorced French empress had pleaded with them to help her daughter Hortense conceal a disastrous pregnancy was so vivid Mélanie could smell the roses at Malmaison. "Is Josephine so strong?"

"When she needs to be."

Mélanie fixed her gaze on the water rushing dark over the stones of the river bed. "I can steal. I can kill. I can do things I never thought I'd be capable of. Things I'm not proud to be capable of. But what Hortense did today—I don't know that I could do that. Put my child into the care of someone else—even someone I trusted—and know that he would grow up without me. Perhaps it's just as well that I'm exceedingly unlikely ever to have a child of my own."

"You're a bit young to be swearing off parenthood."

She returned the flask to him. "Do you? Have children?"

"Not that I know of. We don't exactly live a life that's suited to it. Which doesn't mean I've never thought of it."

"Don't tell me you have a secret longing for a rose-covered cottage and a nursery of fat babies."

A smile pulled at his mouth. "Hardly. But the thought of home has a certain seduction."

"Has it been a long time since you were back?"

"So long I was quite another person."

"That could mean yesterday."

"So it could." He took a swallow from the flask. "I used to think what I wanted more than anything else was my freedom."

"You're the freest person I know."

"Ah, but then you don't really know me at all, do you?"

"Used to think?" she said.

"Lately I find that even I am subject to the occasional clichéd longings. The land one's ancestors trod. The air one breathed in childhood. The smile of one's first love." He reached out and tucked a strand of hair behind her ear.

Mélanie steeled herself against any reaction. "Was she your first love?"

"Who?"

"Josephine."

He smiled for a moment. "I was young enough that she might have been." He returned the flask to his pocket and held out his hand. "Come back to the inn, *cara*. Hortense will need you. All we can do is take care of what needs to be done, one step at a time."

She accepted his hand and let him pull her to her feet. "That's what Raoul says."

"And O'Roarke has an annoying habit of being right."

CHAPTER 1

London
January, 1820

"Mummy! There's a sword missing."

Mélanie Lescaut Rannoch set down her pencil and looked up from the manuscript of *Past Imperfect,* her first play, which was set to open in five days. Dear God. Only five.

Her six-and-a-half-year-old son Colin was in the wings of the Tavistock Theatre, bent over a basket of props, studying the contents with the same intensity with which she'd seen his father scour a crime scene for clues. "It must not have got put away after the rehearsal, darling. See if you see it lying about anywhere. Can you help, Jessica?"

"Right away!" Three-year-old Jessica ran across the stage, feet pattering on the boards, sending up clouds of dust left from rehearsal. Mélanie watched her children for a moment, marveling at the miracle they were, then glanced back at the script balanced on the arm of her seat in the front row of the pit. Covered with scratches and marks of words she was still trying to get right. She was about to embark on an adventure that in its own way seemed more perilous than her years as a Bonapartist agent. Even the years in which she had been spying for the French while married to a British agent. Or the years after she had stopped spying, when she'd lived in fear that the husband she had come to love so much it frightened her would learn the truth of her past. Her husband, the father of her children. She watched Colin and Jessica scouring the recesses of the stage. The same stage on which her husband Malcolm had confronted her two years ago when he'd worked out the truth of her past.

The theatre had been quiet on that night too. In those moments, on this dusty stage where her children now exclaimed with glee in their sword hunt, she'd been sure her life as she knew it was over. That the best she could possibly hope for would be not to lose the children who would always be the center of her world.

Even after she and Malcolm had miraculously managed to rebuild their marriage, the risks had hardly gone away. They'd faced exile and battled both government agents and a shadowy group called the Elsinore League. Not to mention investigating more than one murder and the odd assassination plot.

Even in her quieter moments as a political and diplomatic hostess, she juggled situations where a misjudged seating arrangement or a failure to smooth over a contretemps could destroy an alliance or end a career.

She touched her fingers to the printed pages before her. Arguably any of those adventures had been more perilous than the one she now faced. She was not risking life and limb or liberty, or threatening her marriage. But she knew how to conduct herself on a spy mission. The dangers to watch for, the steps to take to protect herself and her colleagues and those she loved. So often success on a spy mission simply rested on remaining quiet and observing. And perhaps taking the odd paper. Which she'd also been known to do in the midst of a quiet dinner party.

There was nothing quiet about her present adventure. And the papers involved contained words she had written herself. Words that a quite wonderful cast of actors would breathe to life on the stage before them. The risks, one might say, were fewer. Scandal, though her husband assured her that social position didn't concern him for all his work as an MP. Critical failure, which surely she could withstand after everything else she had endured. And, harder to define, a sense of herself. A pride in having created something quite on her own, perhaps for the first time in her life.

She breathed in the air. The dust from the canvas flats, the oil from the rehearsal lamps, the gas from the new lighting system, the lingering smell of the oranges sold in the aisles during performances. This was her world. A world to which she had been a stranger for many years, but the world she had grown up in as the child of actor parents. A world that had nothing to do with the intrigues she'd been thrust into over the past decade through war and destruction.

"Sword over here." Jessica's voice sounded from deeper in the wings on the opposite side of the stage.

"What's it doing there?" Colin asked.

"Brandon or Will must have left it there after they were practicing the sword fight earlier." Mélanie made another note on the script. "Can you bring it back, darling? I'm almost finished and then we can walk home. Daddy should be back from the House soon."

She heard a clatter and then a muffled exclamation from Jessica. "Someone's sleeping."

Mélanie sprang to her feet. One of the stagehands must have drunk too much at the White Rose across the street and fallen asleep instead of returning home. But even as the thought occurred to her, so did another. She hiked up her merino skirts, vaulted onto the stage, and ran across the boards, catching up with Colin as he darted across from stage right.

The light from a rehearsal lamp caught Jessica in the wings at stage left, sending the shadow of her wispy hair and ruffled skirt flickering over the boards far higher than her small person. She was staring at a dark blur in front of her, head cocked to one side. She took a half step forwards.

"Don't, darling." Mélanie caught Jessica up in her arms.

The blur resolved itself into the dark figure of a man sprawled on the boards. The light angled over his face. Lewis Thornsby, a young man about town who had been dangling after one of the younger actresses in the company. Mélanie could see him vividly at rehearsal this afternoon, leaning forwards from a seat in the pit, not far from where she had been sitting just now, high shirt points framing his eager young face. Now he was sprawled on his back, his head at an awkward angle, his expression frozen, his face half-obscured by one of those shirt points and his Byronically cut hair. Without going closer, Mélanie was quite sure he was dead. His eyes were fixed and blood crusted the glossy dark blue of his coat. More blood seeped onto the boards of the stage from underneath him.

"Should we wake him up?" Jessica asked, face pressed to Mélanie's shoulder.

"I don't think he can wake up," Colin said in a small voice.

Holding Jessica against her hip with one arm, Mélanie reached for her son's hand and squeezed it. "Yes, I think we'd best—"

She broke off as footsteps sounded on the stairs from the basement. She spun round, Jessica at her hip, her free arm round Colin, evaluating what weapons might be to hand. More frightened than she'd have admitted to anyone, even to her husband (especially to her husband).

"Mélanie?"

She drew a gasping breath at Julien St. Juste's familiar

accents. "Up here." She had no idea what Julien was doing in the theatre. But then, when did one ever have an idea what Julien St. Juste was doing anywhere?

Julien came into view, pale hair catching the light from the rehearsal lamps. His gaze went from Mélanie to the dark figure in the shadows. "It's Lewis Thornsby," Mélanie said. "Letty Blanchard's beau."

"He's asleep," Jessica said.

"I think it's worse," Colin said.

Mélanie met Julien's gaze for a moment. Julien gave a quick nod, knelt beside Thornsby, shook his head. "You should look at him."

He walked towards them, his smile designed to reassure the children, and oddly just the sort of smile that would do just that.

"Darling, stay with Uncle Julien." Mélanie put Jessica into Julien's arms. Dear God, not many months ago the very thought of ever trusting Julien with either of her children would have horrified her. She gave Colin a quick smile and squeezed his shoulder, then moved deeper into the wings and knelt beside Thornsby. His skin was ashen, his body cool and beginning to stiffen. He had been stabbed in the chest, in the heart or very close it. There was no sign of the weapon, but it had clearly been no accident.

"It's been some time," she said. "I suspect whoever is responsible is long gone. We should send to Jeremy Roth at Bow Street."

"And to Daddy," Colin said.

"Excellent thought, darling. He'll still be at the House."

"Tom's outside," Julien said. "One of the link boys who's used to doing my errands. He can take one message and find a friend to take the other." He flashed a quick smile at the children and then at Mélanie. "Just a precaution. Better we all wait together, I think."

For once Mélanie agreed. She wasn't about to leave until

Malcolm and Jeremy Roth arrived. There was no one she could safely send the children home with, and they'd probably be more frightened if she sent them away in any case. Thornsby had been dead for some time. Killers didn't tend to linger. But the idea of being alone in the theatre with the children was not an appealing one. She dropped down on the edge of the stage, Jessica in her lap, Colin beside her. The light of an oil rehearsal lamp cast a small circle of warmth round them.

"I should have known," Colin said.

"What?" Mélanie asked, settling Jessica against her.

"That something would happen. It always does with you and Daddy."

Colin couldn't know the echoes his words would have. Mélanie reached out and touched his hair.

"And you always manage it," he said.

She leaned down and kissed the top of his head. "We try, sweetheart."

"Trying's all you can ask of yourself. That's what Uncle Raoul says."

And as Julien had once said, Raoul O'Roarke had a way of being right. Mélanie gathered her children closer. So many things to try to do. Make the play a success. Protect her children. And apparently undertake an investigation.

"Right." Julien reappeared a few minutes later. She felt her shoulders relax at the sight of his pale hair and the sound of his crisp voice. Which of them had changed more in the past eight years? In the past eight months? "Malcolm and Roth should be here soon." Julien vaulted up onto the edge of the stage. "Any bets on who will be first?"

Colin frowned in concentration. "Bow Street's closer. But Daddy can probably get a hackney faster."

"A good point. Rannoch knows how to employ the tricks of a gentleman when it's helpful."

"Did you tell Auntie Kitty?" Colin asked.

Julien's eyes widened slightly, but he didn't deliver the protest Mélanie expected about his relationship with Kitty Ashford. "Yes, I told her I'd be ho—back late." He tweaked a strand of Jessica's hair.

"Do you think there's anyone else in the theatre?" Colin asked.

Julien exchanged a look with Mélanie. Most likely the killer was long gone. But under normal circumstances they'd divide forces and search to be safe. The children changed the calculus. There was no safe place to leave them during a search and searching with them risked taking them right into danger. Julien seemed to grasp that as well as she did. Which perhaps, given his relationship with Kitty Ashford and her children, wasn't as surprising as it once would have been.

"I shouldn't think so," Julien said. "I was down in the basement and didn't see anything. Best we all sit tight until Roth and your father get here. What do you say we make shadow puppets while we wait? I imagine Princess Jessica would like that." He exchanged a look with Colin that suggested Jessica could use the distraction. Colin sprang to attention, too absorbed in reassuring his sister to be alarmed himself.

They were in the midst of a story involving dragons, cats, a princess, and a unicorn when Colin's flying dragon shadow puppet froze in midair.

"What was that?" he asked.

Mélanie had heard it as well, and she could tell Julien had too. Footsteps on the stairs again. She put her arms round the children. Julien got to his feet with his usual languid ease, but every line of his body braced for action.

"Mélanie. I didn't know you were still here." Simon Tanner walked onto the stage and stopped in his tracks. "St. Juste?"

Simon didn't sound as surprised as he might have done. After all, Julien more or less counted as a friend of the family these days and Simon certainly was as well. In addition to managing the Tavistock Theatre and co-owning it, he had gone to Oxford with Malcolm.

"Some unexpected developments, Tanner," Julien said in an easy voice. "Perhaps Mélanie can explain while we finish the shadow puppet performance."

Mélanie got to her feet, drew Simon aside, and quickly told him about Thornsby. Simon stared at her. Mélanie pulled him into the wings where he could see Lewis Thornsby's body.

Simon's eyes went wide. "Good God."

"When did you last see him?"

"At rehearsal this afternoon." Simon scraped a hand over his thick dark hair. "Why would he have come back here?"

"I don't know. I saw him leave with several of the others. He must have come back in while the children and I were having supper at the coffeehouse with Manon. Manon and I came back after supper to go over the changes to Act III, and then she went home. I was just finishing up some notes and then the children and I were going to leave as well." Mélanie looked up at Simon. "I didn't realize you were here."

"I stopped by to go through some boxes in the basement. Accounts for Mr. Ford. I must have come in before you and Manon. I didn't see Thornsby." He cast another glance at Thornsby. "Christ, he may have been lying here—"

"If he was lying here when you came in, he was probably dead already."

Simon nodded, though his gaze lingered on Thornsby, his brows drawn. "What's St. Juste doing here?"

"A very good question." Mélanie cast a glance at Julien, who was kneeling between Colin and Jessica, then looked back at Simon. When she'd married Malcolm—an outsider to Mayfair society even aside from the fact that she'd been a French spy—Simon had been one of her first allies in her husband's alien aristocratic world. The son of a painter and an artist's model, the grandson of a Northumbrian brewer, he was an outsider like she was. And because he loved another man—an earl's son and heir at that—like her he was condemned to live a secret life. He'd learned her secrets a year and a half ago, six months after Malcolm had, but she always thought he'd understood a great deal before he learned the actual truth.

"Excellent denouement. Try out some new puppets and we'll work on a sequel after I speak to your mother and Tanner." Julien pushed himself to his feet and strolled over to join Mélanie and Simon. "I wouldn't ask in the general run of things, but was Thornsby a Leveller?"

Simon exchanged a quick look with Mélanie. The Levellers were a group of young Radicals centered round the theatre. Their activities flirted enough with sedition that Mélanie's MP husband Malcolm made it a point to know as little as possible about them. Despite the fact that he was in sympathy with them and had friends among their number. Including Simon.

"Why do you ask?" Simon said in a neutral voice.

"It wouldn't be surprising, given the number of actors and supporters of the Tavistock who are part of the group. But as I said, I wouldn't ask if I hadn't had a look through Thornsby's pockets. I found this." Julien held out a paper. "You'd best decide what you want to do about it before Roth gets here. Or even Malcolm. I'll play it however you both wish."

Mélanie stared down at the paper. It was a sketch of the theatre, most specifically of the boxes from the perspective of another box. The box that was the focal point was the one reserved for royal guests. Lines and mathematical calculations pointed at the royal box.

"What is this?" Simon said, though his tone told Mélanie he already suspected.

"It looks a bit amateurish to a professional's eye," Julien said, "but I'd say it appears to be a plan for how to aim a rife to shoot someone in the royal box."

Simon stared at Julien. "That's absurd. We aren't—"

"You're opposed to the government."

"If you think that equates to assassination, you're sounding very like Carfax for the rational man I took you to be."

Lord Carfax, the father of Simon's lover David, was Britain's unofficial head of intelligence, and since the end of the war, more focused on Radicals at home than abroad. Julien, who had once worked for Carfax, gave a faint smile. "I'd hardly say opposing the government equates to assassination. But I've rarely found any group to be entirely in agreement over tactics. Even some people who are very close aren't in agreement in such matters, as I'm sure Mélanie could attest. On the other hand, as you allude to, it would suit men like Carfax very well to have your friends labeled assassins."

Simon glanced down at Thornsby's still face. "You think Thornsby was a mole reporting to Carfax?"

"Possibly. But just because I found the sketch on him doesn't mean it was there when he died."

Mélanie drew a breath, but it was Simon who swung his gaze to Julien and said, "Are you suggesting Carfax had Thornsby killed?"

Julien scanned the stage as Mélanie had seen him scan enemy terrain. "It's convenient to blame Carfax for things. Convenient and very often accurate. But others could have wanted the Levellers tarnished. Or it's possible an agent of Carfax's made use of the fact that Thornsby was already dead and planted the information on him."

"Good God, how many people do you think broke into the theatre tonight?" Simon asked.

"Quite a number that we already know of." Mélanie regarded Julien. "You still haven't told us what you were doing here."

"Following up on a lead for Bertrand."

Bertrand Laclos smuggled former Bonapartists out of France and was an ally in the fight against the shadowy Elsinore League that they were all involved in. It made a sort of sense. It didn't begin to account for everything. Like her husband, Mélanie was wary of coincidence.

Simon glanced down at the paper again. "We have to tell Malcolm. And Roth. As Malcolm always says, withholding any information can play havoc with an investigation. Not to mention if there really is an assassination plot, the authorities need to know. And if there isn't, and Carfax is behind this, we're not revealing anything he doesn't already know."

Mélanie nodded. "I agree."

"Sound thinking," Julien said. "You also might have been playing right into his hands if you'd withheld it. But you're going to bring a lot of attention down on yourselves."

"We have that already." Simon stared down at Thornsby for a long moment. "We've known for over a month we had a mole in the group probably reporting to Carfax. The thing is, based on the information we had, it couldn't have been Thornsby. The mole was privy to information Thornsby didn't have. So either Thornsby was being set up, before or after he was killed—or there's more than one mole."

"Either way, your first mole is an obvious suspect," Julien said.

Simon regarded him. "Would you really have kept quiet about a plot to assassinate a member of the royal family?"

Julien raised a brow. The long shadows of the wings fell across his face, sharpening the fine bones, rendering it more inscrutable than ever. "You mean would my love of crown and county have compelled me to speak? If you're suggesting that, you know me less well than I thought. I used to play the role I was hired to play. Now I play the role I choose. I've never owned any particular loyalty. But I would rather cavil at turning friends over to the authorities."

Simon returned his gaze steadily. "And Mélanie's your friend."

"You could call her that. You could call *you* that."

A smile, faint but real, curved Simon's mouth. "You're a good fellow, St. Juste."

"If you choose to call me that, it's quite your own affair. All things considered, though, I'm just as glad we aren't lying to Roth and Malcolm. That could strain even my abilities. Even Mélanie's, I imagine."

"You have no idea," Mélanie said.

Quick steps sounded in the aisle. "Daddy!" Jessica shouted.

Mélanie ran to the edge of the stage, swung down, and ran to greet her husband. "You got here quickly."

"I made it a point to." Malcolm caught her hands and squeezed them. His dark brown hair was ruffled and fell over his forehead, as though he'd tugged his hat off quickly, and his greatcoat looked as though he'd pulled it on in a hurry. His gaze darted over her face, taut with concern, then shot to the children and Simon and Julien.

"There's been an accident," she said. "Lewis Thornsby. Julien and Simon were both here."

Malcolm lifted her back onto the stage and swung up behind her. He stopped to hug Colin and Jessica, then followed Mélanie to where Julien and Simon stood beside Thornsby's body. Mélanie quickly explained the sequence of events.

Malcolm stared down at Thornsby. "Before—"

He broke off as Jeremy Roth strode into the theatre, greatcoat flapping about him, sharp features set with worry. And beneath the worry, the light of the chase.

As Roth bent over Thornsby, Mélanie gave him the same update she'd given Malcolm. Roth lifted Thornsby's arm, then carefully set it down again. "Whoever did this knew what they were doing," Julien said.

"He looks to have died about two hours ago." Mélanie looked at Simon and then at Julien. "I'd have been at the coffeehouse with Manon and the children."

"I didn't come back until after that," Simon said.

"Nor did I," Julien said.

"He definitely left the theatre this afternoon with Letty and the others," Mélanie said. "I distinctly remember their all going out the door." Thornsby had been hovering close to Letty Blanchard, offering an umbrella against the threatening rain. "So he came back. Presumably to meet someone. Possibly the killer."

"If not the killer, we have the question of what became of the other person he was meeting," Malcolm said.

"Not to mention the weapon," Julien said. "Whoever did this was extraordinarily lucky or knew exactly where to stab to kill quickly. I'd say we're looking for a knife with a six inch blade."

"I have a constable waiting outside," Roth said. "I'll have him make inquiries in the neighborhood." He looked from Mélanie to Simon. "You said he was hanging about Miss Blanchard. Was it reciprocal?"

Mélanie exchanged a quick look with Simon. "I wouldn't say the feelings were as strong on her side as on his," Simon said. "But she didn't discourage him. It added to her consequence to have a young gentleman dangle after her, I suspect, at least in her mind. "

"So you don't think he came back for a rendezvous with her?" Roth was blunt.

"In the theatre?" Simon shook his head. "I know better than to rule anything out. But I wouldn't have thought it had progressed that far. Or that they'd have chosen such a setting if it had."

Roth considered Simon. "Forgive me. But in the circumstances, I have to ask. Was Thornsby one of the Levellers?"

Simon drew a breath. "You'd best see this. You too, Malcolm." He held out the sketch showing the rifle trajectory.

Roth's sharp breath cut the air. "Since you're showing this to me, I assume there isn't actually a plot that you know of."

"Do you really think there could be?" Simon asked.

Roth's gaze was as steady as a rifle barrel in the hands of a sniper. "No, but I know better than to rule any option out."

"If Thornsby was involved in a real plot, presumably any confederate—anyone wanting to cover up the plot—would have removed the paper," Malcolm said. "So it would seem whoever killed him either didn't know about the paper or didn't care if it was found. Or wanted it to be found."

"Quite," Julien said. "We were having an interesting debate about that before you and Roth arrived."

"It may well be a manufactured plot," Simon said, "but you have to take it to the authorities. And I know that means Carfax. I also realize he may well be behind the plot, and you probably won't be able to tell either way, and that even if he is behind it, he may use it against us."

"Almost certainly," Malcolm said. "Since using it against you would have been the point of such a plot in the first place."

Simon met his friend's gaze. "In which case, if we don't tell him, we're playing right into his hands."

Malcolm clapped a hand on Simon's shoulder. "Not playing into Carfax's hands can be fiendishly difficult." He looked at Roth. "Before we go to Carfax, let's go through Thornsby's things."

"In case there's proof he's a mole?" Simon said.

"It would clarify the situation."

"Given that no one will occupy the royal box until opening, I think we can afford a few hours," Roth said.

Malcolm turned to Mélanie. "I'll get the children home," she said. "Then, I think, if it's all right with Jeremy, perhaps I should break the news to Letty tonight."

Roth nodded. "By all means. The sooner we question her, the better. It would be good to see her reaction to the news. And she'll be far more likely to confide in you."

"Any assignments for me?" Julien asked. He was leaning against a flat pushed into the wings. Viola and Orsino's castle from the Christmas pantomime Mélanie had performed in a month since.

"Not yet," Malcolm said. "But we may. Unless you saw anything else of interest?"

"Not that I haven't related. I stumbled into the drama after the main action occurred. But I'll own to a distinct curiosity. Especially as it concerns Carfax."

Malcolm nodded. "Your insights with Carfax are distinctly helpful. You don't have any reason to think there's a League connection?"

Julien raised his brows. "Do you?"

"Only that the League have a way of following us about. They've shown an interest in the Levellers. And their interests and Carfax's tend to cross. Or converge. Or both."

"I don't know of any connection," Julien said. "Which doesn't mean there isn't one. I'll make some inquiries."

"My thanks." It was another sign of the changes of the past months that Malcolm was thanking Julien quite without irony. "You'd best be on your way. I imagine Kitty's wondering where you are."

Julien raised his brows again but gave a faint smile. "Your family's interest in my domestic arrangements is quite remarkable. I suppose this is what it means to have friends."

Malcolm echoed the smile. "You might say that, St. Juste. They do make it harder to be anonymous. But there are compensations."

Julien nodded, grinned at Colin, touched Jessica's hair, and swung down from the stage.

CHAPTER 2

Lewis Thornsby had had rooms in Piccadilly, not far from the fashionable bachelors' quarters in the Albany where Malcolm had once lodged himself and where Simon nominally still kept rooms, though he spent most of his time with David and David's niece and nephews whom they were raising.

The porter let them in without questions when Malcolm showed his card. There was no need to even mention Roth's Bow Street credentials. The more time they got before the scandal was all over London, the better.

The room was dark and smelled of brandy and cedar. Malcolm held up the candle the porter had given them. Disorder met his gaze. Shirts, waistcoats, cravats, coats, and breeches spilling off chairs, strewn on the floor.

Roth drew in his breath. "A search or—"

"The general untidiness of a young bachelor? I'm not sure." Malcolm took a step forwards, then went still. Even before his mind had consciously formulated what he'd heard, he was across the room and through the door to the next room. He put the candle down on a table inside the door and hurled himself across the room onto a shadowy figure halfway out the window.

The man let go of the sill abruptly as Malcolm hauled him to the ground. The candlelight from across the room flickered over the face. "Kit?" Malcolm stared down into Kit Montagu's blue eyes. "What the devil—"

Before he could say more, a crash sounded from the next room. Another man raced into the room with Roth in pursuit. Roth's quarry leapt over Malcolm and Kit and through the window Kit had been trying to climb out of. Malcolm grabbed the window ledge, pulled himself up, and sprang after. He landed in a crouch in the street, hands smarting as they hit the cobblestones. A shadowy figure was just turning the corner. Malcolm ran after. Three silk-hatted young men staggering out of a carriage blocked the pavement. Malcolm's quarry darted round them and their hackney, losing precious time. Malcolm pushed his way between two of the young men, sending one stumbling on the area steps and the other falling backwards against his third friend, ran towards the street, and used the pavement to propel himself into a jump onto his quarry's back.

"What the devil?" said one of the young men behind them.

"Never mind," another said, "let's get Simpkins inside before he's sick in the street."

Malcolm's quarry had gone limp. "All right, Mr. Rannoch, you'd better ask whatever you were going to ask."

"Billy?" Malcolm stared at one of Carfax's dirty-tricks minions. "I might have known."

"Then you know more than I do," Billy Hopkins said. "His lordship just told me to go to those rooms, look through the young man's things, grab any papers."

"Was that after you killed Lewis Thornsby?" Malcolm asked.

"Is that his name? I didn't kill him. I didn't kill anyone. Not tonight. Not recently."

His tone was so aggrieved Malcolm almost believed him. "What else did Carfax say?"

"Nothing. You think he discusses the finer points of missions with me? He saves that for you. You'd better talk to him yourself if you want to find out."

That was actually a good point. "All right," Malcolm said. "Turn out your pockets."

"Don't be stupid, Mr. Rannoch. I didn't have time to look. I'd just got there when you and Mr. Roth came in, and I jumped into the wardrobe and then Mr. Roth found me."

That was plausible, but Malcolm still searched Billy before sending him on his way. This was how things went with Billy surprisingly often. There was rarely any way to keep him in custody and he rarely had any actual evidence on him.

"One more question," Malcolm said, grabbing Billy's arm, before he could scramble to his feet. "When did Carfax send word to you?"

"Less than an hour since. Maybe forty-five minutes. I'd just sat down with a pint in the Crown & Anchor. Hadn't even drunk a third of it."

So Carfax might have been reacting to news of Thornsby's death rather than covering up because he'd been behind it. Possibly.

Malcolm let Billy go and sat back on his heels. "Tell Carfax I found you before you could finish his errand."

Billy shrugged his shoulders. "Right you are, guv'nor. Any other message?"

"That'll do for now."

"Right. Be seeing you again, I'm sure. Sooner than not, I reckon, with all that's going on."

"I reckon as well." Malcolm got to his feet and pulled Billy up. "Take care of yourself, Billy. We may need you later."

"You always manage to find me, Mr. Rannoch."

"That I do. Make it easy for me and I'll be easy on you."

"Between you and Carfax, you're always easier on a fellow, Mr. Rannoch. But then, you've never offered to pay me."

"No. It's not a bad idea. Except that you'd probably pocket change from both of us."

"I expect I would, Mr. Rannoch." Billy tugged his coat smooth. "A bloke has to keep an eye out for the main chance."

MALCOLM FOUND Roth in the midst of a methodical search of Lewis Thornsby's rooms while Kit sat on a straight-backed chair, watching but scrupulously not touching anything.

Roth looked up from a stack of papers on the writing desk. "Didn't think I could catch you. Seemed more important to start going through things here."

"Quite right." Malcolm closed the door. He'd come back in using the more conventional route.

Kit looked up and met his gaze. "Jem from the White Rose sent me word about Lewis. One of Roth's constables had gone in to ask questions. I didn't know you were investigating. All I could think was what might be in Lewis's things. I mean—" He cast a quick glance at Roth.

"I'm aware of the risks the Levellers run," Roth said in a dry voice. "I would think by now you'd know I'm sympathetic."

"You still work for Bow Street and the chief magistrate still reports to the home office. I don't want to put you in an awkward position."

"Fair enough," Roth said. "Perhaps you and Rannoch should speak in the adjoining room. He can decide what to tell me."

Kit hesitated a moment, then at a nod from Malcolm followed him into the adjoining room. "It feels damnably awkward," Kit said, as Malcolm lit a lamp. "Wouldn't dream of keeping anything from Roth in the regular run of things. He's a friend. But—"

"No, you're right to be concerned for the situation you put him in." Malcolm turned to face Kit. "What was Thornsby involved in?"

"Nothing." Kit scraped a hand over his hair. "Nothing I know of, that is. Nothing outside of what the Levellers were—"

"Generally involved in?"

"Quite. That is—" Kit drew a rough breath. "Thornsby wrote the occasional article. He'd speak up at meetings. He wasn't bad with words. And his heart was in the right place. But he wasn't a leader. And he never seemed the sort to go out and run risks. He seemed more drawn by the appeal of being a Leveller than the practice of it, if that makes sense."

"It does."

"It sounds beastly, doesn't it, with him—"

"Death is always a tragic waste," Malcolm said. "It's particularly so with a young man like Thornsby who seems to have had everything to live for and to have given no cause for anyone to see him as an enemy. But platitudes and worrying about what we say won't help us get at the truth."

"No, I can see that."

"So if you didn't think Thornsby was involved in anything particularly dangerous, why the rush to search his rooms?"

Kit stared at Malcolm with wide blue eyes. "Well, I mean, he was one of us. Even our mildest pamphlets stir government ire. Carfax tried to have us all taken into custody less than a month since. Thornsby was dead suddenly through violent means. I'm no investigator, but it's difficult not to wonder if that had something to do with the Levellers. Even if it didn't, I knew it meant people would be searching his things. Thornsby may not have been a leader, but he could be intemperate. God knows what he might have scribbled down, especially as a draft he never meant to see the light of day."

Malcolm nodded. It was plausible. He had scribbled drafts of speeches and articles that might wreak all sorts of havoc should anyone go through his papers. And yet he wasn't at all sure he'd heard the full story. Kit was a friend, but then, just as Kit counted Roth a friend and wouldn't tell everything to him, Kit might well keep things from Malcolm as an MP. Not to mention as an investigator into a crime about which Malcolm couldn't shake the sense that Kit knew more than he was telling.

"Did you?" Malcolm asked. "Find anything? Because you've heard me say more than once that one can never be sure what will prove to be important in an investigation. And showing it to me isn't showing it to Carfax."

"I know that." Kit's gaze was steady. He hesitated a moment, then reached into his coat and pulled out a paper.

Malcolm glanced at it in the lamplight. It was a scribbled draft proposing abolition of the House of Lords. "I wrote something like this myself when I was at Oxford. Published it too."

"And you had Carfax breathing down your neck."

"Very true. More than we knew." Carfax had set one of Malcolm's closest friends to spy on Malcolm and Simon and his own son. "Do you think Carfax has an agent among the Levellers?"

Kit's gaze slid to the side then back to Malcolm. "We've been afraid of it for some weeks."

Malcolm nodded. "For what it's worth, Simon told me as well." He folded the paper and tucked it into his own coat. "I'll be careful with this. Anything else?"

Kit shook his head. "I didn't have a lot of time before you and Roth burst in."

Kit might not be an investigator or an agent, but he was clever and he'd been through more than one investigation. He'd know the value of turning over one piece of evidence to divert notice from another one was hanging on to.

"Let's see what Roth's found," Malcolm said.

In the adjoining room, Roth had assembled a pile of papers he thought relevant. "Mostly drafts of things Thornsby was writing for the Levellers." Roth looked at Kit. "I won't show them to anyone unless they prove relevant to the investigation somehow. A couple of letters from his father expressing concern about his life in London. A couple of notes from Letty Blanchard. Brief and fairly innocuous but much creased, as though he treasured them. And this." Roth drew one paper from the stack. "Not quite sure what to make of it."

Meet me at the White Rose the day after tomorrow at ten in the morning. You must understand I can't commit more to writing.

"Do you recognize the hand?" Roth asked Kit.

Kit shook his head.

But Malcolm recognized it, and the sight of the note made him grow cold and spun the investigation in a whole different direction. It belonged to Kitty Ashford. Julien St. Juste's mistress. Malcolm's own first love.

CHAPTER 3

As Malcolm stared down at the paper, struggling with the implications, the door creaked open. A sharp gasp followed. Malcolm, Roth, and Kit spun towards the door. A young man stood there, wrapped in an olive-drab greatcoat, hesitating as though unsure whether to attack or take flight.

Thornsby hadn't shared his rooms with anyone. So— "You must be Thornsby's valet," Malcolm said. "We aren't thieves. My name is Rannoch. Inspector Roth of Bow Street, and Kit Montagu."

"Bow Street?" The young man's eyes darted round the room. He had a round face and curling dark hair that gave him the look of a schoolboy. Malcolm doubted he was more than five-and-twenty, if that.

"Yes. Why don't you sit down, Mr.—?"

"Cranley. Where's Mr. Thornsby—"

Malcolm pressed Cranley into a straight-backed chair. Roth poured a glass of brandy from a set of decanters on a table across the room. They told Cranley about his master's death as quickly as possible. He stared at them. Roth pressed the glass into his hand. When Cranley nearly dropped it, Roth guided it to his lips. Cranley took a long drink and stared into the depths of the glass as though searching for answers. "But I just saw Mr. Thornsby—"

"It's a great shock," Malcolm said. "But the more you can tell us, the sooner we can learn what happened to him. When precisely did you last see Mr. Thornsby?"

"This morning. Afternoon, that is. A bit past two. He left to go the theatre. He did most afternoons."

"He didn't return here?"

"Not before I left. It's my evening off, you see. I tidied the flat"—he glanced round at the chaos—"then went round to the King's Arms and met some mates. Had supper at a coffeehouse. The Dark Horse in Piccadilly. Mr. Thornsby always told me to stay out as late as I liked on my nights off—" He drew a sharp breath, took another swallow of brandy. "He is—was—a kind master."

"Do you know what his plans were for the evening?" Roth asked.

Cranley shook his head. "He often went out with some of the actors after rehearsals. He is—was—much attached to one of the actresses. Miss Blanchard." He paused, as though afraid he'd said too much.

"Yes, we know," Malcolm said. "Did she come here?"

"Oh, no." Cranley looked horrified. "Mr. Thornsby would never have gone beyond the line with Miss Blanchard."

What line gentlemen drew with actresses could vary widely and often allowed behavior not different from that accorded to courtesans. Malcolm wasn't sure whether this remark showed Thornsby's feelings for Letty Blanchard, or Cranley's perhaps naive belief in his master, or both.

Kit, who had been hanging back, met Cranley's gaze, then glanced at Malcolm. "I agree. Thornsby's intentions towards Letty were entirely honorable."

That was interesting. But Kit, though clear-sighted, was also quite a romantic and inclined to idealize women, which could be both a positive and a negative.

"Had Mr. Thornsby seemed concerned about anything of late?" Roth asked.

Cranley took a quick drink of brandy, stared into his glass, shifted in his chair.

"You're naturally protective of your master," Malcolm said. "And I applaud your discretion. My own valet has been with me since I was at Oxford and is the same." Leaving aside the fact that Addison was also a very accomplished agent. "For which I am very grateful. But should any harm befall me, I would want him to confide the truth to those investigating."

Cranley gave a quick nod. "Mr. Thornsby was a very cheerful gentleman." He swallowed, perhaps at the realization that he'd used "was" this time without correcting himself. "But he'd been a bit preoccupied of late." He cast a glance at Kit.

"There's been a great deal going on with the Levellers," Kit said. "It's all right. Mr. Rannoch and Mr. Roth know about them."

"Was there anyone in particular he seemed concerned about?" Roth asked. "Or whom he'd quarreled with?"

"Mr. Thornsby always seemed to get on well with people. But—" Cranley dragged his toe over the floorboards. "He had a visitor yesterday. Mr. Carmarthen. One of the actors," he added, just in case they didn't know.

"They were friends?" Malcolm couldn't remember seeing them together much. Carmarthen, a rather intense, sardonic type, seemed quite different from the open, sunny-tempered Thornsby.

"I wouldn't say so particularly." Cranley glanced at Kit again.

"They're both—were, in Thornsby's case—Levellers," Kit said. "But aside from their attending some of the same meetings, I wasn't aware of any particular friendship."

"Do you know why Mr. Carmarthen called?" Malcolm asked Cranley.

"No. Not precisely. I left soon after he arrived to collect some new gloves for Mr. Thornsby. When I came back into the flat, I heard raised voices. I wouldn't have listened normally but I was outside the doors and didn't have a lot of choice. Mr. Thornsby was saying 'I can't believe you'd accuse me of such a thing.' And Mr. Carmarthen said 'It's difficult to assume otherwise.' After that I retreated down the stairs and went round to the King's Arms until I saw Mr. Carmarthen in the street outside. When I went back up to the rooms, Mr. Thornsby seemed—I suppose preoccupied is the best way to put it. But also oddly focused. As though he'd come to a decision. Though about what, I couldn't say."

"You're insightful, Mr. Cranley."

Cranley shook his head. "I know Mr. Thornsby, that's all. But I can't begin to make sense of what's happened."

"None of us can." Malcolm touched his hand. "Did you notice anything else unusual about Mr. Thornsby in recent days?"

"No—that is, I daresay it may mean nothing, but a few days ago—Monday last, I think—I was tidying some papers on Mr. Thornsby's writing desk. I saw a letter with a direction on it I didn't recognize. 19 Rosemary Lane, which surprised me, because it was an odd place for Mr. Thornsby to have an acquaintance. Also, it wasn't in Mr. Thornsby's hand so it wasn't a letter he was sending, but it also hadn't been sent to him, which seemed odd. Not my place to think too much of it, but I couldn't but wonder. Then Mr. Thornsby came in as I was tidying the papers. I felt him staring at me, if you know what I mean."

"Quite," Malcolm said.

"Yes, well I looked up and for a moment I thought he was going to yell at me, which he almost never did. Then he just said, 'It's all right, Cranley, I'll see to it.' I took that as my cue to leave the room. But I heard the poker against the grate and when I next passed the desk, the paper was gone." Cranley looked from Malcolm to Roth. "I think Mr. Thornsby burned the paper. There could be a lot of different reasons."

Malcolm glanced at Roth. "So there could."

ON THE PAVEMENT, Roth looked at Malcolm. "A complicated case on a number of levels."

Malcolm turned up the collar of his greatcoat. The temperature had dropped while they were in Thornsby's rooms. Piccadilly bustled with evening life. Candles and lamps blazed in windows, carriages clattered by, silk-hatted gentlemen and velvet-cloaked ladies moved up and down well-swept steps. Hard to believe the night still wasn't that far advanced. "Yes."

Roth settled his hat against the wind. "It goes without saying that I'd welcome your assistance."

"Which I'm glad to give. In truth, I feel a strong need to discover what happened. But—"

"Thornsby was a member of a Radical group to which other friends of yours belong."

"Who have been targeted by the home office to whom the chief magistrate of Bow Street reports."

"And I, at least in theory, report my findings to the chief magistrate. Then there's the fact that the murder took place at the Tavistock, of which your friend Tanner is an owner. Not to mention being one of the Levellers himself. And the theatre is about to premiere Mélanie's play."

"Quite." Malcolm slid his hands into his greatcoat pockets. "All of which makes for rather more of a tangle than we usually confront in investigations."

"Meaning you may not be able to share everything you discover with me."

"And I imagine you may not wish to share everything you discover with me. Or with Mélanie."

Roth released a breath that frosted in the night air. "It's a fair point. And it won't be the first time we've worked together on those terms."

Malcolm met Roth's gaze and grinned. "So we share what we can—and no blaming the other for holding anything back?"

"Sounds reasonable. I would think by now you'd be used to working with divided loyalties, Rannoch."

Malcolm managed another smile, though a number of unsettling possibilities chased themselves through his mind. "Getting there. But I don't think it's ever really easy."

Roth nodded, though his gaze held a touch of what Malcolm was quite sure was sympathy. "I imagine it isn't."

"DEAD?" Letty Blanchard's Dresden-blue eyes, which had already shown a remarkable ability to hold an audience to the rafters, went wide not so much with grief or horror as with confusion. "Lewis can't be dead. I was drinking ale with him just a few hours ago."

"Is that the last time you saw him?" Mélanie asked.

"Yes." Letty put a hand to her head, sending two hair pins tumbling to the Turkey rug in her small sitting room. "We went to the White Rose after the rehearsal. While you and Manon and Simon were still talking. Not just Lewis and me, a whole lot of us——Oh, my God. He's really dead?"

"I'm so sorry." Mélanie moved from her straight-backed chair to the frayed petit point settee where Letty sat and put an arm round the younger woman. "I'd have a hard time believing it myself if I hadn't seen him."

Letty looked up at her, eyes filled with tears. Not the luminous sort of the stage but a stark torrent that would destroy her eye blacking and leave her nose red and her throat raw. "Was it—did he suffer?"

"I don't think so. It would have been very quick."

Letty gave a strangled sob and clung to Mélanie as though she were a lifeline to normality, then drew back, wiped her handkerchief across her eyes, and blew her nose with defiance. "You want to know what happened tonight."

"When you feel able to tell me."

"Better to talk than to be alone with my thoughts." Letty blew her nose again and dashed a hand across her eyes, leaving a trail of blacking on her fingers. "A lot of us went to the White Rose in a group, but Lewis sat beside me. He usually did. He insisted on fetching me a second pint. And on walking me back to my lodgings."

"Did he stay?"

"Of course not."

Mélanie returned Letty's gaze, keeping her own steady. She couldn't but feel for Letty, but she also knew this was their best chance to get information. "There isn't necessarily any 'of course' about it."

"I wasn't—" Letty swallowed hard, hands fisted in her lap. "I liked Lewis. I knew he was important to the Tavistock. I knew what his notice meant for me. But—oh, poison, I sound the worst sort of witch."

"On the contrary. You sound like a woman who's made calculations about how to survive in the world. You liked Lewis but you weren't in love with him. But you didn't want to discourage his support of the theatre. Or of you."

"That's not—" Letty glanced away, then dragged her gaze back to Mélanie. "I don't mean to sound missish, but I had no desire to become a man's mistress. Not on moral grounds. Not precisely. My family's already scandalized enough by my going on the stage. But I didn't need to add complications to my life. Manon's managed splendidly, but it's difficult enough to survive as an actress without raising bastard children in the midst of it. I know what I want and it's to be a leading lady, not some rich man's trollop." She wadded her handkerchief in her hand. "Dear God, I can't believe he's dead."

"Did he ask you to be his mistress?"

"Not in so many words." She stared at the crumpled linen, the embroidered blue flowers now streaked with eye blacking. "But it was clear that was what he wanted. At least I thought it was. I thought I could dance him along and keep him happy without going beyond the line, but without angering him so much the Tavistock lost his support. Then tonight when he walked me home, he—" Her face crumpled. She glanced away, tears prickling her lashes, fingers white round the handkerchief.

"What? Letty—" Mélanie put a hand on her arm. "Did he try to force himself on you?"

"No." Letty swung her gaze back to Mélanie's face, eyes red but surprisingly clear. "He asked me to marry him."

Despite the actresses she'd seen marry gentlemen, Mélanie hadn't seen that coming. "And you didn't want to do that either."

Letty bit her lip. "I never thought he'd take such a risk. It's not that I was holding out for marriage. It's not that I ever contemplated it at all. But once he asked me—"

"You said you didn't love him."

"No. Not in that way. But look at Manon and Lord Harleton. And Jennifer and Sir Horace."

"Manon's rather madly in love with Crispin. As is Jennfier with Sir Horace, for all I know they're old enough to be your parents."

"I know Manon and Jennifer love their husbands, I'm not blind." Letty twisted the handkerchief between her fingers. "But you can't claim love is the only consideration in marriage, however romantic your own marriage is. I grew up on a sheep farm. Can you imagine what the life Lewis offered me seemed like?"

Mélanie thought of her life with Malcolm. Featherbeds. Fresh fruit in winter. Café-au-lait in bed. Plentiful hot water whenever she wanted it. Well-sprung carriages. Exquisite gowns. A staff to cater to every need. Luxury compared to the brothel she'd once been employed in, of course, but even compared to her childhood in her parents' theatre company or her years as an agent. "I can imagine it." She studied Letty's strained, blotched face. "Are you saying you accepted him?"

"No. He said I could continue on the stage, but I wasn't sure. And however hardheaded and practical I am"—her mouth curved as though she'd heard this description from someone else—"I wasn't blind to what I'd be giving up. Not just perhaps the theatre. The chance to ever—"

"Marry a man you loved?"

Letty's gaze shot away again in a manner that made Mélanie wonder if this man was someone more specific than the general idea of marrying the man one loved. "I told Lewis I needed time to think. I sent him away. I—" She dragged her gaze back to Mélanie's face. "I don't think his family would have approved. Do you think that's why he was killed?"

Until a few minutes ago it would never have occurred to Mélanie as a motive, but now they couldn't discount it. "There are a number of reasons Lewis might have been killed. A betrothal that wasn't even official doesn't seem at all the likeliest. What time did Lewis leave you?"

Letty frowned. "About six-thirty. Perhaps a few minutes after. I remember looking at the clock when I went upstairs to make a cup of tea."

"Did he say where he was going?"

"No. I assume he was going home or to dine with friends or to see his family."

"He didn't mention going back to the Tavistock?"

"No, why would he have done that?"

Mélanie studied the girl Lewis Thornsby had loved. "Did Lewis ever talk about the Levellers?"

Letty drew back slightly on the frayed settee. Wariness shot over her gaze.

"I know about the Levellers," Mélanie said. "I could hardly fail to do so. Surely you realize my husband and I are in sympathy with them."

"Mr. Rannoch is in Parliament."

"So is Roger Smythe, who's a Leveller."

Letty released her breath. "I knew. How can one be about the Tavistock and not know, as you say, for all their pretense to secrecy? To tell the truth, I tried to know as little as possible. Not that I wouldn't like the world to change, but it's enough of a challenge just trying to survive, isn't it?"

"There was a time I felt that way myself." When she'd been holding on to her sanity by her fingernails in the brothel. Before Raoul found her.

"To own the truth, that was another reason I hesitated to agree to marry Lewis. I knew he was involved in something dangerous. Knew it better than he did himself, I think." Letty hesitated, fingered the handkerchief, pushed her fingers through her hair.

"More dangerous than their general activities?"

Letty chewed her lip. "One night a week ago I came back to the theatre to fetch my gloves—I'd left them in my dressing room. I heard Lewis and another man talking. I couldn't make out who the other man was, and I couldn't understand all their words. But I heard Lewis say, 'This is different. This seems like treason.' And the other man laughed. I *think* he said, 'What did you think you signed up for?'"

The sketch of the rifle trajectory shot into Mélanie's memory. "Did you ask Lewis about it?"

"No." Letty rubbed her arms. "I thought I was better off knowing as little as possible about it. Now I can't but wonder— If I'd told Simon or you or someone—"

"We don't know that that's why Lewis was killed."

"No, but it *might* be."

"Letty." Mélanie leaned forwards and laid a hand over the younger woman's own. "When there's been a tragedy it's very common to ask these sorts of questions. To play 'what if?' and imagine all the ways one might have changed things. The truth is, it's impossible to know if anything would have been different. And it's definitely folly to blame yourself."

Letty gave a lopsided smile. "That sounds eminently sensible, Mrs. Rannoch. But it's not so easy to do."

Mélanie found herself smiling in return, heart heavy with memories. "No," she agreed, "it isn't. But at least it can help to try."

Letty nodded.

"Did Lewis have any enemies you know of?" Mélanie asked.

Letty chewed her lower lip. "One doesn't generally think about enemies. I mean, one doesn't expect bad things to happen to one's friends. That is, I suppose one does if—"

"It's a bit different when one is an agent," Mélanie said. "That's true."

Letty nodded. "I never met Lewis's family, but from things he said, I know they disapproved of the Levellers and of how much time he spent about the theatre. I can't imagine they'd have been happy about his involvement with me. At least not about his proposing." She twisted her hands together. "But you're right, much as it worries me, I can't imagine their killing him. They'd be more likely to kill me." Her eyes widened slightly.

"There's no reason to think you're in danger," Mélanie said. "But be extra careful to lock your door for the next few days.

And don't walk home from the theatre alone after dark. I'll talk to Simon. I'm sure we can find someone to walk with you."

Letty nodded, gaze steady with practicality. She was a girl used to facing difficult circumstances.

"What else do you know about Mr. Thornsby's family?" Mélanie asked.

"He has an elder brother who's interested in classics. And two sisters. The younger sister just made her debut." Letty shook her head. "Funny what a debut means for a girl in society and what it means for an actress. His family is comfortably situated. Far more comfortably than I can imagine. But the father has debts, I believe. And the country house and most of what fortune there is go to Lewis's elder brother. But Lewis has—had"—her voice caught—"an aunt—a great-aunt, actually— who was very fond of him. Lady Shroppington. Aunt Shrops he used to call her. It was common knowledge that Lewis was her heir. But of course, there wasn't an entail or anything. She could easily decide to change her will. And though Lewis said she loved theatre and she'd love me, I can't imagine she'd have been happy about his marrying an actress, however much she enjoyed watching the stage from her box. Lewis would have said we could be happy without her money. But then he didn't know what it meant to be poor. I do. And yes, I know that sounds beastly, but it wouldn't have been fair to him either."

"It sounds practical," Mélanie said.

"And people in love aren't supposed to be practical."

"They often aren't. Which isn't precisely the same thing. Do you know who Lady Shroppington will leave her fortune to now Lewis is gone?"

"His brother, I assume. Or perhaps one of his sisters. Or all of them, I suppose. Why—Good God." Letty stared at her. "Surely you don't think Lewis's brother could be behind this? Or his sisters? The younger sister is barely eighteen."

Money proved to be at the root of the motive of a great

many crimes, but Mélanie felt a wave of protectiveness for the seemingly hardened Letty. "We need to explore all the options. There's also the possibility that someone else might think they would benefit if Mr. Thornsby's brother or one of his sisters were the heir."

"Who? A woman who wants to marry Thomas? A man who was courting Hypatia or Helen?" Letty dashed her hand across her eyes. "Sorry. I haven't met them, but I'm so used to Lewis's talking about them I feel I know them. I don't suppose I'll ever meet them now."

"I think they might find it a comfort to meet you," Mélanie said.

Letty stared at her in disbelief.

"To hear about Lewis. From someone he cared for."

Letty shook her head. "I told you. They wouldn't approve of me. And I don't think I was precisely worthy of his regard."

"But they wouldn't be facing his marrying you now. That might make it much easier to be magnanimous. And what would matter to them is that he cared for you. It might be a comfort for them. And for you."

"You're odd, Mrs. Rannoch. In one breath you're suggesting Lewis's family might have killed him. In the next, you're offering compassion to them. And me."

"There are certain questions one must ask in investigating a murder. No matter how much one likes people. Perhaps especially if one likes them, because it can damage one's perspective. But it doesn't do away with compassion. At least it shouldn't. I haven't always been as compassionate as I should."

"I can't imagine your being anything else."

"People can change. I certainly have," Mélanie said. Letty hadn't known her in the old days. When she'd been an agent. Or before then, in the brothel. When it had been hard to find room for anything approaching compassion. "Is there anyone else you can think of who had reason to be threatened by Lewis?"

"Other than those who are afraid of the Levellers? No, no one."

But Letty paused ever so slightly before she said it.

In an investigation, sometimes pauses revealed more than what was actually said.

CHAPTER 4

David Mallinson, Viscount Worsley, regarded the man he loved over the wrought iron nursery beds. Simon was tucking the covers round three-year-old Jamie. He had been recounting the events at the Tavistock while they checked on their four sleeping children. Well, properly, David's niece and three nephews, the children of his late sister, but in reality they had become Simon's as much as David's soon after the children came to live with them.

"Good God," David said. It would have been more of a shock a few years ago—before he and Simon had become embroiled in so many of Malcolm and Mélanie's adventures—but violent death still shook him. David had seen young Thornsby only the day before, when he'd brought the children by the theatre to watch a rehearsal. "You think one of Father's agents planted this drawing on Thornsby?"

"Malcolm raised it as a possibility." Simon smoothed Jamie's hair. "It's nothing like certain."

"But you don't think Thornsby really was involved in a plot to assassinate a member of the royal family?"

"My God, David." Simon straightened up and regarded him

across the bed. "Can you imagine I'd have kept quiet if I'd had the smallest glimmering such a plot existed? Among other things, I don't believe in killing."

"Thornsby could have been involved in a plot without your knowing of it."

"It's possible." Simon glanced round the beds, at Teddy, George, and Amy, sleeping soundly beneath their quilts, then jerked his head at the door. David followed his lover into the passage. "It's barely possible," Simon said when they were out of the nursery with the white-painted door closed. "But it's not the sort of thing the Levellers do."

David made it a point to stay as far out of the Levellers' activities as he could, just as Simon made it a point not to involve him. But he knew they didn't espouse violence. At least they hadn't so far. "But Father would like to discredit them."

"David—" Simon put a quick, warm hand on his arm. "Don't let this drive a wedge between you and your father."

David gave a rough laugh. "Don't you think that was done long since?" When his father had used the truth of Mélanie Rannoch's past to try to drive a wedge between David and Malcolm and between David and Simon. Because Carfax, above all, wanted things ordered as he saw fit. And part of that included David's marrying and fathering an heir.

"You've begun to mend things."

"If by that you mean I can tolerate his presence, and he hasn't actively tried to manipulate us since we returned to Britain, I suppose you're right."

"No sense in tearing it apart again based on supposition. There are too many unknown factors. Even granted it's likely that someone planted that paper on Thornsby, even Malcolm admits we can't be sure it was your father. In fact, he acknowledges it's a bit blunt for Carfax."

David nodded. All that made sense. But he found it difficult to trust his father in anything.

Simon reached for his hand. "Malcolm and Roth are coming to the Tavistock in the morning to talk to the company. And Mélanie will be there, of course. We should know more then. Meanwhile, there's nothing we can do. Best get to bed and face what we have to tomorrow."

David gave a faint smile and let Simon draw him down the passage. He and Simon had learned to navigate the difficult terrain of their sometimes-conflicting interests as MP and Radical. They knew what questions not to ask, knew when to turn a blind eye. After the events of a year and a half ago, they trusted each other more than ever. They were raising four children together. They were as committed to each other as if they'd made vows in a church.

But David was quite sure there was something about tonight his lover wasn't telling him.

VALENTIN, the footman who had been with them since Brussels during the chaos of the Battle of Waterloo, greeted Mélanie with a smile and steady gaze when she returned to Berkeley Square after her visit to Letty Blanchard. "Mr. Rannoch hasn't come back yet," he said, taking her bonnet. "Mr. and Mrs. O'Roarke are still out as well. Blanca and Addison are upstairs with the children. And Lord Carfax called about ten minutes ago. He's waiting in the library." He regarded her for a moment. "I told him you might have to go up to the children before you could see him."

Mélanie smiled and touched his arm. "You're the best of men, Valentin. But no, I should see him." She undid the last of the frogged clasps on her pelisse. "In fact, I'm very curious about what he has to say."

Valentin nodded and slid the pelisse from her shoulders. Mélanie glanced into the mirror over the console table, smoothed the band of black velvet that edged the square neck of her coffee-colored gown, adjusted her hairpins (she was wearing her hair down with the front pulled back as she frequently did now, so it was far easier to repair than a chignon), added a quick swipe of lip rouge from her reticule, then crossed the hall to the library.

She found Lord Carfax—Malcolm's former spymaster, Britain's unofficial chief of intelligence, the man she had worked against in her years as a French spy, the man who had driven them into exile less than two years since—sitting in one of the Queen Anne chairs by the fire, sipping a glass of whisky.

"Lord Carfax." She closed the door with a click that was meant to be audible. "I was wondering when we'd see you."

"Mélanie." Carfax pushed himself to his feet. "Thank you for seeing me."

"I could hardly do otherwise when you're in our library." She moved to the drinks trolley and poured herself a whisky. "May I refill your glass? I imagine you could do with it. I know I could after tonight."

"Er— thank you." Carfax held out his glass, caught off guard, just as she'd intended. "Valentin was good enough to offer it," he added, as she splashed Islay malt into the etched glass. "I wouldn't—"

"Help yourself to our whisky?" Mélanie set down the decanter. "I rather think that would be the least egregious of your sins where this family is concerned. And I'd have to admit at this point one must consider you part of the family."

Carfax flushed uncharacteristically, again thrown off balance, which again was what she had intended. In addition to his other connections to the Rannochs, Carfax was the father of Malcolm's sister Gisèle, a fact they had all (including Carfax) only learned a year ago.

Mélanie took a sip of her whisky and moved to the other Queen Anne chair. "Malcolm isn't here."

Carfax returned to his own chair and settled his glass on the table between the chairs. "I expect he's still out with Jeremy Roth."

Mélanie set her glass down beside Carfax's. "You'll have to ask him when you see him. I don't expect my husband to keep me apprised of his whereabouts. As you must appreciate, we lead quite complicated lives."

"Don't play games, Mélanie." Carfax settled his shoulders against the high back of the chair. "You were at the Tavistock tonight."

"Yes, I was." She smiled at him. "I've been there most nights for the past fortnight. My play is about to open."

"But tonight Lewis Thornsby was found dead."

Mélanie picked up her glass. "How long did it take you to get the news?"

"My dear Mélanie. Given the activity round the Tavistock, you can't imagine I don't have the place watched. My informant saw the link boy head to Bow Street. Sent, I assume by you or Julien St. Juste. So no, I didn't know before you did, and no, I didn't have Thornsby killed. Though I make no doubt Malcolm thinks I did."

"I wouldn't say that."

"Spoken like a diplomatic wife."

She took a sip of whisky. "I did learn a number of things in the years Malcolm and I moved in diplomatic circles."

"As well as perfecting your spycraft, which was already exemplary." Carfax reached for his own glass. "It's probably just as well I found you rather than Malcolm. For a number of reasons. I assume you mean to investigate."

She turned her glass in her hand. The candlelight bounced off the Rannoch crest etched on it. "It would be folly to deny it."

"Good." Carfax took an appreciative sip of whisky.

"Good we're investigating, or good I didn't deny it?"

"Both. I need to know what happened to Thornsby, and you

and Malcolm will undoubtedly ferret out the truth. Then I can work out what to do about it."

"Assuming we tell you."

"There is that." Carfax took another drink of whisky. "What's Tanner got to do with this?"

The mention of Simon, Carfax's son's lover, made the ground suddenly set with mines. Mélanie took a measured sip from her own glass. "Nothing, save that it's his theatre. And he happened to be in the basement going through some papers when the children and I discovered poor Mr. Thornsby's body."

Carfax watched her. "I know you'll protect him. But this business he's involved in with the Levellers could ruin him. And his theatre. And you and Malcolm. And David."

"I don't think you're giving David enough credit."

Carfax's fingers whitened round his glass, but his gaze remained steady. "I'm giving David credit for supporting the person he loves, no matter what."

"Simon's a writer and thinker. Not the sort who takes revolutionary action."

"One can lead to the other. And the line between the two is often blurry. If I were talking to Malcolm, I'd make an appeal to his patriotism. No sense in trying that with you."

"I have no desire to overthrow the British government."

"Don't you?" Carfax adjusted the earpiece of his spectacles. "You disappoint me, Mélanie. Don't tell me you've given up on your convictions."

"Not in the least. But I don't see how a frontal assault on the government would achieve the sort of change I'd like to see. Or that Malcolm would."

"You can't tell me you're entirely in agreement with him."

"Not in the least. I doubt I ever will be."

Carfax leaned forwards, glass held between his hands. "Tanner's involved in something dangerous. I'd say he's in over his head, save that I know just how clever he is, and I suspect he may be far more ruthless than I credited."

"Simon's not an agent."

"No, he's not. Which means he's likely to put a foot wrong. If you're his friend, you'll want to get him out of this before he lands in the briers."

Mélanie thought back to December, when they'd hidden a fugitive in the Tavistock from both Carfax and an Elsinore League assassin. To a tense moment when she'd been sure Simon was lying to her. To moments in the month since when the feeling had persisted. Carfax was far nearer the mark than she was prepared to admit. "My dear sir. You almost sound concerned."

"Can you imagine I'm not? For the country, as well as my son."

"You'll have to do better if you expect me to believe you think Simon is a threat to the country."

"I told you." Carfax's gaze settled hard on her face, unwavering as that of a hawk watching its prey. "He's not an agent, but he's a brilliant and possibly ruthless man. And a believer. It's a dangerous combination. There's no pragmatism to temper the belief. I don't expect you to listen to me, but I do expect you to want to protect your friend. And to protect Malcolm from the consequences if his friend fell afoul of the law. Or was involved in a plot Malcolm himself couldn't support."

"My dear sir. You must know I've made Malcolm an expert in divided loyalties."

Carfax inclined his head but didn't let his gaze waver. "All the more reason, surely, to protect him from more of the same."

"Malcolm and I know better than to try to protect each other."

"Do you? Or do you simply know better than to let the other one see that you're doing it?"

Carfax had a damnable knack for nicking to the bone

without appearing to even lift a knife. "You assume we could deceive each other at this point."

"I have no doubt you could deceive Malcolm. Under the right circumstances, I suspect Malcolm could deceive you. Love can be a weakness. And though I rarely say I'm sure of anything, I'm reasonably sure you love Malcolm. Which is why, going back to my original point, I assume you want to protect him."

"I'd have thought by now you'd have learned the folly of assuming anything. Particularly when it comes to Malcolm and me."

Carfax lifted his glass to her in silent acknowledgement. "St. Juste was there tonight, I understand."

"Does that surprise you?"

He settled back in his chair again. "Julien's being anywhere is hardly a surprise. Though I think you're more apprised of his actions these days than I am. Was Mrs. Ashford with him?"

"Surely you have intelligence on that."

"My dear Mélanie. Even you must realize I don't have intelligence on every detail."

Mélanie took a sip of whisky. Carfax knew about Julien and Kitty's relationship. A relationship she wasn't entirely sure she understood herself. This seemed something she could give him without a great deal of risk. And perhaps in the process find out why he was so interested in Julien and Kitty Ashford. "She wasn't, as it happens. I'm sure you realize Julien and Kitty Ashford don't live in each other's pockets any more than Malcolm and I do."

"Julien and Mrs. Ashford are to all intents and purposes living together." There was a faint line between Carfax's brows.

"Surely even you acknowledge that agents' private lives are their own business. Provided they don't interfere with work."

"My dear Mélanie. Do you, of all people, really think that's possible?"

"Certainly." She met his gaze without flinching. "I never let my feelings for Malcolm interfere with my work."

"A fair point." Carfax didn't blink.

"And neither Julien nor Kitty could be said to be your agent any longer." She made it not quite a question.

Carfax gave a short laugh. "Do you really imagine either of them would work for me at this point? If they did, I'd be rather less concerned. Though still far from sanguine."

"Because you've never been able to control either of them."

"It's a problem with some of the best agents. Your husband included."

What exactly Julien St. Juste was to Carfax remained a mystery to Mélanie. She knew Julien had worked for Carfax, though far from exclusively, and that Julien had then broken free and taken a number of Carfax's other agents with him, by dint of stealing compromising materials Carfax had used to control them. But Mélanie had overheard the exchange between the two men, and both had acknowledged that they could never be entirely free of the other. Why, she wasn't sure. Or how Kitty Ashford, who had also been Carfax's agent in the Peninsula and had worked with Julien there and in Argentina, fit into the picture.

Mélanie took a sip of whisky. "Assuming Malcolm and I keep you apprised of our investigation as we can, will you keep us apprised of yours?"

Carfax raised his brows.

"Whatever your flattering faith in our investigative abilities, you can't tell me you aren't running your own investigation. If we share information as needed it might benefit us both."

Carfax continued to watch her.

"Surely you realize I understand the benefits of collaborating with an opponent," Mélanie said.

Carfax gave a faint smile and lifted his glass to her again. "As

I said, for a number of reasons, it's probably as well I got to speak with you rather than Malcolm."

The door opened on the silence that followed this exchange. The subject of their conversation walked into the library with timing worthy of a stage play. "Carfax." Malcolm paused briefly, then moved to Mélanie's chair and put a hand on her shoulder. "I was expecting to see you tonight."

"I believe Mélanie has filled me in on a number of the details. But I understand you and Roth have been to Thornsby's lodgings."

"Yes. Though we arrived after Billy. He asked me to tell you that he didn't discover anything, by the way."

Carfax, at least, knew better than to attempt denials. "As I told Mélanie, it shouldn't surprise either of you that I have agents watching the Tavistock. When I heard Thornsby's body had been found, naturally I wanted to see what might be among his papers. Not that you don't have better instincts searching for evidence than Billy does, but Billy would hand over everything with none of your sifting and considering. Not to mention protecting your friends. It was a worth a try. I assume you and Roth searched Thornsby's rooms after you sent Billy packing?"

"And you'd like to hear about what we discovered? No, it's all right." Malcolm's hand tightened on Mélanie's shoulder, part warning that he had the situation in hand, part reassurance, perhaps of himself as much as her. "As it happens, I was going to call on you if I didn't find you here. Does 19 Rosemary Lane mean anything to you?"

"Should it?"

"Thornsby's valet saw a letter with that direction on it among Thornsby's things. Thornsby didn't seem to want him to see it and apparently later burned the letter."

"Interesting. I assume you'll pay a call there."

"Roth and I will tomorrow." Malcolm drew a paper from his

pocket and walked over to Carfax's chair. "We also found this. Do you recognize it?"

Carfax stared at the drawing. From her seat across from him, Mélanie could see the lines of the rifle trajectory.

"Where did you find this?" Carfax asked.

"On Thornsby's body. One of my questions is if you put it there."

"Why the devil would I—"

"Oh, for God's sake, sir. Don't pretend you don't know I know you have agents provocateurs in just about every Radical organization in the country."

Carfax took the drawing from Malcolm, walked to the library table, and held it under the light of an Argand lamp. "'Every' is a bit of an exaggeration. Are you accusing me of employing Thornsby to foment such a plot in the hopes of discrediting the Levellers? Or of planting the paper on him after he was dead?"

"Potentially either one."

"Both seem a bit heavy handed." Carfax pushed his spectacles up on his nose. "I suppose it's occurred to you Thornsby might really be involved in a plot to shoot someone in the royal box?"

"That's why I'm telling you about it. That and the fact that Simon insisted I tell you."

Carfax looked down at the drawing again. "Yes, I don't think Tanner would actually try to murder a member of the royal family. The risk he represents to Britain is much more cerebral. And more complicated. I was discussing that with Mélanie before you came in."

Malcolm crossed to Carfax and took the paper from him. "If Thornsby was involved in an assassination plot, he was killed by someone who either didn't know about the plot or who wanted this paper found."

"My dear Malcolm." Carfax returned to his chair and took a sip of whisky. "Are you accusing me of having Thornsby killed?"

Malcolm returned the sketch to his coat. "As you yourself said, it seems a bit heavy handed. You'd have to have known Mélanie and I would end up investigating and that we'd ask the obvious questions about the paper. On the other hand, if Thornsby was working for you and caused trouble, he wouldn't be the first inconvenient agent you've got rid of."

Carfax rested his glass on his chair arm. "Thornsby wasn't working for me. I don't expect you to believe me, but I thought I should at least make the point. His sort of romanticized undergraduate Radicalism can be distinctly dangerous. And it wouldn't make for a good agent. Not unless he was a far better actor than most of the Tavistock's excellent company." He frowned at the spot where Malcolm had stowed the sketch. "I'm going to have to investigate this."

"I trust you will," Malcolm said. "None of us wants an assassination."

"I've been telling Lord Carfax we can share information with him if he shares it with us," Mélanie said.

Malcolm shot a look at her. "Within reason," she said.

"It seems a reasonable arrangement," Carfax said.

Malcolm sat on the arm of Mélanie's chair. "So why did you send Billy to search Thornsby's rooms?"

"I told you. Thornsby was a Leveller. Thornsby met a violent death. It seemed not unlikely the two were connected."

Malcolm folded his arms across his chest. "How did you know Thornsby was a Leveller?"

"My dear Malcolm. I may not have the network I once did, but I am not entirely without resources. I have sources at the Tavistock, as I admitted to both of you."

"You have a source among the Levellers."

"No comment."

"I thought we were sharing information."

"Within reason, as Mélanie said." Carfax took another drink

of whisky. "In the spirit of cooperation, I'll admit to having an agent among the Levellers."

"A great concession, considering, as I'm sure you know, we knew that already. What would really shock me is if you shared the agent's name."

"Would you share the name of one of your agents with me?"

"Fair enough." Malcolm picked up Mélanie's glass and took a drink from it. "Why are you so afraid of the Levellers?"

"Have you read the sort of things they advocate?"

"Yes, they sound very like the sort of things David, Simon, Oliver, and I were writing and speaking about a decade ago. And you were afraid of us. Which surely seems rather silly now."

"Does it? Look in the mirror, Malcolm. Turn round and look at your wife, who is watching you with the sort of pride most men would give a fortune to see on their wife's face. You're a lot of things, but above all, you're a force to be reckoned with. God help us."

"I'd say you're a flatterer, sir. Save that you wouldn't flatter without a reason."

"Well-born young men with delusions that they know how to set the world straight are more likely to upend our world than northern machine breakers or displaced farmers. They're the sort that have all too much time on their hands. And all too much power and all too many resources."

"Are you saying you think the sketch represents a real plot?"

"I'm saying I think it could. I'm sorry, Mélanie. I don't mean to have your premiere disrupted."

"Are you saying you think we should call the play off?"

"On the contrary. If the plot falls apart, we'll never learn who is behind it. With all of us working on the problem, I don't doubt we can get to the truth of the matter in five days." He looked between her and Malcolm. "You're in the midst of an investigation. No sense in wasting your time or mine with an argument neither of us can win. As Mélanie said, there are things we can agree about. Like stopping this plot, whoever is behind it. Like fighting the League."

"There's no reason to think the League have anything to do with Thornsby's death," Malcolm said.

"None that you've discovered? None that I have so far either. But the League are wrapped up in a great deal. They were trying to kill that young woman Kit Montagu's fiancée smuggled into the country last month. And Montagu is one of the Levellers' leaders."

Mélanie glanced at Malcolm. They'd never been quite clear how much Carfax knew about Nerezza Russo and the night they and their friends had saved her from assassination by the League and smuggled her to safety. Mélanie wasn't going to be drawn into questions about Nerezza's present whereabouts.

"You also tried to have the Levellers arrested that night," she said.

"And you warned them."

"No sense in denying that now," Mélanie said. "But Thornsby wasn't in the meeting that night. There's no reason to think he has anything to do with Nerezza or the League."

"No, but the League have a tendency to be in the middle of everything. I'm sure you'll explore the connections." Carfax swallowed the last of his whisky and set down his glass. "And I'm sure you have a number of things to discuss that you can't say in front of me. Or at least don't feel you can. I'll make my goodnights. This has been a very edifying evening."

CHAPTER 5

Sofia Vincenzo looked at Kit Montagu in his mother's lamplit drawing room. Lady Thurston was asleep upstairs. But her shock at Sofia's entertaining a young man alone late at night would be tempered by the fact that Kit was in his mother's own house. And Lady Thurston, despite Kit and his sisters' saying she was a high stickler, had shown herself surprisingly easy-tempered when it came to Sofia and Kit. Perhaps she realized her son, for all his Radical thoughts, was far too much a conventional gentleman in some ways to do anything before they were married. Which rather disappointed Sofia, who would have been ready to go further months ago.

Now Sofia was sitting beside Kit on the sofa, holding his hands, and Kit was too agitated to cavil at their behavior. She could feel the tension thrumming through him. He spoke quickly, as though he needed to spill the story out.

"It's horrible," Sofia said. "Why, I saw poor Lewis only this afternoon when I stopped by the theatre. I was thinking how he was in over his head with Letty, and though I like both of them, they'd never be happy together. Oh, poison, I know that sounds like an odd thing to say, but I can't quite take it in—"

"Nor can I." Kit squeezed her hands. "It must bring back memories."

"Of my father?" Sofia hunched her shoulders. The memory of her father's body on the edge of Lake Como, blood pooling round him, was as vivid as if it had been yesterday, rather than over a year ago. "Not really. I mean, that was so different. It was my father, so nothing can compare. But I knew Father was involved in things that were dangerous. Lewis—"

"Lewis was a Leveller."

She shook her head. "Still."

Kit watched her for a moment. "Are you saying we're all boys playing at being Radicals?"

"Hardly. *Caro*, you know I don't think that. I met you because the Carbonari wanted to work with you. But Lewis seemed to be playing at being a Radical, perhaps. I thought he was drawn to the idea of adventure more than to the idea of change."

"Which may have got him killed." Kit's fingers tightened over her own. "You hadn't heard anything about a plot involving the royal box?"

"Good God, Kit. I'd have told you."

Kit scraped a hand over his hair. "It doesn't seem like Lewis. And yet, he was drawn to adventure, as you say. He was too young to really understand consequences, I think. He might have fallen prey to someone who was trying to foment a plot. Or a pretend plot."

"An agent provocateur? There are so many of them in Radical groups, it would be folly to think we hadn't been infiltrated."

"Or he was framed."

"Because either the killer didn't know the paper was there or wanted the paper found." Sofia scanned her fiancé's face. "*You* hadn't heard any rumblings about anything like this?"

"Beyond the search for the mole in the Levellers? No." Kit drew her closer. "It's going to bring Carfax down on us more than ever. But at least Malcolm and Mélanie are looking into it as well. We'll know more when we get a report from them in the morning. I just wanted—needed—to tell you tonight."

"Of course." Sofia slid her arm round him and pressed her face against his shoulder. She and Kit had been allies before they were lovers. He was a good agent, but she could read him well.

And she was quite sure her betrothed, her colleague, her friend, the man she loved, was keeping something from her.

~

COLIN LOOKED BETWEEN HIS PARENTS. "I don't suppose you've learned anything you can tell us?"

Malcolm grinned and knelt down beside their son. "Not yet, old chap. We haven't learned much at all."

"Is Uncle Simon all right?"

Mélanie saw the instinctive fear that ran through Malcolm. But he said, "Uncle Simon's fine. He's very upset about Mr. Thornsby, and concerned like the rest of us. He went home to talk to Uncle David."

"It's very sad." Blanca, Mélanie's companion, looked from Malcolm to Mélanie and then at her husband Addison, Malcolm's valet. "Mr. Thornsby was a kind man."

"Anything we can do?" Addison asked. In addition to being Malcolm's valet, he, like Blanca, was a skilled agent.

"There'll be leads for of all us to investigate," Malcolm said. "We'll know more tomorrow."

Jessica looked up from the floor where she was playing blocks with Pedro, Blanca and Addison's fourteen-month-old son. For a heart-stopping moment Mélanie was reminded of Colin playing with baby Jessica. "Will we go to the theatre tomorrow?"

"Perhaps later in the day," Mélanie said. "Not first thing in the morning. There's nothing to be afraid of there."

Jessica inched across the floor and climbed into Mélanie's lap. "I'm not afraid when I'm with you."

Half an hour later, when they had tucked Colin and Jessica into bed and read them stories, and Blanca and Addison had taken Pedro to their own apartments in the mews, Mélanie and Malcolm returned downstairs. Malcolm leaned against the newel post in the hall and gave a lopsided smile. "Not the day I anticipated when I got up this morning. I'm sorry, sweetheart."

"I'm all right." Mélanie bent down to pick up a small figure of a lady in a red gown and another of a knight with a Plantagenet crest on his shield that had somehow ended up under the console table. They were favorites of Colin's. "Oh, you mean the play?"

Malcolm crossed to her side and reached out to push her hair behind her ear. "It's rather important to you."

"We'll manage." She leaned her cheek against his hand for a moment, then took his hand and drew him back into the library. "I keep thinking about Thornsby. He looked so young lying there. He'd been so alive a few hours before. And it seems he'd just asked Letty to marry him." She told Malcolm about her talk with Letty.

"Do you believe Letty?" Malcolm asked when she had done. They were back in the Queen Anne chair, the two of them wedged into it together, with her legs draped over Malcolm's lap.

"You mean, do I think she could have been lying about Lewis's leaving her at her lodgings, and that she came back to the Tavistock with him and killed him?" Mélanie asked. "Like you, I know better than to discount anything. But her shock and grief seemed very genuine. I don't think she told me everything she knows, though. When I asked her about Lewis's enemies, I'd swear she bit something back."

"Do you think she'd have married him?" Malcolm asked.

"I don't know." Mélanie lifted her head to look at her

husband. "She was seriously considering it, I think. But she was aware of what she'd be giving up. Not just the chance to fall in love, but the chance perhaps to forge her own life. Still, it was, or seemed to be, a guarantee of a secure life. Letty comes from a background where that means a lot."

Malcolm nodded. "Thornsby was very young. But my impression was that he was sincerely attached to her."

"Enough so to offer marriage. And not, I think, just because he couldn't get her into bed any other way. It's not as though Letty was holding out for marriage. She seems to have been genuinely surprised by the offer." Mélanie hesitated. "I was concerned, hearing her talk, about what might have happened if they'd married. But they might have been happy. She might even have grown to love him. People can, even when they go into marriage for less than ideal reasons. As we know."

Malcolm smoothed a loose strand of hair back from her face. "Finding a way to forge your own life has helped."

"I've been forging my own life from the moment I married you, dearest. I've just been putting together different pieces of it." And yet, all of those pieces had been focused on him. Even as an agent, she'd been working against him. So he had remained her focus. She'd supported him as a diplomatic and political wife. She'd hosted his parties and helped write his speeches. They raised their children together. They worked together as agents and investigated crimes together. The theatre was something different, something that he supported and embraced, but that was hers. Which mattered to her in ways she could scarcely begin to put into words. But she wanted to make sure it didn't bother Malcolm. Because Malcolm had a generosity that would drive him to do anything for her. And he wouldn't admit, even to himself, if it bothered him.

Malcolm kissed her nose. "Have I mentioned how proud I am of you?"

"Once or twice." She reached up to kiss him. "I love you, Malcolm."

He held her to him for a moment, then made a typical Malcolm transition back to the investigation. "A good reminder that there could be motives for Thornsby's death that have nothing to do with that drawing."

"Though the drawing still came from somewhere."

"So it did." Malcolm's voice was hard.

Mélanie drew her knees up and linked her arms round them. "A crude attempt to make a personal crime look like something political?"

"Interesting possibility." Malcolm's brows knotted. "But if Letty is to be believed, Thornsby was involved in something secret, whether or not it relates to the sketch."

"And there's the question of what brought him back to the theatre tonight." She twisted her pendant—a garnet pendant Malcolm had given her in another life, before their exile—on its chain. "Of course, he might have had an appointment at the Tavistock simply because it seemed a quiet place to talk. He could have arranged to meet a friend or a family member there. But it does seem more likely he came back to see someone in the company. Or one of the Levellers, since so many of them are connected to the company and they tend to treat the theatre as their base."

Malcolm nodded. "Thornsby always struck me as well liked. Carfax called him a hothead, but he didn't seem to be so in the way that makes enemies."

"Definitely not a Hotspur," Mélanie agreed. "And not a Hal either. He's not—he wasn't—as dissolute as Hal on the surface, and he wasn't nearly as much of a calculating schemer underneath. At least not unless he was a very good actor, as Carfax said. Do you believe Carfax about Thornsby's not having been his agent?"

Malcolm's frown deepened. "With Carfax, you know I hesitate to believe anything. But for the moment I'm inclined to do so. We found nothing in Thornsby's things to support it. But in addition to Billy, we found Kit Montagu in Thornsby's lodgings."

Mélanie let go of the pendant. "Searching?"

"Attempting to. He said he wanted to go through Thornsby's things before anyone else did because Thornsby was a Leveller. Which is pretty much what Carfax said as well about employing Billy. And while on the surface it makes a certain amount of sense from both of them, I can't help thinking there's more in both cases."

"If Lewis Thornsby was involved in something secret for the Levellers, Kit could have wanted to cover it up and Carfax could want to learn about it. Or if Thornsby was Carfax's agent, Carfax could want to cover that up, and Kit could want to search for evidence if he suspected. Though in that case, I'd have thought he'd have told you."

Malcolm picked up her whisky glass and took a sip. "Thornsby didn't strike me as duplicitous. But then, I've been known to be spectacularly wrong."

Including about his own brother. Mélanie slid her arms round her husband. "You're a good judge of people, darling. Don't doubt yourself."

He pressed a kiss to her forehead. "There's something else." He drew another paper from his coat and held it out to her, fingers taut on the cream laid writing paper.

Less than six months ago, Malcolm's first love had been a nameless, faceless mystery to Mélanie, known only in the sense she knew there must have been someone before her. But now Kitty Ashford was a frequent guest in their house, familiar enough that Mélanie recognized her hand immediately.

"I didn't know Kitty even knew Thornsby," Malcolm said. "Did you?"

"No. That is, she's visited the theatre with the children

occasionally and she's certainly brought them to performances, but I don't remember ever seeing her with Thornsby. But then, though I'd call her a friend now, we're hardly confidantes."

Malcolm gave a wry smile. "I can hardly call her a confidante either. There could be several very innocuous explanations. Save for the all the very complicated intrigues we're all caught up in. And the fact that her lover arrived on the scene just after you discovered the body. What do you think St. Juste was doing at the theatre?"

"I'm not sure. He never really explained this errand for Bertrand that he claimed he was on. I'm sure there's more to it. Though I'll own I was distinctly relieved when he arrived."

Malcolm's arms tightened round her. "I'm inestimably relieved too. Not that you couldn't have handled it, but it would have been difficult with the children."

"They both handled it splendidly, but there were certainly things I wasn't going to attempt with them there." Mélanie shook her hair back from her shoulders. "I'm sure there are connections to what Julien was doing there that we have yet to unravel, but I don't think—"

"That St. Juste killed Thornsby? No, nor do I. We've got to a rather interesting place with him. He's one of us."

Mélanie laughed. "It sounds so improbable but—yes. I gave him Jessica to hold tonight. Without a second thought, save that I was glad someone was there I could trust with her so I could look at the body."

"I'd trust him with the children now too. And yes, that does make me realize how far we've come."

She smoothed a crease from Malcolm's coat. "Carfax asked me a lot of questions about Julien. And about Julien and Kitty. He seems to take an inordinate interest in their relationship."

"Kitty was once his agent too."

"But this seems to go beyond that. Carfax doesn't strike me

as the sort to care about his agents' personal lives unless they interfere with work."

"With Carfax, everything is work. He may well not want Julien involved in Kitty's work in Spain."

"Perhaps." Kitty was deeply involved with those in Spain seeking to move against the restored monarchy, as was Raoul O'Roarke. "It's still strange he's so interested in the details." Mélanie thought about Julien. His quick support tonight and yet his odd detachment from the sketch and its implications. "It's strange," she said.

"What?"

"Kitty believes so strongly in her work in Spain. And one of Julien's points of pride has always been that he doesn't believe in anything."

Malcolm gave a faint smile. "Which could be a problem. Though people can change. And I'm starting to get a strong sense that Julien believes in Kitty. He may be willing to do quite a lot to support her."

"Yes, but just like me, he's going to have to figure out what he wants for himself."

"A good point."

"Even tonight he was apparently willing to keep quiet about a possible plot against a member of the royal family if Simon and I wanted to. Though I think he was glad we didn't, for any number of reasons."

"And knowing you and Simon, he may have realized you wouldn't."

"Have I mentioned your insights are amazing, Malcolm?"

"I can be singularly slow at times." His brows drew together. "I'm going to have to figure out how to talk to Kitty."

"She may even come to you, once she hears Thornsby is dead."

"She may. But I have a strong suspicion—one could say fear—that she won't."

Mélanie watched her husband. "Darling—"

She broke off at the sound of the front door opening. Not as alarming as it once would have been at this hour. After their return from a less formal life in Italy, they'd taken to sending the staff to bed after a certain hour and managing the door themselves. Laura and Raoul must be back from their dinner with Laura's family.

Mélanie and Malcolm went into the hall to find the O'Roarke family, Laura with baby Clara in her arms, Raoul with six-year-old Emily draped over one shoulder, fastening the bolt on the front door with his free hand.

"I'll get it." Malcolm went to help his father.

"Thank you." Raoul steadied Emily. "Hard to believe these days that I used to manage a sword and pistol at once on a regular basis."

And still did so, if the stories of his current work in Spain were even remotely close to the truth. Mélanie looked from Raoul to Laura. Odd to think that they'd been having a conventional evening while the drama at the Tavistock unfolded. "How was dinner?" she asked.

"Quite lovely," Laura said. "The children played together splendidly. Clara demonstrated her crawling prowess. And we had a very interesting conversation about Spain today compared to India twenty years ago."

"Laura's father had a lot of insights." Raoul looked from Mélanie to Malcolm. "But it looks as though your evening was unexpectedly eventful."

"There's no keeping anything from you." Malcolm grinned. "Best get the children in bed. It's a rather long story."

It was some minutes before Raoul and Laura returned downstairs. Malcolm poured whisky for everyone in the library while Mélanie began the story and then Malcolm took up with his and Roth's examination of Thornsby's rooms and their encounters with Billy and Kit.

Laura shook her head. "I remember Lewis Thornsby just yesterday when I brought the children to the theatre."

"I've been thinking the same thing," Mélanie said.

Raoul was frowning. "Interesting about St. Juste showing up."

"Yes, we thought so as well," Malcolm said. "Do you know about anything Thornsby was tangled up in?"

"Other than the Levellers?" Raoul asked. "You both knew him better than I did."

Malcolm watched the man who was his father, as well as Mélanie's former spymaster, over the rim of his whisky glass. "But you have sources among the London Radicals that we don't. And just like Kit, you don't tell me some things. Which is understandable. We're all working out how to work round our various loyalties. But in an investigation—"

"It's important to get at the truth," Raoul said. "Quite right. I haven't heard anything about Thornsby. But I can make some inquiries."

Malcolm nodded. "Do you"—he hesitated, and for a moment Mélanie wasn't sure he'd say more—"do you think there could really be a plot to assassinate a royal at the theatre?"

Raoul continued to hold Malcolm's gaze steadily. Sometimes, even now, it was difficult for Mélanie to read the tangled waters between the two men. "My dear Malcolm. Are you asking if I know about a plot to assassinate a member of the royal family?"

"No." Malcolm scraped a hand over his face. "Maybe."

Raoul's gaze remained steady, but something shifted within it. "Granted we all have secrets, but surely at this point you believe that if I had even a suspicion of such a plot, I'd tell you."

"Probably."

Raoul's mouth lifted in a faint smile. "Given my past actions, I probably deserve that. My darling boy, I don't believe in assassination."

"You believe in change."

"And I'm willing to take drastic measures? If I think they can succeed. Morality aside, the only change assassinating a member of the royal family would cause is to bring down repression on everyone working for any sort of reform in Britain."

Malcolm inclined his head. His gaze held the cool calculation of a professional, overlaying a son's desperate desire to believe. "So you think it's an agent provocateur?"

"I think there's a good chance. But just because an action would be foolish for our cause doesn't mean no one on our side would undertake it. I can make inquiries about that as well."

Malcolm nodded again, and then hesitated, as though framing his words with care. "Do you know of any reason Kitty would have been writing to Thornsby?" His voice was almost too carefully unstudied.

Raoul returned Malcolm's gaze with equally unstudied care. "Though we've all got to be friends, you're more in Kitty's confidence than I am."

"I don't know that any of us is in Kitty's confidence. But you know more about her work in Spain than I do."

Raoul and Kitty were both working with forces in Spain opposed to the Bourbon government. A situation that had grown more intense since the recent mutiny by the Asturian battalion in Cádiz. Raoul had been in England by the time the mutiny started, but Mélanie was quite sure he had had more to do with it than he was admitting. His nephew, Raimundo, was in Spain working with the rebels now, despite having married the widowed Annabel Larrimer only two months ago. "Kitty and I each have our own connections," Raoul said. "And while they do overlap, it's hard to see a connection between Lewis Thornsby and Spain."

Laura had been sitting by in silence. Like Mélanie, she

tended not to interfere in the complexities between Malcolm and Raoul. But now she turned to Malcolm.

"Do you know Lewis Thornsby's family?"

"Only by name. But I believe his elder brother is a classicist. Harry may know him."

"And Cordy may know the family, or at least know gossip about them," Mélanie said. Harry and Cordelia Davenport were an essential part of any investigation. Odd to think they weren't part of this one yet. "I'll talk to her tomorrow—no, I won't. That is, not in the morning. Jeremy's going to talk to the Tavistock company and I should be there."

"I can talk to Cordy," Laura said. "And bring her round to the theatre to see you. She won't want to be left out of an investigation. Any more than I wish to be."

CHAPTER 6

Julien found Kitty, one-and-a-half-year-old Genny on her lap, sitting on the nursery floor, playing lottery tickets with the boys. He bent to kiss Kitty and touched Genny's hair, then dropped down beside the boys, careful not to disrupt the gleaming piles of mother-of-pearl fish. "You missed dinner," Timothy said.

"I know." Julien took a sip from the glass of wine Kitty held out to him. "I ran into some complications at the Tavistock."

"Is Aunt Mélanie all right?" Leo was quick to pick up on worries.

"Yes, all our friends are fine." Julien gave Kitty back her wine glass, though for a moment he felt like downing the entire contents. "I just stayed a bit to help answer questions." It was a constant challenge, Julien had found since being about children more, knowing how much to say. In general, he subscribed to the theory that telling as much of the truth as possible was best. But even with his limited parenting experience, he realized that one had to use finesse in telling children under ten that someone had been murdered.

"Mummy was late too," Timothy said. "We had bread and

cheese and apple slices. We kept some for you." He nodded towards the nursery table. Part of a Stilton, a loaf of bread, and apples were arranged on a Wedgwood platter that took him back to childhood memories he'd just as soon not explore tonight.

"I called on Emily Cowper," Kitty said. "It took longer than I thought."

"Those sorts of calls generally do." Julien leaned back against the side of the nursery settee and held out his arms to take Genny. She climbed into his lap with gratifying enthusiasm and reached for the diamond pin in his cravat that never failed to fascinate her. In truth, that was why he'd taken to wearing it so much.

Kitty got up and moved to the table where she began to assemble a plate of bread and cheese and apples. Julien settled Genny in his lap and examined the boys' cards. "You're missing a prime chance to put your mother in check. Not to mix my game metaphors, but if you let me help you..."

Kitty returned to the floor with a plate of food. Julien ate one-handed and shared apple slices with Genny while they continued the game. Timothy, with help from Julien, vanquished his mother and elder brother and gave a crow of triumph. Genny, who had fallen asleep on Julien's shoulder by that point, one hand clutching his cravat, slumbered on despite the noise.

Julien carried her to her cradle, but it was some time before they got the boys into their nightshirts with their teeth brushed. Finally, in the quiet of Kitty's bedchamber (which practically was really their bedchamber now, though he wasn't going to think about that at present), Julien poured them both a calvados. Kitty came up behind him and slid her arms round him. "Are you going to tell me what happened? Or isn't it something you can tell?"

"No reason not to, now. Didn't want to disturb the children."

Julien turned in her arms and put one of the glasses in her hand. He smiled into her familiar green eyes, a gaze he knew better than he had ever thought to know anyone's. A gaze that knew him better than he had ever intended to let anyone know him.

"Someone's dead," Kitty said. "But not anyone we know. Because while I don't think you'd have told the children, I don't think you'd have actively lied to them. Not if you could help it."

Odd, the faint trepidation he felt. He took a sip of calvados and told her. About visiting the Tavistock. Finding Mélanie and the children. Finding Lewis Thornsby's body. Finding the sketch of the rifle trajectory on the body. Tanner's arrival. Talking to Tanner and Mélanie, and then to Malcolm and Roth. Everything, except the actual reason he'd been at the Tavistock in the first place. Because that would unravel everything.

"How unspeakably awful," Kitty said. "And how beastly for Mélanie to have been there with the children. I don't think she'd quail from anything, but one can't precisely rush into danger with children to think of. And, of course, it would have been unthinkable for her just to leave. I'm glad you were there." She gave a faint smile. "Even if you were there with Mélanie."

"My sweet." Julien kissed her forehead. "I thought we'd settled matters when it comes to Mélanie."

"I don't think matters will ever be precisely settled when it comes to you and Mélanie Rannoch." Kitty's voice was as tart and familiar as the crisp green apples they'd just eaten. "But I stopped being anything approaching jealous of her long since."

"I thought we didn't admit to jealousy."

Kitty laughed. "Speak for yourself, my darling. I'm conventional enough to feel a twinge on occasion. Even if I have no right to it."

"I wouldn't talk about rights." He caught her hand that wasn't holding the glass and kissed it. "It sounds as though we're debating a treaty."

"Quite." She tilted her head back. "How bad is it?"

He took a drink of calvados, weighing his words for a number of reasons. "It certainly creates complications. With Carfax, one way or another, at the very least. But then, when it come to the Rannochs and the O'Roarkes and the Davenports—and us—there are plenty of complications with Carfax, in any case. No matter where this leads, January was bound to have led us somewhere, given everything in play at the end of the year." He frowned into his glass. "Of course, a dead body's always an added complication."

"Oh, Julien." Kitty shook her head and gave a rueful smile. "I'll always love your lack of sentiment."

"Simple statement of fact, sweetheart."

"I'll call on Malcolm and Mélanie tomorrow and see if I can help." She raised a brow. "Unless you think I'll be in the way?"

"On the contrary. It's time for all hands on deck, I think. I imagine they'll both agree."

"Julien." Kitty's gaze darted across his face. "Would you really have kept quiet about this supposed plot if they'd asked you to?"

"You're loyal to Spain. I'm not loyal to any country, remember?"

"Yes, but—"

"Can you see my turning Simon Tanner over to the authorities?"

Her brows drew together. "No…"

"Well, then. I don't own to particular loyalties, but I try not to betray a friend. And these days I'll even admit to having friends."

"You never fail to surprise me, Julien."

"Because I wouldn't stop a plot, or because I'll admit to having friends?"

"Perhaps both."

"I've always rather prided myself on my ability to be surprising. Besides, can you imagine Tanner's actually trying to have someone assassinated?"

"Well, when you put it that way—no." She smoothed his hair from his forehead. "You think Carfax is behind the supposed plot?"

"What do you think?"

"That Carfax would like nothing better than to discredit the Levellers. This seems a bit heavy-handed, though. Especially as he has to have known the Rannochs would get involved. And jump to precisely these conclusions."

"Mmm...I confess to thinking the same thing. We could be looking at intersecting plots. Or another enemy entirely. Though, if Carfax isn't behind the plot, I can't see his staying out of it now."

"Which will pull David Worsley in. And be challenging for you."

Far more challenging than he was going to admit to anyone. Even himself. "I manage well enough round David. I've even dined with him."

"Taking care to turn in the other direction as much as possible."

"Never let it be said I'm entirely lacking in prudence."

"Time to stop talking, I think." She reached up to kiss the side of his jaw. "My day was long. Yours seems to have been worse."

Julien set his glass down, settled his arms round her, and let his mouth find her own. However independent he'd prided himself on being, he'd never been averse to the idea of comfort after a long day. And he could hardly claim to be independent anymore. No sense in dwelling on that now. The risks were already run, the dangers accepted. When had he been one to shy from danger, after all?

He scooped her into his arms and carried her to the bed that had somehow, unaccountably, become theirs. A night of solace counted for a lot. A night with Kitty was always more than solace. And if a small part of him wished she'd told him the truth, he had enough self-knowledge to see that for the folly it was. They'd made no commitments or promises to each other. He was keeping enough things from her, after all. Secrets were inevitable between two spies. He couldn't very well complain that she was keeping something from him.

Even if it did put her at the scene of a murder.

KITTY LAY with her head on Julien's chest, his arm flung hard about her. From the even rise and fall of his breathing, she thought he was asleep, though with Julien one could never be sure. The night they had—reunited, for want of a better word—the night Julien had shot and killed Malcolm's brother, Edgar Rannoch, to save Malcolm, Julien had carried her to bed and held her, both of them fully clothed, the entire night. There'd been something raw that night that neither of them had put into words, and probably never would. He'd left before dawn to talk to Malcolm and Edgar's sister, Gisèle. But he'd come back the next night. And most nights after, barring some absences she wouldn't, of course, ask him about. And they'd done more than hold each other, though despite their past he'd been careful to let her make the first move. Julien had witchcraft in his touch that could unknot the most intense stresses and send her tumbling into happy oblivion. He also had the ability to make her feel safe, in a way she hadn't felt in a long time. Perhaps not ever.

She had been asleep herself tonight, though she'd have sworn it would be beyond her when she'd returned home. But now tension thrummed through her. Secrets had always been part of her relationship with Julien. Even when it began, when they were theoretically allies. Because, of course, agents often had as many secrets from allies as from opponents. And certainly they'd both known secrets were inevitable when they became—whatever they were now.

But tonight had catapulted those secrets into a whole new realm. A part of her wanted to tell him the whole. A part of her, she confessed to herself, wanted to bury herself in his arms and find an anchor in the midst of the turmoil she had unleashed. But the practical part of her mind knew that was no answer. She couldn't risk getting Julien involved, for the sake of her allies. For Julien's own sake. She'd got herself into this, she was going to have to get herself out.

Even if it meant imperiling a relationship that meant far more to her than she'd ever intended.

CHAPTER 7

Malcolm tied his cravat with a haste that would have earned a weary sigh from Addison. For once Mélanie, who usually slept late, was out of the house before him. She had already gone to the theatre to talk to her friend Manon. Odd not to be doing this with her. Mel, as the playwright, was part of the Tavistock company. Malcolm was one of the investigators. They'd had different roles in an investigation before, but never this starkly.

Raoul had left early to make inquiries among his shadowy network in London. Laura had taken the children to the square garden. Cordelia Davenport would bring her daughters round in a bit for lessons, and Malcolm knew Laura planned to talk to her about the Thornsby family. Malcolm needed to find time to talk to Cordelia's husband, Harry, about Lewis Thornsby's elder brother before he and Roth went to the Tavistock.

Malcolm was on the stairs when he heard Kitty Ashford's voice in the hall below. He went quickly down the remainder of the stairs to find Kitty talking to Valentin. "Malcolm." Kitty came forwards as Malcolm reached the bottom of the stairs. She was wearing a moss green pelisse with a high-standing collar and rows of braid that gave it the military look that seemed to be so popular. "Julien told me last night. About Lewis Thornsby. I thought you might need help."

Her gaze held seemingly genuine concern and perhaps a hint of excitement at the prospect of intrigue. No sign that she knew more or had come for any other reason. But then, he'd never been adept at reading Kitty, even when they'd been partners and lovers. Perhaps especially then.

"Let's go into the breakfast parlor," he said. "There's still coffee."

"I saw the children in the park with Laura," Kitty said, as Malcolm held the door open for her. "They were disappointed I didn't bring Genny and the boys, but it didn't seem the day for it. It must have been so horrible last night for all of you."

"Not the night we were anticipating." Malcolm followed her into the peach-walled breakfast parlor, where they had shared many family meals since Kitty and her children—and Julien—had come into their lives.

"I can imagine." Kitty untied the strings on her bonnet. "And it's especially beastly that Mélanie found him. I know she's seen all sorts of horrors, but one doesn't expect to stumble across them in the middle of a London theatre. And with the children, which must have made it so much worse."

"Yes, though I think we're both inured to the fact that they're going to become entangled in our adventures." Malcolm moved to the table to pour coffee. "Mel was very grateful St. Juste showed up last night. As am I."

Kitty smiled, an ironic curve of her mouth that held unvoiced affection. "Julien has a way of being in the right place at the right time." She moved to one of the chairs and set her bonnet and reticule on the chair beside her. "He's remarkably good with children in a crisis."

"He's remarkably good with children most of the time, from what I've seen." Malcolm reached for a second coffee cup. "I've heard Genny call him 'dada.'"

"Genny uses all sorts of sounds for everything. Mélanie told me Jessica called lights 'ma' for years."

Malcolm smiled despite everything. "True enough." He watched Kitty for a moment, giving her time to volunteer more about Lewis Thornsby. Instead, she began to draw off her gloves. With typical grace, but also with the sense of one prevaricating. "I didn't realize you knew Thornsby," Malcolm said as she tugged the last of the lemon kid fingers free.

Kitty unclasped her pelisse and slipped it from her shoulders. "I'd met him." She took the cup of coffee Malcolm was holding out. "One of the nights we were at the theatre and at least one of the times I took the children round to watch a rehearsal. Enough that I could put a face with the name. I'd hardly say I knew him. But I assume you and Mélanie are investigating, and I'm happy to do anything I can to help. Tragic as it is, I quite relish your investigations."

Malcolm splashed some more coffee into his own cup. Odd as it once would have been to imagine, drinking coffee with Kitty in the Berkeley Square breakfast parlor was now a commonplace occurrence. She was more or less one of the family. Which, in this family, didn't necessarily imply any sort of trust.

"Kit." Malcolm took a sip of coffee. "I found this in Lewis Thornsby's rooms." He reached inside his coat and held out the note in Kitty's hand.

Kitty stared down at it.

"Don't say it isn't your hand," Malcolm said.

"Oh, poison." Kitty clunked her cup down, spattering coffee in the gilded saucer. "I know what you're going to say. That one can't withhold any detail in an investigation, however seemingly trivial, however seemingly unconnected. However embarrassing. Because one never knows what else it might be connected to. And I know you're right. So I'll tell you. Though I don't think it has anything to do with Lewis's murder. And it's certainly embarrassing."

"Lewis?" Malcolm said in a neutral voice. He was watching her closely.

Kitty drew in and released her breath. "It was one of the times Julien was away. I went to a play without the children, and then I went round to the green room and Manon invited me to a coffeehouse with some of the actors after the performance. Thornsby and some other young men who hang about the theatre were there."

"You wanted information about the Levellers."

She gave a lopsided smile. "I thought it might prove useful. Those committed to change here might be persuaded to work for change in Spain. And Thornsby was from a well-connected family with influence. He was sulking that night over the young actress—Letty?—who's been leading him a dance. He wanted someone to confide in. There's nothing like thwarted love for confidences. I sat listening to a catalogue of Miss Blanchard's perfections intermixed with his utter despair at her ever taking him seriously and his conviction that he had a rival. I listened, of course, because that's what one does when one's hoping to get to the important information. And because I felt sorry for him. It's been so long, but I remember young love is beastly. It got late and he offered to walk me home, and I agreed because it prolonged the conversation." She took a sip of coffee, returned her cup to its saucer, tucked her gloves into her reticule. Hesitating, which was uncharacteristic for Kitty. "We'd had rather a lot of wine. The children were sound asleep. One thing led to another." She turned the handle of her cup, angling it precisely on the saucer. "I was distinctly annoyed to wake up and realize what I'd done. Not that there'd have been that much harm in it, if we could have both agreed it was a mistake best left in the past. I think Thornsby was horrified too. But because he was horrified, he decided he had a passion for me, to keep the night from being a mere sordid interlude. A lot of rather bad poetry followed. I don't know if you found any of it in his things. I burnt what he sent to me. I knew better than to put anything in writing myself, but I realized we had to talk. Hence the rather vague note you found."

Malcolm sat back in his chair, trying to force the unlikely pieces into a pattern.

Kitty regarded him with raised brows and a lopsided smile. "Shocked, Malcolm? Julien and I've never made any sort of promises to each other. In fact, I've rather come to depend too much upon him, which may be another reason I did what I did with Lewis. To prove my independence. But of course, no matter how open an arrangement one has, one never really likes to hear these details, so I'd just as soon Julien never learned about Lewis. Though I know you can't promise he won't. And I realize that's my lookout."

Malcolm watched his former lover in the cool morning sunlight and the flickering warmth of the fire that burned in the grate. "Damn it, Kitty," he said. "You can lie better than that."

"Malcolm!"

"Not that you can't run rings round me, but surely you knew I'd see through that farrago."

Kitty reached for her cup and tossed down a swallow of coffee. "If I had made it up, I'd have come up with something a deal more imaginative. Not to mention something that portrayed me in a more positive light. Which should support the fact that I'm telling the truth."

Malcolm shook his head. "A good try. But even that won't convince me."

"Why?" She opened her eyes very wide.

"Among other things, because of how you feel about St. Juste."

"Oh, darling." Kitty steadied her cup as her shoulders convulsed with laughter. "Now you're seeing everything through your own lens. I'll admit I'm fond of Julien. Fonder than I ever meant to be. But I'm not you. I'm not even Mélanie."

"No. You're yourself, with your own code. I don't pretend to understand what's between you and St. Juste. But I do know there are lines neither of you would cross. Not without a better reason than this, at any rate."

She shook her head, her gaze warm with rueful affection. "You always want to tie things up with a neat bow."

"On the contrary. I love the delightful messiness of life. Which means that even if two people haven't made conventional vows, they still can find a way to be true to each other."

"That sounds gag-inducing." Kitty slumped in her chair. "Oh, all right. Julien and I haven't made any promises to each other but I do feel a sort of fidelity—God, I can't believe I'm saying that word—to what we have. Enough that I wouldn't have done what I did with Lewis if I'd been thinking clearly. If I hadn't drunk too much wine and been just a bit afraid of how strongly I was coming to feel for my exasperating lover. Enough, as I said, that I'd rather Julien didn't know now."

Malcolm held her with his gaze. "I don't believe you, Kit."

"Oh, Malcolm." She reached out across the table, between the toast crumbs and marmalade pots, and touched his hand. "You're a good judge of people. You're brilliant at it. But you always want to see the best in them. You're right that you know me. And you know I'm capable of compromise."

"We all are."

"And that I'm capable of hurting those I care about. I hurt you."

"That was completely different." Malcolm folded his arms across his chest. "What are you hiding, Kit?"

"Nothing, in this case. When you think about it, you'll realize that. Which makes me rather sad. I'll own I like having you think well of me. But love doesn't always mean happily ever after. Or even fidelity."

"You'll never convince me."

"That's the wonderful thing about you, darling. Your belief in people." Kitty reached for her coffee and took a sip. "But don't let it get in the way of finding the truth."

"Auntie Kitty." Jessica waved to Kitty as she emerged from the Berkeley Square house. Malcolm had left a quarter hour before, but had told her to stay and finish her coffee. Kitty had done so, thinking it best to avoid further conversation for both their sakes. Not that she didn't have experience sharing both hard truths and well-constructed lies with Malcolm, but this conversation sat particularly bitter in her throat. She'd forced down the last of the coffee, put on her pelisse and bonnet, fingers less steady on the clasps and strings than she'd have liked, and then at last left the house.

Jessica's cheerful greeting was a welcome distraction. Kitty went over to the garden, hugged the children, and greeted Laura, who was sitting on a bench nursing Clara. Kitty liked Raoul's wife a great deal, but Laura was entirely too likely to see that something was wrong. Still, she'd be even more likely to do so if Kitty made a hasty exit, and Kitty needed some time to consider her next move, so she sat beside Laura on one of the benches and watched the game of tag that was in progress.

"I wanted to offer my help to Malcolm." Kitty decided it was best to confront the situation head on. "I was horrified by the news about Thornsby, but I confess the idea of being part of the investigation intrigues me."

"I feel precisely the same," Laura said. "Even with a baby. Perhaps especially with a baby." She looked down at Clara, who had one hand fisted round the edge of her mother's nursing bodice.

Colin came running over, as though aware of their conversation. "Are you going to help with the Investigation, Auntie Kitty?" he asked.

"I told your father I'd do anything I could to help," Kitty said. "Julien says you were very brave last night."

"I was scared," Colin said. He cast a quick glance at Jessica to make sure she hadn't heard. "But not so much, because Mummy was there. And Uncle Julien. I mean, I can't imagine any villain outwitting one of them, let alone both of them together, can you?"

"No," Kitty said honestly.

"And then I was curious," Colin said. "I told Mummy I'd help. She said I could distract Jessica. I said I didn't mean that, and she said she'd try to find more I could do. I think I'm old enough, don't you?"

"I think you're a very grown-up six and a half," Kitty said.

"Thanks." Colin grinned. "I'd like to Investigate when I grow up. And be a spy. And a politician. And maybe an archaeologist. And write plays. Oh, there's Uncle Raoul." He waved to Raoul, who was approaching the garden.

Kitty wasn't looking forwards to facing Raoul either, though his arrival might give her a good excuse to depart. But when he joined them in the garden and greeted everyone, Colin said, "Aunt Kitty's going to help with the Investigation. And I am too."

"I imagine you will both be invaluable assets," Raoul said.

"Daddy." Emily joined them. "You're back early. But then, nothing is quite ordinary when there's an Investigation going on."

"Which your father is bound to be pulled into as well," Kitty said.

"Everyone Investigates in this family," Emily said.

"Very true." Raoul grinned at her. "Speaking of which, I'm glad I found you here, Kitty. Could I have a word with you?"

She could hardly say no. And in truth, if he wanted to talk to her, she wanted to know what he had to say.

"Of course." She gave him a friendly, level smile as they crossed the street back to the house. "I made sure you'd have been off on adventures long since."

He returned the smile with one equally friendly. And, she suspected, equally artful. "I'm much more domestic these days."

"Ha."

"At least when I'm in London." He opened the door himself and stepped aside to allow her to precede him into the house.

"Much of the conflict in Spain is being played out in London," Kitty said as they climbed the stairs, aware that she was prevaricating. "Or, at least, the search for support for the conflict."

"But more in clubs and council chambers and drawing rooms."

"And you're in the midst of an investigation."

"There is that." He opened the door onto a small salon with airy sea-green walls. Mélanie's touch was palpable, but then it was in every part of the house. Kitty advanced into the room and took off her bonnet again, remembering one of the first times she had been in this room, waiting for Malcolm. That had been an uncomfortable conversation too. It was also the room where they often sat with the children in the evenings after she and Julien had been to dine. She wondered if that was why Raoul had chosen it, harkening to the family ties between them instead of their relationship as agents,

Raoul closed the door and leaned against it. "Normally I consider it best to leave friends to their secrets. It's the only way to have a remotely comfortable life as an agent. Assuming an agent can have a comfortable life. But there are exceptions. I know you were at the Tavistock last night. And I can guess why."

Kitty's hands tightened on her bonnet. She'd always liked Raoul, long before she learned he was Malcolm's father (really, now she knew, it seemed incredible that she hadn't seen it sooner). And long before she knew he had been a French agent, on the opposite side in the Peninsular War, even if they were now allies against the Bourbons in the shifting landscape that was Spain. She accepted that, like her, he wanted what was best for Spain. But she'd also always known he was dangerous. Perhaps never more so than when he was at his friendliest. "Then surely you can also guess why I might not have told Malcolm. Assuming your guess is correct, which, of course, I'm not admitting at all."

"I have a fairly shrewd notion." His gaze was level and direct. Quite like Malcolm's when he cut straight through to the truth. "And I understand. But Thornsby's murder changes things."

Kitty dropped down in a straight-backed chair, the same one she had sat in waiting for Malcolm all those months ago. "Thornsby's murder has nothing to do with it."

"That you know of."

"Who?" Kitty's voice came out sharper than she intended. "Who among us do you think might possibly have been involved—"

"Impossible to know how the threads may be tangled. You must realize that."

Kitty put a hand to her head. She did, perhaps more than she was acknowledging. "If you're so sure, you could tell Malcolm yourself."

Something shifted in Raoul's gaze that hinted that his relationship with his son had perhaps not always been as remarkable as it now seemed, that even now Raoul was not entirely sanguine about it. "I think he needs to hear it from you. Or Tanner. Otherwise, it could do incalculable damage."

"To what?"

"To his friendships with both of you."

"Is that what Malcolm and I are? Friends?"

"I think you know that. Kitty." Raoul took a step forwards, then checked himself. "I know the pull of competing loyalties. I know the instinct to keep secrets. I've followed it more times than I can name. More recently than I care to admit. But it can destroy lives."

His gaze, which could be so cool and dispassionate, held ghosts that were very present. Kitty suppressed an impulse to close her arms over the frogged braid on her bodice and kept her hands folded in her lap. "We just need another day or two. Maybe less."

"And then? If you don't tell him the truth, he'll piece it together."

Their friendships were all so delicately balanced. She and Malcolm had managed to become friends again, of sorts—oddly going back to what they'd been before they were lovers. And her friendships with all the others in the family were built on her friendship with him. Even her friendship with Raoul, whom she had known longer. It was so long since she'd had friends that it sometimes took her by surprise what those friendships meant to her.

"You can't tell me you don't think it's important," she said.

"Of course, I believe it's important," Raoul said. "How could I not? But as with so many things, it comes down to weighing choices. And I think recent events tip the scales."

She held his gaze for a long moment. "In my shoes, would you tell Malcolm?"

He drew in and released his breath with a harsh scrape. Raoul had always been ruthlessly honest. "I'm not sure. I'd like to think I would. But past experience suggests I might not. I'm not always as good at learning from experience as I should be."

"And you think I can do better?"

"That's up to you."

"So you're not going to tell Malcolm?"

He gave a faint smile. "I was determined eight years ago not to get between you and Malcolm. My feelings on that score haven't changed. So, not yet." His face went serious. "I make you no promises if things shift. I'll try to warn you before I do, but we're all going to have to react in the moment."

She studied him a moment. "You're happy, aren't you?"

He smiled again, this time in a way she hadn't seen in their years in the Peninsula. "Yes, I am. It is possible, you know. However one feels about one's past. You have much less to reproach yourself with than I do."

A bitterness that might be the aftertaste of the morning coffee lingered on her tongue. "That's a matter of perspective."

"The people who care about you would like nothing better than to see you happy. And there are a number of people who do care about you. Very much."

She met his gaze, not trying to veil her own. "I know what I've found here. Believe me. And I'm grateful for it. But as you said, life is always a matter of choices."

"Just don't forget to weigh what would make you happy. And your children."

"Are you saying you think Julien would?" She had never thought to feel such a stab of guilt at saying Julien's name.

"That's for you to work out. There are different types of happiness."

"I don't think you went looking for it yourself."

"No, it found me. And I almost let happiness slip away. I might have done if Laura hadn't been so eminently sensible. And so willing to run risks."

"I'll admit I never thought to see you living the life you are now. But just because you can pull it off doesn't mean I could. Or God knows, that Julien could."

And yet, she couldn't deny that she had been happy this past autumn and winter, far more times perhaps than she ever had before. And most of those moments involved Julien.

With whom she might have just smashed her relationship to bits.

CHAPTER 8

Harry Davenport set down his pen and flexed his fingers. "Malcolm. Come to rescue me from mind-numbing edits?"

"I suspect so. But you may not be happy. A lot's happened since I last saw you." Which had been the previous afternoon when they'd played catch with the children in the Berkeley Square garden. Hard to believe that was less than four-and-twenty hours ago. Malcolm hooked a chair with his foot and dragged it over to the desk so he could sit and tell Harry about last night's events.

"Good God," Harry said when Malcolm had done. His voice held shock and perhaps the faintest undertone—not of hurt, but of a sense of having been left out.

"Yes, it's a long time since Mel and I've been through so much without you and Cordy. Trust me, we'd have told you sooner if we could. It all unfolded very quickly."

"Don't worry, Rannoch. I'm just selfish enough to be sorry I was home last night double-checking footnotes while you were out tackling villains."

"If it's any comfort, I'm the one with sore knees this morning. And chasing Billy, only to have to let him go, is hardly a novel experience. I'm sure we'll have another chance."

Harry twirled his pen between his fingers. "How much do you think Carfax knows?"

"More than he's letting on. I'm not sure how much more." Malcolm hesitated a moment. But this was Harry he was talking to. "I'm not sure how much Kit knows either. Or Simon." Or Kitty, but even with Harry he wasn't yet ready to share Kitty's confession to an affair he still thought was cover for something else.

Harry sat back in his char. "This is bound to be challenging."

"It's a damnable puzzle. And it's Simon's theatre."

"And the Levellers are tangled up in it, one way or another."

Malcolm nodded. "I've warned Roth I won't be able to share everything with him."

"Yes, that's a given. More challenging is what you're going to want to do with the information yourself."

Possibilities he was not yet ready to face swirled like puzzle pieces in Malcolm's brain. "You mean if this assassination plot is real?"

"I doubt it is. But investigations always uncover things. Things a number of people—including sometimes the investigators—would prefer remain decently hidden. But once one's uncovered them, one can't forget. And this investigation happens to be smack in the middle of your friends. Our friends."

With almost anyone else, Malcolm would have protested. Instead, he sat back in his chair and met Harry's gaze across the desk strewn with pages of Harry's latest monograph. "It's been hard, letting Simon go his own way and turning a blind eye. But I've been managing. It's not as though I don't do it almost every day with my father. Not to mention with my wife, if rather less often." He could say that to Harry. There was almost no one else he could say it to.

Harry, being Harry, accepted this as the reality it was. "Yes, but the Levellers are something you might have once been involved in yourself."

There it was, a reality that couldn't but be at the back of Malcolm's mind whenever the Levellers came up. His mind shot back to Italy a year and a half ago. Kit Montagu had hidden his involvement with the Levellers and the Italian Carbonari from Malcolm and then said matter-of-factly that he couldn't be sure which side Malcolm would be on as an MP. And when Malcolm had later expressed his shock at Kit's response to Mélanie, Mel had gently pointed out that Malcolm sat in the Parliament that had passed the laws Kit and his friends were fighting, even if Malcolm hadn't voted for those laws.

Once, Malcolm and Simon and David and their friend Oliver had been not unlike the Levellers. Simon was certainly living up to their youthful ideals. Which meant he couldn't talk about his activities to Malcolm. Or to David. "I don't know that it necessarily follows that I'm more likely to agree with the Levellers than I am with O'Roarke or Mel."

"No, but confronting their activities could be akin to confronting your past. Not always an easy thing. Speaking as one who finds confronting the past damnably difficult. Of course, I have far more to regret than you do."

"Speak for yourself, Davenport. And have I mentioned how annoying it is when you know me better than I know myself?"

"Hardly that. But sometimes the view from the periphery is a bit sharper." Harry swung his feet up onto the desk. "I don't envy your and David's and Rupert's work in Parliament. I'd go mad trying to negotiate, making deals to go a few steps forwards, having to retreat a few steps back. But I'm incredibly grateful you that do it. For the sake of my daughters. For the sake of the future for all our children and all of us. And at times I envy the courage it takes for you to keep doing it."

Malcolm gave a short laugh. He had found Harry wounded

and face down in the mud at Waterloo. "You're one of the bravest men I know."

"There are different types of bravery. The battlefield is nothing compared to this."

Malcolm crossed his legs and stared at his boot toes. They'd got mud-spattered on the walk here. "I wonder sometimes if it's bravery or cowardice. Seeking refuge in a world where I'm viewed as a Radical, yet as you say, I'm only inching things along while Simon is fighting for all the things we believed in."

"You're fighting for them too. Oh, don't get me wrong. Simon's incalculably brave as well. There's a role for both of you. And David and Rupert. And Mélanie and Raoul. As you said, you've all been managing to go along without coming into conflict. Which is why the investigation is challenging."

"Simon could have a lot of reasons for keeping secrets."

"So he could. And you wouldn't lightly betray a friend."

"As my father says, loyalty comes down to a matter of choices. There's also the fact that I might find myself in agreement with whatever Simon's doing." He hesitated a moment. "Or that Mélanie would, and I wouldn't."

"Is that what really worries you?"

Malcolm settled deeper in his chair. "Possibly. Probably. It always hangs over us. Sooner or later we'll face a situation where we don't agree. I always thought it would involve France or Spain. But it might hit much closer to home."

"I can't solve that for you, old man. And you're not going to know how to handle it until you actually confront it. If you actually confront it. No sense in wasting time on it before."

"Easier said than done. But yes. Meanwhile, can you take me to talk to Thomas Thornsby? I think you know him."

Harry grinned. "I'd be insulted if you didn't ask me to. Thomas is far more conventional than I am. But he has a keen understanding. I enjoy working with him. I'm damned sorry he's lost his brother and is caught up in this. But I'm glad I can help."

"You're the best of good fellows. I have to meet Roth and go to the theatre to break the news to the company, but not for another hour or so. Actors aren't early risers. Perhaps we can see Thomas first."

Harry swung his legs down from the desk. "I thought you'd never ask."

Cordelia Davenport stared at Laura. "Good God. I feel like a horrible person. With Mélanie busy with the play and Harry's monograph done except for painstaking edits and this fiendishly cold weather, I confess I've been wishing something exciting would happen to shake things up. But I never wanted—"

"Of course not," Laura squeezed Cordelia's hand. "And I confess I've felt much the same at times. All the holiday flurry over and Raoul and Malcolm and Mélanie all busy—Not that I don't quite enjoy teaching and devising curricula, and planning to open a school is exciting of course, but at times—" She glanced across the library where Colin, Emily, and Livia Davenport were playing with their toy castle and the new carriage that had been a Christmas addition, while Jessica and Drusilla Davenport arranged stuffed animals. It would normally be lesson time, but the children were as excited as she was at a break in the routine. "And, of course, it's dreadful, but wringing our hands won't help poor Mr. Thornsby." She refilled their coffee cups.

"We've known Lewis Thornsby's elder brother Thomas for years," Cordelia said. "He's not anything like as serious a scholar as Harry, at least not yet, but he comes to meetings of the Classicists' Society. I remember thinking when I met Lewis how different they were. Thomas looks as though he scarcely takes his head out of his books. He does have an interest in Edith Simmons, but then she's a classicist too."

"So are you," Laura said.

Cordelia raised her brows, then smiled. "Yes, I suppose so. What an odd thought. When I was a girl, I quite liked classics and my Latin and Greek were quite good. And the lives of the Julio-Claudians were far racier than any French novel. Who wouldn't be intrigued? But by the time I was sixteen I'd have been horrified at the label." She glanced at the girls. "I hope my girls never equate being a bluestocking with being unattractive. I used to like helping Harry with his research when we were first married. It was one of the things we could enjoy together. Well, that and a few other things." She gave another faint smile. "So when we started living together again, it seemed natural to help him."

"You do more than help him," Laura said.

"I think so. Now. I'm a co-author on the latest monograph. I go to most Classicists' Society meetings. That's where I met Edith. I think she thought I was a dreadful society fribble at first, but after I made some remarks on Suetonius, she unbent. You'd like her. She's also a governess. I suspect that if either she or Thomas were better situated in terms of fortune, they'd be married by now."

Laura set down her coffee cup. "That's interesting. Letty Blanchard told Mélanie that Lewis Thornsby was the heir to a tidy fortune from his aunt. She wasn't sure what would happen to it now. But it might go to his brother."

Cordelia's finely arced brows drew together. "These things so often come down to money. Harry would do better talking to Thomas Thornsby than I would, but I can take you to see Edith. She's refreshingly direct." Cordelia reached for her coffee and took a thoughtful sip. "Though I suspect she's also the sort who's very good at keeping secrets."

CHAPTER 9

After unsuccessfully checking at his lodgings, Malcolm and Harry found Thomas Thornsby in the reading room of the Classicists' Society. It was in a small, anonymous building in Marylebone, and perhaps fittingly for the home of a group dedicated to studying the ancient past, it looked to have been little changed since the middle of the last century. Malcolm found it far more restful and less stuffy than most gentlemen's clubs, not least because it did not have a prohibition against ladies. The classical busts in the hall had the look of old friends and the scratched wood and faded upholstery spoke of comfort.

Thomas Thornsby was in the midst of putting papers into a sheaf of foolscap with crisp, precise motions that indicated an effort to hold feeling at bay. He did not seem to notice their entrance at first. He looked up with a start, face drawn. "Harry. I won't be able to make the Society meeting this afternoon. I confess it's the last thing on my mind just now. I only came by to pick up some papers. I need to go back to my parents'."

"Of course. I thought you might be there already, but your valet said you were here. My condolences." Harry was not the sort to easily express his emotions, but oddly such expressions from him had a genuine ring when they could sound like platitudes from others. "I met your brother at the theatre once or twice. He was a good fellow. You know Malcolm Rannoch, don't you?"

"By reputation." Thornsby shook Malcolm's hand. "I understand you're assisting Bow Street with the investigation. I was glad to hear it. Is that why you've come?"

"Not solely," Malcolm said. "I wanted to offer my condolences as well. But yes, I'd be interested in anything you feel able to share about your brother."

Thomas glanced to the side. He was shorter than his brother, with brown hair already beginning to thin at the crown, and a blue gaze clouded with grief. "I'm not sure how much I have to share. Lewis and I had gone in different directions of late. Or perhaps what had been true our whole lives just accelerated. He was never much of a scholar. I have little taste for the theatre. Prefer quiet evenings with my books."

"My brother and I were quite different." Malcolm found he could say that now and keep his voice steady. Just barely. "He died last September."

"I heard." Thomas's eyes warmed with genuine sympathy. "I'm very sorry."

"We're not here to talk about me. I mention it only because I know being different doesn't lessen the loss."

Thomas gave a tight, contained nod, and gestured towards a set of chairs by the fire. "Lewis and I rubbed along well enough going our own ways," he said when they were seated. "He always chaffed me for having my head buried in dusty books, but he was good-natured about it. I was happy he had found something to keep him occupied. I thought he was idling about less. It was only recently that Father pointed out the dangers—" He broke off.

"You mean Miss Blanchard?" Malcolm said.

Thomas colored slightly, hands curled round the arms of his chair. "I wasn't wholly surprised he'd taken an interest in an actress. I don't have my head in my books so much I don't realize that's likely to be some of the lure of the theatre for a young man. But I didn't realize how serious it was."

"Until?" Malcolm asked.

"My father brought it up." Thomas ran his fingers over a nick in the chair arm. "Asked me to see what I could learn from Lewis about Miss Blanchard. I told him I didn't think Lewis could be serious. In my experience, Lewis wasn't serious about much of anything. But I said I'd have a talk with him. Thought I could reassure Father and save us all a kerfuffle. Instead Lewis fairly bit my head off. He said I didn't know Miss Blanchard and I shouldn't presume things about her or how he felt about her. That if I cast aspersions on her character he'd have to take exception." Thomas's brows drew together. "I've never seen Lewis so intense. Truth to tell, it was rather good to see him care so much about something, but I also could see the pitfalls ahead. I told him surely he realized it would have to end sooner or later. Better now, when there was less chance of Miss Blanchard's being hurt."

"What did your brother say?" Harry asked.

Thomas stared across the room at a glass-fronted bookcase, his frown deepening. "He said 'why should it have to end?' I mean, surely even Lewis realized he couldn't continue the liaison indefinitely." Thomas coughed. "If there was a liaison."

"Perhaps a liaison wasn't what he had in mind," Malcolm suggested.

"Oh, come now, Rannoch. My brother may have been feckless and deaf to responsibilities, but I can't imagine even Russell's going so far as to actually marry an actress—"

He broke off, perhaps at the memory that Malcolm's wife had appeared in a holiday pantomime only the month before.

"Crispin Harleton did," Harry said. "And is quite happy."

"Yes, of course. I've met Lady Harleton, she's charming. But —" Thomas shook his head. "Lewis hadn't seemed himself lately. I blamed it on Miss Blanchard. But in truth, I wonder if it wasn't more that group he's been hanging about with. Our family've always been Whigs, but not—"

"Out and out Radicals?" Malcolm said.

Thomas met Malcolm's gaze. His blue eyes seemed more focused than they had. "I may study the ancient Romans, but I don't live in the past, Rannoch. I read the parliamentary debates. I even attend them on occasion. It's quite educational to compare them to the Roman senate."

Harry gave a short laugh. "Excellent point."

Thomas shot a look at him, then turned back to Malcolm. "I heard you speak on capital punishment. You made a powerful case. I'm in sympathy with much of what you support, though I wouldn't go quite as far you in many cases. In truth, a few months ago I'd have said my own views were more liberal than Lewis's. To the extent Lewis had political views, which he never seemed to much at all. Then, suddenly, he was hobnobbing with Simon Tanner and his set and spouting things at the dinner table that seemed designed to set my parents' hair on end. I like Tanner, by the way. What I've read of his plays and of his political writing. I can't imagine what he'd see in Lewis."

"Perhaps Miss Blanchard's being at the Tavistock drew your brother to the Levellers," Malcolm said.

"One might think so. But Lewis actually met her because he was spending time at the Tavistock. My brother who never seemed particularly interested in the poor or downtrodden suddenly became a burning Radical."

"There are degrees of everything," Malcolm said. "Simon would be the first to say more than one of the Levellers is flirting with the glamour of Radicalism and hasn't got much sense of progressive reform."

Thomas frowned. "Perhaps."

"Speaking from the advanced age of two-and-thirty, young people often look for some way to rebel at that age," Harry said.

"Is that what you did?"

Harry gave a dry smile. "No. I just buried myself in my books and then fell improbably and unsuitably in love and made a mess of my life and my wife's and my daughter's before I managed to put things to rights somehow. But then, I always was something of an oddity."

Thomas's frown deepened. "I never felt the need to rebel either. I just sought refuge in my books. I can't say my parents were thrilled, but they didn't pay much heed. It's a gentleman's occupation after all, even if Father would rather have seen me riding to hounds. Perhaps Lewis did want to rebel. I should—" His right hand curled into a fist, the nails pressing into his palm. "I'll still find myself thinking there are things I should ask him. But the damnable thing is I'll never be able to be sure now. I suppose he'll always be a cipher."

"It's one of the hellish legacies of unexpected death," Malcolm said. Edgar would always be a cipher. Not that he could imagine Edgar's ever explaining himself in a way Malcolm would have been able to understand if Edgar had lived. Not that, for all his opposition to violence, he could imagine conversing with his brother without giving way to the need to throttle him. The questions would have haunted him one way or another. But the void yawned more starkly with Edgar gone. "Was your father concerned about Lewis?" Malcolm asked.

"Oh, yes. Mama too. I do think they thought at first that some of it was to provoke a reaction, but as time went on, they were concerned he was going too far—out of reach, I suppose you'd say. Damaging his prospects. Partly they were afraid Aunt Henrietta wouldn't like it. My aunt, Lady Shroppington. Lewis was her heir, you know." Thomas drew a breath.

"So we've heard," Malcolm said. "Who is now?"

"I don't know." Thomas sounded as though he was only considering it for the first time. "It will be up to her. Aunt Henrietta controls her own fortune. Lewis was always a favorite of hers. She indulged him." For a moment in Thomas's tone and gaze Malcolm could see a younger brother who had charmed their aunt and been able to get away with things his more sober and better-behaved elder brother wouldn't have dreamed of attempting. "But Father thought there'd be a limit to what she'd tolerate. The last time she dined with the family she was kind enough to Lewis, but after dinner she asked me a number of questions about what he'd got himself into."

"With Miss Blanchard?" Malcolm asked. "Or with his friends at the theatre?"

"Both. She said it had been agreeable watching Lewis grow up, but she was beginning to think it was time he started acting like an adult."

"Naturally you were concerned on your brother's behalf," Malcolm said.

"Yes. But it was a bit more." Thomas straightened his shoulders against the worn leather of the chair. "The family fortunes have been straitened for some time. Father made some unfortunate decisions after Waterloo with his investments. Lewis's inheritance seemed to protect not just him, but the whole family. However much he may have surprised me of late, I can't see his not making sure his sisters had adequate dowries." Thomas's brows drew together, and Malcolm could almost see the weight of his sisters' prospects settling on his shoulders.

"Difficult being responsible for a family," Harry said. "I suppose in some ways I was fortunate to have no one but my uncle. And also that my parents left me well provided for. As the father of daughters, I'm particularly aware of how difficult the world is for young women without fortune. You must now feel the responsibility for your sisters."

Thomas nodded. "I'll have to come up with dowries for them somehow. And the estate will need repairs when I come into it."

"All of which must make your own choice of marriage partner more complicated," Harry said.

Thomas shot a surprised look at him. Malcolm wouldn't have put it quite so bluntly, but perhaps Harry's words were just what was needed to jolt Thomas into confiding.

"Marriage can be a matter of economics for men as well as women," Harry said. "It shouldn't be a matter of economics for anyone, but sadly all too often it is."

Thomas drew back slightly in his chair. "I have no thoughts of marriage."

"My dear fellow. I've seen you with Edith."

"Edith is my friend."

"Yes, it's always best when one can be friends with the person one is head over heels in love with."

"Damn it, Davenport—"

"I wouldn't push you to talk about it. God knows I understand keeping feelings quiet. But it's become part of the investigation."

"There's no understanding between Miss Simmons and me."

"Of course not. Whatever your brother's intentions may have been towards Miss Blanchard, you wouldn't make any declaration to a woman without being able to offer her marriage."

Thomas drew in and released his breath. Malcolm sat back and watched. Harry's pushing had produced far more than his own more measured approach would have done. "I'd gladly live in poverty with Edith," Thomas said in a low voice. "I think I could be quite happy. I even think Edith might be happy."

"I'm quite sure she could," Harry said quietly. "She's used to the life of a governess."

"Yes, but I can't drag my family into poverty with me."

"There's always the chance Lady Shroppington will make you her heir."

Thomas gave an unexpected shout of bitter laughter. "And you think I'd have killed my brother on that chance? You haven't met my Aunt Henrietta. More to the point, you haven't seen her utter contempt for me. If my parents tolerate my scholarship, Aunt Henrietta scoffs at it. She liked Lewis's being a young man about town. She encouraged him to have a bit of dash. I imagine she'd have turned a blind eye to a liaison with an actress. She just didn't expect him to become so deeply entangled. It's barely possible she'll decide to settle her fortune on one of my sisters. But she's far more likely to look outside the Thornsby family entirely."

"Did your brother have enemies?" Malcolm asked.

Thomas didn't scoff at the very idea, but he did frown. "Lately I've felt I didn't know Lewis as well as I thought. But enemies? The sort who would kill? It's difficult to comprehend." He passed a hand over his face. "The whole thing is difficult to comprehend. But I suppose—" He looked from Harry to Malcolm. "How dangerous were these Levellers? Are these Levellers?"

"Impossible to be sure," Malcom said. "But I would have said not very." He wished he were still quite so sanguine. "Do you think your brother would have become involved in anything violent?"

Thomas was silent for a long moment. "I'd have thought not. But as I said, I'm not sure I trust my judgment anymore. I'm not sure I know—knew him anymore. At this point—" He stared at the gilded book spines behind the glass across from him. "At this point I can't say with any certainty that I think Lewis was incapable of anything."

~

"Do you miss it?" Harry asked as he and Malcolm descended the steps of the Classicists' Society.

Malcolm jammed his hands into his greatcoat pockets. The wind had whipped up, promising rain. "I believe I've admitted to you—if to no one else, including my wife—that at times I miss being an agent."

"Yes, you're not fooling anyone there, old fellow, including Mélanie, I'm quite sure. But I didn't mean being an agent. I meant being a fire-breathing Radical."

Malcolm shot a look at his friend. "I wasn't very fire-breathing."

"I've read your articles. Plenty of your speeches in the House still conjure up a muse of fire."

"I don't think that's quite what Shakespeare meant."

"Perhaps not, but I like the allusion." They reached the pavement and turned down Baker Street. "The point stands. You're a powerful voice, but you don't have the freedom you did in your student days."

"Who does?" Malcolm glanced up and down the street. A nurse with three young children, two ladies with shopping parcels, two gentlemen with umbrellas. A solidly English scene, of a certain sort. A crossing sweeper at the next corner, shoulders hunched against the quickening wind. That said a lot about England as well. "We didn't really plot anything. We talked, we wrote."

"We don't know the Levellers are plotting anything," Harry said.

Malcolm stared at a haberdasher's sign whipped by the wind for a moment. "When I first learned in Italy that Kit was a Leveller. He said he'd been afraid to tell me because I was an MP. And because I worked for Carfax. That was when I realized how far I'd gone from the ideals of my youth. Can you imagine Kit's going to work for Carfax? Or Castlereagh?"

"Kit's older than you were when you went to work for them,

and he hasn't gone through what you had. And we both know people are capable of unexpected things."

"Even granted that."

"You stopped working for Carfax and Castlereagh."

"Far later than I should have done."

"You're your own man in Parliament."

"More or less. I suppose—" Malcolm stared at the charcoal sky. "Mel said once that the arguments in Parliament are circumscribed. That one has the illusion of debate because there are discussions, but the boundaries are defined and whole perspectives are left out."

"Mélanie's right. MPs don't have the perspectives of well over half the population. Women, for one thing. Anyone who isn't at least nominally an Anglican. Most people who don't own property. But that's all the more reason we need people like you to push the boundaries."

"As long as we push them, rather than smugly assuming whatever point we're making is the outside edge of what's possible."

Harry watched him for a moment. "You're wondering what you'll do if the Levellers are plotting something and you discover it, aren't you?"

"How could I not be? Not to mention what Mel will do if she uncovers it first and whether or not we'll be in agreement."

Harry nodded. "It's more comfortable studying ancient Rome in a lot of ways."

"I agree with you there." Malcolm was silent for a moment as they trudged over pavement still muddy from last night's rain. "I need to meet Roth and get to the theatre. But before I go—Thomas Thornsby strikes me as decent man. Not that I trust my judgment so very much. What did you make of the interview?"

"Me? I'm his friend."

"Perhaps all the more reason to get your viewpoint."

Harry frowned across the street. "I like Thomas. I don't think he's a killer. But then, one's never the best judge of people one likes. I'm quite sure he loves Edith, more intensely than he'd admit. He makes a good point that he had more of a chance of the future he wanted if Lewis was Lady Shroppington's heir. But it sounds as though, even if Lewis had lived, he wasn't likely to continue as Lady Shroppington's heir."

"Quite," Malcolm said. "So you think there's a chance Thomas killed Lewis before Lady Shroppington could disinherit him, in the hopes she'd make Thomas her heir?"

"I don't like to think it," Harry said. "I don't think it's logical. But I also don't think we can ignore the possibility. Especially if Thomas knew Lewis had decided to propose to Letty Blanchard. How often have people surprised us?"

Malcolm thought of his brother. "Quite."

CHAPTER 10

Manon Caret stared at Mélanie across her dressing room. "*Mon Dieu*. I can't believe I went home last night and left you to that."

"You could hardly have known, *chérie*."

"No, but I hate to think of you facing all that—and you had the children with you." Manon took the kettle off the spirit lamp on the chest before the settee in her dressing room, added some more hot water to the teapot, and then refilled Mélanie's cup as though to offer the comfort she hadn't been able to give the night before. "I knew so many boys like Thornsby in Paris. Well, here too, but since I've been with Crispin they don't dangle after me as much. But they'd haunt the green room and crowd into one's dressing room with bouquets and tag along to cafés with the actors when they were invited. They tended to be surprisingly respectful—well, the ones like Thornsby. Of course, they could be a nuisance when they invaded rehearsal (and management never likes to send them off, because they support the theatre), and I've been known to complain once or twice about how they'd get underfoot. But honestly, right now all I can think is how poor Lewis's mother must feel."

"I know." Mélanie took a sip of tea and felt the warmth shoot through her. Odd how once one had children, one viewed situations through the lens of a parent. She doubted Lewis's parents' reaction would have been foremost in her mind before she was a mother herself. Manon had been a mother far longer than Mélanie—she'd had two daughters in Paris before Mélanie had ever met her and now also had a baby son with her new husband. But in addition to being mothers, she and Manon were both former agents and thought like agents as well as parents. "However much of a puppy Lewis seemed, he wasn't a child. And he was involved in some very grown-up things. You don't know why he came back here last night?"

Manon drew the folds of her flowered shawl about her shoulders. "I assume it was something to do with the Levellers. I try to stay out of their intrigues. Yes, I'm still a Republican, but God save us from amateur Radicals. Unless he was meeting Letty?"

"She says not. She also says he asked her to marry him last night."

Manon's brows rose. "Well, that's surprising. I suppose I shouldn't be surprised by a gentleman's proposing to an actress at this point, but somehow Thornsby didn't strike me as having the same substance as Crispin. And God knows Crispin's loving me still takes me by surprise every day. In the best way possible."

"Thornsby's proposing to Letty surprised me too," Mélanie said. "And I suspect his family wouldn't have been happy. Which opens new avenues of suspects."

"If they'd wanted to stop the marriage, they'd have been more likely to kill Letty."

"True." Mélanie turned her cup in her hand. "Do you think Letty was in love with someone else?"

Manon frowned. "What makes you ask?"

"She said she hadn't decided on marrying Thornsby. She

admitted part of her was drawn to the position—she even said she wanted what you had."

Manon snorted. "Then she should have held out for a man she loved. God, I sound like a lending-library novel cliché, don't I? But marriage is challenging enough. I can't imagine undertaking it with a man one didn't love."

"And to Letty's credit, I think she understood that. She wasn't sure she was prepared to give up the theatre. And she wasn't sure she was prepared to give up marrying a man she loved. She didn't say as much, but I had a faint sense that she might have meant a specific man, not a theoretical construct."

"Interesting." Manon pushed her dark gold side curls back from her face. "Letty tends to have a crowd of young men about her in the green room. Not surprising, she's young and bewitchingly pretty. I try not to gossip, but one does notice things in a company that spend as much time together as we do. Letty and Will Carmarthen have always had wonderful chemistry onstage. They do in this play. That doesn't always carry offstage—only look at Brandon and me—but before Lewis Thornsby started dangling after her, I wondered if something was developing between Letty and Will."

Which was particularly interesting, given the quarrel Thornsby's valet had recounted between Thornsby and Will Carmarthen the day before the murder. Mélanie nodded and returned her cup to its saucer. "We should note reactions when Malcolm and Roth talk to the company."

Manon met Mélanie's gaze. "That's part of the reason Malcolm's arriving with Roth, and you're here with the company, isn't it? So you can observe."

Mélanie gave a smile that may have come out more bitter than she intended. "Once an agent, always an agent."

Manon refilled their teacups. "So you're undercover again."

"With people who are my friends and colleagues." Mélanie

took a sip of tea. It was hot and burned her mouth. "You'd think by now I'd be used to it."

THE NEWS of Lewis Thornsby's death had inevitably spread by the time the company gathered on the stage of the Tavistock to hear Roth and Malcolm's announcement. Actors weren't called early, and though Roth had managed to keep it out of the scandal sheets for now, Roth's constable had been making inquiries in the neighborhood the night before, and all it took was one or two loose tongues for the news to get out. So it was a sober group that crowded into the drafty theatre, clutching mugs of coffee or tea or, in more than one case, tankards or flasks. Mélanie hugged Bessie, one of the seamstresses, who was red-eyed and stricken. Mélanie remembered Bessie bringing Lewis a cup of tea on more than one occasion. She suspected the girl had nourished romantic feelings for him, though she'd seen no sign they were reciprocated.

Jennifer Mansfield, another of the Tavistock's leading actresses, came over to Mélanie and Manon. "I'm so sorry you and the children found poor Mr. Thornsby, Mélanie. Though probably better than that someone else did."

"I said much the same." Manon was holding her shawl close about her, though normally she seemed impervious to drafts.

"I tried to persuade Horace to stay home with the children. But of course he insisted on coming." Jennifer glanced at her husband, one of the Tavistock's leading patrons, standing to one side talking earnestly to Simon. "I hope he isn't driving Simon mad."

"Simon's used to it," Manon said.

"Simon is a saint," Jennifer said with the dazzling smile that had been charming audiences in Paris and London for three decades. "And I speak as someone who loves Horace dearly."

Mélanie glanced round the company. Strange to be on the other side of this. Usually she and Malcolm were the ones asking the questions. But she had to stay a part of the company. It was vital for the success of the play. And, a small voice within her mind said, it also might position her better to investigate. As Manon had pointed out in their talk in the dressing room, to all intents and purposes she was undercover. Which was something she'd once enjoyed. Well, to be brutally honest, she still enjoyed it. She was just more aware of the costs.

Malcolm and Roth had slipped into the room, so quietly even she was scarcely aware of it. She met Malcolm's gaze for a moment. He smiled at her, the sort of quick, instant communication they had during an investigation. Thank God, they were still partners. Ridiculous how relieved she was.

Simon called the company to order, achieving quiet in a remarkably short space of time. Simon was an effective leader, but also everyone was keyed to hear what would be said next. Simon briefly mentioned Lewis Thornsby's tragic death, then asked Roth and Malcolm to say more.

Roth and Malcolm gave an account of the events, trading back and forth with an aplomb worthy of a pair of actors, but saying nothing about their search of Thornsby's rooms or their encounters with Billy and Kit.

Not surprisingly, Brandon Ford, who played the hero opposite Manon in *Past Imperfect,* first broke the silence when they were done. "What the devil was Thornsby doing here last night?" Brandon scraped a hand over his dark hair, making it even more Byronically disheveled than usual.

"An excellent question." Roth surveyed the company. "Does anyone know? Had anyone arranged to meet him here?"

Silence hung over the company, rare for a group of actors who tended to love the sound of their own voices.

"I try to stay as far away from the theatre as possible when Tanner lets us go home." Brandon took a swig from his tankard.

"Sorry that sounds disrespectful. God, I can't believe this has happened. But I certainly didn't hang about last night."

"There wasn't a meeting," Tim Scott, one of the stagehands said. "Was there?"

Silence and several veiled looks greeted his pronouncement.

"For what it's worth," Malcolm said, "we know about the Levellers. And we aren't here to shut them down."

"That's true enough," Brandon said. "But there wasn't a meeting last night. Leastways, not one I knew about." He glanced round the room. No one volunteered anything. More interestingly, no one gave a sign that they were holding something back. At least, not obviously.

"Which of you went to the White Rose with Thornsby last night?" Roth asked.

This time several raised their hands. Letty Blanchard, who was sitting with her hands locked tight together in her lap. Tim Scott. Bessie, still red-eyed. Brandon. Jim Taylor, who played comic characters. George Darnley, the assistant stage manager. And Will Carmarthen, the young actor Lewis Thornsby's valet had said he'd heard quarreling with Thornsby and who Manon had said might have had a romantic connection with Letty.

"When did you last see Thornsby?" Roth asked them.

Quick looks were exchanged across the bare stage. "When he left the White Rose," Tim said. "We all went our separate ways. Well—" He broke off at a look from Brandon. The company protected each other.

"Lewis left with me," Letty said. "But you already know that."

"And no one knows of any reason he'd have come back here?" Malcolm asked.

"Without Letty? Why would he—I mean..." Tim trailed off.

"Letty was his main interest here." Brandon shot a shrewd but not unkind look at Letty. "I think they already know that."

"What's next?" Simon asked.

"We'd like to talk to each of you individually," Roth said. "In case there's something you remember that perhaps you don't realize is pertinent."

"Or in case we killed him," Brandon said. "I mean, someone did," he added in the silence that followed. "And most likely, someone at the theatre."

"Possibly," Malcolm said in an easy voice. "But presumably Thornsby came back here last night to meet with someone and that could be someone unconnected to the theatre."

"Assuming that person killed him," Brandon said.

"At this point, we're trying hard not to assume anything," Malcolm said.

CHAPTER 11

Cordelia's description of Edith Simmons had prepared Laura for the scholarly type of young woman without a fortune who often ended up a governess. Usually the life of a governess went with restraint, self-imposed, as Laura knew to her cost from her own days as a governess, if one was not born with it. The most vibrant woman quickly learned the art of fading into the background, or she was likely to find herself without a position. The sober clothes helped. But one learned to tame one's personality as well. Even in a household as open as the Rannochs'.

It was quiet when they reached Green Park, not many having ventured abroad on such a blustery morning, but children's cries cut the air. Livia gave a cry of excitement and led the other children towards a girl of about eight and a boy of about six racing over the muddy ground. A tall young woman was not watching from the sidelines as most governesses would be (assuming they permitted their charges to romp at all), but running about with the children, so that it was only her height that indicated she wasn't one of the schoolroom party herself. Drusilla ran over and flung her arms round the young woman.

The young woman bent to hug her, slipped and landed in the mud, pushed herself to her feet without self-consciousness, and walked over to Cordelia and Laura. Her tawny hair, which looked as though it was difficult to contain in the best of circumstances, slipped from its pins about her face, and mud caked the hem of her serviceable dark blue pelisse (Laura had once lived in one very like it).

"Cordelia." The young woman stretched out her hands. "It's good to see you. And particularly good to see the children. Difficult to be low-spirited with Drusilla tumbling into one."

"I know just the feeling," Cordelia said. "She's saved me from low spirits more than once. I don't believe you've met Mrs. O'Roarke? Edith Simmons."

"Mrs. O'Roarke." Edith Simmons smiled and paused to exclaim over Clara, whom Laura was holding. "Cordelia and Harry have spoken about you and your husband." She looked from Laura to Cordelia. "You know, don't you? About Lewis."

Cordelia touched her hand. "I'm so sorry, Edith."

Edith glanced at the children, now happily performing their own introductions. "Thomas sent me word this morning. He wanted to warn me before the news got out. It doesn't seem to have reached the scandal sheets yet. But I imagine it will soon."

"Sensational news has a way of doing that, unfortunately," Laura said.

"Yes." Edith looked between them. "Not that I don't appreciate the sympathy, but I expect this isn't just a social call. Assuming one can call a visit to Green Park a social call. Or just a call of sympathy. You're involved in the investigation into Lewis's death, aren't you?"

"I wanted to see you," Cordelia said. "But yes, the Rannochs are assisting Bow Street."

"Oh thank heavens. That's exactly what I'd been hoping for, knowing your friendship with the Rannochs. It's horrible for Thomas's family, but this will make it much easier. Oh poison, that sounds dreadful, doesn't it. As though it's easier to talk to someone in the same social sphere, somehow. But that's not really what I meant. Though from what I know of the Thornsbys, I expect it will help them to talk to someone in the beau monde. But I meant it will make it feel less official. If that makes sense."

"Eminent sense," Laura said. "Would you rather talk to Cordelia alone? I can watch the children."

"Oh, no. I'd much rather have the benefit of your sense and I imagine you'll have to share information anyway." Edith glanced again at the children, who were now playing hide-and-seek. "To own the truth, it's a great relief to talk. I've been longing to do something all morning. And of course I couldn't do anything, so I brought the children to the park so all of us could run off our frustrations."

"Did you know Lewis well?" Cordelia asked.

"I scarcely knew him at all." Edith smoothed her hands over her blue skirt. "I met Thomas through the Classicists' Society. Thomas could hardly invite me to call at his home, and in any case, I gather he and Lewis didn't see much of each other. The only time I even saw Lewis was when he stopped by at the end of a meeting to collect Thomas because they were dining with their parents. But Thomas talked about Lewis." She hesitated a moment, as though suddenly uncertain for all her directness. "Thomas and I talked—talk—a great deal."

"Yes, I know," Cordelia said.

Edith flushed. "I think perhaps it was easier for him to talk to me because I was outside his family. Nothing he said was going to impact my relationship with them because I didn't know them. That wasn't going to change unless—" She broke off. "In any case, I know he was concerned about Lewis."

"About Lewis's involvement with the theatre?" Cordelia said.

"Yes, that. That is—there's a group associated with the theatre Lewis was part of. I suppose you—"

"We know about the Levellers," Cordelia said.

Edith folded her arms over her chest. "I thought they sounded rather splendid. But Thomas was afraid Lewis was involved in something dangerous, and I do understand his concern. Winston, careful of the little ones!" she called as her boy charge and Drusilla went rolling down the hill.

"Dru's equal to anything," Cordelia said. "Believe me, I can tell cries of delight from cries of distress. Did Thomas have other concerns?"

Edith hesitated. "There was a girl." She scanned Cordelia's face, then glanced at Laura. "You know already, don't you? I couldn't understand why Thomas was so concerned about this actress. But he said Lewis seemed increasingly cut off from his family. And of course I couldn't but be concerned about that. Not that—I mean I don't really know them, as I said. But Thomas and I—" She turned away, glanced at the children as though seeking distraction, but they were playing agreeably with no need for intervention.

"Edith," Cordelia said in a soft voice. "Had you and Thomas talked about marriage?"

Edith gave a strangled laugh. She dragged her gaze back to Cordelia's face, almost as though at once forcing herself to do so and relieved to speak. "Talked about it? In an oblique sort of way. Thomas is the sort who wouldn't have a discussion about those sorts of feelings at all without offering marriage, but he couldn't offer marriage. So we mostly discussed it in the sense of Thomas's pointing out what he couldn't offer me. He has his sisters to provide for somehow. And an estate to look after, at least when he inherits it. It's heavily encumbered. Being a classicist is hardly a profession that pays. Neither does being a governess."

"It's beastly," Laura said. "How personal relationships become tangled with economics."

"Yes," Edith said. "It is. One of the reasons I find myself in sympathy with these Levellers Thomas was talking about. It's all very well to think about being happy in a garret. I actually think I could be happy in a garret in the right circumstances. Thomas doesn't need a great deal as long as he has his books. But he has his family to think of. I don't think I could be happy if they weren't provided for, and I know he couldn't. Not that I'm sure I'd marry him anyway if it was a possibility. I mean—one gives up a lot to marry, doesn't one?"

"I can't say I ever really thought about it," Cordelia said. "Not at the time. I had it in my head I had to marry, that it was the only way to independence. Even if it wasn't the man I wanted. The man I thought I wanted. I'm shocked every day at how lucky I've been. Now—" She glanced at Livia, racing after Colin, and Drusilla wrestling with Jessica. "I hope my girls feel they have more options."

"I thought about it." Laura said. "So much that—despite having lived as a governess—I was determined never to marry again after my first husband died." She tucked a fold of blanket round Clara, who was looking round the park with wide eyes. "It took a rather extraordinary man to change my mind."

Edith scanned Laura's face with a gaze at once coolly ironic and that of a scholar seeking answers. "Because you loved him so much it was all worth it?"

Laura felt herself give an involuntary smile. "That was part of it. I wouldn't have married without it. But I also wouldn't have married without believing that he'd never use the intolerable legal powers the law puts at a husband's disposal against me."

Edith's eyes widened in acknowledgment. "Yes, precisely. Most people can't understand how there could seem to be more freedom in the life of a governess than that of a wife. But sometimes I think there is. I trust Thomas implicitly. And I know he values my scholarship. But it would be different if I were his wife. There'd be a role he'd need me to play. He'd have expectations. Even if he doesn't see that, I do." She hugged her arms. "Of course, I may just be saying that to comfort myself because anything actually happening between us is so very unlikely."

Laura saw Cordelia hesitate, her role as a friend warring with her role as an investigator. "It must have been difficult, Lewis's being his aunt's heir."

Edith met Cordelia's gaze, her own level. "And you're thinking Thomas might have killed his brother so he could have his aunt's fortune. I can quite see that, obviously you're looking for motives. I could talk a lot of twaddle about Thomas's love for his brother and how he's the sort of man who would never do that. And I'd be speaking the truth. But I daresay you wouldn't believe me, and I'm not sure I would in your shoes. Truth to tell, I wouldn't want you to. You'll never get to the bottom of this if you don't question everything, and for Thomas's sake I desperately want it solved. But the thing is, just on a practical level, there's no guarantee Lady Shroppington will make Thomas her heir. In fact, it seems rather unlikely. She has no desire to rescue the family's faltering fortunes. According to Thomas, she's made that clear often enough. There are cousins on the other side of the family. And she might leave her fortune out of the family entirely. Whereas, if Lewis had inherited, Thomas was confident he'd have helped the girls with their marriage portions and helped with the estate." Edith hesitated a moment, glanced at the children, tugged at the faded dark blue brim of her bonnet. "I think he had hopes that with the girls settled and some support for the estate, it might even have been possible for us to marry. But since he can't let himself talk openly of marriage, I can't be sure. And as I said, I wasn't sure what I'd have done if he'd been able to ask me. I think I was afraid to consider it."

"Do you know of anyone else who might have benefited from Lewis's death?" Laura asked.

"Do I?" Edith's brows rose. "I told you, I scarcely knew Lewis."

"But you know Thomas well. Did Thomas say anything else about his brother? You said he talked a lot about him."

"Yes, he did. But it was mostly about the theatre and the Leveller group and Letty Blanchard. And a bit about how he felt he didn't know his brother anymore."

"Do you think Lady Shroppington might leave her fortune to one of the girls?" Cordelia asked.

Edith frowned. "It's possible, I suppose. But according to Thomas, she's never taken much interest in them. He says he could see her deciding to benefit a distant godchild or even one of her footmen. She can be eccentric, apparently."

"And yet it sounds as if she didn't care for Lewis's entanglement with an actress."

"People can be like that, can't they?" Edith pulled her gray wool scarf tight about her throat as the wind whipped up. "Appreciative of eccentricity on their own terms while still wanting those about them to preserve the forms. What they see as the forms. From what Thomas says, Lady Shroppington was fond of Lewis, but I also think she had a clear idea of the life she wanted him to live. She was indulgent about his sowing his wild oats, as it were, but now she wanted to rein him in and have him conform."

"You sound as though you know her well," Cordelia said.

Edith colored. "Not really. Not at all. I've never met her or seen her. But I've heard a good deal about her from Thomas. And as a governess, I know the type."

"So do I," Laura said. "I used to be a governess. One learns to fade into the background. But that lends itself to observing. And because one fades into the background, people can be careless of what they reveal."

"Yes, that's it precisely," Edith said. "I like teaching. I enjoy the children." She smiled at her two charges. "I can't say I care for fading into the background. But it is intriguing to observe people. One feels alone, but there's a certain freedom to it. A freedom I fear I would give up if I were married."

"I know Lady Shroppington," Cordelia said. "She and my grandmother are friends. She didn't speak to me at the height of my scandalous days, but she's unbent now I'm living with Harry again. I'm not sure whether or not I'm glad she did, but it should help in the investigation. And yes, I can quite see her wanting Lewis to cut a dash and be a bit wild, but expecting him to come to heel when she called. I imagine she may even have had her choice of bride picked out for him."

"Thomas never said so," Edith said, "but I wouldn't be surprised." She drew a breath that had the bite of the January wind. "A part of me desperately wants to marry Thomas. So much so it hurts." She looked from Laura to Cordelia. "I suppose I shouldn't have admitted that to you. Because there's no way I can prove Lady Shroppington won't leave Thomas her fortune. So I've just given myself an excellent motive for murder."

William Carmarthen was in the wings on one side, practicing with a fencing foil. Malcolm couldn't but wonder if it was the foil Colin had found in the wings last night. Not that that necessarily hinted at anything. Will and Brandon had a sword fight in the third act of Mélanie's play.

Carmarthen set down the foil at Malcolm's approach. He had an intent, quicksilver face beneath a shock of chestnut hair. "Is it my turn to be interviewed? I didn't know Thornsby well. I went to the White Rose some nights. I looked in last night, but I left before Thornsby did."

"You and Thornsby were both Levellers."

Carmarthen gave a dry smile. "Along with half the company,

and half those who hang about the green room like Thornsby. As I'm sure you know, Mr. Rannoch."

Carmarthen's tone was easy but there was an edge to it. Malcolm took a step forwards, into the shadows of the wings. Roth was talking to Tim Scott across the stage. They'd divided forces to complete the interviews more quickly. "You called on Thornsby the day before he died."

Carmarthen went still for a moment. "Ah. The valet. Should have realized you'd have spoken to him. Yes, I did."

"And he heard you quarreling."

Carmarthen leaned back against a canvas flat that might be Juliet's balcony, hands braced behind him. "Doesn't look good to have quarreled with a murder victim, does it?"

"There can be any number of reasons for people to quarrel," Malcolm said.

"Christ." Carmarthen spun away, then looked back at Malcolm, eyes bright with a combination of grief and anger in the shadows. "I'm sorry Lewis is dead. I mean, one would have to be a pretty cold-hearted monster to wish that on anyone. But we weren't friends. And yes, I wasn't in the best humor when I went to see him the day before yesterday. Though I didn't mean the talk to go as it did."

Malcolm regarded the younger man. "Why did you go to see him?"

Carmarthen was silent for a moment. "To ask him about Letty."

Five words that revealed a multitude. Had he been delivering the line onstage, the subtext behind the name Letty would have been masterful.

"You're fond of her yourself," Malcolm said.

"Of course. I work with her."

"Do you show such concern for every young woman in the company?"

"I—" Carmarthen drew in and released his breath. "Oh, the

devil. Someone's probably going to tell you. Can't have secrets in a theatre company. A less adept writer than your wife would say I'm head over heels in love with Letty Blanchard."

"And Letty?" Malcolm recalled Mélanie's suspicion that Letty Blanchard loved someone else.

Carmarthen's mouth curved with memories at once sweet and bitter. "I think she may have had a passing fondness for me. At least, once. When we were—when we were first acquainted. We were Celia and Oliver opposite each other, and sometimes that sort of thing can carry over. But then Thornsby started hanging about the green room. He dazzled her. Or what he seemed to offer did."

"His position?"

Carmarthen's mouth twisted. "Letty looks at Manon Caret and Jennifer Mansfield and sees herself as an actress married to an aristocrat. Perhaps it's not to be wondered at, given that we live our lives making fiction as real as possible, but she doesn't see how incredibly rare Manon's and Jennifer's marriages are. Not the least because they're remarkably happy, but more to the point because gentlemen aren't in the habit of marrying actresses they trifle with. I made the mistake of trying to point that out to Letty, and she fairly bit my head off."

"So you decided to talk to Thornsby?"

Carmarthen grimaced. "Not my most sensible action. But I told him if he had a scrap of affection for Letty he wouldn't trifle with her. We hadn't much in common, but he struck me as decent enough that I thought he might see reason. Instead, Thornsby got huffy. Said he had nothing but honorable intentions." Carmarthen frowned and scraped a boot toe over the floorboards. "At the time I laughed and said that might work with Letty, but it wouldn't with me. But now I have the oddest feeling he may have been telling the truth. That he really did mean to offer her marriage." He cast a quick look at Malcolm. "Do you think that's true?"

"I can't know what was in Thornsby's head. And I can't divulge anything we've learned."

"Meaning you think he might have been going to. Or that he did?" Carmarthen cast a quick glance towards the stage where a number of the company were disposed, sitting on the floor or on rehearsal chairs, sipping coffee or something stronger. He scraped a hand over his hair. "God. I never meant to get between him and Letty. That is—" He stared into the shadows with the air of one scouting a terrain he didn't fully understand. "I don't think Letty loved him. But if she wanted to trade a chance at love for security, that's her own affair. And if Thornsby would have been happy with what she could give him, I suppose that's his. I don't think it would have made either of them happy in the end. But perhaps that's my jealousy talking."

His voice was low and conversational. But Malcolm could hear the taut pain of unrequited love beneath. "Did you tell Miss Blanchard about it?"

"Are you mad? I may not have a lot of pride, but I have a bit. It was up to her if she wanted to marry Thornsby. I've been avoiding her as much as possible ever since my talk with Thornsby. That's why I left the White Rose early last night." Carmarthen glanced away. "God, poor Letty. Whatever she felt for him—and she may have loved him more than I'd like to admit—she was certainly fond of him. But of course anything I say to her now will come across the wrong way."

"I wouldn't discount the power of comfort, sincerely offered."

Carmarthen dragged his gaze to Malcom's face and gave a twisted smile. "That sounds splendid, Rannoch. But the reality is likely to be angry tirades and accusations that I've ruined her life. I like Letty, you know. Quite apart from—everything else. But the damnable thing about love is that it can make friendship impossible."

"I wouldn't say that."

"If you're going to say you're friends with your wife, that's quite different. You evidently are friends with Mrs. Rannoch, from everything I've seen, and that's splendid. But can you imagine being friends with a former love when the love had burned out or otherwise ended?"

Malcolm thought of Kitty. And then of Raoul and Mélanie. "Yes," he said. "I can. Not that it would be easy. Not that there wouldn't be echoes. But I think one can get beyond them. Or learn to live with them. Or both."

"You're an idealist, Rannoch. Or a remarkable man. Or both."

"Or a deluded fool."

"That too. Though somehow I don't think so." Carmarthen watched him for a moment. "So I'm sure you know that I know I've just given you a motive for having murdered Thornsby."

Malcolm held the young man's gaze in the shadows. "I take it you aren't confessing."

"Good God, no. I abhor violence." Carmarthen cast a glance at the fencing foil. "Offstage, anyway. And all other things aside, I'd never have put Letty in that position." He looked back at Malcolm. "But I suppose I'd say that anyway. If I were guilty. I suppose I'd say anything."

That was quite true. And it was impossible to forget Carmarthen was an actor. A very good actor indeed.

CHAPTER 12

"*If only I could make you see what you—that is, I—* Sorry." Brandon broke off and turned to Mélanie and Simon. "I always seem to mangle that part."

"I need to rework the speech." Mélanie looked up from the script. Her play centered on a fashionable married couple who each learned the other was not what they seemed. Very close to home, though neither was a former spy in the play. The hero, Gideon, was in fact a former valet who had taken his master's place—a plot device inspired by Mélanie's father's love of Beaumarchais's Figaro trilogy. The heroine, Fiona, was in fact the mother of the little girl she was raising as her niece. Manon's young daughters Roxane and Clarisse were playing Fiona's secret daughter and the younger daughter she had with Gideon. Manon and Brandon brought Fiona and Gideon to life more brilliantly than Mélanie could have dreamed possible, but Brandon struggled with the scene in which Gideon bared his soul to his wife.

"It's a good speech," Brandon said. "There's just something about it that makes my mind go blank."

"You could always launch into the St. Crispin's Day speech

like you did that time you forgot your lines when you were supposed to be sending me off to a nunnery," Manon said.

"That was a rehearsal. And it was bloody hard to keep two versions of Hamlet straight. I had twice the lines you did."

"Don't remind me. I spent an unconscionable amount of time lying on the ground while you wept over my grave. Though I quite liked the speech Shakespeare gave Hamlet in that version. Made it clearer how he felt about Ophelia. Not that I think it's that unclear, in any case."

The four of them—Brandon, Manon, Simon, and Mélanie—had retreated to one of the rehearsal rooms to work on a key scene while Malcolm and Roth conducted interviews. They were opening in four days and had no time to waste. So of course Mélanie needed to be here, working on the play, not interviewing suspects. Which would also put her at odds with the company. None of which shook her feeling of being sidelined in an investigation.

Simon pushed himself away from the wall he'd been leaning against. "Let's take a few minutes. I think it's hard for everyone to concentrate right now."

"You have a genius for understatement, Tanner." Brandon reached for his flask, then set it down. "I think I need coffee. Anyone want anything from the White Rose?"

"You can be an angel, Brandon," Manon said. "The usual. A lot of milk and sugar to hide the fact that it's not French."

"Milk, no sugar," Mélanie said.

Simon reached for his coat. "I'll go with you."

Mélanie gathered up her script and pencil and turned to the door to see her husband standing in the doorway.

"Sorry," Malcolm said.

"No, it's all right." She moved towards the door. "We're taking a break."

"Do you need to talk to one of us?" Simon asked.

"Not yet. I know where to find you." Malcolm flashed a grin

at Simon, Manon, and Brandon that couldn't quite erase the fact that while they had all dined at his table, he was interviewing them about a murder.

Manon went to the White Rose with Brandon and Simon. Malcolm joined Mélanie in the rehearsal room. "Is it going all right?"

"As well as it can be, considering we're all thinking about Lewis Thornsby one way and another." Mélanie scanned her husband's face. It was as intense as it always was during an investigation, but there were shadows round his eyes that hadn't been there last night. "Have you learned anything? Anything you can tell me?"

Malcolm gave a faint smile. "There's nothing I can't tell you, sweetheart. But we haven't learned a great deal. Roth and I are going to Rosemary Lane to investigate the address Thornsby's valet saw on the paper he thought Thornsby burned. We may talk to the company more later. So far, our main discovery is that Will Carmarthen admits to having been in love with Letty Blanchard."

"That's not entirely a surprise."

"You knew?"

"Not for a certainty. But I could at least tell he was fond of her, and Manon mentioned it this morning. I wonder—"

"If he was the man you thought Letty was worried about giving up if she married Thornsby? I wondered the same thing. Carmarthen says he went to see Thornsby to warn him off trifling with Letty, only to have Thornsby claim not to be doing anything of the sort. It's possible that confrontation got him to propose to Letty last night." Malcolm leaned against the wall where Simon had been standing a few minutes before. "Whatever Letty feels for Carmarthen, Carmarthen admitted to being quite desperately in love with her. And then admitted he'd just given himself a motive for murder."

"Will doesn't strike me as a killer. Of course I'm a bit biased because I like him. And he's quite brilliant in the play."

"I like him too, and he doesn't strike me as a killer either. But it's a possibility we have to consider."

Mélanie studied her husband. The light from the Argand lamp on a table to one side caught his face from below, making the shadows round his eyes and beneath his cheekbones look even more pronounced. "Darling? You look worried, and somehow I don't think it's about Will."

Malcolm grimaced. "How well you know me. No, it isn't. I like him, as I said, and I think it's possible there's more to his quarrel with Thornsby than he admitted to me. But liking people and realizing they have secrets is part of any investigation." He frowned at a framed poster for *The Steward's Stratagem*, one of Simon's most successful plays, on the wall opposite. "Kitty came to Berkeley Square this morning after you left. She says she and Lewis Thornsby had a liaison. Well, a night together. That Thornsby wanted to make into more than it was. I don't think she's telling the truth."

That certainly accounted for the shadows. As always, when it came to Kitty and her husband, Mélanie chose her words with care. "It can't have been an easy story for her to tell. Why don't you believe her?"

Malcolm gave an almost sheepish smile. "Because I think St. Juste means more to her than that."

Mélanie watched her husband for a moment. His gaze was fixed on the chipped gilt paint on the table, a former prop piece stripped of theatrical illusion by daylight. "Caring for someone—even loving someone—doesn't necessarily guarantee fidelity."

"No. I know that. But—" He shook his head. "Kitty accused me of being a romantic. Of seeing them through the lens of our relationship, I suppose."

"They aren't us, darling."

"No, of course not." Malcolm's shoulders shifted against the pine-paneled wall behind him. "But I'd swear what's between them is genuine. They're—you've seen them together."

"I have."

"And?"

Mélanie remembered the last time Kitty and Julien had dined in Berkeley Square. Only last week. Kitty taking a sip from Julien's glass of port, Julien flicking a lazy finger against Kitty's cheek. Kitty putting Genny into Julien's arms. Julien wrapping Kitty's cloak round her shoulders. "One can never know what two people mean to each other. How that will impact their ideas about fidelity. Let alone their practice. But—I've felt what's between them too. They're both very controlled people. And I think they both take the relationship more seriously than they'd admit to anyone. Including perhaps themselves."

"Precisely."

Mélanie moved to Malcolm's side and slid her hand into his. "It's still no guarantee of anything, Malcolm."

"No." He looked down at their entwined fingers, his mouth curved in a rueful smile. "I realize that in insisting on the depth and constancy of Kitty Ashford's and Julien St. Juste's feelings—in claiming to know them at all—I look like a fool. And yet—"

"Not a fool, darling." Mélanie reached up and smoothed his hair off his forehead. "It's easy enough to believe in the fidelity of people everyone expects to be faithful. Much harder to believe in those no one expects such behavior from. It takes keen insights."

"Or madness."

"People have been writing keen insights off as madness for years."

Malcolm laughed and kissed her hair. "And of course, if I'm right, it means Kitty's lying about her relationship to Lewis Thornsby. That she'd rather I thought her careless and heedless, that potentially St. Juste did as well, than that we learned the truth." His arms closed right round Mélanie for a moment. When she looked up, his gaze had hardened. "Whatever that truth may be."

~

ROTH GLANCED at Malcolm as they made their way in a hackney to the address Cranley had given them in Rosemary Lane. "What did you make of the company?"

"They're actors." Malcolm reached for the strap as they rounded a corner. "Very good actors, which complicates matters. Possibly the most difficult group to investigate, next to a group of agents. Maybe more so."

"And half of them are mixed in with the Levellers," Roth said. "At the risk of crossing lines we said we wouldn't cross, what do you make of the Levellers' activity?"

"That there are things going on they aren't talking about. Possibly that they don't all know about. From secret societies to Radical protesters to the House of Commons, factions and secrets seem to be inevitable in any group over a certain size. And that size may be as small as four."

Roth nodded. "Do you believe Carmarthen?"

"I believe him when he says he loves Letty Blanchard to distraction. Which could have led him to do all sorts of things. And he's also an exceptionally good actor among a group of good actors."

Roth frowned. "You think he's using his love for Miss Blanchard as cover for something else?"

"He's a Leveller. Lewis Thornsby was a Leveller. There are all sorts of ways their paths could have intersected."

"But you believe he loves Miss Blanchard."

"I do. I could be wrong. But using romantic relationships as cover is one of the oldest tricks of an adept agent."

Roth glanced through the fogged glass of the window. "We

keep hearing that Thornsby didn't seem that serious about the Levellers. Everyone from his brother to his comrades seems surprised about his involvement."

"Yes. And yet he seems to have stumbled into some very complicated intrigues." Not the least of which was that involving Kitty Ashford. Which Malcolm had yet to share with Roth. Or with anyone but Mel. Which was probably foolish. Still.

"Some people do just stumble into tangles," Roth said.

"It's certainly possible. Or it could be that Lewis Thornsby was more complicated than any of us thought."

They had reached Rosemary Lane. The wind blew a length of bright cotton from a nearby stall into a mud puddle a few feet off as Malcolm swung down from the hackney. A boy about Colin's age, clad in mismatched boots and a coat two sizes too big, caught the cloth up and ran back to the stall. He scrubbed the mud with his fist and tacked the cloth to a peg next to a faded pelisse and a yellowing once white gown. A thin woman with a worn face who presided over the stall gave him a quick smile and returned to haggling with a woman with bright red hair over how much she'd give her for a blue velvet dress the woman was exchanging for a green dress that looked rather more worn. Similar scenes were going on at stalls and barrows all along that side of the lane. Another gust of wind sent great-coats and pelisses, gowns and chemises flapping like pennants where they hung in front of shops. As Malcolm paid off the hackney driver, he caught more than one glance run over his greatcoat and beaver hat, both of which would fetch a tidy sum with Rosemary Lane's old clothes dealers. Roth picked his way round a faded square of carpet piled with boots and shoes and studied the sign that hung over the narrow building that was Number 17. A scarlet-bound volume and the faded words Hapgood's Novels and Books of Interest. "Interesting that

Thornsby had the address of a bookstore. Perhaps the Levellers are using it to pass messages?"

"Perhaps Mr. Hapgood is another Leveller?" Malcolm said. "Or perhaps Thornsby was merely searching for a hard-to-find book." His gaze moved to the floor above the shop. Narrow sash windows, a table visible behind one, a chair back at another. "It looks as though there are lodgers above."

"You think one of the Levellers might lodge here?" Roth asked, scanning the windows.

"It's a possibility. Which doesn't answer the question of how much Hapgood knows."

Without further speech, they crossed the street and opened the door of Hapgood's shop. The musty, leathery smell of old books greeted them. The smell of Malcolm's favorite rooms since childhood. A smell he'd always associate with his boyhood visits to Raoul, either at hotels or in rooms Raoul had stayed at in Malcolm's grandfather's houses or at Dunmykel.

The only sources of illumination were whatever wintry light the windows let in and two oil lamps, one set on a table in the center of the room, the other on a counter at the back. A man sat behind the counter, but at first all Malcolm could make out was the dark blur of a figure.

"May I help you gentlemen?" the man asked in a deep voice.

Malcolm threaded his way between bookcases and tables, wondering how anyone managed to see enough to examine the books that were offered for sale. "Do I have the pleasure of addressing Mr. Hapgood?"

"I don't know if it's a pleasure, but I'm Hapgood." He was a wiry, compact man, with thick, close-cut salt-and-pepper hair and a strong, blunt-featured face. He looked to be in his late fifties or early sixties. Less likely he was a Leveller. They tended to be young.

Hapgood was seated on a high stool behind the counter,

turning the pages of a book set directly beneath the lamp. He did not close the book as Malcolm and Roth approached.

"We're looking for information about this gentleman." Malcolm pulled out a sketch Mélanie had done of Thornsby. "We thought perhaps he'd been to visit your shop."

Hapgood pulled the sketch into the lamplight. "What's he done?"

"What makes you think he's done anything?" Roth asked.

"You gentlemen look as though you have more important things to do with your time than to go about asking questions without good cause."

"He was murdered last night," Malcolm said.

"Good lord. " Hapgood's brows shot up. He stared at Malcolm and Roth for a long moment. "And the two of you—"

"Are trying to find out why he was killed and by whom," Roth said.

Hapgood looked from Roth to Malcolm. "And you are—?"

"This is Inspector Roth of Bow Street. My name is Rannoch. Malcolm Rannoch. I'm—"

"I know who you are. I've read your speeches. There was one a couple of months back against suspension of Habeas Corpus that I particularly admired. Not that you had a prayer of stopping its suspension."

"Thank you," Malcolm said. "And yes, I knew I didn't."

Hapgood closed the book he had been reading. "It must be difficult, all that work and passion, only to see your ideas voted down."

"My wife would tell you I have a fondness for taking a lance to windmills."

Hapgood gave an unexpected smile. "My character reading may not be the most acute, Mr. Rannoch, but I'd imagine you're the sort who can tell a windmill from a dragon."

"When the wind is southerly."

Hapgood gave a grunt of acknowledgment.

"Where have you seen the victim?" Roth asked.

"In my shop. And above it. Mr. Montford has rented a room for the past month."

"That's his name?" Roth said. "Montford?"

"That's the name he gave me. What name do you know him by?"

"Lewis Thornsby," Malcolm said. "When did you last see Mr. Montford?"

Hapgood scratched his head. "Three or four days since. He's out a good deal. Did he have lodgings elsewhere in London under his own name?"

"In Piccadilly." Malcolm felt something soft brush his leg. He glanced down to see a tabby cat winding itself against his boots. He bent to stroke the animal. "Did the supposed Mr. Montford tell you anything about his life?"

"He'd been abroad for several years as a private tutor. His charge having gone off to university, Montford had returned to England to look for work. Or so he said."

"You had reason to doubt him?" Roth asked.

The cat jumped onto the counter. Hapgood scratched its ears. "Not until what you gentlemen told me just now." He regarded Malcolm and Roth with an unblinking gaze. "I'm very sorry to hear he met his death, but I must say I'm also curious as to his reasons for living a double life."

"So are we," Roth said. "Did Montford ever receive visitors?"

Hapgood frowned. The cat lay down on its side and began to wash. "No one I noted."

The cat batted at a fold of Roth's greatcoat. "What else can you tell us about Thornsby? Montford," Roth said, petting the cat.

"Very little, I'm afraid. He kept to himself, and as I prefer to do likewise we didn't converse much." Hapgood rubbed the bridge of his nose. "I suppose you think I should display more grief at his death, but truth to tell, while I knew nothing ill of him, we weren't well acquainted."

"Did he ever have ladies visit him?"

"Not to my knowledge. Though he looked to be the sort of man who'd know how to be discreet."

Yet there was something guarded in Hapgood's expression. Malcolm couldn't swear he was lying, but nor could he be confident the bookseller was telling the truth. At least not the entire truth.

"We'll have to see his room," Roth said.

"I assumed you'd wish to." Hapgood pulled open a drawer beneath the counter and produced a tarnished brass key. "Third door at the top of the stairs. They're at the back of the shop. The stairs, that is."

Malcolm and Roth made their way past ranks of books and up the narrow stairs. The corridor at the stairhead held no illumination save the light from a window that faced the next house over. The window had been left half open, perhaps in an attempt to drive out the damp that pervaded the house and threatened the books belowstairs. A gust of cold air greeted them.

They walked down the passage to the third door. Malcolm reached for the knob. Before he could turn it, the door swung open, and a dark figure hurtled through and knocked him to the floor.

CHAPTER 13

Malcolm slammed into the floorboards and heard Roth hit the ground. By the time he pushed himself to his feet, their assailant was climbing through the open window at the end of the passage. They reached the window in time to see a greatcoated figure dart out of the alley into Rosemary Lane. Too late to give chase. He'd be lost amid the barrows and stalls and sellers and shoppers and they hadn't seen enough to identify him.

Roth leaned against the wall, handkerchief pressed to his nose, which was streaming blood. "I don't know whether to be relieved or sorry that Mélanie didn't accompany us."

"Relieved because she didn't see the two of us bested by a single man, or sorry because if she'd been here it might not have happened?"

"Precisely."

"Are you all right?" Hapgood's voice came up the stairwell followed shortly by Hapgood himself. The cat trotted behind him.

"There was someone in Montford's room," Malcolm said. "You didn't know he was there?"

"If I had known of it, surely I'd either have warned you or attempted to delay you, assuming I was the man's confederate. He escaped?"

"Out the window," Malcolm said. "Not our most shining moment."

"Are you injured?" Hapgood asked with unexpected crispness.

"Only bruises and a bloody nose," Roth said, voice muffled by the handkerchief.

"And the damage to our pride." Malcolm looked out the window again. "Mud on the side of the building. That didn't come from his escape—he jumped. So it looks as if he climbed in. I doubt he's your confederate, Hapgood, unless you're singularly inhospitable to your confederates. You'd better see if you think anything was taken from Montford's room."

Malcolm stepped through the open doorway into a room filled with the smells of citrus and sandalwood and some sort of spice. Cloves, perhaps, or cardamom. Blended with a subtlety that indicated expense. Different from the cedar shaving soap scent in Thornsby's rooms in Piccadilly. Changing his scent in a different persona implied a degree of finesse that suggested Thornsby may have been very different from the guileless young man he had seemed on the surface. A lamp had been left lit on the chest of drawers. The room was scrupulously neat save for the writing table drawer, which had been pulled from its tracks and set on the tabletop. A search by a professional, interrupted in midstream.

Hapgood entered the room after Malcolm and surveyed the scene. "I can't swear to what might be missing from his personal effects. The room looks as I remember. But I was only in here once." He glanced at the drawer that had been removed from the desk. "Do you think whoever searched the house is likely to come back? There's a very pleasant young woman who rents the room across the hall. Sings at the King's

Theatre. Lovely voice. I don't like to think of any harm coming to her."

"I'd advise you to use extra caution in locking up," Roth said. "And to warn the young lady. I can assign a patrol to keep watch on the house."

"I'm obliged to you." Hapgood scooped up the cat, who had jumped up on the bed and was kneading the blanket. "If I can't be of further service, I'd best return to the shop. I know it doesn't look like it, but I do have customers every now and again."

Malcolm surveyed the room. A trunk at the foot of the bed, a shaving kit on the chest of drawers. The leather looked to be good quality. "How's your nose?" he asked Roth.

Roth took the handkerchief away from his face. "Seems to have stopped bleeding." He stared at the bloodstained handkerchief for a moment, then stuffed it into his greatcoat pocket.

"Papers or clothes?" Malcolm asked.

"I'll take the papers." Roth struck a flint to the taper on the writing table. The clean smell and pristine white indicated beeswax rather than tallow.

Malcolm opened the doors of the wardrobe. The garments that first met his eye spoke of Mr. Montford the former-tutor-in-search-of-employment. Coats of sturdy, slightly scratchy wool, well made but several years out of date, cut for comfort more than fashion, different from the fashionably cut Bond Street attire Thornsby had affected. A single greatcoat, beginning to wear through at the elbows.

"Thornsby knew the value of dressing for a part," Malcolm said. "He may well have purchased this wardrobe in Rosemary Lane. Anything in the writing desk?"

"A couple of letters from a Timothy Compton at Cambridge, telling Montford he'd never have been able to keep his head above water at university without the excellent preparation. Thornsby seems to have been a bit of an egotist in his forgeries.

Very adroitly done, though. There's even a bit in Latin. Typical sort of undergraduate blather. At least, what I've always assumed to be typical undergraduate blather."

"Self-consciously clever and convinced one has attained great maturity? It sounds like it. Anything else?"

"Another letter, from Aunt Mathilda in Shropshire, detailing his cousin Susan's lying-in and cautioning him not to catch a chill in the dreadful London damp. Pens, ink, pen knife, writing paper. I'll try the chest of drawers."

Malcolm carried the lamp over to the trunk. He lifted the lid to release a faint scent of lavender. Clean, starched shirts, neck-cloths, and drawers with frayed seams. Waistcoats that were beginning to fade, one with cracked buttons, another with a torn lining. The trunk did not seem as deep as one might expect. Malcolm ran his fingers over the lining. The bottom snapped away.

In the hidden compartment beneath were the possessions of Lewis Thornsby, young man about town. Coats of cassimere and superfine, a greatcoat of merino wool with a velvet collar. "So he could make a quick change here?" Roth asked, looking over his shoulder from the writing desk.

"Presumably. Though you'd think he'd have been worried Hapgood or someone would see him coming or going," Malcolm said.

No sign of papers. He ran his fingers over the lining of the false bottom and at last felt a telltale crinkle. He tugged at the silk lining and it came away in his fingers, loosely tacked to the frame of the trunk. Too loosely. Had the man whose search they'd interrupted been here before them?

If so, he hadn't taken his discoveries with him. Beneath the lining was a stack of papers. "If you're finished with the chest of drawers, come take a look at these," Malcolm said, carrying the papers and the lamp over to the writing desk.

"So far, my most interesting discovery is a bottle of excellent cognac." Roth joined him at the writing desk. The loose sheets of paper were creased, as though they'd been much folded. Malcolm spread the first out. A jumble of characters met his gaze, block capitals grouped together with the odd number thrown in.

"Can you break it?" Roth asked. This was not the first time he and Malcolm had examined a code together.

"Not easily. I'll take them to my cousin Aline. She'll be quicker." Malcolm continued to flip through the papers. All were in code and appeared to be in Thornsby's hand, until at the bottom he found what appeared to be a laundry list—shirts, handkerchiefs, sheets, pillowcases—written in another hand, fastened with a metal clip to several more sheets of paper. The laundry list had been torn four ways across and then glued together.

"What the devil—" Roth said.

"Rescued from a waste basket," Malcolm said. "Spies are constantly sorting through debris. In Vienna, agents for almost every country spent hours piecing together the contents of diplomatic wastebaskets. I can't tell you how many times I was asked to decode papers which turned out to be no more than a bill from the bootmaker's or a menu for a dinner party. But if Thornsby saved this—"

He removed the clip, carefully, so as not to damage the glued pieces, and examined the papers beneath. The contents of the laundry list had been copied onto the first paper. Beside it were a series of jottings in Thornsby's hand that Malcolm recognized as the notes of someone struggling to decipher a code. A rough table was sketched on the next paper. On the third paper, each line of the laundry list had been transformed into a place name and date. Lancaster, 3 November; Long Eaton, 21 November; Nottingham, 8 December; Clitheroe, 14 December; Rochdale, 22 December.

"Apparently Thornsby decoded this," Malcolm said. "And thought it important. The question is why?"

~

MALCOLM FOUND his wife sitting at the writing desk beside the fireplace in the Berkeley Square library, pen in hand.

"You're home." In the midst of an investigation, not to mention rehearsals, that was something of a surprise.

"I'm doing some rewrites and I thought I could focus better here. Laura and Cordelia stopped by the Tavistock with the children, and I walked back with them. They'd been to see Edith Simmons—a friend of Thomas Thornsby's."

"Yes, Harry and I saw Thomas this morning. I gather Edith would be his betrothed if he were in better circumstances."

"So do I. Though apparently she has some qualms about the restraints of marriage. An interesting sounding young woman. Colin was particularly excited to be part of things. He talked to the children Miss Simmons is governess to and learned that Miss Simmons had been crying and also that Thomas Thornsby is very kind and once gave them each a shilling. Cordy and Laura are upstairs with the children now." Mélanie regarded her husband. "What did you and Jeremy learn in Rosemary Lane?"

"Quite a lot, as it happens." Malcolm pulled a chair over, sat beside his wife, and told her about their visit, the attack, and Lewis Thornsby's second identity as Montford.

Mélanie's gaze widened with a shock Malcolm wasn't used to seeing on his wife's face. "Lewis Thornsby was living a double life?"

"An exceedingly well-constructed one. Complete with letters to verify his persona should anyone search, a different scent, a full wardrobe change."

She shook her head. He could see her sifting the pieces. "You'd think someone leading a double life wouldn't surprise me, of all people. But Lewis Thornsby—"

"I doubt anyone suspected you," Malcolm said. "I'd like to think it wasn't totally obvious when I was undercover."

"No, of course not." Mélanie pushed her fingers into her hair where it fell over her shoulders. "But we're trained agents. We're—"

"Supposed to be able to spot this sort of thing. In theory. Yet you deceived me." He sat back in the chair he had pulled up beside the writing desk and kept his voice easy. "Under the right circumstances, I might even be able to deceive you."

Mélanie's gaze stayed steady in the flickering firelight. "I'm quite sure you could, darling. I suppose—I wonder if either of us ever seemed as uncomplicated to those we met on missions as Thornsby did on the surface. That's a terribly self-centered thing to say, isn't it? But Thornsby wasn't a trained agent—"

"That we know of."

"He was barely out of university. Of course, you'd been out even less time when you went to the Peninsula."

"And St. Juste was stealing state secrets, assassinating the odd target, and seducing a future empress in his teens."

"Well, Julien's an exception to just about everything." Mélanie frowned. "And I'm not sure who did the seducing, Julien or Josephine."

"Fair enough. The meticulousness of the persona Thornsby had set up suggests he was trained by someone. I agree a young man fresh from university probably wouldn't think of tricks like using a different shaving soap and creating elaborate cover documents to deceive searchers. All of which leaves the question of why set up a second identity in London?"

"To move in different circles? Which is interesting, because he was already one of the Levellers under his own identity."

"To spy on someone. Or to undertake a plot."

Mélanie's gaze darted over his face. Level, but he saw an echo of his own fears. "A plot for the Levellers?" she asked.

"We can't overlook the possibility. But it also could be against them."

"Which would mean Thornsby was undercover as a Leveller, but also needed a second identity for something further."

Malcolm frowned at the muddy toes of his boots. "If you'd infiltrated a group under your own persona, why would you set up a second identity?"

"Because I needed to do something that couldn't be traced to my real identity. Or to secure the trust of people who wouldn't trust me in my true guise. You're right, he could be doing both of those for the Levellers or against them. But it seems very elaborate lengths to have gone to—"

"Unless the prize is very valuable indeed." Malcolm reached in his pocket and pulled out the papers he'd brought back from Rosemary Lane. "Roth and I found the lodgings Thornsby used as Montford. We surprised someone in the act of searching."

Mélanie took studied the coded papers. "You've tried to break these?"

"Not yet. I think I'll take them to Aline and see what she can do. I also found this in his rooms in Rosemary Lane, though I'm not sure what to make of it." Malcolm pulled the glued-together sheet and Thornsby's decoded version from his coat. "Roth and I wondered if they could be drop dates."

Mélanie scanned the list. "There's something familiar about at least one of them, but I can't quite remember what. Perhaps—"

She broke off as the door opened to admit Cordelia. "Look who I found in the hall when I came down from the nursery," she said.

David followed Cordelia into the room but hesitated a few steps behind her, as though not quite sure of his welcome. "I confess I felt singularly useless at home," he said, "with the children doing lessons, and Simon at the theatre. I came round to see if there was anything I could do."

Malcolm got to his feet and surveyed his friend. They had made tremendous progress, but their friendship was still a fragile thing, something they were trying to nurture and rebuild. Much as he and Mélanie had once done with their marriage, though he wondered if he and Mel had ever been quite so estranged as he and David had become. Odd how different betrayals could cut differently. Mélanie was his wife and had spied on him. David was his friend and had simply failed to accept what Mélanie had done. Yet that had created a deeper breach—perhaps because it was easier for Malcolm to understand Mélanie's actions than David's.

And yet in the old days, David and Simon had largely been outside their investigations. Long before he knew the truth about Mélanie, David had often been horrified by the life of an agent. Now, knowing the truth about the League, knowing Gisèle was his sister, David was part of the fight and more of a pragmatist. He and Malcolm might not have fully recovered what they had once had, but David was far less shocked by the life of an agent and far more ready to be an ally.

"How well did you know Thornsby?" Malcolm asked.

"Not well." David took a step forwards into the room. "I'd spoken with him in the green room once or twice, but usually I take the children home and don't linger. He seemed agreeable enough, but for someone who apparently was one of the Levellers, he didn't seem particularly knowledgeable about political matters. He hadn't even heard of your capital punishment bill."

"Apparently he was living a double life," Malcolm said.

"Good God," Cordelia said.

"Thornsby?" David said, with the same shock Mélanie had shown.

Malcolm gave a quick account of his and Roth's visit to Rosemary Lane.

"Is everyone you know a spy?" David demanded when he had done.

"Thornsby's just about the last person I'd have thought

would be," Malcolm said. "Though we don't know he was a spy, precisely."

"Why else would he have set up a second identity?" David asked. "Isn't being undercover practically the definition of being an agent?"

"More or less," Malcolm agreed. "Though there could be other reasons."

"Such as conducting a love affair," Cordelia said. "Plays and operas are full of it. Look at Count Almaviva. Though if Thornsby was being Montford to woo a lady in secret, it obviously wasn't Letty Blanchard."

"No," Malcolm agreed. "It would have to be another love affair, which, given what we've learned about Miss Blanchard, would also indicate a level of deceit." He avoided Mélanie's gaze because there was Kitty's story, not that he believed it. "And from Thornsby's level of skill in setting up his persona, it does appear he was trained by someone."

"You searched his rooms?" David asked. "I mean, the rooms he had in this other identity?"

"We haven't found much so far. A few papers."

David glanced at the list of dates which Malcolm had set on the marble library table. "Was this one of them?"

"Yes. It looks to be something Thornsby took from someone else and decoded. We thought they might be drop dates."

"Lancaster, 3 November," David read. "That's the date of the protest meeting that turned into a demonstration."

"The exact date?" Malcolm asked.

"I'm sure of it. Will Carmarthen got himself in a bit of trouble and I had to go up to Lancaster and speak to the magistrate to get him released from jail. Don't you remember? Simon and I were dining with you when we got word about it two days later. Mélanie was saying that she still didn't understand Guy Fawkes Day when the footman came in with the message."

"I remember," Cordelia said. "You had to leave in the middle of dinner."

Malcolm nodded. The exact date had been lost in the emotional chaos following Edgar's death, but he well remembered Simon's frown and muttered curse on scanning the note about Will Carmarthen. Even then, Malcolm had been sure Carmarthen was one of the Levellers.

Mélanie was scanning the other dates. "Long Eaton, 21 November. Wasn't there a fire in a factory at Long Eaton?"

"A textile mill," Malcolm said. "I don't know the exact date, but it was in November."

"The 11th," David was staring down at the paper, an odd look on his face. "The Tavistock company went on there after Lancaster."

"And there was Luddite activity round Rochdale last December," Mélanie said, looking at yet another entry. She turned to David, whose face had darkened. "David—"

"Ned Blakeney's from there." Ned was another of the actors in the Tavistock company."

"Another of the Levellers?" Malcolm asked.

David's mouth tightened. "I avoid asking Simon certain questions, just as he avoids asking me. But yes, I think so." David stared down at the list, brows knotting together. "Are you saying you think Father was right and Thornsby really was involved in Radical plots? With Carmarthen and who knows which others? That the assassination plot is real and not something designed to discredit the Levellers?"

Mélanie ran her fingers over the glued-together paper. "Thornsby decoded this. Which doesn't make a lot of sense if he's behind the incidents."

"Unless the list was put together by someone trying to uncover what was behind the incidents rather than the person who orchestrated them," Malcolm said. "Assuming they were orchestrated. Assuming the list means what we suspect. In any case, it's worthwhile talking to Carmarthen."

"Have you talked to Simon about this?" David asked.

"I've talked to him about a lot of the investigation," Malcolm said.

David met Malcolm's gaze, with less shock and more understanding than he'd have displayed in their investigations a couple of years ago. "But you're not sure you can trust what he's telling you."

"I'm not sure of that with anyone in an investigation."

David nodded. "The Levellers—"

"The Levellers are working to do a lot of good. As, I hope, are you and I, in our own way. And you're right, it's been better for us to work without knowing too much of what the other was doing. Unfortunately, with the investigation, we can't continue to do that. Loyalties can conflict. And it's not always a simple question of one loyalty coming first. There are always choices. My father taught me that. As did my wife." He reached for Mélanie's hand.

David looked between them. "I don't know how you got through it."

His gaze held an understanding Malcolm had never thought to see. But also fear for the future. Mélanie touched his hand. "Nor do I, often. But it can be done."

"It's amazing what people can get past," Cordelia said. "Sometimes just by muddling through."

David gave her a quick smile, then turned back to Malcolm. "I don't mean to keep you. You'll want to get to the theatre and talk to Will."

"Simon sent the actors home for the afternoon," Mélanie said. "All but Manon and Brandon. But he'll know where Will lodges."

"It's a Tuesday," Cordelia said. "He'll probably be at Paul and Juliette's tonight."

Malcolm exchanged a look with Mélanie. "That might be a good place to find him."

Writer Juliette Dubretton and painter Paul St. Gilles held a salon every Tuesday evening. Malcolm and Mélanie attended when they could, and Will Carmarthen was usually to be found there, as were a number of others in the Tavistock company.

"It might be a good place to collect information in general," Mélanie said.

Malcolm glanced out the window. The shadows were lengthening over the Berkeley Square plane trees, but evening was still some way off. "We have a few hours." He looked at Cordelia. "Would you be willing to call on Lady Shroppington with me?"

"Of course. I was going to offer to." Cordelia wrinkled her nose. "In the general scheme of things, I'd do a great deal to avoid calling on Lady Shroppington. But in this case, I should be positively disappointed not to be part of it."

"I need work on the revisions and then go back to the theatre," Mélanie said. "And in any case, I suspect my theatrical associations wouldn't help with Lady Shroppington."

"I fear not," Cordelia said.

"I can see what my mother knows about the Thornsbys," David suggested.

"That would help," Malcolm said. "Thank you."

David met his gaze and nodded. And with that exchange, perhaps a tiny bit more had been repaired.

CHAPTER 14

Lady Shroppington lived in Brook Street in a stuccoed terrace house with an Ionic portico that seemed a surprisingly modern abode for a dowager.

"Her husband always refused to purchase a London house," Cordelia said as she and Malcolm climbed the freshly scoured steps. "She bought the house when he died. Rather a declaration of independence, I thought. It never struck me as a love match. But then, in one's teens, one rarely thinks of one's parents' generation as having love matches, let alone one's grandparents' generation."

The footman recognized Cordelia and took them in without checking to see if his mistress was at home, which suggested to Malcolm that Lady Shroppington knew about his role in the investigation and had anticipated his calling on her. The footman led them across a high-ceilinged entrance hall and up a gilt-railed staircase to a first-floor sitting room with scagliola columns, peacock blue wall hangings, and striped chintz furniture.

"Cordelia." Lady Shroppington addressed them from an armchair positioned so the light from the windows fell at a flattering angle across her face. "About time you called on me. I can see your mother in you as you get older. And your grandmother. Though you're more striking than either."

"You are too kind, ma'am." Cordelia stepped forwards and bent to kiss Lady Shroppington's cheek. "I don't believe you've met Malcolm Rannoch."

"No. Though I've certainly heard of you, Rannoch. From your foreign marriage to your work in parliament to your wife's habit of gallivanting about the stage, you have a way of making yourself talked of."

Lady Shroppington surveyed Malcolm. Even seated, she was plainly not a tall woman, but she had the ability to dominate the room. She was a pretty woman, but her features, which Malcolm suspected had had a girlish softness in her youth, had hardened into lines of determination. Her blue gaze said she knew how to play the social game but didn't necessarily feel she needed to anymore. She was a generation older than his mother and Cordelia's mother and his aunt Frances. She'd have been a child during the Jacobite uprising in 1745, a young adult when the American colonies broke away, in her fifth or sixth decade by the time of the French Revolution. There was a crumpled handkerchief beside her chair and even the flattering light betrayed a faint redness about her eyes, but her face was set in a controlled mask.

Her gaze went from Cordelia to Malcolm. "I must say I'm a bit surprised to see Cordelia with a gentleman other than her husband. Or perhaps I mean I wish I could say I was surprised."

That was plain speaking for the drawing room, but then Lady Shroppington's generation tended to be franker about these matters than the younger generation. And plain speaking and scandal could be one refuge in the face of grief. God knows everyone needed something.

Cordelia gave one of her irrepressible laughs. "Dear ma'am, pray don't worry. I'm quite besotted with Harry, and he's surprisingly devoted to me. I came with Malcolm because he needed to talk to you, and I thought it might be easier for both of you to have me present."

"Hmph. You want to talk about Lewis, of course. Suppose I was trying to distract myself by talking about Cordelia. Thomas told me you were assisting Bow Street, Mr. Rannoch. Glad they have someone of your quality involved."

"I'm very sorry for your loss, Lady Shroppington. Lewis Thornsby was an engaging young man."

"He was, but people always find platitudes to say about the dead. He's no more agreeable for having got himself stabbed to death, and we want to arrive at the truth. You'd better sit down. The new footman has a good leg, though not a great deal in the brain pan, but he should manage to come in with the tea shortly."

"I understand you were particularly close to Lewis," Malcolm said as he and Cordelia moved to straight-backed chairs close to Lady Shroppington.

"I don't have children of my own. Never been sure, watching my friends with their offspring, if that was a blessing or a curse, but no sense wasting time on it now. My husband left the settling of our fortune in my hands, so I needed to pick an heir. My nephew's younger son made sense—Thomas already has an estate he'll inherit, and Helen and Hypatia are pretty enough they should marry well if they have a scrap of sense—not that they necessarily do, girls seem sillier and sillier the older I get, or perhaps that's me. Oh, here's the tea."

Conversation stopped while the footman set the tea tray on a table close to Lady Shroppington's chair. Lady Shroppington watched the door close behind him. "In any case," she continued, picking up the teapot. "Lewis seemed a sensible choice."

"Seemed?" Malcolm said.

Lady Shroppington poured out a cup of tea with a steady

hand. "He'd got a bit wild. Well, young men will do that, as I'm sure you know from your own experience. Some young women too." She gave the cup to Cordelia. "Easier for the men, of course, as Cordelia could tell you. And mostly they grow out of that sort of behavior and of spouting off that sort of nonsense." She handed Malcolm a second cup. "With some exceptions, of course."

"If you mean me, I'm flattered you're so aware of my work."

"Difficult to ignore it, Rannoch, try as one may." Lady Shroppington squeezed lemon into her own tea. "You find your way into the papers tiresomely often. But in any case, it wasn't that Radical nonsense that Lewis was caught up in that concerned me so much as the young woman he'd been hanging about. Not that a young man's dancing attendance on an actress is so surprising or even alarming. But from some comments he made, it seemed she had given him some wholly inappropriate ideas."

"How do you know it was Miss Blanchard who gave him the ideas?" Cordelia asked.

Lady Shroppington took a measured sip of tea. "I can't imagine it would have occurred to Lewis on his own. No matter what Radical nonsense he was exposed to, he had some basic understanding of the forms."

Malcolm set his cup down. "He might have considered that the forms meant offering marriage to a girl to whom he was sincerely attached."

"There are lines one doesn't cross." Lady Shroppington met his gaze without blinking. "Oh, I know your wife took to the stage at Christmas. It caused a bit of a flutter over Mayfair tea tables. And I wouldn't care to see a daughter or daughter-in-law of mine do so. But she can afford to flout convention. She's your wife. The Rannoch name will always protect both of you, at least to a degree. Though I can't imagine she'll be as much of an asset to your political career as she once was."

"Mélanie's insights are an invaluable asset to my political career. I don't need the rest of it."

"Humph. You may find yourself talking differently as your career progresses. But your career and your daughter's chances on the marriage mart are your business. I can't imagine such an outlandish idea as offering marriage to a girl of that sort would have occurred to Lewis on his own. I still can't quite believe he was contemplating it, save that he told me so himself. Don't look so shocked, Cordelia. Your own behavior is one thing. At least you did it after you were married. And you're a Brooke. This girl was a nobody. And an actress."

"Is," Malcolm said. "She's still very much alive."

Lady Shroppington pursed her lips, almost as though it was in bad taste for Letty Blanchard to still be alive when Lewis was not. "Do you think she had something to do with Lewis's death?"

"There's no reason to suspect that." Malcolm was not going to give Lady Shroppington ammunition against Letty, whatever his suspicions.

Lady Shroppington set down her cup. "I told him it was impossible. And that if he persisted in this madness, I'd have no part in it. I assumed that would make him see sense. The boy had no prospects of his own. Instead he seemed to have thought he was acting out one of the romantic dramas his lady love performed on the stage. Giving up all for love may make for an amusing evening at the theatre, but it's hardly the stuff of real life. Even at two-and-twenty, Lewis should have seen that."

Cordelia added more milk to her tea. "Real life can vary."

Lady Shroppington met Cordelia's gaze, her own hard and direct. In that moment she looked less like a social arbiter and more like a spymaster, though in truth, both required a rather similar degree of ruthlessness. "The rules of society don't change. One has to live within them. To your credit, you learned that. It sent you back to your husband."

Cordelia set down her spoon. "Dear ma'am. That isn't what sent me back to Harry. I realized I loved him."

"Love." Lady Shroppington drew out the word as though it were a foreign concept. "It hardly guarantees stability. Occasionally it can occur conveniently, as apparently it did for you. I imagine you'd say you love your wife, Mr. Rannoch, and you appear happy enough, though I wonder what you'll think in a few years if she continues down this course. Lewis's so-called love was anything but convenient. I was fond of him"—her fingers tightened for a moment round the handle of her cup—"but obviously I wasn't going to allow an actress to succeed me as mistress of Shroppington Manor."

"Did you tell him so directly?" Malcolm asked. "Not just that you wouldn't accept the marriage, but that you'd cut him off?"

"In no uncertain terms. I believe in plain speaking, as I assume you've both seen. No sense in setting up false expectations. I told Lewis if he insisted on this folly, I washed my hands of him." She took a sip of tea. Her fingers shook just the slightest bit. "That was the last time I saw him."

"I'm sorry," Malcolm said.

She set her cup down with a controlled clink. "You think I'm regretting it? On the contrary. I regret that Lewis is dead. I want the perpetrator brought to justice. But I have no qualms about opposing Lewis's folly."

Strong words from a supposedly devoted aunt. But Malcolm had seen many reactions to grief. Retreating behind a shell of hardness could be a way of protecting oneself. "Had you decided what to do with the inheritance instead?" he asked.

"What business—Oh, I see." She adjusted a side curl that was escaping her beribboned cap. "A new heir would have had a motive to get rid of Lewis. I hadn't decided. Thomas is stable enough, but a bit eccentric with his head buried in dusty tomes. He might take it into his head to use the money to open a library or a school or some such thing. Helen and Hypatia can be flighty. Can't be sure they wouldn't make choices as unsuitable as Lewis's. There's my husband's nephew, George. I'd thought to leave the inheritance to my family, but I may reconsider. I'm in good health, I have time to watch them and consider. So you see, none of them would have had a motive to get rid of Lewis. Not that I can imagine—but then, I couldn't imagine Lewis's wanting to marry that actress either."

"Did your nephew have any enemies that you knew of?" Malcolm asked.

She did not, as many bereaved relatives did, react with shock to the question. Her brows—carefully plucked into a fine arch—drew together. "I've been wondering, of course. How could I not? Lewis's family are commonplace enough. My nephew, Lewis's father, fills the role of country gentleman well enough, but he isn't cut out for much more. Neither is his wife, Lewis's mother, for all her pretensions to London society. So it has to be something he got caught up in at that theatre." She plucked at the dark fabric of her gown. "I know a lot of this Radical nonsense is undergraduate posturing, shocking the elders for the sake of shock. And I do realize the talk of us being murdered in our beds is talk. But you can't tell me they don't flirt with dangerous ideas, Rannoch. Or perhaps I should say *you* don't, given your politics."

"Danger can be in the eye of the beholder, Lady Shroppington. Though I do hope my ideas and those of the Levellers are ideas that hold the possibility of change."

"That's precisely why they're dangerous." Her fingers tightened on the paisley folds of her shawl. "It has to be that lot at the theatre that's responsible for what happened to Lewis. Perhaps he had enough sense to object to some of their plans. Or perhaps it was because of the girl. From something he said, I think Lewis was worried she was interested in another young man in the group. Which wouldn't surprise me. That sort of girl almost always has more than one string to her bow."

"Did he mention a name?"

"No, nothing so specific. But I gathered it was someone the girl had been entangled with before Lewis met her. Which in itself should have been enough to tell him the sort of girl he was dealing with."

Malcolm bit back a number of sharp comments. "Does the name Montford mean anything to you?"

Her brows drew together again in seemingly genuine contemplation. "There was a Thaddeus Montford who was the curate near Little Epping and used to give the dreariest sermons when I went to house parties at the Kittredges' and then trod on one's toes if he was invited in the evening for dancing. But he'd be approaching ninety now, and I can't imagine he has a connection to Lewis."

"It was apparently a name your nephew used incognito."

"Lewis? Incognito?" Lady Shroppington wrinkled her nose as though Malcolm had suggested Lewis had gone into trade or joined a traveling theatre company or run off to Paris with a painter. "Why on earth would he want to do such a thing? And how would he have the wit to carry it off?"

"He apparently had more abilities than many people credited," Malcolm said. "He had taken rooms in Rosemary Lane under the name Montford."

"Rosemary Lane?" Lady Shroppington sniffed as though the smell of the lane had invaded her sitting room. "Nonsense. Young men may frequent gaming hells and houses of ill repute and all sorts of raffish locations. They may venture into Seven Dials or St. Giles. But why on earth would Lewis go to Rosemary Lane? It makes no sense."

"It's a very good question," Malcolm agreed. "He evidently had business he wanted to undertake under a different persona."

"Lewis? Business? Lewis had no business at all—I refuse to dignify his activities at the Tavistock with that name. He had a good enough mind, but he never put it to much use. Even if it occurred to him to set up a second identity, I can't imagine his having the wit to carry it out." She put her cup down again with less control. "You don't think he was planning to marry that girl under another name and run off with her, do you?"

"I suppose it's possible," Malcolm said, "but it doesn't seem likely. He was of age and could have married Miss Blanchard under his own name had he chosen to do so. His family might have cut him off, but he'd have had no fortune as Montford either."

"Humph. I doubt the girl would have had him with no fortune. Though she might have thought I'd change my mind. This Montford business sounds like some confusion to me." Lady Shroppington frowned. "Lewis was good at playacting. I'll never forget him as Harlequin in Christmas theatricals one year. I thought that was what drew him to theatre. But to have the organization to carry off what you're suggesting—it's preposterous." She picked up her cup and took a sip, then clunked it back into its saucer. "Preposterous."

"I WAS HARD PRESSED NOT to shake her," Cordelia said as she and Malcolm descended the steps of Lady Shroppington's house. "At the same time, I think she's a great deal more shattered by his death than she lets on. So a part of me feels dreadfully sorry for her."

"Your feelings match mine precisely." Malcolm gave Cordelia his arm. "I'd like to apologize for my sex, Cordelia."

Cordelia smiled as she curled her gloved fingers round his arm. "My own sex must lay claim to Lady Shroppington."

"But her attitudes are built on the fact that men can get away with—and are frequently lauded for—things that can ruin a woman."

Cordelia tightened her grip on his arm. "Groups are made up

of individuals, Malcolm. You aren't responsible for the group, whether or not you're among its ranks."

"Perhaps not, but as one of the privileged I have a responsibility to try to change things."

"Which you try to do. Which you do."

"You're kind, Cordy."

"Nonsense. I might be kind because I'm excessively fond of you, but I'm also very well aware of everything you do in and out of Parliament."

"Talking."

"Saying things that need to be said. They can't be debated at all if no one brings them up."

"Even if the debate ends there?"

"I don't think debates ever end, Malcolm. Especially in the House of Commons."

"You have a point."

"Malcolm." Cordelia looked up at him as she negotiated her footsteps over the paving stones. "Did you glance at the cards of invitation tucked into the glass over Lady Shroppington's mantle? There were quite a few—she obviously has a wide acquaintance. But the crest of one caught my eye. It was from the Beverstons."

Malcolm drew a breath. Lord Beverston was one of the senior members of the Elsinore League. "Interesting."

"Of course, the Beverstons also have a wide social circle. It doesn't prove anything. But it does mean Lewis might have known Beverston. And others in the League." Cordelia's brows drew together. "We've talked about Carfax's wanting intelligence on the Levellers. But we know the League were looking for intelligence on them as far back as over a year ago when we met Kit Montagu in Italy."

"So they were. It wouldn't be surprising for them to have tried to plant an informant among the Levellers. Which doesn't prove they did, and doesn't prove it was Thornsby. But Thornsby's dual identity as Montford suggests he was working for someone. I'll ask Roger what he knows about Thornsby's possible connections to Beverston. I need to talk to Roger about Thornsby, in any case." Roger Smythe, Beverston's son, had become one of their best allies against the League. He was also a member of the Levellers.

Cordelia's brows tightened beneath the green satin brim of her bonnet. "If there is a plot going on among the Levellers, do you think Roger knows about it?"

"I think it's very likely he does," Malcolm said.

CHAPTER 15

Simon was rehearsing onstage with Brandon and Manon when Mélanie returned to the Tavistock. She stood in the wings watching them work on the scene in which Fiona and Gideon confronted each other over their secrets, then went into the nearest dressing room to read over the revised version of the speech she had finished in the Berkeley Square library after Malcolm and Cordy had gone to talk to Lady Shroppington and David had left to speak to his mother. And if her mind had strayed more than once to what they all might be doing, she had still managed a revision of the speech she was fairly happy with.

About ten minutes later, she heard footsteps and looked up to see Brandon in the dressing room doorway.

"I think you'll find this version flows more easily." She held out the paper to him.

Brandon took it but didn't immediately scan the words. "I didn't mean to complicate things."

"You haven't. You've pointed up a problem. Which we needed to know."

"It's a good speech. A damn good speech. But I can't keep the words straight."

"Then there was something wrong with the speech. You're too good an actor to stumble."

"You're a good fellow, Mélanie." Brandon glanced down at her revision. "This is good. I think I'll do better with it and it keeps the spirit of the original. Maybe the next production you can find someone who can carry off the original as written."

"I'm fortunate to have you."

"You've obviously learned a lot, married to a diplomat."

"The lovely thing about the theatre is that we can say what we think instead of walking on eggshells."

"Ha." Brandon gave a quick laugh. "Nothing like a bunch of needy actors to make one guard one's tongue. Though that's nothing compared to talking to patrons in the green room." He frowned. "I think perhaps it was Gideon's motivation I wasn't getting. It's clearer now."

"Yes, I was thinking the same thing." Mélanie looked down at the scribbled-over sheet before her that held her first draft of the rewrite. "Sometimes it's so clear in my head I don't realize I haven't actually made it clear on paper."

Brandon nodded. For a moment it seemed he would turn to go, but he hesitated, leaning against the door jamb. "You're investigating with your husband, aren't you? Thornsby's death?"

"To the extent I have time."

"I didn't know him well." Brandon shifted his weight from one foot to the other, in a way he would never do onstage except in the service of a particular character. "I said that this morning and it's true. But I saw him the day before he died. Well, we all did obviously, he was at the theatre. I mean I saw him later that day. Or rather I heard him."

Mélanie set down her pen, careful not to do so too hastily. "At the theatre? Or elsewhere?"

"Here. I wanted to practice one of my speeches on the stage."

Brandon drew the toe of a dusty boot over the worn floorboards. "I do that sometimes, to try to get a sense of the space. Of the character. I can feel it better alone onstage." He flushed. "That sounds a bit pretentious. But you know damn well it isn't as easy as I try to make out. I don't worry about making a bloody fool of myself if I'm alone. I can take risks I wouldn't, even in front of Simon and Manon. But when I came in, I heard voices in the basement. Thornsby and someone else. They were arguing."

"Why didn't you say anything sooner?"

Brandon shifted his weight again as though still not sure whether or not to speak. "Because the other person was Kit Montagu."

Mélanie kept her hands steady and her voice level, even as her stomach plunged as though she'd gone tumbling down a hillside. "What were they arguing about?"

"I don't know precisely. I was too far away to make out all of it. But I heard Kit say something about 'pulling the wool over our eyes.' And Thornsby say something about 'proving.' Look, I know Kit's a friend of yours. He's a friend of mine now too. I like him. He's a bit of an idealist, but then, I suppose we all are or we wouldn't be risking arrest with the Levellers. He has some actual understanding of the theatre and he doesn't pretend to know more, like so many of the young aristos who hang about the green room. Or the not so young ones, like Sir Horace, of whom I'll actually admit I'm rather fond. But Kit's something quite unusual. He believes in his work. He believes in pretty Sofia Vincenzo, who is quite remarkable herself."

"Did you think of asking him about what you overheard?"

"I was debating if I should. We get used to keeping to ourselves in the theatre, living on top of each other as we do much of the time. I thought perhaps I should just leave it alone. Then Thornsby was killed. I assumed if it was important, Kit would tell you. Or—"

"Or he wouldn't, and you didn't want to betray him."

"What do you think I just did?" Bitterness cut through Brandon's voice.

"Told the truth. Which is vital to the investigation."

"He's my friend. He's your friend too. And your husband's. I don't know why I—"

"Because you know it's important we get at the truth."

"So there's justice for Thornsby? Don't tell me it's that simple. Not in a world with so much injustice."

"Partly for Thornsby," Mélanie said. "Whatever his secrets, he deserves that much. So do his family. But also for the sake of the Tavistock. For the sake of all the people who may have suspicion hanging over them indefinitely if we don't learn what happened."

Brandon nodded. "So you're going to tell Malcolm and Roth?"

"I have to."

"I knew that. I didn't quite want to admit it, but it was obvious. I'm sorry I didn't come to you sooner."

"I'm glad you came to me now." Mélanie studied Brandon. For all his pose of selfish unconcern, he had keen insights. "Brandon—what did you think of Thornsby?"

Brandon's mouth twisted ruefully. "Not a great deal, I'm afraid. I can't pretend to be a beacon of liberty. I'm an actor before anything else. But I have enough sense of what needs to be done in the world to respect men like Kit and Roger Smythe. And Tanner, who manages to be a playwright and an agent of change. Thornsby was playing at it." Brandon frowned. "At least that's what I thought. I couldn't really hear what he said to Kit, but it was quite a different tone from what I was accustomed to hear from him." Brandon paused for a moment, frowning. "Almost as though he were a different person."

~

Clouds were beginning to mass in the sky as Raoul walked back to Berkeley Square. Rather like a flock of ravens. He shook his head at the fanciful thought. Perhaps it was the stories he'd been reading to the children. This was the second time he'd returned to the house today. Unusual, but then, as Emily had said this morning, nothing was usual in an investigation.

Young voices carried on the quickening wind as he approached the Berkeley Square garden. He saw a familiar sapphire-blue bonnet and a flash of titian hair escaping it. His wife was in the garden with the children, including the Davenport girls, but there was no sign of the other adults in the family.

"Mélanie went back to the theatre," Laura said, as he dropped down on the bench beside her. "And Malcolm and Cordy have gone to talk to Thornsby's aunt." Her gaze flickered over his face. Clara was in her lap, but she looked as much a seasoned agent as a mother. Not that the two were mutually exclusive. "Did you learn anything?"

"Mostly by omission." Raoul stretched out his arms to take Clara. "I can't find any evidence to support a plot to assassinate a member of the royal family at the Tavistock. Even in what people aren't saying. There seems to be general consensus that that would have the worst implications for any sort of reform in Britain." That was all quite true. He had merely left out the confirmation he had received of his suspicions regarding Kitty Ashford.

Laura's shrewd gaze told him she suspected he was holding something back. But then, it was hardly the first time. Raoul shifted on the bench and touched his fingers to Clara's head. Impossible to deny a pang at the thought that secrets and lies were an accepted part of his relationship with his wife. Which was foolish, because they'd both known that would always be the case long before they'd married.

"Uncle Julien!" Jessica's greeting carried across the garden.

Raoul turned his head to see Julien St. Juste approaching the garden gate.

"You didn't bring Genny and the boys," Jessica said, running to greet St. Juste. "And Auntie Kitty didn't bring them this morning."

"No, you must accept my apologies." Julien closed the gate behind him and knelt down in front of her. "It's been a bit of an unexpected day. We'll bring them soon."

The other children ran over. St. Juste exchanged greetings with them, with the same ease with which he'd greet a group of royalty or diplomats or agents or assassins, then strolled over to the bench where Laura and Raoul sat. "You two—you three—are an advertisement for domesticity. No doubt quite misleading, like most advertisements. I don't suppose you've seen Kitty. It's times like these I find myself longing for a good drop system to exchange messages."

"She was here this morning," Laura said. "But she left about ten. Raoul talked to her last."

"She didn't say where she going," Raoul said. Which strictly speaking was true, though he could make some guesses. "I know she talked with Malcolm and wanted to help with the investigation."

"It's no matter." Julien's voice was easy. Perhaps a shade too easy. "I just found myself near Berkeley Square and thought I would check."

"Mummy." Emily came running over, followed by Colin and Livia. "We're thirsty. May we have lemonade?"

"I'll get it," Raoul said.

"No, you stay and talk with Julien and have some time with the children." Laura got to her feet. "I can bring something stronger back as well."

Julien gave a lazy smile, quite as though they weren't in the midst of a murder investigation and he weren't wondering what his mistress was involved in. "Have I mentioned you're an exceedingly astute woman, Laura?"

"One can never hear it too often." Laura smiled and went out the gate towards the house, promising the children she'd bring cakes as well as lemonade.

Julien settled himself in Laura's place on the bench. "You're a lucky man, O'Roarke."

Raoul looked down at Clara, who was tugging his cravat free of his waistcoat with great concentration. "Don't think I don't know it."

Julien continued to watch him, gaze narrowed as though against the sun, despite the gray sky. "How the hell do you do it?"

Raoul returned the younger man's gaze. In the quarter century of their acquaintance, through being allies and enemies, watching Josephine fall from power and the empire itself fall, betraying each other's secrets and saving each other's lives, this might be the first time Julien had asked for his advice. "How do I do what?"

"All that." Julien glanced at the center of the garden. Colin was helping Jessica and Drusilla build a castle out of sticks. Emily and Livia were dangling a toy for Berowne, the cat. "Being a father. Being a husband. Making it work."

Raoul gave a short laugh. "One might argue whether or not I do make it work." He unhooked his watch and gave it to Clara to play with. "In fact, one could make a fair argument I don't."

"Don't be self-deprecating, O'Roarke. I've seen you with your wife and your children. I know what you mean to them. I know what they mean to you. Perhaps more important, I've seen what they get from you and you get from them. The man who was playing on the drawing room carpet last week, the man whose wedding I went to last April. The man sitting here now holding his baby. I'd never have thought the man I met in Paris twenty-five years ago—even the man I knew in the Peninsula and at Waterloo—could become that man."

The past danced before his eyes for a moment. Choices made and not made. Things admitted to and things concealed. "I'm the same man I've always been. Perhaps people just see me differently."

"Or you let people see more of you."

Raoul returned Julien's gaze. For all the unusual emotional questions, that blue gaze was as sharp as ever. "Possibly." Raoul hesitated, unfamiliar words bottled up in his throat. He didn't talk easily about these things. He closed up at most efforts to draw him out. But talking about feelings was probably even harder for Julien than it was for him. "I could never have envisioned it either. Twenty-five years ago. Ten years ago. Five years ago. Even two and a half years ago, when Laura and I first—I knew how I felt about her, but I couldn't have seen the way from there to here. It happened a bit at a time. A moment of mutual need. A realization that I was happy. That she seemed happy. A declaration I couldn't stop myself from making." He cast a quick glance at Emily, who had picked up the remarkably compliant Berowne and was spinning in a circle. "If it weren't for Emily, it probably would have happened much more slowly," he said in a low voice. "Or never become what it is at all. I thought we could keep it without strings on Laura's side. But as you may appreciate, it's difficult to keep relationships without strings when there are children involved. Emily—I think she decided I was her father before I realized it was a possibility. People started treating Laura and me as a couple before we consciously admitted we were one. I remember watching Malcolm put his arm round Mélanie and realizing I could do the same with Laura. Going to Italy, where it was easier to be together openly. Realizing how far I'd come, and that I couldn't go back and wouldn't want to." Raoul looked at Emily, who had dropped down on the ground beside Livia, then down at tiny Clara. "If I'd contemplated it all from the start, I'd never have tried. But then, that's true of most things that are complicated in life."

"Says the farseeing strategist."

"Strategy is often a matter of reacting well after one blunders."

"Because you've thought through twenty-five scenarios before you moved."

"And sometimes because it's the twenty-sixth scenario that occurs. But then, you should know that. Your whole life is one long improvisation. And you can adapt better than most to the circumstances in which you find yourself."

St. Juste had been watching Colin, Jessica, and Drusilla build a fortification of stones about their stick castle, but at that his gaze swung round to pin Raoul like a dagger thrust. "Is that what you think I'm doing with Kitty and the children? Adapting to circumstances?"

Clara was examining the watch fob that held a lock of Malcolm's baby hair. "From what I've seen," Raoul said, "what you're doing with Kitty and the children is making a life."

"Which you just said was improvisation."

"Improvisation can make a life."

St. Juste's gaze went back to the children. Two of the sticks had fallen over. Jessica was crying in frustration. Colin moved one of the rocks to prop them up. "You must worry—"

"That'll I'll fail them?" Raoul watched Jessica clap her hands and Colin press a kiss to her forehead. "Every day. Though perhaps less so than a year ago. That they'll be hurt because of me—Laura wouldn't thank me for it, but yes. As I said, I'm still not sure one could say I'm making anything work. But I do know I'm far happier than I have any right to be."

"I thought everyone had the right to be happy. Isn't that one of those principles you're always fighting for? The slave owner who is somehow a spokesperson for individual liberty said something of the sort in his declaration."

"A palpable hit on two counts, St. Juste." Raoul touched him on the shoulder. "I'm hardly a font of wisdom, but if I've learned anything, it's that you can't be sure when you start where you're going to end up. You create a life a bit at a time and it's constantly changing. You don't have to start with all the answers. Or even any of them."

"That sounds annoyingly wise." Julien gave a short laugh that was quite unlike his usual sangfroid. "I don't have the least idea how to do it. But I seem to be managing to muddle through, at least much of the time." He paused for a moment. "It's a long time since I've played a role I wasn't sure of. An intriguing challenge. Though this isn't really a role at all."

"No. I've seen enough of you to be quite sure it isn't. And I speak as one who is frequently not sure of anything where you're concerned. From the outside, I'd say you've already taken a number of steps towards creating a life."

"Perhaps. But as you say, that life is still evolving."

Raoul glanced at the children. Emily and Livia had joined Colin and the younger girls and they were all taking toy knights and ladies out of a basket and setting them up in the stick-and-rock castle. Berowne was washing himself nearby. "Don't make the mistake of thinking it has to evolve into anything that looks like what everyone—or anyone—else has. If nothing else, being round this group should have taught you that."

"Being round this group has rendered me sadly domestic. It's obviously catching. But I find I don't mind very much. Which may mean I'm besotted. Or mad. Though I imagine a lot of people would say I've always been mad."

"All the most interesting people are." Raoul studied Julien for a moment. "I don't think you've ever been afraid of risks."

Julien leaned back on the bench, gaze on the children. "There are risks and there are risks. I'm not sure someone with my past has any business dragging anyone else into it. Let alone four people. But I'm selfish enough not to let that stand in my way. It's actually not my fears that are likely to be a problem."

"Kitty doesn't strike me as the sort to be afraid either," Raoul said.

"She's quite fearless. But we all have our quirks. She may not think I'm up to the job. Or worth the risk. Or both. I don't know that she trusts me. In fact, it's rather obvious that she doesn't."

"My dear fellow," Raoul said, as the door of the house opened and Laura appeared, carrying a hamper, "none of us can fully trust the others. That's part of being an agent. Even an agent who's managing to carry off matrimony."

Laura came back into the garden and set down the promised collation for the children, then joined Raoul and Julien carrying a bottle of wine and three glasses. "What did I miss?"

"The two of us being sadly prosaic." Julien gave a lazy smile and took the glasses, while Laura opened the bottle. "You'd never guess we were agents in the midst of an investigation."

MALCOLM FOUND HIS COUSIN, Aline Blackwell, sitting on the floor of her study, demonstrating equations to her four-year-old daughter, Claudia, with a set of blocks.

"Uncle Malcolm!" Claudia ran over to hug Malcolm. "What's one hundred and twenty take away fifty, and then plus thirty?"

"I'm sure you can work it out." Malcolm scooped her up.

"Well, of course I can." Claudia fixed him with a direct gaze that was the twin of her mother's, set beneath level dark brows that were also the twin of Aline's. "I'm testing you."

"Oh, well then. One hundred."

"You're smart, Uncle Malcolm."

"I'm not half as good at numbers as you and your mother."

He sat down on the Axminster carpet beside Aline, Claudia in his lap. "In truth, I came because I need your mother's help."

"I thought it was probably that." Aline drew her legs up and hooked her arms round her knees, as she had so often when they were in the schoolroom. "Otherwise, you'd be too buried in the investigation to call."

"You know about the investigation?" Malcolm asked. That was quick even for Mayfair, given that the story had still been out of the papers this morning.

"We've just been to see Mama. Raoul had stopped to see Archie this morning." Aline's mother, Malcolm's aunt Frances, was married to Harry's uncle Archibald Davenport. Archie was a former agent who had been undercover with the Elsinore League.

"I should have realized how fast news travels in this family." Malcolm reached into his coat and pulled out the coded papers they'd found in Rosemary Lane. "Do you think you can break these? We found them in rooms the victim was keeping under a secret identity."

Aline studied the papers. "I'll get to work right away. I may ask Sofia to help. It will go faster with two of us." She looked up from the papers. "Mama said Mr. Thornsby was a Leveller so I suppose Kit is involved?"

"Yes, he can hardly fail to be," Malcolm said.

The question was just how deeply.

CHAPTER 16

Malcolm found Roger Smythe in a corner of the Thistle Inn, not far from the House of Commons. And not alone. As he threaded his way between the tables, Malcolm recognized the sandy head of Roger's companion even from the back. He and Roger had their heads close together over pints of porter that looked scarcely touched. The dark wainscoting below the white plaster left them in comforting shadows.

"Rannoch." Roger saw Malcolm first. "Kit's been telling me about Thornsby. I'm still having a hard time taking it in."

"Have you learned anything?" Kit swung round in his chair. His face was haggard as though he had slept little, his eyes dark with concern for his friend. His going to see Roger made perfect sense. But Malcolm was still not entirely sanguine about the reasons his idealistic young friend had broken into Thornsby's rooms hours after the murder.

"Quite a bit, actually." Malcolm dropped down on the bench beside Roger, facing Kit, and signaled the waiter to bring him a pint of porter. "Does the name Montford mean anything to you?"

No recognition flashed on either man's face. "There's not a Leveller named Montford," Kit said. "At least, not unless we have a member I don't know about."

"In a sense, you do," Malcolm said. "Thornsby was living a double life under the name Montford, with lodgings in Rosemary Lane. I assume that wasn't for Leveller purposes, as far as you know?"

Kit and Roger exchanged glances. "Good God," Kit said. "No."

"Definitely not." Roger ran a hand over his sleek dark hair. "Thornsby always seemed so disingenuous."

"He certainly gave that impression," Malcolm said. "These rooms and the identity he concocted indicate he was good deal more complicated."

The waiter deposited a tankard of porter in front of Malcolm. He took a sip. "Can you think of anything that would interest Thornsby in Rosemary Lane? The rooms are above a used bookshop run by a man called Hapgood."

Kit shook his head. "I've never heard the name. Or anything about Rosemary Lane."

Roger continued to frown into his tankard. "I can scarcely credit it. Lewis was never the sort for—"

"You knew him?" Malcolm said. "That is, before he was a Leveller?"

"Oh yes. I've known him since we were boys. I suppose you could say since he was a baby. His parents and my parents dined together from time to time, but his great-aunt, Lady Shroppington, was—is—much more of a family friend. She and my grandmother—Father's mother—made their debuts together. She's Father's godmother."

That was interesting. "I didn't realize," Malcolm said.

"No reason you should." Roger sat back against the bench. "I didn't bring Lewis into the Levellers, as it happens. He just started hanging about the theatre, and the next thing I knew someone brought him along to one of the Leveller meetings."

"Do you know who?"

Roger frowned. "I can't say I recall. I'm not sure I ever knew. Do you, Kit?"

Kit frowned, gaze knotted across the single candle on the table. "No. I'm trying to remember when I first met him. I think it was last autumn in the green room one night, after it emptied out. After a performance of *The Steward's Stratagem*. I remember seeing Lewis across the room, but I don't remember anyone's bringing him in. He was simply there."

"Could he have walked into a Leveller meeting without knowing anyone?" Malcolm asked.

"We don't make it difficult for people to attend," Roger said. "That would rather go against the whole idea of everyone's being equal. There are smaller groups that meet more secretly, but it wouldn't have been hard for him to attend one of the larger meetings like the one Kit mentioned, if he found out when and where."

Malcolm took another drink of porter. It reminded him of his student days when he and his friends had frequented coffee houses and taverns, though he drank plenty of porter and stout these days. "Do you think there's any chance Thornsby could have been spying for your father?"

"Lewis?" Roger laughed, then sobered. "Do you have evidence he was?"

"Not precisely. Cordelia and I called on Lady Shroppington just now and Cordy noticed a card of invitation with the Beverston crest. You've confirmed the connection. Russell's second identity and the skill with which he set it up strongly suggest he was working for someone. If he didn't do it in the service of the Levellers, as you both confirm, one option is that he's working for Carfax. That doesn't fit how Carfax is behaving, but then, Carfax is hard to read. But once we realized his connection to your father, it occurred to us that the League might also want to plant a source within the Levellers."

"My God," Roger said. "Of course they would. I don't know why—"

"Possibly because we were too busy worrying about Carfax." Kit turned his tankard on the table top.

"Carfax admitted he has a mole in the League," Malcolm said. "What if there are two moles?"

Roger drew a hard breath. "One working for Carfax and one working for the League?"

"God help us." Kit took a long drink from his tankard. "But yes, that would make a certain sense."

"The League don't like reform," Malcolm said. "But they aren't as wholly dedicated to opposing it as Carfax is."

Roger grimaced. "No, they're dedicated to advancing their own interests."

"Precisely." Malcolm leaned forwards and looked between the two younger men. "So why are they so focused on the Levellers? They were trying to blackmail Percy and Mary Shelley to get information about the Levellers a year and a half ago."

Roger's mouth twisted. "It's certainly not because I'm a member. Father's never been much interested in my activities. You're right, the League's goals tend to be pragmatic and focused on personal gain. So one can only assume they feel the Levellers stand in their way somehow. I'd like to say I know—I'd like to say I believed—we have that much power, but in truth, I don't have the least idea why they would care."

"Nor do I," said Kit. "I'd never even heard of the League until I went to Italy. Until I met you and Mélanie. And Sofia." He took another drink from his tankard and stared into the depths. Sofia's father had been working for the League. "But they certainly seemed interested in us then. I could believe they planted a mole in our midst. I'd never have believed it was Lewis Thornsby. At least, not until this."

Malcolm sat back against the high bench and took a drink

from his tankard. It was a good porter, though on the bitter side. "How well did Lewis know Kitty Ashford?"

"Mrs. Ashford?" Roger frowned. "I'm sure he knew her, they were both about the Tavistock enough, but I can't imagine he knew her well. Can you?" He looked at Kit.

Kit pushed his tankard from one hand to the other. "I don't—"

"It's an investigation," Malcolm said. "I need the truth."

Kit met his gaze in the flickering candlelight. "I think—I think Thornsby admired Mrs. Ashford."

"He did?" Roger took a drink from his tankard. "From what I saw, Thornsby had eyes for no one but Miss Blanchard."

"There are—um—different types of admiring, sometimes," Kit said.

"Meaning Thornsby wanted to bed Mrs. Ashford but wouldn't have dreamed of offering such advances to Miss Blanchard unless he married her?" Malcolm said.

Kit's fingers slipped from his tankard. "Good God, Rannoch."

"Some men divide women into the two categories," Malcolm said. "The fact that I deplore it doesn't make it any less true." His brother had certainly been one of those. With disastrous results, where Kitty was concerned.

"If you put it that way—yes." Kit couldn't quite bring himself to meet Malcolm's eyes.

"Do you have any reason to believe Thornsby actually was bedding Mrs. Ashford?"

Kit clunked down his tankard, spattering porter over the tabletop. "My God, Rannoch, we're talking about a lady. A friend of yours."

"Yes. And if she's connected to a murdered man, I need to know how. For Kitty's sake as well as the sake of the investigation."

"Have you asked Mrs. Ashford?" Roger asked. "Forgive me, I

know that would be damnably awkward, but in the circumstances—"

"I have," Malcolm said. "She says there was something brief between them that Thornsby took more seriously than she did. I don't believe she's telling the truth."

"Don't believe she took it less seriously than Thornsby or don't believe he took it seriously either?" Roger asked.

"I don't believe it ever occurred. I think Kitty's covering up something else."

Kit pulled out his handkerchief and blotted the spilled porter. "I can't speak to that. But I can attest that Thornsby admitted to an—attraction to Mrs. Ashford. I think it confused him—he asked me about it once. If I noticed other women once I met Sofia."

"That's different," Roger said. "Everyone notices—"

"Yes, well, in Thornsby's case I think it was more than that." Kit stared at the sodden handkerchief. "He said he wasn't sure if Miss Blanchard would ever forgive him. That he wasn't sure he'd ever forgive himself." He looked at Malcolm. "I'm sorry. I wouldn't for the world have said anything to sully—"

"Oh, Kitty won't mind. In fact, she'll be relieved to have her story confirmed, I expect." Malcolm took a drink from his tankard. "I'm still not sure I believe it, though. Among other things, Thornsby had apparently just asked Miss Blanchard to marry him."

"If he was conflicted he might have rushed into that as a way to settle the conflict," Roger said.

"He might," Malcolm conceded. He reached into his pocket and pulled out a copy he'd made of the list of dates Thornsby had decoded. "Do these mean anything to you?"

"November 3 is the protest meeting where Will got arrested," Kit said without hesitation. "In Lancaster."

"Yes, they all seem to be the dates of Radical disturbances, from what we can make out. Will was at several of them. So were others in the Tavistock company."

Kit sat back in his chair. "Are you suggesting the Levellers were behind all of these?"

"Were they behind any of them?"

"Of course not."

"There's not necessarily any 'of course' about it, Kit," Roger said. "Not if you're Rannoch. He has to ask the questions."

"I know." Kit reached for his tankard and took a drink. "I'm sorry. But whatever Carfax may say, we're not in the habit of causing violent disturbances."

"Could Will Carmarthen or others be involved in doing so on their own?" Malcolm asked.

Kit opened his mouth as though to protest, then frowned. "One can't be certain of anyone—that's what you'd say, isn't it? But I have no indication that he was. He's bright, he has a caustic tongue at times, he gets frustrated with the slowness of action, but he's shown no willingness to do anything violent."

Malcolm reached for his tankard. "He has an interesting history. According to Simon, he showed up at the Tavistock one day last spring and asked for an audition. Simon was about to politely decline when Will launched into the St. Crispin's Day speech and stopped him dead in his tracks. He engaged Will on the spot. But he says he has no idea where Will came from or where or if he acted before." Malcolm looked between Kit and Roger. "Has he said anything to either of you?"

"No, now that I think of it," Roger said. "Will's always been a bit quiet. Not about reform and not about the theatre, but about his personal life. That is, his life before he came to the Tavistock. Most of the other Levellers—both the actors and the stagehands and those who aren't from the theatre—drop a comment here and there. A dinner with their parents, their sister's wedding, playing with nephews and nieces, time at university. I've never heard Carmarthen say anything."

Kit sat back in his chair and folded his arms across his chest. "What are you implying, Roger? That Will may have been planted amongst us?"

"Christ, Kit. You know I like Will. What's more, I respect him. He has a keener mind and better instincts than many of the Levellers. And a more generous spirit. But given everything we're learning, how can I not but wonder?"

Kit scraped a hand over his hair. "It doesn't prove anything."

"No, of course not. But have you ever heard him talk about his past?"

Kit frowned for a moment. "No. At least I don't think so. But there could be lots of reasons for that."

"There could," Roger agreed.

Malcolm took a drink of porter. "Carmarthen admits to being fond of Miss Blanchard."

Roger reached for his tankard. "Yes, I suspected as much. Surely you did, Kit."

"I—ah—tried not to notice."

"Difficult to do that without being blind," Roger said.

"And though he didn't come out and say so," Malcolm added, "I had the impression the affection had been reciprocated, at least for a time."

Roger shifted on the bench. Like Kit, he had strong instincts about the respect due to ladies. Admirable in general. But a bit challenging in an investigation. "I—ah—I had that impression too."

"Until she met Thornsby?"

"Possibly even after." Roger wiped a trace of liquid from the side of his tankard. "I saw her looking at him one night in the green room—"

"Thornsby's valet heard Carmarthen and Thornsby arguing two nights ago," Malcolm said. "Carmarthen admits to it and says he went to confront Thornsby about his intentions towards Miss Blanchard."

"Says?" Kit asked. "You think he's lying?"

"Not necessarily. His account was very convincing. But he's also a very good actor. And we only have his word for the substance of his confrontation with Thornsby. He appeared at the Tavistock suddenly with no explanation for his background and quickly became part of the company and one of the Levellers. He's connected to a number of incidents on a list Thornsby had apparently decoded."

Kit and Roger exchanged glances.

"Just because it sounds damning doesn't necessarily mean it is." Malcolm said. "Evidence can seem to correlate without actually being connected. Believe me, I know. I was once arrested for murder." Of his half-sister. That had been its own particular hell. He'd only survived thanks to his wife. Who he hadn't yet learned was a French agent.

"But you're going to talk to Will again," Kit said.

"I'm going to talk to Will again. I'd appreciate your not warning him. Or mentioning the list of dates and places to anyone at present."

"Of course," Roger said.

Kit gave a curt nod and pushed back his chair. "I must go. Sofia's waiting for me. Unless you need more, Rannoch?"

"No, not now. I appreciate what you've given me."

"Going to the House, Rannoch?" Roger asked. "I'm walking that way."

Malcolm hadn't intended to, but he sensed Roger wanted to talk further, so he nodded. They left the inn, said goodbye to Kit, and started along the street.

"It's a damnable business," Roger said, turning up the collar of his greatcoat. The wind had whipped up. Winter seemed to cut unusually sharp this year. "So many friends involved."

Malcolm studied Roger. "Could Thornsby have been involved in something with the Levellers you didn't know about?"

For a moment something flashed in Roger's eyes that might have been recognition. But he said, "Anything's possible. But I've always been fairly well apprised of the Levellers' activities."

"You're an MP, Roger." Malcolm glanced at the Houses of Parliament in the distance, the place he spent much of his life, a center of pride and frustration and occasionally hope. "Simon keeps things from me because I'm an MP. He keeps things from David. Could there have been something afoot they were deliberately keeping from you?"

Roger turned away for a moment. "I said we met in smaller groups. And of course there are activities we don't all share with each other. But Lewis wasn't close to anyone who might have been orchestrating such activities. Truth to tell, no one took him very seriously. Least of all me. I suspected he was doing this partly to be close to Letty, partly to shock his father, and only tangentially because he had any concerns about injustice."

"Yes, that was my impression as well," Malcolm said, "though I didn't know him as well, obviously. And his having an undercover identity implies he wasn't the man either of us thought."

"No." Roger frowned. "But if he had that undercover identity in the service of the Levellers, surely I'd have known of it. Have you asked Simon?"

"Yes."

Roger watched him for a moment. "But you don't think he's telling you the truth. And you don't think Kit is. At least, not the full truth."

"I think we all pick and choose which parts of the truth to share, consciously or unconsciously. And how to shape it. That's why an investigator has to talk to so many different people. I don't know that we ever arrive at the truth, but different perspectives help us get to a closer approximation." Malcolm hesitated a moment. "Under normal circumstances, I'd say you were very right to keep things from me. But Thornsby's murder changes the equation."

Roger continued to watch him. "Is it just that? Or are you afraid we may be involved in something you'll feel you need to stop?"

"Christ, Roger," Malcolm said without entirely planning his speech, "how could I not have been afraid of that from the moment I learned about the Levellers? Not so much that I'll feel I should stop it as that it will be something I legally should stop but am all too inclined to let go. Simon's been one of my best friends since I was at Oxford. I'd have been a Leveller myself in those days."

Roger nodded, hands jammed in the pockets of his greatcoat. "Kit's one of my best friends. Has been since we were at Oxford. We started the Levellers together. Kit wasn't overjoyed when I stood for Parliament—you know that. I told him it wouldn't make a difference. That there were different ways to fight for the same things." He shot a look at Malcolm. "I still think I was right about that. But I was wrong that it wouldn't make a difference. I can't help but think about it. What the law is. What I'm duty-bound to do. How far I can stretch things. I haven't come to a full-on confrontation between my two worlds." He looked at the churning sky. "At least I hadn't until today."

Malcolm waited and didn't say anything. The wrong word could send Roger back into silence.

"You're probably right that there are things they don't tell me," Roger said. "And it's also certainly true there are things I'd as lief they don't tell me." He went still for a moment, turned to Malcolm, who had stopped beside him. "I said I doubted Lewis was involved in a Leveller plot I didn't know about. And that's true. But a week ago, Lewis came to me and said he had reason to believe some of the others were involved in a plot that could be treasonous."

It was something Malcolm had suspected. It fit with a number of the facts. So there was no reason for him to feel as though he'd been dealt a punch to the gut. "Did he say who he thought was involved?"

Roger dragged his gaze back to Malcolm as though in meeting Malcolm's gaze he was forcing himself to confront the reality of the situation. "Kit. And Simon. He wasn't sure who else."

"What was the nature of the plot?" Malcolm kept his voice even as a gust of wind howled round them.

"Lewis said he wasn't sure. He said he'd come back to the theatre one night in search of Miss Blanchard, who was rehearsing late. He found the door unlocked, so he thought they were still rehearsing. He heard voices from the stage, but as he got closer, he realized it wasn't the rehearsal. He heard Kit say, 'We're flirting with treason,' and Simon say, 'We were always bound to at some point,' and ask Kit if he wanted out. Lewis thought Kit said something like, 'No, we've come this far.' Lewis told me he moved closer to try to hear better and he stepped on a creaking board. He head Simon and Kit ask who was there and he said all he could think to do was beat a hasty retreat and hope they wouldn't follow. He said he'd been stewing for over twenty-four hours about whether to confront Simon and Kit, or say nothing or tell someone else. Finally, he'd decided to tell me."

"Nothing like having someone dump a dilemma in your lap. What did you say?"

Roger grimaced. "I asked a lot of the same questions you're asking now. I told him I needed to think about how to proceed, that I'd look into it and get back to him. Not to tell anyone else for now. I was still mulling it just now when Kit came to tell me Lewis had been killed."

"You didn't say anything to Kit?"

"I almost did. I might have done if you hadn't come in. He's my friend. My best friend. But there's only going to be one chance to confront him with this and gauge his reaction. And you can do that better than I can. The same goes for Simon."

Malcolm nodded. "A lot of things are classified as treason. A lot of things that shouldn't be. A lot of things you and I might do ourselves, under certain circumstances."

"Yes, I know," Roger said. But Malcolm could see the other possibilities chasing themselves behind his eyes.

"I don't know Kit as well as you do, but I know his decency. God knows I know Simon's. I trust them both."

"But you're concerned?"

Malcolm hesitated. "I've been surprised too many times by too many people. So I always wonder. Of course, the fact that Lewis was undercover changes things a bit."

Roger frowned. "You think he was making it all up? Acting as an agent provocateur for Carfax or the League, trying to sow discord among the Levellers?"

"It would be comforting to think so. And I could see a plot by Carfax or the League to do as much. But Letty Blanchard told Mel she overheard Lewis talking to someone else about something he said was 'treason.'"

"Who?"

"Letty said she couldn't make out who. But the person apparently said, 'What did you think you signed up for?'"

Roger frowned. "You think Lewis told another of the Levellers, who was advising him to turn a blind eye?"

"That's one explanation. Or it might not be this supposed plot of Kit's and Simon's that was the treason at all. Lewis might have been talking to his handler. He might have been protesting something he was being asked to do."

"And calling it treason? The League might ask him to commit treason, but surely Carfax wouldn't."

"You don't know Carfax very well if you think that. He'll cross just about any line in pursuit of what he thinks must be done. Including crossing his own government."

"In which case, this whole conversation Lewis told me he heard between Kit and Simon might be made up."

"Perhaps."

"That would be a relief. But—" Roger frowned.

"What?" Malcolm asked.

Roger shifted his weight from one foot to the other. "I was horrified by what Lewis told me. And I was shocked. But at the same time, a part of me wasn't surprised. Because the truth is I've suspected Kit was keeping something from me for some time." He released his breath. "That's part of why I didn't do anything to follow up on my talk with Thornsby sooner. I was hurt at first, but then I told myself we were going to have to have secrets from each other in my position, as you did with Simon. That Kit was protecting both of us and I should do the same."

Malcolm hesitated. But Roger had confided so much he could not but do the same. "I've had a similar sense about Simon. Or rather, my wife did and told me."

Roger nodded, as though a truth he'd been trying to deny had settled on his shoulders. "So they *are* plotting something."

"Probably. Which may have nothing to do with Thornsby's murder."

"But now we're going to have to find out. And even if it's nothing to do with the investigation, we'll have to decide what we're going to do."

Malcolm nodded.

They started walking again. Roger frowned at his boot toes. "Do you think Lewis and Will were in this together? That they're both moles for Carfax or the League?"

"It's one possibility. They wouldn't be the first allies to fall in love with the same girl. Or their quarrel might have been about their work, and Letty Blanchard was a convenient excuse."

"And you think Mrs. Ashford fits in somewhere."

Malcolm drew a breath. The air was rank with smells from the river. "How do you think Kitty Ashford fits into this?"

"She's your friend, Rannoch."

That was true. He'd have once thought he and Kitty couldn't be friends, but in the past months they had grown to be. Which made all of this so much more complicated. "I'm not sure my being her friend is helping me see the situation clearly."

"Because you don't want to believe there was—er—something between her and Lewis? I know Kit seemed to think there was, but for what it's worth I never had any sense of it. But you say she told you it was true."

"I think she was lying. To cover up some other connection to Lewis Thornsby. And it wasn't an easy lie to tell. Which means whatever she's trying to cover up is something she's even more determined to keep from me."

"Surely she wouldn't be working for Carfax or the League."

"I don't think so, no."

Roger's eyes narrowed. "Kit said Julien St. Juste was at the Tavistock when Mélanie found Lewis."

"He arrived just after."

"And St. Juste and Mrs. Ashford—"

"Are living together. Yes, that makes the questions even more complicated."

"Do you think St. Juste is telling you the truth about what he knows about Lewis's death?"

"The whole truth? Oh, no, I'm quite sure he isn't. But then, Julien St. Juste rarely tells the whole truth about anything."

CHAPTER 17

Mélanie turned from her dressing table to look at Malcolm. He'd found her in the breakfast parlor when he returned from seeing Roger and Kit, eating a light dinner with the children and Laura and Blanca and Addison, before they went to Paul and Juliette's. She'd known at once that he had something important to tell her, but he'd waited to swallow a few mouthfuls of shepherd's pie and admire Jessica's latest drawings before they went to change for the evening. When they'd gone into their own room, he'd at last given her an account of his talks with both men.

She stared at him now he had finished, one garnet earring on, the other dangling from her fingers as she pieced together the information. "Are you going to talk to Simon?"

He grimaced. "That prospect weighed on me all the way home. I want to wait at least until after we talk to Will tonight. Once Simon—and Kit—know what we know, they'll close ranks."

"They might have an explanation."

"They'll undoubtedly have an explanation. Just as Kitty did. And then we'll have to figure out if it's the truth." Malcolm pulled off his coat and tossed it onto the frayed green velvet chair that he always resisted her efforts to have recovered. "You know, with everything we've been through, sweetheart, neither of us has ever had to investigate the other. I find myself intensely grateful for that."

"There is that." She smiled and found she could do so without bitterness. Somehow it was getting easier between them. Instead of laughing at the past because the alternative was unthinkable, they could do so with relative ease. "Anything Thornsby said about Simon and Kit has to be suspect, considering we know Thornsby was living a double life and very likely spying on the Levellers."

"True enough." Malcolm threw his waistcoat after his coat and pulled his shirt over his head. Sadly, this was not a moment when she could appreciate the sight. "But Roger suspected Kit was concealing something, and you had the sense Simon was. That suggests to me that there's at least a grain of truth in what Thornsby told Roger."

Her fear last December when she'd first suspected Simon was concealing something from them shot through her again. "It's hard to make the pieces add up." She stared at the earring dangling from her fingers, then flicked open the clasp and threaded it through her ear. An automatic task that seemed suddenly harder. "I suppose if Thornsby was an agent provocateur he might have told the story to Roger to provoke dissent among the Levellers."

"And if he was an agent provocateur he might have been listening in on conversations and overheard a real argument between Kit and Simon." Malcolm went to the chest of drawers and took out a clean shirt. "As I said to Roger, a lot of things are treasonable. A lot of things we wouldn't find questionable. That we think should be done. So even if Thornsby was telling the exact truth about what he overheard, it doesn't remotely prove

Kit and Simon are doing something we'd disagree with." He pulled the shirt over his head.

Mélanie watched his head emerge from the clean linen, wondering if he'd hesitated just a bit over the word "we." She couldn't be the only one who wondered what they'd both do when they learned the truth of whatever their friends were plotting.

"No." She picked up her brush and ran it over her hair. "What about the list of places and dates?"

"Thornsby could have taken the coded paper from someone in the Levellers and decoded it."

Mélanie set down the brush and tucked a pin into her hair. She'd left it down with just the front pulled back, as she tended to wear it these days. They were only going to Juliette and Paul's, after all. "You think the Levellers were behind all those incidents? Despite what Kit and Roger said?"

Malcolm was doing up his shirt cuffs. "I think it's possible."

"If they were, it seems odd they'd keep a list like that, even in code."

"It does," Malcolm agreed.

Mélanie reached for her rouge pot and dabbed rouge on her cheeks without looking in the mirror. "What if someone in the Levellers put the list together because they thought the incidents had been orchestrated? Perhaps by an agent provocateur."

"Possible." Malcolm went to his wardrobe and pulled out a silver-striped waistcoat. "Has Will Carmarthen ever told you anything about his past?"

"No." Mélanie frowned at her eye-blacking brush, thinking back through her interactions with Will. Fragments of conversation in the green room, in coffee houses, during breaks from rehearsal. "I've talked to him quite a bit about characters in plays—from Shakespeare's to Simon's to my own—but not at all about his own life." She turned to the glass and deepened the blacking round her eyes. "But surely if he was a plant, he'd have a constructed backstory. Look at what you found in Thornsby's Montford rooms in Rosemary Lane, and that wasn't even a life he was living full-time."

"Yes, that is odd." Malcolm was doing up the buttons on the waistcoat. "But Carmarthen seems to be tangled in a great deal of this one way or another. Even if he wasn't involved in the incidents on that list, he was close enough to a number of them that he may know something."

Mélanie set down the brush and turned to look at her husband, who was pulling on a black cassimere coat. "Malcolm, you don't think that Simon—"

Malcolm tugged his coat smooth. "You've said you can't be sure what you'd do in various circumstances, Mel. I can't be sure of myself. How can I be sure about Simon?"

Mélanie pulled her gown on over her satin slip and fastened one of the silver buttons that ran down the front. The metal shimmered in the light from the tapers on her dressing table, bright and sharp as memories cut into her brain. "Raoul used to talk to me a lot about the Irish uprising. Especially when he'd had a few glasses of wine. I think he kept trying to make sense of what had gone wrong." She could see him, wine glass in hand, leaning towards her across a table or sprawled on the floor by the fire.

"He used to talk to me about it too, when I was a boy," Malcolm said. "It wasn't the fact that it turned violent that infuriated him. Difficult for an uprising not to be violent, he'd argue. It was the disorganization."

Mélanie nodded and did up another button. "The lack of communication between the factions, the wanton destruction that served no purpose—"

"You think he'd claim the acts on that list we found in Rosemary Lane served a purpose?" Malcolm pushed the wardrobe doors closed.

"I'm not sure. But I don't know that he'd have shrunk from

them if he thought they'd achieve the ends he wanted." She smoothed her hands over the burgundy silk of her gown. She knew Raoul could be ruthless. She knew she could be ruthless herself. The question was how ruthless Simon could be. "Whom do you identify with in *Julius Caesar*?"

"Portia," he said without hesitation. "I never know what my spouse is plotting."

She gave a faint smile that did not reach the coldness inside her. "Then we're consistent, at least. I've always felt an affinity for Brutus."

"So when Napoleon Bonaparte made himself Emperor, you thought about assassinating him?"

Mélanie met her husband's gaze across their bedchamber. "That's my Malcolm. No fancy footwork, just a nice, clean thrust to the heart. No, obviously. But I can imagine—"

"Killing someone for a good cause?"

Her fingers clenched on the soft silk. "What else is war?"

"Except that in a war, someone else is trying to kill you."

"Someone has to start the killing. Raoul would say that we've been at war against poverty and injustice for years."

"Fair enough." The wood creaked as Malcolm leaned his shoulder against one of the bedposts. "Antony thinks that Brutus's motives set him apart from the other conspirators. But it doesn't change his thinking Brutus was wrong."

"And yet in the end he calls Brutus the noblest Roman. Brutus put his cause above the life of his friend."

"And his wife died because of it. Most causes come down to people, in the end. If you overlook the people for the cause, then how do you warp the cause?"

"But how can you change anything by playing by the rules, when the rules are being set by the people running the system you're trying to change?"

For a moment she had a clear memory of sitting round their dining table downstairs one evening the previous autumn.

David and Simon and Harry and Cordy had come to dine. Raoul and Laura had been there, of course. The port had long since been brought, but none of the women withdrew from the table in Berkeley Square these days. David had been discussing a speech he planned to make in support of Lord Althorp's motion for an inquiry over the Peterloo carnage. Simon had clunked down the decanter and said, *Where the hell is that going to get you? Even if it passes, do you think it will change anything?* The usual irony had been quite gone from his face and voice.

David had taken out his handkerchief and blotted up the port that had splashed from the decanter. *It's a start,* he'd said, in a hard, even voice.

That's brilliant, David. Simon had stared at David with the full force of the caustic wit Mélanie had never seen him turn on his lover. *The government used troops to break up a peaceful meeting. Women and children were trampled in the streets. And you're going to make a speech saying they shouldn't have done it.*

It had been Raoul who'd said, *There can be a value in putting things into words.* But a few weeks later, when the bill had failed to pass, Simon hadn't said anything. He hadn't needed to.

Mélanie did up the last button on her gown. "Sometimes I think I've become the most shocking coward."

Malcolm took a step forwards and reached out a hand to cup her cheek. "My darling, you're a lot of things, but you're no coward."

"I just enjoy living a life of luxury in a system I claim to disapprove of."

He tucked a strand of her hair into its pins. "The sacrifices one makes for marriage."

"I'm not sure how funny that is."

He set his hands on her shoulders. "I'm not sure how funny I meant it to be."

Before she could reply, the door opened and Jessica came hurtling in and flung her arms round both their knees. She was wearing the pink tulle princess dress Blanca had cut down from one of Mélanie's old dresses. Which she wore whenever she could.

"Are you ready?" Colin followed her in, Emily beside him. "We've been ready for ages." He looked between them. "We're Investigating tonight, aren't we?"

"We're certainly keeping our ears open." Malcolm touched Colin's hair while Mélanie scooped Jessica up. Laura came in, carrying Clara. Her gaze went from Mélanie to Malcolm for the briefest moment. Mélanie sent her a silent promise to update her as soon as they could. Laura returned the smile. "It's raining," she said. "I brought umbrellas."

"It's too bad Daddy isn't back." Emily looked over her shoulder at her mother. "He always likes Juliette and Paul's."

Without looking round, Mélanie could feel the tension that ran through Malcolm. It wasn't that unusual for Raoul to be out all day without saying where he was going, but he tried at least to be back in the evening for the children. And with the uncertainty about the investigation, they were all on edge.

"You know he never knows how long things will take him when he's making inquiries." Laura's voice was easy, perhaps determinedly so.

"He's Investigating," Colin said.

"I know," Emily said. "I just wish he could Investigate with us."

"I expect he'll be back to say goodnight before you go to sleep," Malcolm said in a voice as easy as Laura's.

Emily nodded. "Oh, there's the carriage," she added, with the sharp hearing of the young.

A short time later they pulled up in front of Paul and Juliette's terrace house in Henrietta Street. A sedate, uniform house, but its orderly sash windows, neat chimneys, and shiny blue door contained a family that were decidedly unorthodox.

Gavin, the family manservant, who had joined the household

after Malcolm helped get him acquitted of charges of thievery three years before, ushered them into the slate-flagged entry hall, took their dripping umbrellas, and helped them out of their outer garments.

"They're all in the drawing room," he said, nodding towards the stairs. "You know the way."

The children ran ahead with the ease of family, which in a sense they were in the Dubretton-St. Gilles household. The strains of a new song by their friend Schubert, which Mélanie had given Paul the music for, drifted from the drawing room. The air smelled of colza oil from the urn-shaped hanging lamps, drying wool garments, Cotswolds cheese, and sherry.

"I'm so glad you're all here." Juliette swept up to them in a stir of gold satin and citrine earrings that glowed in the candlelight. Strands of dark hair escaped their pins and fell about her face, probably because she'd been working rather than because of time spent at her dressing table, but with an equally artful effect. She bent down to return Jessica's hug. "Pierre and Marguerite and Rose have been asking about you all day."

"We'll find them." Laura exchanged a look with Mélanie and threaded her way through the crowd to the parlor that was set aside for the children's games at Juliette and Paul's parties, though the younger generation always mingled freely through the house.

Juliette looked after them with a smile, then turned to Malcolm and Mélanie. "I wasn't sure you'd make it, with everything that's happened. Poor Mr. Thornsby."

"Did he come here often?" Malcolm took Juliette's hand and leaned forwards to kiss her cheek. "I don't remember seeing him."

"Only a couple of times, but the last one was just last week. I have a clear memory of his sitting at the piano turning the pages of the music for Letty Blanchard. One never thinks—" She looked between them. "Between the play and the investigation

I'm sure you aren't here simply because it's Tuesday evening. Whom are you looking for?"

"Will Carmarthen," Mélanie said. "And we'd have done our best to be here, regardless."

"Carmarthen?" Paul St. Gilles joined them. He had sandy hair and keen blue eyes that burned with equal parts intensity and kindness. "He's in the drawing room." Paul shook his head. "Funny how easily I say drawing room. Three years out of Paris and I'm practically an Englishman. It's good to see you both. I saw Laura and the children. Where's O'Roarke?"

Where indeed? "You know O'Roarke," Malcolm said in the same easy voice he'd used talking about Raoul earlier. "It's unusual when he does share where he's going."

Paul grinned but his gaze said he perhaps saw more than he let on. He touched Malcolm's arm and kissed Mélanie's cheek. "With everything else, we're looking forward to the play."

"It's quite brilliant," Juliette said. "I was fortunate to have a preview of the script, and the children loved the rehearsal I brought them to."

"You're very kind," Mélanie said.

Juliette smiled. "I can be when necessary, but with you I don't have to."

The company were ranged about the drawing room with the ease of familiarity. The intense, fair-haired young man at the piano played for rehearsals at the Tavistock. Lord Palmerston, the secretary at war, was lounging against the wall on the opposite side of the room, exchanging flirtatious banter with Cecily Summers, who was also in the Tavistock company. He looked up, nodded at Malcolm, and blew a kiss to Mélanie. Juliette and Paul's elder daughter, Marguerite, moved about the room, replenishing drinks with aplomb.

They found Will Carmarthen perched on an age-mellowed crimson velvet sofa in a corner of the room talking with a broad-shouldered man with a shock of thinning hair the color of damp birch leaves, a sharp-featured face, and a quick hazel gaze. George Bartlett was a barrister, known for the erudition of his arguments as well as the inflammatory nature of the cases he chose to take on. He'd defended Gavin, the manservant, three years ago.

Bartlett noticed them first as they approached the sofa. "Malcolm. Mélanie."

Will gave a grin that almost masked the flash of concern in his eyes. "Didn't expect to see you here tonight. I thought you were busy assisting Bow Street."

"We found ourselves with a bit of time," Malcolm said.

"Nothing like convivial company to clear the head," Bartlett said. "Malcolm, here's a new one for you. 'The good of the people is the chief law.'"

"Cicero."

"Damn it, boy, you're too well read. You take all the fun out of things. Wonderful quote, must use it in a closing. It's good to see you both. We've missed you. Haven't turned too Whiggish, have you?"

"Perish the thought," Malcolm said. "You'd never say so if you heard the talk in the coffee room at Brooks's."

"I was in the coffee room at Brooks's once. Damned stuffy. That was a good speech on the evils of the corn laws, though it didn't go quite far enough."

Mélanie, who had argued as much with her husband, held her tongue.

"You, on the other hand," Bartlett continued, turning to Mélanie, "didn't hold back a bit in the article on marriage rights. Took even me by surprise."

"Yes, well, I'm a woman. I can afford to be more extreme because no one takes me seriously. And the *Political Register* is a bit different from the House of Commons."

"Shouldn't be, m'dear, shouldn't be. In a just world, it wouldn't be."

"The troublesome question, of course, is how to bring that just world about," Mélanie said.

"Without resorting to unjust means? Question for the ages. Plato would say—"

"Do stop pontificating, George. You'll scare them off." Hetty Bartlett slipped her hand through the crook of her husband's arm. She was gowned in bronze lustring cut to show her figure to advantage. Her thick ebony hair was dressed in a style that looked as if it might have been copied from a Renaissance oil, and her dark eyes sparkled brighter than the topaz ring that gleamed on her hand. The daughter of a forward-thinking engineer and a former slave, she had grown up in Jamaica and Italy, performed as a singer, and then turned novelist. "Talking of ways to change the world, I hear your play is about to set London about its ears," she said to Mélanie.

"I only hope people find it coherent," Mélanie said.

"It's hard enough to be coherent. But you have a knack for getting your point across while doing so. And making people laugh."

"Also for writing dialogue that actually sounds like natural speech," Will said. "Even if Brandon does mangle it. Sorry, Mel."

"No need to apologize. He actually helped me improve the speech. Oh, there are Kit and Sofia." Mélanie caught sight of the young couple as she glanced across the room. "I didn't know they'd be here tonight." Had Kit come to warn Will after his talk with Malcolm? She met Malcolm's gaze for a moment. "I should speak with them. I haven't seen either of them since the terrible business with Lewis Thornsby."

CHAPTER 18

Malcolm felt Will Carmarthen's gaze on him when Mélanie moved across the room to talk to Kit and Sofia, and Hetty drew George Bartlett away to speak with friends. "I was actually hoping for a word with you, Carmarthen."

"I'm happy to be of help," Will said as Malcolm settled himself on the sofa. "But I told you what I could about Thornsby earlier today. We didn't mingle much. His circles are a bit above my touch."

"Hardly that, Carmarthen. You have a knack for fitting in to most society." Malcolm returned Will's frank regard. He was clearly educated, but whether the education was self-acquired or university taught remained unclear, as did everything else about his past.

"Perhaps," Will said. "But our confrontation about Letty aside, I didn't spend much time with Thornsby. I don't think I'd have fit in well with his friends."

"How did you fit in at the jail in Lancaster?"

Will's back stiffened. Then he relaxed against the sofa cushions. "What does that have to do with what happened last night at the Tavistock?"

"Why don't you tell me?"

"Do you want me to make up a story? I could come up with a damned good one if I put my mind to it, but I don't see how a farrago of lies would be of much help to either of us."

Malcolm dived a hand into his pocket and pulled out his copy of the decoded list he and Roth had found in the rooms Thornsby had occupied as Montford. "Do these dates mean anything to you?"

Will scanned the list. "They're dates of Radical disturbances. I was involved in several. On one occasion, as you alluded to, I spent a few nights in jail in Lancaster. I owe my release to the kind offices of your friend Worsley. Don't think I'm not grateful. But what the hell does that list have to do with last night's murder? Don't tell me you believe the idiots who say Thornsby was killed by bloodthirsty Jacobins."

The puzzlement in Will's face appeared utterly genuine, but Malcolm was not sure. In a lot of ways, Will reminded him of himself a decade ago.

"We found the list in rooms Thornsby had been using," Malcolm said. "Does the name Montford mean anything to you?"

Will frowned as though genuinely searching his memory, then shook his head. "No. I don't think it's anyone at the Tavistock. Or any of the Levellers."

"It's an alias Thornsby was using."

"*Thornsby* had an alias?" Will said. "For God's sake, why?"

"That seems to be the general reaction to his having had an alias. And *why* would be the pertinent question. He'd taken rooms in Rosemary Lane under that name."

Will gave a short laugh. "I wouldn't have thought Thornsby could even find his way to Rosemary Lane. He certainly didn't have need of anything secondhand. Sorry." He raked a hand over his hair. "I keep forgetting he's dead."

"His being dead doesn't change who he was in life."

"No, but it makes me realize I wasn't always fair to him. I'd have said the rooms and the second identity were some sort of elaborate gambit to seduce Letty, except that doesn't make sense given that Letty knew precisely who he was and where he lived. And as I told you this afternoon, I'm no longer sure he was trying to seduce Letty. Although—" He frowned. "If he wanted to marry Letty in secret but not tell his family, he'd have needed a place they could live together as husband and wife without questions. He was the sort who would care about no one's looking askance at Letty."

"An ingenious idea." One Malcolm admitted hadn't occurred to him. "But Miss Blanchard is known. You think she'd have agreed to live quietly in Rosemary Lane?"

Will's mouth twisted. "Possibly, if she was dazzled enough by what she thought she might eventually gain as Thornsby's wife. Or if she loved him more than I've wanted to admit. But she wouldn't necessarily have had to. She could have gone about her life at the theatre, Thornsby could have gone about his as a man about town. They'd just need a safe identity when they—wanted to be together as a couple. Thornsby might have thought that with time he could persuade his family to accept Letty. But he didn't want to wait for marriage and everything that went with it."

Malcolm nodded. "I hadn't thought of it that way, but it's possible. Though Thornsby established his Montford identity with a care that suggests to me he was trained as an agent. And it doesn't explain that list of Radical disturbances."

Will studied the list again. "You already knew Thornsby was a Leveller. Which to some means a Radical, a Jacobin, a Sans-Culotte—"

"Those names are a bit French Revolution, aren't they?"

"A lot of people can't get past the French Revolution. You think Thornsby was involved in the disturbances on that list?"

"I think there's an explanation for what he was doing with the list. I'm not in the least sure what the explanation is."

"You're starting to talk like someone at the home office, Rannoch. Seeing conspiracies everywhere. Imagining we're all connected. Look about you." Will's gaze swept the drawing room and the open doors to the parlor. "Do you see ten people who could find a half-dozen topics to agree on, let alone plan a conspiracy? Lack of agreement has been the curse of Radicals back to the United Irish Uprising."

Raoul shot into Malcolm's mind, so vividly Malcolm could almost imagine he was in the room. Which Malcolm very much wished he was, for a number of reasons. "Why the United Irish Uprising in particular?"

"Because it seems less obvious than saying the French Revolution." Will regarded him for a moment. "Aren't you going to give me the lecture?"

"What lecture?"

"About how you were just like me when you were my age, but now you see the dangers of too much agitation, and if I were sensible I'd stand for Parliament like you and Worsley and Roger Smythe and work for reform through legal channels."

Someone was singing "Dove sono" at the piano. Whoever it was had a pretty voice, but lacked the passion Mélanie brought to the aria. "When I was your age," Malcolm said, "I spoke and wrote a bit, largely for an audience who already shared my beliefs. I hardly think I had your flair."

"That's not the way I hear it. You and your friends—Tanner and Worsley and Lydgate—caused quite a bit of consternation among government types like Carfax and Castlereagh and Sidmouth."

"I'd take that as proof of their paranoia rather than of any power on our side."

"And then when your reckless undergraduate days were behind you—"

"I ran off to the Continent, mostly because I couldn't face the demons at home. I met my wife and got quite good at picking locks and decoding documents. But as far as living up to the ideals I'd espoused in my undergraduate days, I can't claim I made a very wise choice. In fact, one could say for a time I turned my back on everything I believed in. For what it's worth, I do think you'd be quite effective in Parliament."

"Yes, well, we can't all afford to buy our way in. Sorry, that was a low blow."

"No," Malcolm said, "I'd call that above the belt."

Will sat forwards on the sofa. "I like you, Rannoch. More important, I admire you. But you're never going to get Parliament to reform a system that favors its own members to so great a degree."

"So what's your alternative?"

"I don't know. At this point, I wouldn't rule anything out, though."

"On a number of issues of the day, the official positions of the Whigs and Tories are so close as to be almost indistinguishable. Yet the fact that we have two parties gives us the illusion of debate, while neatly excluding from the discussion any opinions that fall outside that narrow spectrum."

"That's quite well put. Are you trying to mimic something I'd write?"

"No, I'm quoting something I wrote myself."

"When you were a heedless undergraduate?"

"Last week."

"One can argue that anyone who doesn't actively oppose an unjust system is complicit in the tyranny," Will said.

"So one can. Have you read Cagano?"

"A former slave. He claimed every man in Great Britain was

responsible in some degree for slavery. I wonder what Hetty Bartlett would say. Or your friend Josefina Lopes."

"You'll have to ask them. For that matter, Carfax's late sister-in-law was the daughter of a former slave."

Will frowned. "Carfax's younger brother's wife?"

"His elder brother. Carfax inherited the title when his brother died shortly after the death of the brother's only son." It was a long time since Malcolm had thought of Arthur Mallinson, David's older cousin. If Arthur had lived, David's life would have been a great deal simpler. "As a second son, Carfax had gone into the army. That's how he got into military intelligence. And then, even after he inherited the title, he never really left it."

"And his brother married the daughter of a slave? He must have been quite different from the present Carfax."

"Actually, in their politics they were much the same. Carfax's brother married the daughter of a wealthy Jamaican planter who had married a former slave. The late Lady Carfax came to Britain as a great heiress."

"And money has a way of trumping everything. Even prejudice."

"She died when I was a baby, but I imagine she still had to deal with prejudice. Or at least with being an outsider in the beau monde. I don't know what she'd have said about Cagano's comment, but I certainly wouldn't disagree with him."

"So what's your solution?"

"I don't know," Malcolm said. "I haven't ruled anything out either. But as a former diplomat, I incline to compromise rather than confrontation."

"Diplomacy can become a quagmire."

"So can war."

"But it offers the possibility of victory."

"Violence can have unintended consequences."

"In other words, if you let the ends justify the means, the ends become warped?"

"Whom do you identify with in *Julius Caesar*?" Malcolm asked.

"The plebeians. They're pawns, whoever's in power. But I feel a certain sympathy for Brutus's fear of tyranny."

"And yet in the end, Brutus and his companions assassinate Caesar and Rome still ends up with an emperor. A colder, more calculating emperor, as Shakespeare portrays him. Morality aside, violence tends to convince those in the middle that any sort of reform will lead to blood in the streets. Which in turns lends support to tyranny."

"Very well done, Rannoch. That's one of the best arguments for inactivity I've heard in an age."

Malcolm regarded Will. "So you don't know of any connection among these events?" he asked, gesturing towards the list.

"They all caused a lot of consternation at Whitehall and Westminster and in Mayfair drawing rooms. A lot of the same people were present at all of them. None was as well organized as it should have been. Other than that—No."

"You don't suspect any of the Levellers might have been involved?"

"I probably wouldn't tell you if I did, but as it happens, no, I don't. Philosophically, we don't advocate violence. And I know you'll say we can't be sure of all our members, but practically we aren't organized enough to pull any of those incidents off."

"Which doesn't account for a splinter group."

"You're right I can't be sure of it. But it would have to be a splinter group I don't know about."

"Was Kit there for any of the incidents?"

"Surely you've asked Kit? Or you can—he's across the room with your wife."

"I'm asking you."

Will's gaze settled like a dagger point on Malcolm's face. "Good God. You suspect Kit."

"I'm trying very hard not to suspect anyone without evidence. And not to make assumptions about anyone's innocence either."

"Kit came up to Lancaster with Worsley after I was arrested —you probably know that. But he wasn't there before. And he wasn't at any of the other incidents, that I know of."

"What about Thornsby?"

Will's brows drew together. "That's the odd thing. Thornsby actually was in Lancaster. Well, I suppose it's not so odd. Letty was performing. Thornsby and a couple of the other Levellers who weren't in the company had come up to Lancaster and were staying at a hotel. A much more elegant hotel than where the company were billeted."

"Tell me about what happened. How you came to be arrested. I haven't heard all the details."

"We heard about a protest meeting. We were all drinking in a tavern after an afternoon performance and a bunch of us decided to go along to the protest. It's not my sort of thing, normally. I'm all for change, but I don't like the energy in a crowd. But everyone else was going and I was curious about how these things happened in Lancaster and I wanted to show support. And I'd had a couple of pints. It was already crowded by the time we got there, and speeches were underway. There were a lot of shouts and applause, but it seemed pretty orderly at first. We were standing towards the back and it was hard to see and hard to make out the words with all the noise and the fact that a north country accent isn't in my repertoire."

Will shifted in his seat. Malcolm made a mental note that wherever Will was from, it apparently wasn't the north country, unless this was elaborate subterfuge.

"Then all of a sudden, I heard a shout that didn't sound like support for the speaker," Will said. "The crowd started pushing backwards. I tripped and realized I'd fallen over Tim Scott who'd got knocked to the ground. I tried to pull him up, but people kept pushing into us. All of a sudden, a pistol went off. Suddenly the crowd pulled back round us. There was a man bleeding on the ground alongside Tim and me, and a pistol lying there. I crawled over and bound my cravat round the wounded man's leg, while Tim pulled out a flask to splash brandy on the wound. The next thing I knew, someone grabbed me from behind and people were asking where I got the pistol, and a man in a blue coat I'd never seen before was saying he saw me shoot the pistol. I had handcuffs on and was being pulled off to jail before I had time to think. Tim tried to get me free, but I told him the wounded man needed help more. I was sure it was a misunderstanding, but a few hours later Tim came to see me with Letty. They'd bribed the turnkey to let them in. They said the man in the blue coat was sticking to his story and there was another witness. The charge was attempted murder. Letty said she was sending to Simon. She got Thornsby to pay for an express."

"What do you know about the people who informed against you?"

"Nothing." Will took a drink from his glass of claret and frowned into the dregs. "Tim and Letty started searching for them. Worsley and Kit tried to get their names. They seemed to have melted into thin air. Worsley got the names from their statements, but even with that they couldn't trace them. Then the charges were dropped and everyone stopped trying." He looked up and met Malcolm's gaze. "And yes, it feels like a setup."

"Of you?"

"I don't know. If so, no one's ever tried again. It could have just been general agent provocateur action against Radical protests. But if you're thinking Thornsby might have been involved in setting it up, he worked hard to get me acquitted.

Not only did he send the express, he helped Letty and Tim look for the informants. If that was all part of an elaborate setup, he did a lot to sabotage his own efforts. If Thornsby hadn't sent the express, Tanner might not have got it in time to send Worsley. If Worsley hadn't got there, I'm not at all sure I'd have got off. And I was arrested for a capital offense. So I suppose you could say I owe Thornsby my life. Which makes me feel a bit of a worm for not having been more grateful when he was still alive to thank. I mean, I thanked him, but I went on—"

"'You can't blame yourself for your thoughts, Carmarthen."

"No, I suppose not. But I attacked him for his intentions when he'd shown good intentions towards me. Perhaps he realized he had no reason to be jealous of me where Letty was concerned. Or perhaps he was simply a better person than I am."

"Whatever else he was," Malcolm said, "Thornsby was clearly complicated."

"Yes." Will shook his head. "The irony is that part of the reason I was sure it wouldn't work for him and Letty is that he'd bore Letty to death. But I begin to think I was quite wrong about that." He stared across the room at a landscape of Paul's, a lonely ship on a storm-tossed sea, the moonlight gleaming off the water in a way that shimmered with mystery. "God knows what else I was wrong about."

CHAPTER 19

Mélanie found Kit Montagu and Sofia Vincenzo sitting side by side on a settee, both holding glasses of sherry that looked scarcely touched. Normally she wouldn't have dreamed of interrupting the young couple, who got little enough time alone. But this was anything but a normal time.

"Mélanie," Sofia said. Her smile was friendly, but Mélanie caught marks of strain about her eyes. "It feels like we haven't seen you in an age. I know it was only two days, but so much has happened."

Mélanie drew a chair closer to the settee. "How well did you know Lewis Thornsby?"

"Not well at all, really. I'd only met him two or three times since I came to Britain last month. But all the Levellers feel like friends." Sofia's gaze went to Kit. Mélanie thought she caught a flicker of a question in it. Then Sofia looked back at Mélanie. "Aline's asked me to help decode the papers Malcolm found in Mr. Thornsby's rooms in Rosemary Lane."

"Thank you," Mélanie said. Sofia, who had broken Elsinore

League codes on her own, bid fair to be as formidable with numbers as Aline.

"I'm glad there's something I can do to help. Do you think Mr. Thornsby's death is connected to the League?"

Sofia's father had been part of the Elsinore League, so she was quicker to jump to that possibility than some were. "It's possible," Mélanie said. "We don't have any definite connection. But it seems Thornsby may have been working for someone. Possibly—probably—to infiltrate the Levellers."

Sofia pulled her shawl about her, a rich Italian silk in red and blues that took Mélanie back to the days on Lake Como when she had first met Sofia and Kit. "We haven't had to confront that," Sofia said. "Not with the Levellers or the Carbonari." She glanced at Kit again, then looked back at Mélanie. "I told Kit. I think I need to tell you. I heard Lewis talking with Mrs. Ashford the day before yesterday. I'd come to a rehearsal and I was waiting for Kit, who was talking to Simon. I went into the green room, and I heard voices. Raised voices. I could tell from the tone they were arguing. I drew back, but I heard Mrs. Ashford say, 'You can't be sure of that,' and Lewis say, 'No but I can make assumptions.' I retreated quickly. I'll confess I was curious, but it wasn't any of my business." She looked at Mélanie for a moment. "There could be all sorts of explanations."

"There could," Mélanie agreed. "But anything to do with Lewis could be relevant. Thank you for telling me."

Sofia nodded. Her gaze was dark with concern and somehow Mélanie suspected it wasn't just to do with having betrayed Kitty's quarrel with Thornsby.

"I didn't—" Kit looked at his fiancée as though searching for the right words. "I didn't want to tell you, Sofia, but Malcolm knows, so I assume Mélanie does. I think Thornsby had—er—feelings for Mrs. Ashford."

Sofia frowned. "But—"

"If you're thinking of Letty—"

"For heaven's sake, Kit, I know a man may feel things for more than one woman. Or a woman for more than one man. But that exchange I overheard didn't sound at all like a lovers' quarrel. Even more than the words, the tone on both sides wasn't that of people who had feelings of the sort. Or had ever had them."

"They could have been quarreling about something else," Kit said.

Sofia shook her head. "Even so. There's a certain tone—"

"I know what you mean." Mélanie took a sip from the glass of sherry she'd acquired on her way across the room. "Although everyone is different."

"They didn't even sound like two people who knew each other well," Sofia said. "Not that lovers necessarily have to— Well, they don't." She cast a glance at Kit. "One doesn't have to be experienced to know that. But there was something about the tone between Mrs. Ashford and Lewis that made me think they'd never shared anything of the sort. I could be wrong, of course. But my instincts are usually good." She looked at Mélanie, her confidence wavering for a moment to reveal the girl who was barely over twenty. "I don't like telling tales about Mrs. Ashford. But I also don't like the idea that she could have been playing Mr. St. Juste false. I know that makes me sound like a silly romantic—"

"No," Mélanie said, "it makes you sound like someone who cares about her friends. I hope to goodness we can all manage not to lose sight of that in the midst of the investigation."

Sofia's dark gaze fastened on Mélanie's face. "That's the thing, isn't it? Because the investigation is going to end at some point. And we're all going to have to live with the truths that are uncovered. Whatever those may be."

"MÉLANIE?" Marguerite, Juliette and Paul's older daughter, materialized beside the settee after Sofia and Kit moved off, holding a decanter. "Would you like some more sherry?"

"No. Yes. It can't hurt, at this point."

Marguerite refilled her glass and perched on the settee. "Your dress is pretty. It's sort of like a pelisse but also an evening gown." She ran a gaze over Mélanie's burgundy silk gown, which buttoned up the front but was softened by bands of burgundy lace running down the front and a deep border of burgundy lace along the skirt. "I saw a picture of one like it in the *La Belle Assemblée* you gave me the last time you visited. 'Dress in a peculiar shade of red.' It had a cloak that went with it, with black braid and lace, and a hood with blond lace and silk roses. In the capu-something style."

"Capuchin," Mélanie said.

"That's it. I looked it up in the dictionary and it said it was a hood for monks, but I think it's prettier how you're wearing it."

Mélanie smiled at the girl. "I'll send a new *Belle Assemblée* round for you."

"Thanks." Marguerite ran a practiced gaze over Mélanie's gown. "That dress goes with an evening costume, doesn't it?"

"So it does. I think *La Belle Assemblée* called it a dinner dress."

"I'm surprised you had time to change for the evening since you and Malcolm are investigating the murder that happened at the Tavistock last night."

"Marguerite. Who's been talking to you?"

"Oh, everyone's been talking about the murder. Well, almost everyone. A lot of people from the Tavistock are here, and they all know about it. I don't think it's what Sofia and Kit were arguing about though."

Mélanie looked into Marguerite's blue eyes, every bit as sharp as either of her parents'. "Sofia and Kit were arguing?"

Marguerite glanced at Kit's abandoned sherry glass. "I heard them when I went to refill their drinks earlier. They didn't realize I was there at first. Kit was worried about Sofia's going home alone and Sofia was upset because Kit wouldn't say why he couldn't leave with her."

Mélanie glanced round the room. Kit and Sofia were still in the group round the pianoforte. Sofia was talking to Cecily Summers. Kit was engaged in conversation with Lord Palmerston and Hetty Bartlett. Kit and Sofia were side by side but their backs were to each other. "Kit's going somewhere special?" Mélanie asked.

"Sofia thought so. She seemed angry—No, not angry exactly. She seemed scared."

MALCOLM WAS MAKING his way through the crowd looking for Mélanie when his wife caught him by the arm. "Darling. I thought I'd never get you to myself." She put her lips against his cheek. "Where's Will?"

"He went into the small parlor." Malcolm stooped his head close to his wife's own. "He's talking with Harriet de Boinville."

"Kit's going somewhere when he leaves here." She backed him against the Grecian molding, her hands on either side of his face. "Somewhere he wouldn't tell Sofia about. Marguerite overheard them arguing."

Malcolm stroked his wife's hair. He could see Palmerston grinning at their display of connubial affection. "If Kit's worried about eluding Sofia, not to mention us, he'll probably try to slip out the back," he murmured into her ear.

"Darling." Mélanie looked up at her husband. "We're talking about following Kit."

"So we are." Malcolm tucked a strand of walnut-brown hair behind her ear.

"Who is a friend."

"A friend who's lying to us about a murder." He cupped his

hand round her cheek. "Christ, Mel, under the right circumstances I'd follow you."

She drew a breath that might have been a laugh. Or a sob. "Point taken."

"And I have no doubt there are circumstances under which you'd follow me." He drew her hand up to his mouth and kissed her knuckles. "We need to know what Kit's up to. And he's not going to tell us."

Mélanie's sea-green gaze settled on his own. "You're right. I'm going soft. I don't think I ever really thought like a political wife, but I'm thinking like a playwright."

Malcolm grinned. "Nothing wrong with that."

"It's dulling my skills."

"Sweetheart." He kissed her nose. "Nothing could do that."

They returned to the parlor designated for the children, where they found Laura sitting on the floor in a swirl of dark green velvet, Emily and Jessica on her lap. Colin was holding Clara, and all of them and several other children were engaged in a game of dominoes, which had spread to create an elaborate pattern on the Turkey rug.

Mélanie dropped down beside them. "Mummy." Jessica climbed over to her. "I found a double-six!"

"Splendid, darling." Mélanie pulled Jessica into her lap. "It looks as though Daddy and I are going to have to leave early, but there's no need for you to do so."

Colin raised a brow at her across the domino game. "Be careful."

"Always." Malcolm touched his son's hair and looked at Laura.

"We'll be fine," Laura said. "Lots of distraction here."

"Speaking of distraction—" Mélanie looked from Jessica to Emily. "Do you want to help while Laura and Colin cover here?"

The girls jumped up eagerly. Malcolm put Jessica on his shoulders. Emily caught Mélanie's hand, and they all went into the drawing room and joined the group about the piano, the picture of a carefree family bent on amusement, not investigation. Malcolm swung Jessica down so she and Emily could dance. A quarter-hour later, when Sofia's attention had been claimed by Marianne Hunt, Kit excused himself and wandered down the passage towards the gentlemen's retiring room. Malcolm twirled Emily. Mélanie spun Jessica in a circle. Then the two girls caught hands and ran into the crowd. Mélanie exchanged a quick smile of pride with Malcolm as they melted into the crowd in the other direction.

"Jessica and Emily couldn't have done that better if we'd trained them," Mélanie murmured to Malcolm as they went down the backstairs to the kitchen.

"I think we all have been by example from when Jessica was born and Emily came to live with us," Malcolm returned. "I'm not sure whether to be proud or panicked at how adept they are."

In the stone-floored kitchen they exchanged a cheerful greeting with Mrs. Ford, Juliette and Paul's cook. Then while Mélanie darted into the hall, Malcolm took up a position in the shelter of an oak tree in the back garden. The rain had let up, but the air had grown colder, frosting against his skin and numbing his gloveless fingers. A few moments later, Mélanie joined him, wearing her pelisse and carrying his greatcoat.

"I left your hat," she said. "It would be in the way. Your gloves are in the pocket."

"A bit like the Cantabrian Mountains." Malcolm shrugged into the greatcoat and pulled on the gloves.

"The Cantabrian Mountains were much colder. Malcolm, for heaven's sake, what are you doing?"

"Trying to keep us both warm." He tightened his arms round her.

"There are advantages to cold," she said, her voice muffled by his cravat. "Remember—"

She broke off as the area door creaked open. Kit emerged and slipped through the garden gate. They followed, with the careful, near-silent footfalls they both had perfected long since. Kit went through the mews to Duke Street. Gusts of wind bent the leafless trees and sliced through their layers of clothing. A hackney rattled by, but Kit made no attempt to flag it down. He crossed Oxford Street and then turned down Grosvenor Street and Upper Grosvenor Street to Park Lane, past houses blazing with candlelight and lamplight. Malcolm half-expected him to go into one of the houses, but instead he turned through the Grosvenor Gate into Hyde Park.

The moon emerged from behind the clouds in intermittent flashes. The gravel was slippery underfoot. Malcolm kept his senses tuned to the trees and shrubs on either side. Nighttime attacks by footpads were a common occurrence in Hyde Park. An owl called in the distance. A squirrel raced up a tree trunk and along a branch, shaking loose a hail of raindrops. A dark blur that might have been a fox or a badger darted into the shelter of the trees. A couple of larger dark blurs huddled beneath the branches. Malcolm ran a wary gaze over them, but they appeared to be lying motionless. Even in winter, the park was a refuge for those with nowhere else to sleep.

Kit left the path. They followed onto grass slippery with frosted raindrops. Twigs and fallen leaves crunched underfoot. A sound caught Malcolm's attention above the whir of the wind. It took him a moment to realize it had been a human cry. They had reached the slope of ground above the Serpentine. The undulating mass by the water's edge was more than just wind-tossed trees. A brawl was in progress. Three men, or perhaps four. Difficult to tell the numbers in the dark.

Kit, a dozen yards ahead, ran forwards. Malcolm stared at the brawlers, trying to sort out who was fighting whom. A gunshot ripped the air, closely followed by another. No one fell, but the combatants froze for an instant. It looked to be three against one. Three against two, as Kit launched himself at a man's back.

Malcolm exchanged a quick glance with Mélanie. "Unequal numbers," she said. "And whatever he's up to, it's Kit."

Malcolm nodded and pulled off his gloves. They ran down the slope. Kit was grappling with one of the men. He seemed to have a good purchase on the man's arm, so Malcolm ran to the two men who were pummeling the original victim. One was trying to pinion the victim's arms. The victim twisted away. The other attacker swung a cudgel towards the victim's head. Malcolm grabbed the cudgel-bearer's arm and spun the man round to face him. The man gave a grunt of surprise, jerked away, and swung the cudgel at Malcolm. Malcolm ducked and grabbed the cudgel. The heavy wood came away in his hand. Out of the corner of his eye, he saw the second man reach for Mélanie's throat. Mélanie tossed the contents of her scent bottle in the man's face.

Mélanie's attacker screamed. Malcolm's original opponent hurled himself at Malcolm and slashed at his arm with a knife. Malcolm twisted away and banged into rough, crumbly tree bark. His boots skidded on the frost-crusted leaves. As he felt himself falling, he grabbed his attacker and pulled the man down with him.

They pummeled each other, rolling over fallen leaves and icy ground and hard tree roots. The impact carried them to the water's edge. They slammed into cold, hard ice. The cudgel went flying. Malcolm's opponent scrambled to his feet. Malcolm grabbed at the man's ankles. The man stumbled to his knees, caught up the cudgel, and swung it at Malcolm's head. They both fell back on the ice, which gave way beneath them. His opponent scrambled away. Malcolm plunged into freezing water.

He fought his way to the surface and caught at the edge of

the ice. It stung his fingers. His sodden boots and greatcoat tugged him downwards. The ice crumbled in his grip.

A cudgel blow caught him on the back of the head. He recovered his vision to see his opponent sent flying across the ice, cudgel still in hand. A firm hand was extended to grip his own.

"Allow me," said Julien St. Juste.

CHAPTER 20

Mélanie turned to see her onetime lover pulling her husband from the freezing water. Her own opponent had run off through the trees when she wrested his knife away from him. Kit, his nose bloody and coat torn, was holding the third man with his arms pinioned behind his back. The man looked groggy. She had seen Kit bashing the man's head against a tree trunk. Kit's compatriot, the subject of the initial attack, was using his own cravat to bind the man's arms.

Julien and Malcolm had found something with which to lash the wrists of Malcolm's attacker before he could scramble up from the ice where Julien had flung him. They marched him onto the bank. Julien was holding him by the arm and Malcolm had a knife, probably recovered from his attacker, in his hand. Malcolm was dripping wet and shivering, but he was managing to hold his knife hand steady and she could not see any blood, though the light was too dim for close scrutiny.

Kit's confederate took a step away from his now bound captive. *Her* now bound captive, Mélanie realized, recognizing the woman's high-cheekbones, delicate nose, and decisive chin.

"I'll say this for you, Julien," Kitty Ashford said. "You have a remarkable sense of timing."

"Thank you," Julien said. "They had the weapons on their side. Challenging."

"Who hired you?" Malcolm asked Julien's captive.

Julien's captive's gaze flashed to that of Kitty's prisoner. "Out for pickings," he muttered.

"I don't think so," Kitty said. "You seemed to have a very specific target in mind."

"Just the first rich idiot who happened by." The man was broad-shouldered and barrel-chested, and his voice had the sound of north London.

"I'm cold," Malcolm said, "and I'm tired. There are more of us than you and we have the weapons now." He pressed the knife-point against the throat of the man Julien was holding. "Let's do this the easy way. Tell us who hired you."

The men exchanged glances again. "You wouldn't," said Kitty's captive. He was slighter than his companion and his voice sounded more youthful. "You don't look like a man who'd kill in cold blood."

"No?" Malcolm said. "Perhaps not. But let me put it this way. Refuse to talk and we'll take you to our friends at Bow Street and have you up on charges of attempted murder. The penalty is hanging and I happen to be personally acquainted with the chief magistrate. Tell us what you know and we'll let you go free."

Both men let out rough laughs. "What do you take us for?" Julien's captive said.

"Men who know a good bargain when they see it."

"And what bloody guarantee do we have that you'd keep it?" the man demanded.

"My word. Who hired you?"

The pause before they spoke was long enough for a gust of

wind to shake the trees overhead and douse them with shards of ice.

"Don't know his name," said Julien's captive. "Gentleman. Leastways, spoke like one. We never did see his face. Not much of it, anyway. Met us in the alley behind the White Hart in St. Giles. He had his hat pulled low over his face and his coat collar turned up and he stood in the shadows. Sounded as though he had a cold."

"When was this?" Malcolm asked.

"'Bout six tonight. He told us the job and handed over the money. We were to have more sent to us tomorrow if we were successful."

"Successful at what?" Mélanie said.

The men fell silent again. Julien's captive rolled his gaze towards the knife Malcolm was holding to his throat. "Him—the one we jumped first—wasn't supposed to leave the park alive."

"The man who hired you told you I'd be in the park tonight?" Kitty asked.

"Sometime between nine and midnight." Julien's captive stared at her. "Bloody hell. You're a woman."

"Would that have made you turn down the job?"

"Well, it'd have made me think twice about it."

"What else did the man tell you?" Julien asked in a voice as even and lethal as the knife Malcolm held.

"Told us to wait by the Serpentine. Said we could keep all the money we found on him—her—but we were to bring him anything we found in writing. He made sure none of us could read."

"Where were you to find him again?" Kitty asked.

"We weren't. He said he'd find us."

Malcolm reached into his pocket, pulled out his card case, and flicked it open with one hand. He took the knife away from his captive's neck and held out a cream-colored card. "If this man ever contacts you again, you'll let me know."

The captive stared at him. Julien exchanged a look with Malcolm and undid the man's bonds. Kitty did the same for her prisoner.

"I did give you my word," Malcolm said to the two men.

The men stared at him a moment longer, as though perhaps the cloudy sky were obscuring his true motives. Then they turned and ran before Malcolm or any of the others could change their minds.

Kit stared at Malcolm. "Good God, Rannoch."

"I take my word rather seriously." Malcolm struggled out of his sodden greatcoat and squeezed the water from its folds.

"But they tried to kill Mrs. Ashford—"

"Malcolm's right," Kitty said. "It was professional, not personal. The sort of thing Julien might have done."

"'Have done' being the operative words," Julien said. "And not *precisely* the sort of thing."

"They were much less adept than you," Kitty said. "Thank goodness. But it would be a bit hypocritical to put them beyond the pale because of their skill level. Besides, I don't think any of us fancies having to explain ourselves to Bow Street."

"Quite," Malcolm said. His gaze suddenly sharpened in the moonlight. "Kitty—"

Julien had already moved. He caught Kitty as her knees gave way. "Stay with me, Kitkat. Mélanie!" His voice had a sharpness Mélanie had never heard before. He was tugging at his cravat one-handed while he held Kitty. "She's bleeding."

"A flesh wound," Kitty muttered, but she was sagging against Julien as he pressed the cravat to her chest. Malcolm yanked off his own cravat and gave it to Mélanie. Mélanie bent down and bound Malcolm's cravat over Julien's to staunch the bleeding. Malcolm held the bandage in place while Julien held Kitty.

"Two of them had pistols," Kitty said. "I managed to trick them into firing early, but one of the shots winged me. Then someone got me with a knife. Not the most organized of attacks. If they had hired a marksman to lie in wait in the trees with a rifle, he could have picked me off easily. Still, I suspect they'd have succeeded in the end if you hadn't all happened along. I'm all right, Julien."

"My intrepid darling, you're nothing of the sort."

Mélanie knotted off her makeshift bandage. The flow of talk didn't deceive her. She'd once seen Raoul direct an entire skirmish with a musket ball in his shoulder, only to collapse from loss of blood when the enemy were routed. Julien's and Malcolm's gazes said they knew the same. "You need to see a doctor," Mélanie said. "Or at least I need my medical supply box. Malcolm, you look quite fetching dripping wet, but it won't be very helpful if you catch pneumonia. We need to get inside."

"Yes," her husband said. "Kitty, can you walk as far as Berkeley Square? We can meet you and St. Juste there."

"Don't be ridiculous. Of course I can." Kitty's voice was level, but Mélanie was close enough to hear the labored sound of her breathing. "Meet you? Where are you going?"

Malcolm looked down at Kitty for a moment, face tight with concern, then glanced at Kit. "Where were you meeting the others?"

"Others?" Kit repeated. The fitful moonlight bounced off his gaze. He had been standing by in silence, as though torn between wanting to help, concern for Kitty's state of undress, and the quite sensible realization that there was little he could do.

"You and Kitty weren't meeting by the Serpentine," Malcolm said. "You were both on your way somewhere."

"Don't try to argue with him, Mr. Montagu." Kitty straightened her shoulders against Julien's chest, though she made no attempt to pull away from the curve of his arm. "It's time we told the truth." She regarded Malcolm for a moment. "You can do what you want with me, but do I have your word you won't turn my companions over to the law?"

"You know I can't promise that," Malcolm said.

"If you think they don't pose an imminent risk."

Malcolm was silent for a moment. "All right. Yes."

Kitty nodded. "I'm afraid it's a bit of a walk."

"For God's sake, Kitty—"

"I'm perfectly capable of walking." Kitty swiveled her head round. "Julien, you've always been a bit more sensible about these things than Malcolm. Tell him I'm not about to collapse."

Julien's brows were drawn but his mouth quirked slightly. "You wouldn't let yourself collapse."

"Precisely."

"Cold comfort," Malcolm said.

"The bandage stopped the bleeding," Mélanie said. "As long as we get a clean dressing on before infection sets in, she'll be all right."

"Thank you, Mélanie." Kitty pulled away from Julien. "Let's go."

Kit put out a hand as she stepped forwards. "Are you sure—"

"Yes," Kitty said.

Mélanie wasn't sure whether they were talking about Kitty's wounds or revealing whatever they were involved in. Or both.

Julien moved to Kitty's side and put his arm round her. Kitty made no attempt to pull away again. She led them away from the water, through a dark landscape where flashes of moonlight threw twisting tree branches into relief against a charcoal sky, to the walled Deer Pound. Three men were waiting, grouped tightly together. Difficult to tell for a certainty, but they appeared to be arguing. Suddenly, four additional men rushed onto the scene. One of the original three fell to the ground. Another launched a left hook at one of the newcomers. Kitty started forwards. Julien pulled her back. "They can handle it." He looked from Malcolm to Mélanie.

"Go." Kitty pushed Julien. "I promise I'll stay out of it."

Mélanie was already running, Malcolm beside her, Kit close

behind. Malcolm grabbed a man who was attacking a tall man with clear, sharp-cut features that were plain in the moonlight. Simon. Mélanie grabbed a branch and brought it down on the head of a second man grappling with a shorter, gray-haired man she'd never seen before. She looked up to see a third attacker rushing at Malcolm from behind with a knife drawn. One of Simon's companions ran between, grabbed the knife-wielder's wrist, and sent him spinning. In the same instant, Kit screamed and the fourth attacker went running, propelled by Julien.

The other three attackers hesitated a moment, then fled after their friend.

"Probably little sense in chasing them." Julien held out a hand to Kit, who had been knocked down. "I doubt they know more than the first group."

"Quite." Malcolm turned to the man who had rescued him from the knife-wielder. The man was turned away from Mélanie, but the angle of his shoulders brought a shock of recognition.

"O'Roarke," Malcolm said. "I have to say I didn't expect to find you here. Good evening, Simon." Unlike his greeting to Raoul, Malcolm's voice betrayed no surprise, but Mélanie could hear the fear and pain that underlay it.

A weight like a musket ball settled in her chest as she looked from Raoul to Simon.

"Hapgood." Malcolm addressed the gray-haired man, then turned to Mélanie. "Mr. Hapgood, who happens to own the building in which our friend Thornsby was lodging as Montford. Hapgood, my wife, Mélanie Rannoch. I assume the rest of you are all acquainted."

"Jesus, Malcolm," Simon said. "What happened to you?"

"Someone tried to kill Kitty." Malcom turned to Kitty, who had joined them in the Deer Pound. Julien was already at her side and had an arm round her again. "She's much worse off than I am, she's just better at hiding it."

Simon took a step towards Kitty. "Are you—"

"I'll live," Kitty said. "But I wasn't anticipating the attacks."

"None of us were," Simon said.

"It's time we told the truth," Kitty said. "Past time."

Simon met her gaze and gave a curt nod.

"Thank God," Raoul said.

Malcolm shot a look at him.

"He's not part of this," Kitty said. "He advised me to tell the truth some time ago. Well, actually this morning, but it seems like centuries ago. And like you and Mélanie, I assume he followed one of us tonight."

"Hapgood, actually," Raoul said.

"O'Roarke got here just before the attack," Simon said. "I don't know if you'll believe us—"

"I think I do." Malcolm looked at Raoul. "You wanted to warn them against us?"

"No," Raoul said. "Well, not exactly."

"As I said." Malcolm held his father's gaze for a moment.

"Explanations are undoubtedly called for," Kitty said, "but not here. Malcolm, do you think you can walk as far as Berkeley Square?"

"For God's sake, Kitty, I'm not the one who was shot and knifed."

"No, you were dunked in freezing water. You're obviously shivering, and as Mélanie said, you're at risk of pneumonia. But unlike you, I'll take your word for it that you can make it to Berkeley Square."

Julien grinned and tightened his arm round Kitty.

Mélanie took Malcolm's arm. "I'll catch him if he's about to collapse."

Kit looked among the group. "But—"

Raoul touched his arm. "Explanations later, as Mrs. Ashford said."

They trudged through the park, out the Grosvenor Gate and

past the cool white townhouses of Upper Grosvenor Street to Grosvenor Street and the wide expanse of Grosvenor Square. A party of guests emerged from one of the candlelit houses. Of one accord they all ducked into Charles Street to avoid being seen. God help them if they encountered any of their friends. Even her and Malcolm's reputation for eccentricity might not be able to live this down.

They continued along Grosvenor Street and turned down Davies Street. Malcolm had his arm round her. She could feel the shivers that wracked his body, and his steps were a trifle erratic, but he remained upright, as did Kitty. In a short time, Mélanie realized, she was going to have to confront the truth of whatever the hell Kitty and Simon and Kit had been involved in. Not to mention Raoul. And how Malcolm would react to it. And how she would react herself.

They were almost at the point where Davies Street met Berkeley Square when a voice stopped them. "Here now! What are you lot doing?"

It was a night watchman, lantern raised, brows drawn.

Malcolm seemed to have been concentrating solely on keeping his footing, but at that, he raised his head. "We're on our way home. My name's Rannoch. Malcolm Rannoch. My wife. And some of our friends. We've been at an entertainment."

The watchman gave a rough laugh. The lantern cast light over his ruddy face. "You expect me to believe—"

"Yes," said Malcolm. "I do."

The watchmen peered at them. His gaze moved past Mélanie, then came back to linger on her. There were advantages to having one's likeness displayed in print shop windows. "Bloody he—" He coughed. "Begging your pardon, ma'am. Madam. Mrs. Rannoch. Sorry to have troubled you."

Mélanie shepherded the erratic band up the steps to the fanlit door of the Berkeley Square house without further incident. Laura opened the door, relief evident on her face. Along with a number of questions.

"Kitty's been hurt," Mélanie said. "We should send to Hill Street for Geoffrey."

"Of course—" Laura began.

Kitty shook her head. "You can tend to it, Mélanie. You did an excellent job patching up Julien last month."

"This is worse."

"All the same. We don't want to bring anyone else into this. Even someone like Geoffrey Blackwell."

Mélanie had to concede that was a valid point. She nodded. "Go into the library. I'll get my medical supply box. Laura, could you boil some water? Malcolm, you need to change before you do anything else or you'll be ill. Raoul, can you hunt up dry clothes for the others?"

She started upstairs to get her medical box without waiting to see if they acceded to her requests.

CHAPTER 21

"You can stop being brave now," Mélanie said, when she and Malcolm were in the privacy of their bedchamber. She'd already picked up her medical box, but when she saw how Malcolm's hands were shaking, she tugged off his coat and went to work on his waistcoat buttons with more dexterity than she'd ever shown in an amorous encounter.

"I'll live." He pulled his shirt over his head. "Kitty could have been killed."

"It was horrible." She grabbed a towel from the washstand and wrapped it round him. "But she wasn't. As long as the wound heals cleanly, she'll be fine."

"This time."

"The same's true for all of us." She handed him a fresh shirt, then began to fumble with the clasps on her pelisse, which was not exactly dry either. "There's no doubt Thornsby was lodging with Mr. Hapgood?"

"Hapgood admitted as much to Roth and me this afternoon, though not that he knew who Thornsby really was."

Mélanie pulled off her pelisse. "What do you think—"

"No sense in speculating until we talk to them." He looked at the torn lace on her sleeve. "You're going to have a bruise on your shoulder."

"Minor damage. I'll mend, and Blanca can mend the gown."

He stretched out a hand to touch her face. "We listen to the evidence and we each make up our own mind and act as we see fit. Same as we've always done."

"And if we make up our minds differently?"

Malcolm pulled on his dressing gown. "It won't be the first time we've been on opposite sides. Only this time, the battle will be out in the open."

Laura had already brought in a jug of hot water by the time Mélanie got to the library. Laura or Julien had given Kitty a glass of whisky, which Kitty was sipping as though determined to prove she could hold her hand steady. Julien sat beside her on the sofa, gaze trained on her, not touching her, but a hands-breadth away. The others hadn't come down yet.

"I'll make coffee," Laura said. "I imagine everyone could use it. Along with whisky."

Kitty gave a faint smile. She had got her coat and waistcoat off. The makeshift bandage was stained red, as was the shirt, but the blood had begun to dry. Mélanie set down her medical supply box and also a clean dressing gown she had brought with her. "Do you mind if we cut the shirt? It will be easier."

"By all means," Kitty said.

The bullet scrape on her shoulder really was little more than a scratch. The knife cut was more serious. The bandage was soaked through with blood, but the wound appeared to have stopped bleeding. It was a long, jagged cut, but it did not appear particularly deep. It would not require stitches. Mélanie doused a towel with vinegar. Julien reached for Kitty's hand. Kitty's fingers closed round his own, white-knuckled, but she sat still while Mélanie cleaned and bandaged the wound.

"The dressing needs to be changed twice a day," Mélanie said, knotting off the ends of the new bandage.

Julien nodded. He was holding the linen steady while she tied it.

"Compresses at night would be good." Mélanie snipped off the ends. "And if you don't want to go to a doctor, come back to see me in two days."

"Given what we're all involved in, I suspect I'll see you well before that," Kitty said. "You're a wonder, Mélanie, thank you. Now perhaps you could hand me that dressing gown you were kind enough to bring before the others come in? Malcolm and Raoul and Simon and even Mr. Hapgood would be all right, but I think poor Mr. Montagu would be shocked to find me in déshabille."

With Mélanie's and Julien's help, Kitty was discreetly swathed in the rose-colored silk dressing gown and holding a refilled glass of whisky by the time Malcolm rapped at the door and then ushered in Simon, Hapgood, Kit, and Raoul. Simon and Hapgood had removed their greatcoats and wore their own clothes, now very nearly dry. Raoul, like Malcolm, was wearing a dressing gown over a clean shirt and trousers. Kit was clad in a shirt and trousers of Malcolm's.

"I'm quite back in one piece," Kitty said with a smile that would charm the most hostile diplomat. "Mélanie can work wonders."

Laura came in with the coffee tray as they all seated themselves. Raoul took it from her and set it on the sofa table.

"Right," Malcolm said, as Laura and Raoul poured out the coffee and passed it round. "We can talk while everyone gets settled. What were you doing in the park?"

Simon carried his coffee cup over to the drinks trolley and splashed brandy into it. "This is your scene, Malcolm. You're always explaining how the criminals orchestrated the crime. Surely we deserve as much."

"All right," Malcolm said. "But it's largely supposition."

"Isn't it always?"

Malcolm drew a breath, sharp enough that Mélanie looked up from adding milk to her coffee. His damp hair fell over his forehead in the way that always made him look like a schoolboy, but his face was uncharacteristically hard. "You and Kitty and Hapgood and Kit are involved in something. Exactly what, we aren't sure, save that it has to do with a series of Radical disturbances in recent months. And that Carfax fits in somewhere."

"What—" Simon clunked the brandy decanter down. "Never mind. Go on."

"Thornsby was interested in the disturbances. He'd found a coded list of them and decoded it. He confronted Kitty about something, probably to do with the disturbances, and also wrote to her. He may be an agent provocateur working for Carfax or the League. Will Carmarthen fits in somehow, but I'm not sure if he's working with you or is an agent provocateur as well, or if he's simply an innocent bystander caught up in the whole thing."

Kitty drew a sharp breath, but that might have been because she'd shifted and pulled on her wound.

Simon strode back into the center of the library. "Look, Malcolm, your story's a coherent scenario. As a dramatist, I appreciate the narrative construction. But as one of the principals, I feel compelled to point out that it contains barely a shred of truth."

Malcolm folded his arms and regarded the man who had been one of his closest friends for over a decade. "Then tell me your version of the truth."

Kitty and Simon exchanged glances. Simon inclined his head at Kitty.

"I need hardly tell you that freedom of the press is in considerably worse straits in Spain now than it is in England," Kitty said. "Which is saying a lot. But a number of Spanish journalists are writing things that need to be said. And heard. Including friends of mine. Friends of yours." She looked at Malcolm. "Flavio Ruiz. Hector Quimeso. The articles they're writing are things that the British Government would also be quick to suppress, given the chance. They both sent papers to me in December. I told them I'd do my best to see the articles published."

"And you did see them published, didn't you?" Malcolm was watching Kitty intently. "There've been a number of pamphlets of articles from Spain circulating recently. I actually wondered if Raoul was involved. I should have guessed you were. And you went to Simon?"

"I didn't have the resources to have them printed on my own. I'd already got myself in trouble in Argentina for publishing my own pamphlets. Julien remembers." Kitty cast a brief look at Julien who was sitting quietly beside her. He was watching Kitty with an intent gaze that gave little away, but Mélanie was fairly sure most of this was news to him too. Kitty touched his hand, then looked back at Malcolm. "Simon and I had talked about the situation in Spain, and his frustration at Britain's lack of support for those seeking change and fears that Britain could intervene on the other side. From the things he said, and what I'd heard about the Levellers, I assumed not only did he know printers, but he probably knew some who would print not just plays, but papers that the government might be interested in suppressing."

Malcolm's gaze moved from Kit to Hapgood.

"I have a press in my basement," Hapgood said. "Used for unofficial purposes."

"And you—" Malcolm turned to Kit.

"Did the odd bit to help out," Kit said. "I'm actually the one who knew Hapgood first. He published some pamphlets of mine a couple of years ago."

"The ones that caused you to have to flee Britain for Italy."

"Er—yes. I introduced Hapgood to Simon."

Kitty took a drink of whisky with tight fingers. "Getting these articles published has become even more vital since the mutiny in Spain. I received more recently that were particularly explosive." She hesitated a moment, looked at Raoul for the first time since she'd begun her story, looked back at Malcolm. "They're notes of secret meetings Carfax had with counterparts from Spain and Italy about the possibility of British intervention if the revolutionaries take control."

Malcolm drew a breath. Mélanie met her husband's gaze across the room. On the one hand, it was hardly surprising. Of course any rumblings of revolution would make Carfax think about interfering. They already knew he'd been gathering information on the Carbonari and about the revolutionaries in Spain. On the other hand, technically the British government was committed to nonintervention.

Mélanie glanced at Raoul. The connection to Spain potentially put him more in the middle of this, but he was sitting by quietly, gaze shifting between Simon and Kitty.

"Getting those notes printed would make it more challenging for Britain to interfere." Malcolm looked at Raoul. "How much did you know about this?"

"I told you." Raoul was sitting very still on the sofa. Laura was equally still beside him. "I didn't know what they were doing until tonight."

"I know what you told me. That was before we knew this was about Spain. And notes of secret meetings."

"I'm not the one who intercepted the notes. More's the pity. I knew Quimeso and some of the others had sent papers to Britain. I suspected what Kitty and Simon and Hapgood and Kit were doing. But I didn't have proof. And I wasn't part of it." He took a drink of coffee. "Not that I wouldn't have been if asked."

"We couldn't have asked you to keep secrets from Malcolm." Perhaps surprisingly, it wasn't Simon who said it, but Kitty.

"It would be far from the first time," Malcolm said. "Or the last, I suspect.

"Still," Raoul said. "It's appreciated."

"It's the truth," Kitty said. "And what Raoul told you is true. Unless you think we're all making this up for some reason."

"No." Malcolm turned his cup in his hands. "It may be folly for me, of all people, to talk about knowing people, but I think I know you all well enough to recognize a story that has the ring of truth." He looked at Simon. "Why in God's name didn't you tell me?"

"Why the hell do you think?" Simon said. "For the same reason I didn't tell David. You're both in Parliament. Supposedly upholding the law of the land. It would be a rather ugly burden to inform you I was in the process of breaking it. Besides—"

"You weren't sure what we'd do?"

"To be blunt, no."

"Jesus, Simon." Malcolm's gaze locked on his friend's. "We're on the same side."

"Sides get a bit blurry."

"I think we've established that we're both opposed to Carfax."

"Who was conducting British government business in these meetings, even if unofficially. Those are the sorts of missions he used to send you on."

"He used to send Kitty on them too." Malcolm's gaze shifted to his former comrade and lover.

"Fair enough," Kitty said. "We've all changed. But I'm not part of the government."

"No," Malcolm said. "But I wouldn't—"

"Aren't you always saying no one can be sure what anyone would do under the right circumstances?" Kitty asked.

Simon scraped a hand over his hair. "And Carfax is David's father. Just as Kitty and I both knew we couldn't ask O'Roarke to keep secrets from you, I couldn't put David in the position of knowing in advance we were about to publish notes of his father's meetings. Of course, you could also say I shouldn't have published them at all on those grounds. But I couldn't hold back either."

"No," Malcolm said, and though he didn't look at Mélanie she knew he was thinking of their conversation just now in the bedchamber. "I can see that. And David wouldn't want you to act differently."

"I hope so," Simon said. "I also couldn't ask you to lie to David. Not after everything else the two of you have been through."

Malcolm inclined his head. Then he looked from Kitty to Simon. "Where does Thornsby fit into it?"

"I wish to God I knew," Kitty said.

"You mean he wasn't in on the plot?"

"Thornsby?" Simon shook his head. "He was far too impulsive for anything of the sort. At least, he seemed to be."

Malcolm turned to Hapgood. "Thornsby was staying in your house."

"I know. Now. Thanks to you and Mr. Roth."

"You mean you didn't know it until Roth and I called on you?"

"How should I? He called himself Montford, as I told you."

"Simon would have recognized him. Or Kit. Or Kitty." Malcolm's gaze swept the three of them.

"I never saw him," Simon said. "I didn't even know Hapgood had a tenant."

"Nor did I," Kit said.

Kitty took a sip of whisky. She was still pale but her hands were steadier. Julien sat watching her closely, probably both to monitor her health and to appraise her story. "I never went to Hapgood's at all," Kitty said. "That was why we were meeting in the park tonight. It was the first time I met Mr. Hapgood." She smiled at Hapgood. "I haven't thanked you for your assistance yet, have I? Or apologized for what I pulled you into."

Hapgood flashed a smile at her. "My life is quiet enough, Mrs. Ashford. I appreciate some adventure." He looked back at Malcolm. "Montford—Thornsby—wasn't home much. Which makes more sense, now I know he was leading a double life."

Malcolm met Hapgood's gaze and nodded. "Do you think he was spying on you?"

Hapgood stared into his coffee cup, brows drawing together. "I didn't at the time. Would have taken action if I had. But thinking back—I found him in the shop one day, turning the pages of a book in the classics section. Said he was reliving moments from his undergraduate days. Didn't think so much of it. But in retrospect—After you and Mr. Roth visited me this afternoon, and I learned Montford had been living a double life and had been murdered, I had all sorts of questions. I wasn't sure why the devil he'd lodged with me or who he was, but it all began to look a bit suspicious. I sent messages to Tanner and Montagu and Mrs. Ashford suggesting we meet this evening."

Malcolm scraped a hand through his hair. "That's such an implausible story it almost has to be the truth as well."

"Or a very, very clever lie," Julien said.

"That too," Malcolm said.

Hapgood reached for his coffee cup. "I can't answer for the others, but I'm not that good a liar."

"Somehow I doubt that, Mr. Hapgood. And yet—" Malcolm regarded the bookseller, then turned his gaze to Mélanie. She stared back at him. He'd said they'd both make up their minds for themselves. But she couldn't be any surer of her own mind than he could of his.

"Surely it's occurred to you that he could have deliberately chosen to lodge at Hapgood's without being in league with us," Kitty said. "We could be his targets, not his accomplices."

"Oh, it's occurred to me," Malcolm said. "And I admit it looks more likely now." He watched her for a moment. "Sofia

Vincenzo heard you quarreling with Thornsby. What was it really about?"

"I told you—"

"I know what you told me."

Kitty drew a sharp breath, glanced at Julien, winced again. Perhaps at the pull on her wound. Perhaps not. "I told Malcolm that Lewis Thornsby and I spent an unexpected night together when you were away. That he had to make more of it than it was to justify his behavior so he decided he fancied himself in love with me."

"Well, that's one way to account for it," Julien said. "I'd have thought you could come up with something better. So perhaps it's the truth."

"That's what I tried to tell Malcolm. He was convinced I was lying. But Malcolm's inclined to romanticize things."

"Which neither you nor I is," Julien said.

"Sofia said you and Thornsby didn't sound like people who'd ever been intimate," Mélanie said.

"Sofia is an astute young woman," Kitty said. "But no one can be sure in such a situation. But—oh, poison. I don't know if it's Malcolm or Sofia, or sitting here beside Julien, or the fact that I almost died tonight and I really don't want my legacy to be that all of you think I dallied with Thornsby." She hunched her shoulders and took a sip of whisky. "Sofia's right. I never slept with him. I scarcely even talked to him until Thornsby confronted me the night before last and said he knew Kit and Simon and I were involved in something. He said he wanted to help. When I implied that the best help he could give was by staying out of it, he implied that if he couldn't be sure of what we were doing, he might have to tell someone else to make sure it wasn't something treasonous. I told him I had to talk to the others and promised to send word to him soon. When I got home, I sent him a note asking him to meet me at the White Rose in two days—this morning. That's the note Malcolm found. I had to think quickly and make up something when Malcolm confronted me about it. I didn't do very well. And then I asked Mr. Montagu to back my story up." She looked at Kit. "I'm sorry for putting you in that position."

Kit swallowed. "I wanted to help. But—"

"Don't look at me," Julien said. "I should be the least of anyone's concern in this."

Kitty regarded her lover. "Are you going to tell them the rest?"

The candlelight seemed to bounce off Julien's eyes. "What rest?"

"That Simon and I were meeting in the Tavistock the night Thornsby was killed. Possibly while Thornsby was killed." She shivered. "I assume you showed up so promptly after Mélanie discovered the body because you were following me."

Julien shifted his position on the sofa. "Yes, as it happens. Call it professional curiosity. Or perhaps personal curiosity would be more accurate."

"And then you followed me again tonight."

"It seemed the best way to learn what was going on."

Kitty's gaze raked his face. "How did you know—No, I suppose it would be better to ask how you could *not* know something."

Malcolm looked from Kitty to Simon. "When did you get to the theatre?"

"About six," Simon said. "Kitty sent me a note in the morning to meet her after rehearsal."

"I was trying to work out what to say to Thornsby the next day," Kitty said.

"Which of you got to the theatre first?" Malcolm asked.

"I did," Simon said. "I waited in the alley until Kitty arrived. We went inside and down to my office. We didn't see or hear anyone. But we also didn't search the theatre."

Malcolm nodded. "And then?"

"We talked for about half an hour. We agreed that this made it even more imperative to get the notes of Carfax's meetings with Spanish and Italian officials printed and out into the world. Kitty said she'd stall Thornsby as long as she could. I walked back upstairs with Kitty at about six-thirty. I still had some papers to go through, so I locked up behind Kitty and went back down to my office."

"That fits with what I saw," Julien said. "I followed Kitty and took up watch in the theatre, though I didn't risk going close enough to overhear them. I saw Tanner let her out. I waited a bit because I had it in mind to look round the theatre. And I thought Kitty might notice if I followed her home."

"I woefully failed to notice your following me there," Kitty said.

"You were preoccupied. I didn't want to press my luck. After a while, when Tanner was still absorbed in his papers, I decided it was safe to venture out. I heard Mélanie and the children when I did. And judging by the condition of Thornsby's body, he must have been dead by the time Tanner and Kitty arrived. So unless the three of us are involved in something together, you have a timeline, and we're in the clear. At least Kitty and Tanner are. I supposed I could have killed him earlier."

"Any of us could have killed him earlier," Kitty said.

"You couldn't," Julien said. "You were with me the rest of the day."

"We'd have to have been in on it together," Kitty said. "And my having to meet Thornsby the next morning gives me a motive."

"And me," Simon said.

"And me," Julien added.

Kitty looked at him.

"There's a lot I'd do for you, sweetheart. But I think Malcolm realizes at least Tanner would have had qualms about cold-blooded murder."

Kit shifted in his chair. "Er—" He coughed and took a drink of coffee. "You showed me a list earlier today, Malcolm. A list of Radical disturbances, including the one where Will Carmarthen got arrested. You said you found it in Thornsby's rooms. Is that true?"

"Yes," Malcolm said.

"And so you assumed that Thornsby had something to do with the disturbances."

"I didn't assume it. It was one explanation. We're still trying to figure out the meaning of the list."

"Yes. I may be able to shed some light on that." Kit turned his cup in his hand. "Thornsby approached me two days ago as well."

"In the theatre?" Mélanie asked.

Kit's eyes widened.

"Brandon overheard some of it."

"You didn't say."

"We didn't find out until this afternoon."

Kit gave a quick nod. "I don't know how much Brandon overheard, but I found Thornsby going through papers in Simon's office."

"What?" Simon said.

"I know," Kit said. "When I accused him, Thornsby told me he thought he had evidence Carfax had engaged agents provocateurs who were behind several violent incidents at recent Radical events. I asked him why he was going through Simon's things. He said he knew some of us were involved in something else and he wanted in. He basically offered to trade his evidence about the agents provocateurs for letting him in on what we were doing. Which didn't really make sense if he was on our side. I said there wasn't anything to let him in on, and he said he knew I was lying. I asked him what evidence he had about the agents provocateurs. He said he could bring it to me tomorrow. I was going to wait and see what he had before I told anyone else. But then the next night he was killed." Kit looked at Malcolm. "I was waiting at the White Rose to talk to him when Roth's constable came in, and I learned Thornsby had been killed. That's why I went to search his lodgings. I couldn't tell you without unraveling the whole plan to publish the papers. I couldn't make that decision on my own. I was waiting for tonight to talk to Simon and Kitty. I told myself one day's delay wouldn't ruin things."

"A day can be vital in an investigation," Malcolm said. "But I do see your dilemma. Given that none of you trusted me."

"It's not as simple as trusting, Malcolm," Kitty said. "You should know that better than anyone." She looked at Kit. "Thornsby seems to have been extremely eager to be part of what we were doing. If he wasn't working for Carfax, I wonder why."

"If he wasn't working for Carfax, as looks increasingly likely, he may well have been working for the League," Malcolm said. "The League are eager for evidence to use against Carfax. This doesn't seem quite of a level that would warrant such seriousness. But you were attacked tonight."

"Who knew all of you were meeting in the park tonight?" Mélanie asked.

Kitty, Simon, Kit, and Hapgood exchanged glances.

"Only ourselves," Simon said.

Malcolm looked at Kitty. "Is this the first time you've been attacked since you've been in London?"

Kitty took a sip of whisky. "Don't you think I'd have told you if I had been?"

"Not necessarily."

"Possibly not. But as it happens, I wasn't." She looked at Julien. "Julien can attest that these are the first injuries I've received in some time."

Julien returned her gaze steadily. "That doesn't mean you haven't been attacked without being injured. And let's not even attempt to pretend you'd have told me if you had been. You wouldn't be the woman I love if that were true."

Kitty's gaze widened and locked on his own. She shook her head as though this wasn't the time to examine his words. "I might have told you."

Julien lifted her hand to his lips, then folded it between his own. "Might."

Kitty looked from him to Malcolm. "You'll both just have to take my word for it. As Malcolm's said, sometimes we do have to trust each other."

"Your printing pamphlets of Carfax's secret meetings changes things."

"But surely—" Laura had been sitting by in concerned silence, but now she spoke. "I can see Carfax's not wanting the pamphlets printed, but his wanting to work against revolution in Spain and Italy is hardly surprising, as Malcolm said. Would he really have people attacked to stop something getting out that confirms what most people suspect?"

"Officially, the British government is committed to nonintervention on the Continent," Malcolm said. "Some government ministers would like to intervene, I suspect, but it's far from unanimous. If France decided to move into Spain to help their Bourbon cousins and Britain backed them, we'd essentially be supporting exactly what we fought Napoleon for doing."

"What Britain allegedly fought Napoleon for doing," Raoul said.

"Yes, there's that. But there's also concern that Tsar Alexander might use intervening in Spain or Italy as an excuse to move Russian troops deeper into the Continent."

"Carfax wouldn't need an army to do the sort of thing he does," Kitty said.

"No, but if it became public, there'd be more attention on him. The whole issue would be brought to the fore. Which could make it harder for him to do the sort of thing he wants to do behind the scenes. On the other hand, as Kit brought up, Thornsby seemed eager to get his hands on the papers. He was working for someone. That someone—perhaps the League—could have been behind the attacks tonight. The question is why the papers are so important."

"You said you asked for more proof, Kit," Mélanie said. "Perhaps the drawing of the rifle trajectory that Thornsby had was part of the proof."

"You think Carfax was going to have an agent provocateur assassinate a member of the royal family?" Kit asked in horror.

"I wouldn't put it past him, if he thought the payoff was sufficient," Julien said. "But it's more likely he meant to have the plot foiled at the last minute. If there is a plot. It does look more as though we have a pattern of agent provocateur attacks."

"Thornsby got the coded list somewhere," Malcolm said. "He could have got the drawing from the same source. But we still have the fact that if whoever killed him knew about the drawing, they must have wanted us to find it. Which argues against the person he got the drawing from being the person who killed him. If—"

He broke off as the library door opened abruptly. "I'm sorry," Valentin said. "But Mr. Laclos is in the hall with Miss Russo and Mr. Smythe. Mr. Benedict Smythe. Normally I'd have bought them right in, but—" He hesitated.

But Kitty was wounded and in déshabille, and he wasn't sure if all of those in the room were meant to be seen. Valentin had impeccable instincts. "Send them in," Mélanie said, wondering what other surprises the night could possibly hold.

CHAPTER 22

Valentin shot Mélanie a quick grin and shortly after ushered Bertrand Laclos, Nerezza Russo, and Benedict Smythe into the library. They were all still wrapped in their outer garments, as though they'd been in too much of a hurry to relinquish them to Valentin. Nerezza's bright red hair was coming unpinned. Bertrand and Benedict looked as though they'd tugged their hats off without ceremony. Bertrand had been in and out of London all month, but Nerezza and Ben had been remaining in seclusion at the Cotswolds estate of Bertrand's lover Rupert Caruthers. Nerezza had fled Italy with Sofia's help in December after helping the Carbonari in Naples and running afoul of the minister of police, only to learn that the Elsinore League—or at least one faction in the League—were trying to have her killed for reasons that had yet to be explained.

The new arrivals stopped short, even Bertrand, who was usually equal to anything, taken aback by the crowd in the library.

"It's been an interesting evening," Malcolm said. "I think you know everyone but Mr. Hapgood." He introduced the three new arrivals to Hapgood as they seated themselves. "We're in the midst of an investigation."

"Yes, that's why we've come," Bertrand said.

"I insisted he bring us." Nerezza tugged at the ties on her cloak. She was sitting bolt upright on a settee. "It's true about Mr. Thornsby?"

"I'm afraid so." Malcolm looked at Benedict, who was sitting beside Nerezza. "I'm sorry. You must have been friends. I saw Roger today and he said your families were close."

"Good God." Ben dug his fingers into his thick fair hair. "I never thought—yes, I'd known Lewis forever. We had different circles of friends at university, but we were still friends. I just saw him—"

Nerezza reached for Ben's hand. He twined his fingers round her own. "I wish you could have talked to him that last time," she said. "You couldn't because you were so busy hiding me. Which is why we've come. Because I recognized Mr. Thornsby."

"You knew him?" Malcolm asked in surprise. Nerezza had been in Italy until a month ago.

"Yes. No. Not really." Nerezza folded Ben's hand between both her own. "I saw him in the theatre the night all of you hid me. I didn't say anything about it at the time, there was too much going on. But later, after we got to Rupert and Bertrand's house I asked Ben about him. Because I recognized him."

"From where?" Malcolm hesitated. "Was—"

Nerezza, always direct, gave a quick smile. "No, I wasn't involved with him too. That would be a bit too much. But I saw him in Italy. We never spoke. But he knew a man I was involved with." She cast a quick glance at Ben. He smiled at her. "I saw them talking."

"Who was the man?"

"Alexander Radford." Nerezza accepted a cup of coffee from Laura. "I haven't heard anything else about Mr.

Thornsby or Alexander Radford since I got to Britain. Mr. Radford doesn't seem to be connected to Beverston or any of the others, so I didn't think about it particularly until I heard Mr. Thornsby had been murdered. It could all be a coincidence, but Bertrand thinks Mr. Thornsby was one of the Levellers, and you told me the League are targeting the Levellers—"

"Yes," Malcolm said.

Nerezza took a quick drink of coffee. "Is Thornsby's death connected to the Levellers?"

"It looks increasingly likely it is," Malcolm said. "And we know the League are targeting you. Presumably because of something you know or saw in Italy. And it doesn't seem to be to do with Beverston, unless he's playing a very complicated game, as he helped save your life and get you away."

Benedict was frowning. A month since he'd never heard of the Levellers or known of Nerezza's connection to his father. "You say there are two factions in this Elsinore League."

"At least two," Malcolm said.

"And my father's involved with one, and someone else you don't know is running the other and trying to take control of the League."

"Apparently." Malcolm looked at Julien.

"Don't look at me, I'm a lot of things, but I'm not a League member," Julien said.

"You're in closer communication with them than the rest of us," Malcolm said.

"They've tried to engage my services. I don't think they have an illusion they can do so anymore."

"But my sister still manages to have their confidence. Or at least, a way to talk to some of them." Malcolm continued to watch Julien. "And she'll talk to you more than to me."

"Family can be complicated."

"It's all right," Malcolm said. "That is, it's not really all right at all, but I know Gelly's doing something she doesn't feel she can share. And I respect that she has her reasons."

"My brother was working for the Elsinore League," Benedict said. "John. But not for the same faction as Father."

"Apparently," Julien said. "That's not based on any inside information but on what we all saw in the alley by the Tavistock in December." The night Julien had stepped in front of an assassin's bullet to save Nerezza, and Beverston had shot the assassin.

"But John was betraying the League to Carfax," Benedict said.

"That much seems clear," Malcolm said.

"So how much does Carfax know?"

Malcolm exchanged a look with Julien and then with Mélanie and then with Raoul. "An excellent question."

"The Elsinore League are after Nerezza." Benedict took a drink of coffee without looking down at the cup in his hands. "Did they have Lewis killed too?"

"Possibly." It was Julien who answered this time. "Or he may have been working for them."

"It doesn't sound like that would have stopped them from killing him," Nerezza said.

"An excellent point," Malcolm said.

"*Lewis* was an agent?" Ben said.

"He seems to have been. He'd set up a second identity under the name Montford."

"*Lewis,*" Ben repeated.

"People can surprise you," Bertrand said.

Benedict turned to look at Bertrand. "Yes, but you're—I mean, all of you—" He gestured round the company. "You all have a knack for it. Lewis was just—Lewis."

"Sometimes the greatest skill is making people think one doesn't have any skills at all," Bertrand said.

"What did this Alexander Radford, whom you saw Thornsby talking to, look like?" Malcolm asked.

Nerezza frowned. "Middle height. Not as tall as you—about Mr. St. Juste's height. Sandy hair. Hazel eyes. Sharp hazel eyes. They looked blue in some lights and green in others. Middle years—about Mr. O'Roarke's age, maybe a bit older. He always seemed to be laughing at the world."

"Did he say anything about his life? Where he was from in England?"

"You don't recognize his name?"

"No." Malcolm glanced at the others. They all shook their heads.

"It may have been an alias," Malcolm said. "But sometimes even undercover people will reveal details about themselves. I know I've done so."

"Sometimes it's easier to reveal things undercover than in one's own persona," Raoul said.

Nerezza's frown deepened. "He said the English could be a stuffy lot, and that he wouldn't have thought he'd miss Britain, but at times he did."

"That sounds like me," Julien said.

Several sharp looks were directed at him.

"I didn't mean it *was* me," Julien said. "Nerezza obviously knows it wasn't."

"You're assuming she'd recognize you," Kitty said. "She wouldn't if you didn't want her to."

"I'm not sure about that," Julien said. "Go on, Nerezza, what else did this so-called Alexander Radford tell you?"

"That he'd once thought he had to run from the past to be safe but that he'd realized the only true way to safety, if there was one, was to vanquish the past."

"Easier said than done," Julien murmured.

"That the two people he'd loved most in his life were perhaps his greatest enemy and the product of his greatest betrayal." She looked among them. "He talked a lot. Mostly in—" She glanced at Ben. "When he was tired. I couldn't make sense of most of what he said. I think you're right that that's why he felt he could talk to me."

"One often does," Mélanie said. "With someone you think you'll only see for a night or a week or even a month. It's a sort of escape."

Malcolm shot a look at her and nodded with understanding. That was Malcolm. He never judged.

"He sounds like an interesting man," Laura said. "And a complicated one."

"Could he—" Benedict looked round the room. "Could this man be the leader of the other faction in the Elsinore League?"

The room went still with the silence of a missing puzzle piece clicking into place.

"I mean," Ben said, "he seems to have been keeping secrets and Nerezza knew him, and this faction in the League want Nerezza dead, apparently because of something she knows, and if it's that she knows this man, perhaps that she could recognize him—"

"You're very astute, Benedict," Raoul said.

"It's just a thought," Ben said. "I mean, you all know better than I do—"

"It's a damnably acute thought," Malcolm said. "You may have stumbled on a truth none of us had quite managed to piece together."

"It wouldn't have made sense without my story about Mr. Radford," Nerezza said. "But if he's the one trying to have me killed—" She broke off. "It's an odd thought. I mean, I knew someone was trying to have me killed, but the idea that it's someone I knew—" Ben put an arm round her. Nerezza reached up to squeeze his hand. "But if Mr. Radford is the one trying to have me killed, is he also the one who had Mr. Thornsby killed? Because Mr. Thornsby seemed to be friendly with him. In fact, now I know about the League, I'd say Mr. Thornsby perhaps was working for him."

"That seems increasingly likely," Malcolm said. "But as you said, that doesn't mean Mr. Radford didn't have Thornsby killed."

"To keep his identity secret?" Ben asked. "That's why we think he's after Nerezza, right? Because she could recognize him?"

"That seems likeliest," Bertrand said. "Or it could be that he thinks he revealed something to her that could be used against him."

"Do you think Carfax knows about Alexander Radford?" Simon asked Malcolm.

"I don't know," Malcolm said. "But for a number of reasons, I need to talk to him. As soon as possible."

Simon looked steadily at Malcolm across the library. "Are you going to tell him about the papers?"

Malcolm returned Simon's gaze, his own equally steady. "How soon can you get the papers published?"

Simon, Kitty, and Kit all looked at Hapgood. "If I set type tonight, we can have them out tomorrow," Hapgood said.

Malcolm nodded. "Good. Mélanie and I promised we'd share what information we could with Carfax. Which doesn't mean everything. And much as secrecy may complicate an investigation, those papers need to be published. As quickly as possible."

CHAPTER 23

Malcolm came downstairs from putting on a neckcloth, waistcoat, and coat to call on Carfax, to find Mélanie and Kitty in the library. Mélanie had invited anyone who wished to to spend the night, and Nerezza and Ben had taken her up on it. Bertrand was going to the London house he shared with Rupert, but it was still partially closed up, for though Rupert had returned to London for Parliament, the rest of the family were in the country. Laura had taken Nerezza and Ben upstairs to get settled. Bertrand had taken Simon, Kit, and Hapgood home in the carriage he'd arrived in. Raoul and Julien had gone to the mews to ready one of the Rannoch carriages for Kitty and Julien.

"I told Julien I was perfectly capable of walking, but he insisted," Kitty said. "I never thought I'd say this about Julien, but he's inclined to fuss."

"You're not in fighting condition and I'd hate to see St. Juste have to manage attackers on his own," Malcolm said.

Kitty smiled.

Mélanie got up from the sofa where she'd been sitting beside Kitty and moved to the door. "I know it's only a short distance, but you'll attract too much notice if you get in and out of a carriage in a dressing gown. I'll get you a gown and pelisse you can put on easily."

Which was very adroitly done, Malcolm thought, but perhaps designed to allow him to talk to Kitty. He looked at her as the library doors closed behind Mel. She was still pale but some color had returned to her cheeks.

Kitty reached for her whisky. "Don't you start fussing too, Malcolm. At least not more than you already have."

Malcolm set his greatcoat—thank God he had two, because the first was still drenched—over a chair back. "I knew it."

"That we were publishing articles from Spain?"

"No, I didn't have the least idea of that, and confess I imagined something far more alarming. That there was an explanation other than the one you gave me for your interaction with Thornsby."

Kitty shook her head, setting unpinned strands of dark gold hair falling about her face. "It doesn't mean I'm what you thought I was, Malcolm. Just that, in this particular case, I didn't violate your principles."

Malcolm pulled a chair closer to the sofa where she sat. "You can violate my principles as much as you want. You don't owe me anything. It's your own principles I'm concerned with. Because of how that will make you feel about yourself."

Kitty took a sip of whisky. "Darling Malcolm. You're assuming that I have principles."

"You do, sweetheart. Far more than you'll let on. Among other things, they made you send me away eight years ago."

Kitty set the glass down on the sofa table by Mélanie's medical box. "But I did that to protect myself."

"I'm arrogant enough to think I had something to do with it."

"Oh, of course, you did, Malcolm. But that doesn't mean I'm a figure of romance, or that my relationship with Julien is the sort of fairytale happily-ever-after that yours with Mélanie is."

Malcolm gave a whoop of laughter. "Now who's talking in romantic terms? My relationship with Mel is a lot of things—including the core of my life—but it's far from a fairy tale, and how can we talk about anything ever-after when we're still muddling through life?"

Kitty smiled, head tilted to one side. "It's a matter of perspective. You and Mélanie are living a fairy tale compared to anything Julien or I could imagine. But then, we don't all want the same thing."

"Precisely. Mel and I are still working out what we want. You and St. Juste have a lot of time to work it out for yourselves."

"Even if that doesn't include each other?" Kitty smoothed the sleeve of her borrowed dressing gown. "That will disappoint you, won't it?"

"I hardly think what does or doesn't disappoint me should have anything to do with what you want." He reached forwards to tuck her hair behind her ear, where it had fallen loose from its pins. "I want you to be happy, Kit. Whatever that works out to be."

Kitty shook her head. "Oh, Malcolm. Since when have I had the luxury of thinking about happiness?"

SIMON LET himself into the Craven house in Brook Street with his latchkey. That is, it had been the Craven house. The home of David's sister Louisa and her husband, Lord Craven, a rather cold house in more ways than one and not particularly like a home, despite the presence of four children. It was less cold now, and not just because of the thick red-and-gold Turkey rug they had added in the hall. And it was starting to feel like home, Simon realized as he closed the door, much as their flat in the Albany once had done. That precious flat had symbolized his and David's ability to craft a life together. He'd have sworn leaving the flat would have meant they had lost the chance of sharing a life together. And yet here they were, raising four children in what had once seemed a cold mansion.

A lamp burned on the hall table and a light shone from the library. The footmen and Tim Marston, who had been David's valet since Oxford, would have gone to bed long since. As the Rannochs had done, David and Simon had taken to insisting the staff not wait up, and even Marston had eventually relaxed his standards enough to go along with them.

Quick footsteps sounded and David came out of the doors from the library. "Simon, thank God." David's gaze moved over Simon's face. "I was staring to worry."

"Sorry. I didn't think I'd be this late." Simon moved to David's side and kissed him. Because he wanted to. Because it was still a wonder that they could kiss in this house. Because he wasn't sure where the conversation was headed. "Children asleep?"

"I even got Jamie down."

"I'm impressed." Simon moved past David into the library. A welcome fire glowed in the grate and a book lay abandoned on the arm of David's favorite chair. "Once the play opens, it will be easier to have story time. I suppose they hear that a lot."

"They're used to it. But I thought you didn't have a rehearsal tonight?"

"We didn't." Simon shrugged out of his damp greatcoat and tossed it over the sofa back.

David stared at Simon's mud-stained clothes. "For God's sake, where have you been?"

"Attending a secret meeting to plot illegal activities with dangerous subversives."

David's gaze flickered over his face. "Oh, Christ. You mean it."

"More or less." Simon went to the drinks trolley and poured two glasses of whisky. "You'd better sit down, this is going to take a bit. I think I've told more lies in the past few days than in the entire time you've known me."

David drew a sharp breath, but accepted one of the whiskies and returned to his chair. Simon sat opposite him with the other whisky (which he needed for any number of reasons) and told him about Kitty and the pamphlets smuggled out of Spain, Hapgood and Kit Montagu, Carfax's secret meetings, and the events of the evening.

"No one's hurt?" David said when he had done.

"Kitty lost a lot of blood, but she didn't need stitches and Mélanie thinks she'll be all right."

David stared across the room at an oil of the Seine in winter that had been painted by Simon's father. They'd brought it with them from the Albany flat. "I know there've been times in the past you haven't told me things. When you thought I was better off being able to deny any knowledge of your activities."

"Occasionally. " Simon leaned forwards and touched his lover's face. "We may not have made vows in a church, but I know what I owe you."

"You wouldn't take vows made in a church seriously anyway."

"Probably not. That doesn't change the general point."

David put up his hand and covered Simon's fingers with his own. "I trust you with my life. I think you trust me with yours."

"But?"

David drew their clasped hands down to the chair arm. "But I know there's a part of you that despises me for being part of a government that would hang us for what we do every night."

"Every night may be a bit of an exaggeration. Especially since we've had the children."

"That doesn't change the general point."

"You aren't part of the government. You're in the Opposition. And I don't think I could ever despise you, even if you turned Tory. Well, maybe then."

David gave a faint smile, but his gaze remained serious. "This started in December," he said.

"Yes. I got the first papers the night of the pantomime."

"You've been keeping these secrets a long time." All through the holidays. All through their first Christmas with the children in London. Walking to the Rannochs' on Christmas night. Boxing Day dinner at Mivart's Hotel, which Raoul still hosted though it was no longer his London home. Sledding in Hyde Park. New Year's Eve at Frances and Archie Davenport's. New Year's Day at Harry and Cordy's. Where Kitty had given him some more papers.

"Not compared with the time a lot of our friends keep secrets," Simon said. "But yes, it's been a challenge." He tightened his grip on David's hand, as though he could bridge the chasm David had alluded to. "I couldn't put you in the middle, David."

There was a time when David would have said that was a ridiculous way to talk. Now he inclined his head. "You thought I wouldn't have wanted these papers published?"

"I thought you wouldn't be sure what you should do. I thought it might be good for you to be able to deny any knowledge of them. And with these last, I thought it might seem like a betrayal of your father."

David gave a short laugh. "Is it really possible to betray Carfax?"

"He's still your father."

"Who betrayed everything I hold dear when he tried to use Mélanie to drive a wedge between me and Malcolm and separate me from you. Who tried to murder an innocent young man solely to cover up his own past actions, and didn't cavil at shooting into our friends' drawing room with children and two pregnant women present."

"He didn't actually shoot the rifle himself."

"I thought you'd be the first to say ordering something is the same as doing it. In any case, I doubt Father would have hesitated to fire the rifle if he hadn't needed his own deniability and wasn't in the habit of not doing his own dirty work." David tossed down the last of his whisky. "Do you think Father was behind the attack on Kitty?"

Not so long ago, even knowing Carfax, David would have been horrified at the idea. Now he said it quite calmly, though his fingers were white round his glass.

"I don't know," Simon said. "It's not that I think he'd have hesitated—Kitty's an agent, after all, and to Carfax that probably makes her fair game—"

"To my father everyone is fair game."

"But if he's that desperate to suppress the papers, it's even more complicated than it seems. And I'm not sure why he'd assume Kitty had the papers on her tonight. She didn't, as it happens. So unless he was planning to kill all of us and thought that would end the publication, I'm not sure what his endgame would have been."

David pushed himself to his feet and splashed more whisky into his glass. "He might have meant to kill all of you. You said there were two sets of attackers."

"There were. But it's hard for me to imagine Carfax's thinking he could count on taking all of us out."

"He wouldn't have known Malcolm and Mélanie would be there. Or St. Juste or O'Roarke. This Hapgood sounds middle-aged, you and Kit aren't trained agents—"

"True enough. Kitty's undoubtedly the best fighter among those of us who were supposed to be present."

David picked up Simon's glass. "Kitty could have been killed."

"Yes. We were all well aware of it. St. Juste looked ill. And I never thought to see him so terrified."

"He's afraid of losing the person he loves. I can sympathize." David refilled Simon's glass. "What's going to happen with the papers?"

"Malcolm wants to make sure they're published."

"That's good." David touched his glass to Simon's. "I do as well."

CARFAX, as usual, was in his study in Carfax House when Malcolm called. "Amelia and Lucinda are at the theatre," he said when the footman ushered Malcolm in. "Drury Lane, not the Tavistock. Easier often these days for them to go out on their own. Bit of a relief, actually." He pushed his spectacles up on his nose. "I take it there's news?"

Malcolm pushed the door to. "Was Lewis Thornsby working for the League?"

Carfax set down his pen. "That's an interesting idea."

"Don't play games, sir. We haven't got time for it."

"I should think not. I'm an exceedingly busy man. I don't play games."

"Your whole life is a game. Was Thornsby working for the League?"

"My dear Malcolm. Surely I don't need to remind you that I am just as much the League's enemy as you are. How would I know who was working for them?"

"Doing it much too brown, sir." Malcolm hooked a chair leg with his ankle and dragged the chair in front of Carfax's desk. "You're investigating the League just as much as we are. You were having Thornsby watched."

"He's a Leveller."

"There are a lot of Levellers."

"Don't remind me."

"Sir. You had a reason for choosing Thornsby. He wasn't obviously a leader. Were you paying as much attention to Simon Tanner and Kit Montagu and Roger Smythe?"

"I always pay attention to Tanner. For obvious reasons."

"You had Thornsby's rooms searched."

"Thornsby was murdered."

"Sir."

Carfax sat back in his chair. "All right. I had my suspicions about Thornsby. He was Lady Shroppington's heir and she's close to the Beverstons. But they were no more than suspicions. I didn't want to prejudge your investigation."

"But you have your own source among the Levellers."

"I believe I admitted as much."

"Did you ask your source about Thornsby?"

"Yes. He didn't know."

Malcolm folded his arms across his chest. Carfax raised a brow. "Believe me or not."

"Does the name Alexander Radford mean anything to you?"

Carfax frowned in what looked like genuine puzzlement and may have actually been so. "Is he one of the Levellers?"

"He may be the man who is trying to take control of the Elsinore League. Or an alias for him."

Carfax's eyes narrowed. "Interesting."

"And Lewis Thornsby was seen with him."

"In London?"

"In Italy. By Nerezza Russo. I thought perhaps that was why you were so keen to take her into custody."

"What? Oh, no, I was just doing a favor for the minister of police in Naples, who had dallied with her. I know she's been staying with Caruthers and Laclos. I don't feel any need to pursue that. Not that I necessarily have illusions I could extract her from Caruthers and Laclos. They're both very capable agents."

From Carfax that was high praise. "Yes," Malcolm said. "They are."

"She knows who this Radford is?"

"She knew him as Radford. She doesn't know who he really is. I suspect the League—or his part of the League—are after her because she could recognize him."

"And the description—"

"Fifties to sixties. Sandy hair. Middle height. Sharp hazel eyes that could appear green or blue in different lights. Ironic manner. From things he said to her, it sounds as though he may be someone who's been living in exile from Britain, whether self-imposed or imposed from without."

"Well, we know a number of people who've done that."

"And apparently he wants to come back."

"We know a number of people who've done that as well. Thankfully." Carfax frowned. "Beverston is connected to Thornsby. But Beverston is in the other faction."

"Yes, I know. Thornsby could have changed sides. Or he could have been trying to get information about Radford for Beverston."

"Which would have given Radford a motive to have had him killed."

"Or Beverston, if Thornsby had changed sides."

"You think this is what Thornsby's Montford persona was about?"

"Possibly."

Carfax tented his fingers together. "One way or another, he was betraying the Levellers. So that still gives any of them a motive to have killed him."

"That would be convenient for you, wouldn't it?" Malcolm held out a copy of the list of Radical disturbances. "Do these mean anything to you?"

Carfax glanced at the list. "They're Radical disturbances. That turned violent, as such protests often do. Where did you find it?"

"In Thornsby's things."

"If you're suggesting he was behind the incidents—"

"He appears to have decoded the list, which makes that less likely."

Carfax glanced at the list again. "The one in Lancaster is when David got young Carmarthen acquitted."

"How much do you know about that?"

"That someone shot a pistol during a demonstration. That it still isn't clear whether it was Carmarthen or not."

"And the other incidents?"

Carfax smoothed the edges of the list. "As I said, I've heard of all of them."

"You don't happen to have been behind them, do you?"

Carfax raised his brows.

"I know you employ agents provocateurs. It's just a question of if you did here."

"It's easier to believe that than that your comrades actually turn to violence, isn't it?"

"I have no illusions that people with whom I'm in sympathy don't turn to violence on occasion. It doesn't necessarily mean I'm in sympathy with the violence. I tend to think it produces the opposite result of what's intended. Which is why you employ agents provocateurs to orchestrate such incidents."

"My brother used to say the youth of England would be its salvation or its downfall, and he couldn't be sure which."

"It may depend on one's viewpoint." Carfax's brother had, if anything, been even more reactionary than the current Lord Carfax. "Which did he think his own son would be?"

Carfax's eyes narrowed. "I think his not being sure about Arthur was part of why he said it."

"It's a pity he didn't have the chance to find out. I liked Arthur." Though it was difficult now to imagine anyone but Hubert Mallinson as Lord Carfax, he had only succeeded to the title when his brother died, following the death of the brother's only son, Arthur, in a sailing accident. Malcolm could still remember how the mantle of being the heir had seemed to physically weigh David down when he returned to Harrow, no longer David Mallinson but Viscount Worsley.

"One of the tragedies of someone's dying young," Carfax said. "One never knows what he'd have made of himself." He leaned back in his chair. "Was there more you wanted to ask me about?"

A great deal, such as if Carfax had been behind tonight's attack. But as he couldn't mention the night's events without mentioning the papers—and Carfax wouldn't tell him the truth anyway—Malcolm merely said, "Not yet."

"You aren't any closer to knowing who killed Thornsby?"

"We've learned a lot about him—including that he was seemingly far more complicated than just about anyone who knew him realized—but no, I can't say we're closer to knowing who killed him."

On the way out, Malcolm stopped before a painting that hung in the hall beside the stairs. A dark-haired lady in a peach-colored gown and a boy of about eight with her gleaming dark hair and fine-boned features. The lady was the Countess Carfax. Not Amelia, David's mother, but Pamela, Carfax's brother's wife, who had died when Malcolm was a baby, probably shortly after the portrait was taken. As Malcolm had told Will, like Hetty Bartlett and their friend Josefina Lopes, Pamela Carfax had been the daughter of a former slave, but unlike Hetty and Josefina, she had been a considerable heiress. Her father had been a wealthy planter who had sent his only child to England to make her debut. Malcolm studied Pamela's portrait, wondering how she had found it trying to fit into London society. Not an easy task, he knew from his own wife's experience. Pamela's eyes were kind, but he thought he caught an echo of sadness in them. Her hand was curled tenderly round her son's head. Arthur Mallinson looked to be about eight in the painting, before Malcolm could remember him, for he had been eight years Arthur's junior. Arthur had his mother's face, but his eyes were a bright, piercing blue.

Arthur had been kind to David and Malcolm, in an indulgent way. Arthur's death had changed David's life, but Malcolm had felt the loss of Arthur on his own account. He smiled at the portrait for a moment. Even at eight there'd been a certain mocking irony in Arthur's smile and in the gleam in those arresting blue eyes. Malcolm found himself staring, struck by something in that smile he couldn't quite articulate. He shook his head, accepted his hat from the footman, and descended the steps of Carfax House.

CHAPTER 24

Kitty spent a long time kneeling between the boys' wrought iron beds. She smoothed their hair, breathed in the scent of soap and little boy, pulled the covers up round Leo, tucked Timothy's stuffed dog back into the crook of his arm, sat back on her heels and watched the even rise and fall of their breath. Finally she kissed them both. When she pushed herself to her feet, she winced at the stab of pain in her side. Julien was there in an instant and somehow she was standing with an ease she wouldn't have thought possible. She pressed his hand but didn't trust herself to meet his gaze. Not yet.

She went through to her bedroom. Their bedroom. Genny was asleep in her cradle, but she stirred at Kitty's approach. She often woke to nurse when Kitty returned late. Surely it wasn't selfish to pick her up. Kitty scooped her daughter into her arms and held her close for a moment. Genny snuggled into her. Kitty buried her face in Genny's soft hair and sank down in the armchair beside the cradle. Genny nestled in for a few moments, then started to pull at the neck of the gown Mélanie had lent her, which had a nursing bodice. Kitty undid the buttons.

Julien didn't say anything, didn't do anything, save put a shawl round her shoulders as she sat with Genny. Then he sat himself, a little way off. When Kitty looked up from their daughter, she saw him watching both of them as though committing the moment to memory. Their gazes locked for a moment. She almost spoke then, but she didn't trust herself. She looked down at Genny nestled in her arms and drew back into the small circle that was herself and her daughter, within the glow cast by the candle Julien had lit on the table beside the chair. She needed a few more minutes to gather up the tattered remnants of her self-possession before she said what needed to be said. Though first she had to figure out what that was.

She waited until Genny's head flopped against her arm and Genny's breathing turned soft and even. When she started to move, Julien moved faster (faster than one could see, as he often did) and had a hand under her elbow as she got to her feet. It was easier this time. Perhaps because she'd moved more slowly, perhaps because she'd been sitting rather than kneeling. She could do this. She put Genny down in her cradle. Julien didn't stand beside her as he often did. In fact, once she was on her feet he drew a little way off again. She pulled the blankets up about Genny, bent carefully to kiss her (successfully managing to control her indrawn breath, or at least close to successfully), then returned to her chair to find that Julien had returned to his chair as well. He was watching her with a steady, unreadable gaze. "Go ahead," she said in a voice that was meant to be ironic but came out cracked and dry as old love letters. "Tell me I'm a fool."

"I don't think you're anything of the sort." Julien was sitting very still, the way he did when he didn't want to betray anything. "You made a series of challenging decisions. You ended up in danger, more danger than you probably anticipated, though I know you aren't afraid of danger. You could have been killed—"

"Julien—"

"You could have been," he said in a voice as hard as the flat of a sword blade. "I'm not saying you would have been if the rest of us hadn't shown up, but—"

"It would have been distinctly challenging." She hunched her shoulders and fought off a sudden shiver. "I admit it." She did up the flap on the bodice of her borrowed gown.

"We all run risks," he said in the voice he would use to analyze a mission. Though his eyes had never looked quite so dark in the midst of a mission. She wasn't sure she'd ever seen them look quite so dark before. "We're all—you, me, the Rannochs, the O'Roarkes, the Davenports—going to continue to run them in the life we lead. But I hope you remember your children need you."

Kitty glanced at the cradle and then the door to the nursery. "My God, of course I do."

"*I* need you."

She stared at him. He still wasn't moving, wasn't blinking, wasn't doing anything to acknowledge the enormity of what he'd said. His blue eyes had turned to cobalt. "Julien—"

"I'm not saying I couldn't live without you, but I damn well don't want to have to try." His light, flexible voice turned rough in a way she had never heard. "We aren't playing at this, Kitkat. At least, I'm not. I thought you understood that by now."

"I—do."

"I'm not trying to burden you. Well, I suppose I am, if there's a chance it will keep you from going off into danger without proper backup."

Kitty's fingers tightened on the shawl he had put round her. "I didn't know I needed backup."

"Precisely."

She sat back in her chair. "Why the devil were you following me?" Nothing like an attack when one needed to defend oneself.

Julien shifted in his chair. "Call me an overprotective fool, but I was concerned. And I wanted to know what you were doing."

She kept her gaze on his face, on firmer ground now. "You didn't ask me."

"You didn't tell me."

"No, but—"

Julien gripped the arms of his chair as though about to get up, then sat back. "I'm not used to this. I'm not used to being a—partner. I was trying not to interfere, but to be there if you needed me."

"It didn't occur to you that you might blunder into something?" The words came out faster and sharper than she intended.

"When have you ever known me to blunder into anything?"

She tugged at the shawl. "You have a point. Possibly. But if you're trying to share my life, this is hardly the way—"

"Sharing's an interesting word." Julien folded his arms over his chest.

"Meaning I haven't been doing enough of it? We're both going to have secrets, Julien. We knew that going into—whatever this is. It was always going to be one of the challenges."

"And a challenge I'm woefully unprepared to meet." His mouth twisted with what might have been acknowledgment or bitterness or regret. Or all three. "Fair enough. You made me no promises."

"Lewis and I weren't—"

"You needn't explain."

"I needed a story to account for things to Malcolm." She found herself leaning forwards, willing him to believe her. "That one was a bit obvious, but it was the first that came to mind and it had the merit of rousing Malcolm's chivalrous instincts so he was less likely to talk."

"Practical. Not, as I said, that you've ever made promises to avoid such behavior. Or that I have. It's always more awkward in reality than in theory, but I imagine we could get past it if we had to."

For some reason her breath had tangled up in her throat. "I wouldn't—"

"No need to make promises now, sweetheart. In fact, much better not to do so. As you pointed out, we don't owe each other anything. Including the truth."

And yet, when she'd lied to him, she'd felt more conflicted than she had any intention of admitting. Kitty regarded him, holding the shawl about her with taut fingers. "It wasn't my story to share."

Julien leaned back, hands braced on the chair. "I can see that. And we never agreed to share—anything."

"They weren't my secrets. It didn't seem fair to ask you to keep them."

He nodded. "Though one way and another we keep a fair number of each other's secrets."

Her son's parentage. Julien's very identity. "Personal secrets." Her fingers tightened on her elbows. "This was my risk to run."

He gave a faint smile that somehow had the bleakness of a wasteland. "I'm no stranger to running risks."

"Spain's my fight. Not yours."

Julien raised a brow. "I've been known to help fight your fights. I think I've been rather useful at times."

"You've saved my life, and furthered my cause, and protected my comrades more than once. Including tonight. But I didn't want to presume."

"Thoughtful." He watched her a moment longer. "Though you've been quick enough to ask for help in the past."

"You have enough you're dealing with on your own. You haven't asked for my help with the League. At least, not with most of it."

"A good point."

She watched him. "Surely you didn't think I could have been

working for the League. Or for Carfax again—"

"No. Not without some extraordinary circumstances. It was different during the war. Britain was your ally and Carfax ran British intelligence." He hesitated. "I know you make your own choices. I was trying to stay out of your way."

"Not entirely."

"Call it the urge to meddle. Or call it concern." Suddenly, he was kneeling in front of her, so close she could feel the warmth of his breath. "I'm not going anywhere, Kitty. It's your own business what dangers you rush into. But I'm here beside you."

She continued to watch him. Her own breath was still bottled up in her throat. "It's always going to be like this, Julien. I can't stay on the sidelines. I get tangled up in things. I choose to tangle myself up in things. I seek out fights if they don't find me."

"I know." His gaze moved over her face in that odd way it sometimes did that was like a caress. "It keeps life interesting."

"But I'll always have secrets."

"My darling. Do you imagine I won't?"

"You've never been driven the way I am, Julien."

"Meaning I haven't been committed enough to anything to run crazy risks for it? It's a fair point. I used to wonder at the trouble Mélanie and O'Roarke got themselves into over their beliefs. And then Malcolm. Possibly the worst of the three of them."

"But Malcolm draws personal lines I don't. You're always going to wonder about me, Julien."

"I hope so. I'd hate for you to get boring."

"Julien, even I recognize the importance of trust in a—"

"In a relationship? Is that what this is?"

"You know perfectly well that we aren't—" She broke off, because it was so hard to articulate what they were and what they weren't.

"Just because you can get by on your own doesn't mean you

have to." Julien closed the rest of the distance between them and took her in his arms, his breath warm against her hair.

She buried her face in the warmth of his shoulder. "We're not—"

"Stop fussing about what we're not and start focusing on what we are." He kissed her hair. "Rather happy, among other things." He settled his cheek against her hair. "You can go on tilting at windmills. I'm quite prepared to help."

"You don't—"

"I know where I belong." He settled beside her in the chair, holding her against him. "I don't have any desire to be anywhere else."

Kitty pulled back and looked at him. For how long? That was what she kept wondering.

"We've been managing very well," Julien said. "We can go on managing. Whether or not we suit anyone else's idea of what's appropriate."

"Since when have you given a thought to what's appropriate?"

"Precisely." He lifted his head, gave her a crooked smile, then put his mouth to hers.

KITTY TURNED to look at the head on the pillow beside her. His eyes were closed, his face relaxed in that way it only got in sleep. He'd flung one arm about her. When she shifted, he shifted slightly but kept his hand at the small of her back.

Edward had rarely spent the night in her bed—usually on occasions when he'd drunk too much to rouse himself and return to his own chamber. Even Malcolm had seldom spent an entire night with her, thanks to exigencies of their time together. And now here she was, used to Julien's being here. Used to the warmth of his breath on her hair, used to drifting into sleep with his arm round her and her head in the hollow of his shoulder.

For most of her four-and-thirty years she hadn't let herself lean on anyone, but in these past weeks she'd let herself lean on him. On everything from his help putting the children to bed to his help strategizing missions. To his saving her life and bandaging her wound tonight.

In December, she'd accused them of playing at domesticity. She knew better than that now, perhaps had done even at the time. There was no pretense in Julien's affection for her and the children. But nor was she fool enough to believe that the man who played cards with the boys and blocks with Genny, who carried the children and got up in the night to change nappies, even the man who had saved her tonight and helped bandage her wounds, was the real Julien. Not the sum total of him. For the moment, being part of a family filled some sort of a need for him. It didn't mean he wasn't the man she had first met in Spain or known (in so many senses of the word) in Argentina. Just as her seeking solace with him didn't mean she wasn't fundamentally a woman who functioned on her own. Which didn't mean either of them couldn't enjoy it for the moment...

She touched her finger to the corner of his mouth. Weakness? Perhaps. Self-indulgence? Almost certainly. But letting herself lean on him didn't mean she couldn't go back to looking after herself. Of course, she'd never meant to let it go this far. And it was going to hurt so very much more than she'd ever thought possible to let go.

MALCOLM CLOSED the door of the Berkeley Square house and put his hat on the console table. A light still showed from the library. He went in and saw his father on the sofa with a portable writing desk and a cup of coffee.

Raoul looked up with a quick smile. "Making notes of everyone I know of who was at the Radical disturbances on the list. So far, no pattern is emerging. Did you learn anything from Carfax?"

"I don't think he knows who Alexander Radford is, though I can't swear to it. There was a lot I couldn't say without revealing what we know about the papers." Malcolm shrugged out of his greatcoat. "How long have you known?"

"About the papers?" Raoul set the portable writing desk aside. "I've had suspicions for a while. I saw Kitty talking to Simon the night of the pantomime opening. I wondered when the first papers were published. I thought it best to know as little as possible." He hesitated. "I talked to Kitty this morning. I suggested she tell you the truth. I think she might have done if you hadn't worked it out first."

"Well, in the end she did." Malcolm dropped down on the sofa beside Raoul. "I was a long way from actually working it out. Did you think about telling me yourself?"

Raoul tented his hands together and rested his chin on them. "How would you have felt if I'd told you one of your oldest friends and your former lover—who is also a friend—and a young man who looks up to you were involved in a secret plot they hadn't shared with you?"

"Surprised and I suppose a bit betrayed. That's hardly a novel experience for me at this point, though. Are you saying you decided it was better for me to feel betrayed by you than by them?"

"No." Raoul settled back on the sofa. "Not exactly. I was hoping you wouldn't feel betrayed by anyone. And I also thought we could make more progress in the investigation without the distraction of hurt feelings. As soon as you found out, their plans would shut down and we'd lose any chance of finding out if there was more to it than I suspected."

"You're assuming I'd have confronted them. I might have

done what you did and followed them. I did follow Kit."

"Fair enough," Raoul said. "I may have been thinking too much as a father. Or too much as a spymaster, wanting to learn what they were doing myself. Sometimes I find it difficult to be sure myself. More than sometimes."

Malcolm reached for the glass of whisky he'd left on the sofa table. "Fair enough. I could remind you that I'm grown up. And that we're supposed to be allies. But I wonder if you'll ever fully accept either."

Raoul returned his gaze steadily. "It can be difficult to accept that one's children are grown up. And difficult to trust allies. And as we've said, we're not always going to be allies."

Malcolm scraped a hand over his hair. "I was damnably afraid. Of what Simon might be involved in. And Kit and Kitty. Of having to try to stop them. Of your being on the opposite side. Of Mel's being on the opposite side, perhaps."

"Mélanie wouldn't—"

"Mélanie might, if she saw things differently from how I did. She wouldn't be the woman I love if she didn't." Malcolm turned his glass in his hand. "But more than all of that, I think I was afraid I'd learn whatever they were involved in, and know I should try to stop it as an MP but not want to." He held the glass out to Raoul. "Sometimes I wonder if I should be a Leveller."

Raoul accepted the glass and took a drink of whisky. "Incremental change can be damnably frustrating. That doesn't necessarily make it less valuable. On the contrary, perhaps."

"You've been fighting in non-incremental ways your entire life."

"I've seen my cause go backwards more than forwards in many cases." Raoul put the glass back in Malcolm's hand. "We've said it before. People are needed both places."

"I just sometimes wonder where I'm needed." Malcolm swallowed the last of the whisky. "Or perhaps I should say where I want to be."

"That's something I can't answer for you. But I'd have said you were happy in Parliament."

Malcolm set the glass down. "Most of the time. When I'm not bashing my head against a wall."

"My dear boy. I've been bashing my head against multiple walls since before you were born. So far, I have a persistent headache and the walls show little damage."

"Spain may change."

A shadow of concern flickered across Raoul's face, along with carefully masked hope. "It may. I've seen change. The question is sustaining the change."

"I'd be happy just to achieve it. I hope publishing the papers will help."

Raoul tossed down the last of his coffee. "As you pointed out, it will make it harder for Carfax to take covert action in Spain or Italy. Which could be very helpful indeed." He hesitated a moment. "That was bravely done, Malcolm. I don't expect it was easy."

"Actually," Malcolm said, "I didn't need to think twice about it. Which perhaps goes with my wondering where I want to be." He started to get up, then said, "Father? Did you ever meet Pamela Carfax? Carfax's late brother's wife."

"I never met her officially, but I saw her driving in the park once on a visit to London when I was about eighteen. She was a beautiful woman. And even at eighteen, I could tell she didn't appear happy."

"Knowing the late Lord Carfax, I don't think it was a happy marriage. I was looking at a painting of her tonight at Carfax House. With her son Arthur when he was a boy. Something about it keeps puzzling me, but I can't work out what. Carfax mentioned his brother tonight, which he doesn't do often. Perhaps that's why I'm thinking about Pamela and Arthur."

Malcolm was still thinking about Pamela and Arthur Mallinson as he and Raoul banked the fire and put out the lamps and climbed the stairs to the second floor. His mind kept returning to the painting and the mocking glint in Arthur's smile. He said goodnight to Raoul and opened the door of his and Mélanie's room. As he stepped through the door, he stopped, one hand gripping the doorknob, blinded as he'd once been when he worked out that his wife was a French agent. It wasn't as personally painful a realization, but the implications were just as shattering. He shook his head. No. Surely he was wrong. He didn't have the sort of evidence he'd had about Mélanie. And yet—

He forced his fingers to unclench and stepped into the bedchamber.

Mélanie was sitting up in bed, hair tumbling over the seafoam silk of her dressing gown, making notes on a script. "Darling. Did you learn anything from Carfax?"

"As usual, a great deal of possibilities, nothing of substance." Malcolm bent to pet Berowne, who was curled up on the bed, and cracked open the nursery door to look in on the sleeping children. "I don't think he knows who Alexander Radford is. And I don't think we need to worry about him where Nerezza's concerned."

"That's something, at least."

Malcolm came back into the bedroom and sat on the edge of the bed. "I'll call on Beverston in the morning. I don't know how much I'll be able to get, but even denials will be interesting."

Mélanie leaned against him. "I need to be at the theatre in the morning. But I can talk to the actors."

"Excellent." Malcolm pressed a kiss to her hair. He missed doing more of the interviews with Mel, but in this case it was good, perhaps. Because the other call he had to make in the morning he couldn't tell her about.

If he was right in his suspicions, it changed everything. And he was going to have to figure out what to do about it.

CHAPTER 25

On an early January morning, Hyde Park was not crowded, though it looked far more tranquil than it had in the dark less than twelve hours before. Fog hung over Rotten Row, but Addison, who had been making his usual inquiries in coffee houses and taverns frequented by valets and footmen, had informed Malcolm that Lord Beverston rode here almost every morning, rain or shine. Malcolm guided his horse Perdita through the fog, beneath leafless trees with branches still dripping from last night's rain. He saw a lone figure ahead and spurred Perdita to a canter.

"Rannoch." Beverston swung his head round as Malcolm reined in beside him. "I don't think I've seen you here at this hour. And I imagine you're too busy just now for morning exercise. So I assume this isn't merely a social visit?"

"Did you recruit Lewis Thornsby into the League?" Malcolm asked.

Beverston raised his brows. "Everything that happens isn't to do with the League. But assuming I had recruited Thornsby, why on earth do you think I'd share it with you?"

"Because presumably you want to learn who killed him."

A shadow flickered across Beverston's face that seemed to have nothing to do with the trees overhanging the path or the clouds overhead. "Thornsby was a young man with a bright future. It's a tragedy."

"You knew him well."

"I wouldn't say that."

"You're on good terms with Thornsby's aunt, Lady Shroppington."

"I'm on good terms with a number of people."

"You've known Lewis Thornsby since he was a boy."

Beverston put up a hand to brush a drop of water from the brim of his hat. "You've been talking to Roger, haven't you? No need to conceal it, I know you're friends. Yes, I have known Lewis his whole life. But as I said, I have a number of friends. And it should come as no surprise to you that I'm not accustomed to spending as much time in the nursery as you and a number of your friends. Even Archie Davenport, apparently, which I wouldn't have expected. In any case, I didn't spend a great deal of time dandling my friends' children on my knee or tossing balls with them. Or teaching them to read every subversive book ever written, as O'Roarke did with you."

"A pity, the subversive books make for a wonderful education. What does the name Alexander Radford mean to you?"

Beverston's gaze flickered. "Who is he?"

"It's an alias of the man who is probably trying to take over the League. But you already knew that, didn't you?"

The wind shifted and the tree branches whipped overhead, but Beverston's gaze remained steady. "There's a war going on in the League, Rannoch. You aren't part of that. I can't make you part of it. For my own sake. But also for yours."

"You don't want me to hurt your ability to win."

Beverston gave a faint smile. "That too."

"Nerezza saw Lewis Thornsby with Alexander Radford in Naples."

Beverston drew in and released his breath with a sound like the cracking of a dried branch. "I didn't bring Lewis into the League, as it happens. What happened to my son John was tragedy enough. I preferred to keep my family and anyone approaching family out of it."

"But someone else recruited him."

Beverston gave a curt nod.

"That must have seemed quite a betrayal."

"Are you thinking I killed him because of it?" Beverston guided his horse round a puddle. "I wouldn't kill for such a melodramatic reason. Revenge doesn't really get one anywhere."

"It would have removed him from the field of play."

"He was little more than a pawn."

"He had the makings of an excellent agent. He'd set up a second identity under the name Montford."

Beverston's brows drew together.

"You didn't know?"

"No."

"Who recruited Thornsby?"

Beverston hesitated a moment. "I wasn't sure for a long time. I learned from sources of my own fairly recently."

"Who was it?"

Beverston regarded Malcolm for a long moment, his dark eyes tinged with what might have been compassion. "Your brother."

It shouldn't be a shock. Malcolm had known Edgar was working for the man trying to take over the League, the man they now called Alexander Radford. But the very idea of Edgar as an agent still seemed alien in so many ways. "How did you find out?"

"One of my men got into his things before you did, after he was killed. We didn't learn a great deal. But my agent did find a communication from Thornsby."

"Saying what?"

"Reporting on the Levellers."

Which they had known Thornsby was doing. But somehow the confirmation of his betrayal made it worse.

"Edgar was abroad until just before his death."

"Thornsby had traveled abroad. He was on the Continent for much of last spring and summer. You said that's where Nerezza saw him with this man you're calling Alexander Radford."

"Was Thornsby an agent provocateur?"

"Thornsby wasn't working for me."

"Do you think Edgar was setting up agent provocateur missions?"

"Your brother was doing a great many things. I don't think I knew the half of them."

"And the League would like to see Radicals discredited."

"There are some very dangerous ideas running round the country now, Malcolm. Those of us who were young in the eighties and nineties may be more aware of the risks than your generation. Except for men like your father, who were part of the danger a generation ago."

"One might say the same problems need to be addressed as a generation ago."

"Yes, I imagine you would. As would my elder surviving son. I suspect you may both see it differently when you're my age and have more of a sense of what you have to lose. Although that certainly hasn't been the case with O'Roarke."

"Agents provocateurs do damage."

"Agents provocateurs help a vulnerable public see the dangers of agitation."

"My God, sir. You don't actually believe that, do you?"

Beverston relaxed his hands on the reins, letting his horse lengthen her stride. "It's not a question of what I believe, Rannoch. It's a question of what I can persuade others to believe. Agents provocateurs help with that."

"Do you know who Alexander Radford is?"

Beverston hesitated, gaze fixed on the sodden tangle of interlaced branches ahead. "Some secrets we can share, Rannoch. Some we can't."

"Meaning it would be worse for you if I knew the truth."

"We all have to calculate what we reveal. And what we don't." Beverston's gaze shifted to the rain-splashed path ahead. "If Nerezza told you she saw Thornsby with Alexander Radford—is she in London?"

"No comment."

Beverston shot a look at him. "Surely by now you realize I don't mean Nerezza any harm."

"You didn't mean her harm a month ago. Or at least, it suited you to protect her. That's no guarantee for the future."

"I was fond of Nerezza. I still am. Benedict's fond of her and at present, after what my family have been through, I'm inclined to try to give my children what makes them happy if I possibly can. I'd also as lief keep Benedict as far away from everything else that's happening as possible, and his protecting Nerezza oddly does that." Beverston frowned for a moment. "Actually, Benedict's rather impressed me this past month."

"Yes," Malcolm said. "He's impressed me too."

Malcom returned Perdita to the mews in Berkeley Square, then walked round to the house in Carnaby Street where Kitty had taken lodgings. He was a frequent enough visitor that Kitty's maid admitted him without hesitation. He found Kitty, St. Juste, and the children at breakfast in a cheerful chaos of toast crumbs, spilled porridge, coffee cups, a stuffed dog, and a stuffed unicorn. All quite unlike what one would expect of Kitty and St. Juste. At least, not of Kitty and St. Juste as Malcolm had first known them.

"Uncle Malcolm!" Timothy sprang up and ran over. "Mama was hurt last night."

"Yes, I know." Malcolm bent to hug Kitty's younger son. "I've come to inquire how she is."

"Much better after a good night's sleep." Kitty's color had improved more, Malcolm was glad to see, though there were lines of strain about her eyes. Her fingers were curled round the handle of a coffee cup.

"I'm relieved to hear it," Malcolm said.

"You all had an adventure last night." Leo regarded Malcolm with a steady gaze that held a number of questions.

"We did. Rather more of one than we bargained on. That's the thing about adventures. They're often more enjoyable to remember than when one is in the midst of them."

"That's because Uncle Malcolm is sensible and practical," Kitty said.

Genny—good God, *Genny*, why had her name never struck him before—banged her spoon against her porridge bowl. Malcolm bent to acknowledge her.

"Have you come because you need Mama for something?" Leo asked. "I think she should rest."

"I quite agree, though I doubt your mother does. But actually, I've come to talk to your—to St. Juste, if he has a moment."

"Certainly." Julien pushed back his chair. "I need to go out for a bit, in any case." He looked at the boys. "Keep an eye on your mother, scamps." He reached for his coat, which was tossed over a chairback, ruffled the boys' hair, bent to kiss Kitty, flicked a finger against Genny's cheek, and then strolled from the room after Malcolm, pulling on his coat.

They made their way out of the house and along Carnaby Street to the peaceful precincts of Golden Square without ever discussing where they were going. "She looks better," Malcom said.

"Yes, I think she is." Julien's steady voice couldn't quite

disguise the underlying worry. "I changed the dressing this morning and there's no sign of infection so far. I'd feel better if she didn't exert herself for a day or two—or a week or two—but this is Kitty. And we're not in circumstances that lend themselves to quiet. Kitty, of course, said she'd be as careful as I'd be in the same circumstances. Which is cold comfort. Though she's probably more sensible than I am."

"Just a bit."

Julien gave a faint smile. "Did you see Beverston?"

"This morning. He denied recruiting Lewis Thornsby. Which I actually think I believe, because he claims someone else recruited Lewis Thornsby to work for Alexander Radford—who is indeed the man trying to take over the League."

Julien let out a whistle. "Interesting. Did he say who recruited Thornsby?"

Malcolm hesitated. "Edgar."

Julien stopped walking for a moment. "Well, given what we know about your brother, I suppose that's not really surprising. And I suppose it's not surprising we've encountered him again in the course of the investigation. I'm sorry, though. For you. And Kitty."

Malcolm kept his gaze on an inn sign up ahead. Gilt paint of what seemed to be a crown, more than half-obscured by the soot and grime of London. "It's not as though I don't think about Edgar almost every day. I wish Kitty could forget him, though."

Julien was silent for a moment, during which Malcolm could feel the weight of myriad conflicting impulses. "I don't think she ever will. But I don't think she's haunted by it."

Malcolm shot a quick look at his former lover's current lover. "You've helped her."

"She's helped herself. She's too strong to let a man like Edgar break her." Julien looked away, in one of those moments when he seemed almost about to let his mask slip. "I'm glad for whatever I've been able to do, though."

Difficult to say more without intruding on St. Juste's and Kitty's privacy. They had reached the square garden. Malcolm glanced at the white statue of a figure in classical military dress. Or pseudo-classical military dress, as Harry said. It was said to be George II, though some claimed it was actually Charles II. Like many things, it was a matter of perspective. "Do you think Edgar could have trained Thornsby?" Malcolm asked.

"He was your brother. What do you think?"

"I'd have laughed at the idea. Just as I'd have laughed at the idea that Edgar could have been a secret operative called the Goshawk or been an agent of the Elsinore League. I obviously didn't know him at all, and no sooner did I realize it than he was gone. Now I'll never have the chance to confront any of it."

"I'm sorry." Oddly, the words that could be a platitude had the solid ring of reality from St. Juste.

"I didn't mean it that way, St. Juste. If you hadn't killed Edgar, I'd be dead. I owe you a debt I can't possibly repay."

St. Juste nodded. For once he didn't seem to have an ironic response at the ready.

Malcolm watched him in the gray light that shifted as the clouds moved overhead like images flashing by from the past. "I don't think I appreciated how hard it must have been for you."

St. Juste skirted a pile of refuse on the pavement. He had a catlike knack for staying clean. "Everyone keeps saying that, and I can't tell why. It's not the first time I've killed someone, and the need here was more straightforwards than in many cases. He wasn't my brother."

"No." Malcolm paused, and then said the words that could upend all their lives. "But you'd known him since he was a boy."

Julien went as still as the statue.

CHAPTER 26

Malcolm studied the man who called himself Julien St. Juste in the shifting shadows of the morning. "I remember your tossing me up in the air when I was about Jessica's age. And helping me climb a tree when I was Colin's."

Julien remained absolutely still, though when he spoke his voice was startlingly normal. "I've been wondering how long it would take you to work it out."

"You must have thought me woefully slow."

"Never that."

"The hair is a great disguise. And of course the fact that I thought you were dead made me less likely to suspect it was you. I'm glad you're not, by the way."

"Thank you." Julien turned, leaning against the back of a bench, face still in shadow. "When did you work it out?"

"Last night Carfax started talking about your father and how he said he wasn't sure if the younger generation would be Britain's undoing or its savior. When I was leaving Carfax House I looked at that painting of you and your mother that hangs by the stairs. Something struck me about your smile in it, but even then I didn't put it together until after I got home. Once I did—to say I felt a fool is putting it mildly. Does Gelly know?"

"Oh, yes. I told her."

Malcolm stared at the other man, who was almost defined by never admitting anything to anyone. "That's rather a lot of trust."

"She's earned it. And I suppose—" Julien stretched his hand into a shaft of sunlight and regarded his nails. "We all need someone to confide in."

"That's quite an admission." Malcolm continued to watch the man who was his sister's cousin. "Did my mother know?"

Julien kicked his foot against the bench. "I always liked your mother. When I was Arthur, and when I became Julien St. Juste. And not for the obvious reasons one might expect a young man to like a beautiful woman. Yes, she knew. She worked it out for herself when I met up with her working against the League. I was younger and hadn't changed as much."

"You trusted her with your secret."

"I didn't have much choice. But yes, to the extent I trusted anyone, I trusted Arabella."

"And she trusted you with her secret."

"Gisèle? Yes, I was rather surprised by that. I think she felt someone needed to know. After all, I was Gisèle's cousin."

Malcolm took a moment to frame his next question, for a number of reasons. "Does Raoul know?"

"Surely at this point you think he'd have told you?"

"Perhaps. Probably. But he could have thought there were risks. He could have made promises to you. Or to my mother, or both."

"And O'Roarke's the sort who keeps his promises. If he can. Though he wouldn't admit it. He likes to delude people into thinking he's ruthless. At least he used to. He's rather let the mask slip now." Julien turned and sat on the bench. Malcolm sat beside him. Carriages rattled by. A few intrepid pedestrians hurried across the square, but it was mostly deserted. "O'Roarke's never given me any indication he knows who I am," Julien said. "In France or in the Peninsula or here. Arabella never told me she told him. And somehow I don't think she would have."

"Nor do I. She didn't tell him about Gisèle either."

"Have you told Mélanie?" Julien asked, his voice almost too casual.

"Not yet." Malcolm hesitated. "I think a part of me didn't truly believe it until I talked to you."

Julien turned his head and lifted a brow. "A bit ironic isn't it? With all my pose of independence, I was Carfax's creature."

"I don't think you were ever Carfax's creature."

"Not entirely. But more than I'd like."

"Did he help you stage your death?" There was still so much Malcolm didn't know about Julien St. Juste. Arthur Mallinson.

"Oh, no. I did that. I needed to. Father was going to have me arrested for treason."

For all the shocks of the day, for all the mysteries of Julien's life, Malcolm stared at the other man.

"Not that there weren't plenty of advantages to disappearing," Julien said. "But I'm not sure it would have occurred to me without that." He stared at a rare splash of mud on his immaculate boots. "You remember the *Unicorn* Rebellion in Barbados?"

Even at the age of seven, Malcolm had heard of it. A group of escaped slaves had commandeered a British naval ship, the *HMS Unicorn*, and sailed her to freedom in Canada. They had taken the ship when most of the crew were onshore, but most of those who had been on board had been killed, including the captain, as had a number of people on the plantations the slaves escaped. "It was the talk of London," Malcolm said. He remembered his mother and Raoul bent over a newspaper account together, his mother's exclaiming over the loss of life,

Raoul's saying, *How many lives would have been lost if they hadn't escaped?*

Julien stared across the dry winter flowerbeds. "My father had invested in munitions. He was shipping them to the Caribbean. My mother's maid was still in our household, and she was in communication with slaves on my grandfather's plantation—which my father owned by then—who were among the ringleaders in the rebellion. I figured out how to smuggle them a message to let them know where the weapons were stored. The house my mother grew up in burned down that night. My grandfather's brother's son—my cousin—was managing the plantation for my father. He and his wife and two of his sons died. I have enough of a conscience that that will haunt me forever. But some of the slaves who escaped to Canada were my cousins as well. I exchange letters with one of them. She has five children who are growing up and able to forge their own lives. I'm sorry for a lot of things I've done. But I'm not sorry for my actions over the *Unicorn*."

"Raoul would agree with you. I rather think I do."

Julien shot a look at him. "Loss of life weighs more with you than with anyone I know."

"Without the weapons, the rebels would have been massacred. And an unconscionable number die in the course of everyday life on plantations."

Julien fixed his gaze on a leafless tree branch. "I'd like to say I did it out of a deep-seated belief in abolition. Which I certainly support, to the extent I support anything, and I support rather more than I'd have admitted to even a few months ago. But the truth is it was at least half to get back at my father. He killed my mother, you know."

Malcolm felt himself go still. "He—"

"Oh, he didn't do it with his own hand. He didn't even order someone else to do it. But she was miserable. From the start of the marriage, I suspect. Certainly for as long as I could remember. England was cold and damp. She missed home. I remember her talking about it. The warmth of the sun. The beaches where the water was actually warm. Josephine talked about the same things when she talked about Martinique."

"I never thought—" Bits and pieces of what Malcolm knew about Julien St. Juste merged with bits and pieces of what he knew about Arthur Mallinson. "You and Josephine had the Caribbean in common."

"Not precisely. I'd never been to the Caribbean. But I'd heard enough from my mother that I could understand what Josephine was talking about."

"Did she—"

"Did Josephine know who I was? No. I'd have been mad to reveal it. But I think her being from the Caribbean helped me understand her and that understanding infused our relationship." He said it so easily, this man who was accustomed to disdain any references to any sort of human relationship. "She'd been in an arranged marriage as a young girl, just as my mother had. She talked about being an outsider when she first came to Paris. My mother was an outsider who had to navigate an alien society, just as Josephine did. It was years later before I really understood how hard that must have been for her." He swung his head round to look at Malcolm. "I suspect it's been hard for Mélanie as well."

"Yes," Malcolm said. "It has been. Harder, I think, than I realized for a long time."

Julien nodded. "Hard for Kitty as well, I would imagine. Living in British society after she married Ashford. Living here now." His gaze swept the square like that of one scouting terrain. "You know the beau monde. Outsiders never really belong. You can sip tea with them. You can dance at their balls. You can marry their children. But you're never really one of the club."

"No you aren't." Moments from his life with Mélanie shot

through Malcolm's memory. Walking into a ball with her on his arm. Driving in a carriage. Taking their place in a box at the theatre. Looks he hadn't really registered because he'd never cared what anyone thought of him and never had to, because whatever he thought of the beau monde, his place in it was assured. "But I wouldn't discount what Kitty can manage."

"I wouldn't discount Kitty in any way. But managing isn't the same as being happy."

"I think Mel would say she's happy now. Especially now we're not playing so much at trying to belong." Why the devil had they, for so long? Simply because they thought they should?

Julien shot a glance at him. "Mélanie at least has you. My father never really tried to disguise that he'd married my mother for her fortune. He'd make the most cutting remarks to her. In front of me. In front of guests. I'm not sure which embarrassed him more, the fact that her mother was African or the fact that her father made his fortune in trade. He enjoyed the fortune, but he wasn't proud of how they came by it. I don't know it for a certainty, but I suspect he hit my mother. She certainly had more bruises than one would expect in the normal course of life." He drew a breath. His fingers had curled inwards. "When I was five, she almost ran away with a footman she'd fallen in love with. She only stayed because of me. At least that's what I gather from the servants' gossip I pieced together later. Apparently she was actually on the point of slipping out of the house when I woke up and called out and she changed her mind." He shook his head, his gaze locked on the distance. "Funny the difference a childish nightmare could make. I remember how she'd smile at Gavin—the footman—and how sad she seemed after he left. Then she died trying to have another baby. Which of course wouldn't have happened if she'd had the sense to run off."

"Julien." Malcolm put a hand on the other man's arm. "It isn't your fault that your mother didn't want to leave her child. All of us who are parents would probably have made the same decision."

Julien gave a quick nod, though he didn't quite meet Malcolm's gaze. "I understand that a bit better now I'm—now I've got close to Kitty's children. But the fact remains if she'd left, she might well still be alive. Or at least have been happier in her last few years."

"Or miserable because she was separated from her son."

"Perhaps. In any case, her marriage was a misery, and I blamed Father. All his self-righteousness and he couldn't keep his hands off the maids. Or my governesses. Or pretty much any available female who wasn't protected by rank and fortune. Or any with rank and fortune who was willing. I'd been trying to attack him for years."

"You weren't even sixteen."

"I think I was thirteen when I started picking the lock on his dispatch box, looking for information I could use against him"

"You had a lot to be angry at him for. And your mother—"

"My mother was never a slave. But her mother was one until my grandfather freed her. My grandmother's mother was the mistress of the man who owned her. Assuming one can use the word 'mistress' to describe someone who could scarcely have said no. Assuming she had even the illusion of choice and he didn't simply force her into his bed when they made my grandmother. For that matter, I don't know that one could say my grandmother went to my grandfather willingly, considering that I doubt he'd have freed her if she hadn't agreed to be his wife."

"I know what it's like to have an ugly history." Malcolm said.

"And out of it, I was born to a world of privilege. I could have focused my efforts on combating my father's slave holdings. Or I could have bided my time until I could inherit from him and free his slaves. Instead I was focused on a way to bring him down."

Malcolm regarded Julien as he completed this dispassionate statement. "You also struck a blow for freedom. I know your abilities, but even so, that's quite something to have pulled off before your sixteenth birthday."

"Yes, well, I didn't precisely pull it off. Uncle Hubert figured it out. He came down to Carfax Court and told Father. They were closeted together for hours. Uncle Hubert was ready to hush the whole thing up. Father insisted I had to face the consequences. For the good of Britain, supposedly. And maybe because he was afraid of what I might expose about him. He'd been overcharging the war office for guns for years. Ask your friend Palmerston to look into the accounts In any case, it seemed prudent to remove myself from their control. I slipped out of the house and took out a sailboat."

"You did all of this alone?"

Julien hesitated. "No, Sylvie helped me."

"Sylvie St. Ives?"

"She was Sylvie de Fancot then. She and her family were staying at Carfax Court. She helped me set up the whole thing."

"She'd only have been—"

"Thirteen. And quite brilliant already."

"You were friends."

"Of a sort. We both knew what it was to be outsiders. We weren't lovers yet, by the way. That came later. But Sylvie helped me set up my supposed drowning. I got to France on a smuggler's boat. I knew all the local smugglers, that's where I'd get my brandy. I managed to take some money and some candlesticks and three of my father's snuffboxes to sell. For a month it was rather a lark. I met a woman about twenty years older than I was who was happy to help with my bills and happy to share other things. She's the one who taught me how to dye my hair. Her own was a quite spectacular gold."

"As one who's struggled with dyed hair undercover, I'm in awe of how you've managed."

Julien gave a twisted smile. "I started to turn gray early. That's made it easier. In any case, after a month's idyll, I walked into the local café one day to see Uncle Hubert. He said he hadn't come to drag me back to Britain. He had no desire to see me put on trial. It would be bad for the family and a waste of my talents. His word."

"And your supposed death left him heir to the earldom."

"My being hanged would have done the same, but yes, it did. I'd never had much interest in being Lord Carfax—I wanted to be as far as possible from the man my father was, so why should I want his title?—so that didn't much concern me. Uncle Hubert said he'd keep my secret."

"If you went to work for him."

"Once a spymaster…Though even then it was clear it wouldn't be an exclusive arrangement. He gave me an initial assignment—to retrieve some papers from the local garrison—and he helped me get credentials to set myself up in Paris. But from the start it was clear I'd choose my employers. I didn't share information about Josephine with him. At least, not all of it. As I got older and took on more jobs, his control lessened. But he could still reel me in when he wanted to. He had papers that proved what I'd done. Which gave him a certain control over me—tempered by the fact that I was living a different identity, in any case. Unfortunately, the papers also gave him control over Sylvie."

"I always wondered how she came to work for him," Malcolm said. "I thought it was her family's straitened circumstances."

Julien's mouth tightened. "That was only part of it. She couldn't leave if she wanted to. Sylvie has a lot to answer for, but what Carfax did to her as a girl is damnable. She's probably right that if she'd married Lydgate it would have been a disaster, but I do think she should have had a chance to try. I don't think much of what he did to Lydgate either. Though Lydgate could have broken away, at least at the start."

"Yes," Malcolm said, Oliver Lydgate's betrayal still rank in his throat, "he could have done. Though he was penniless when Carfax recruited him. That's something I've never known."

"Nor have I, precisely."

"You've been on your own, far more than I ever have, at least in terms of fortune. And so years later you and Sylvie and Oliver all wanted to break away from Carfax."

"As did other of Carfax's agents we'd come to know. Craven, of all people, gave me an idea of where we could get papers that would give us leverage over Carfax. Even I couldn't manage it on my own."

Malcolm thought back to the exchange he'd heard between Carfax and Julien in Hyde Park a year and a half ago. "So you got the incriminating evidence back."

"Most of it. Carfax still knows what I've done, so as he pointed out to me that night in Hyde Park, I'll never be entirely free. But then, I knew what he'd done, and the truth of who I am could destroy him, in a sense. I'm sorry, by the way, that I didn't get him to protect Mélanie when I was negotiating. I didn't know he knew about her. My letting it slip to Sylvie was one of my more criminally careless moments."

"It's all right." It was the obvious response, but Malcolm found he meant it. "Italy was good for us in a lot of ways. And Aunt Frances got Mel a more thorough pardon than you could have negotiated with Carfax."

"That last is true. I still can't forgive myself for telling Sylvie."

"We all have lapses."

"You're a better man than I, Rannoch. That was a lapse I shouldn't have made. In any case, I was far less under Carfax's control after I traded papers with him. But I could never entirely break free."

Malcolm studied Julien. The fine-boned face beneath the

distinctive shock of fair hair he now knew was dyed was still the face of the eight-year-old boy in the painting who had been Viscount Worsley. "Don't you want it back?"

"What?" Julien gave an uncharacteristically rough laugh. "The title? Carfax Court? Can you see my presiding over an estate and sitting in the House of Lords?"

"I can see you doing just about anything, St. Juste. Arthur."

"Can you see my wanting to?"

"That depends. You, of all people, should know we can change."

Julien stretched his legs out in front of him and contemplated the toes of his boots. "I ran away for a reason. A number of reasons. To protect myself. But also because I had no desire for the life I was destined for. And little use for what my father had made of it. As I said, I wanted to be as different from him as possible."

"I can't see your being an Earl Carfax who was remotely like your father. Or like your uncle."

"I suspect they'd agree with you." Julien fixed his gaze across the square. Two young men with high shirt points had emerged from a coffeehouse and were walking along the pavement as though they'd imbibed more than coffee. "Do you know the Canaletto at Carfax Court?"

Malcolm pictured the painting of a Venetian canal that hung in the grand salon. "It's a beautiful piece. One of my favorites."

"Your—Alistair procured it for my father."

Malcolm gripped the side of the bench. The wind seemed to have shifted, cutting against his face. "St. Juste. Are you saying your father was an Elsinore League member?"

Julien met Malcolm's gaze, eyes narrowed against the sun, or perhaps against the possibilities. "I'm not sure. The last time I saw my father I hadn't even heard of the League. But Alistair came to the house. Probably more than you realized."

"I'm sure more than I realized. I was scarcely aware of my—of Alistair's activities."

"Alistair supplied my father with works of art. We know he did that for League members. He may have done it for others who weren't League members, but it's suggestive. And it might help explain Uncle Hubert's obsession with the League. I don't think much of Uncle Hubert, but he has twice the understanding my father had. If not four or five times. If Father was a member of the League, I suspect being on the outskirts would have driven Uncle Hubert mad."

"I always thought being outside the League bothered Carfax. But I never thought of your father's being an insider."

"If the League had been sensible, they'd have made Uncle Hubert a member and co-opted him. But they obviously didn't see what he'd develop into. And he might have turned on them anyway. He's fairly focused on what's good for him, but he does give a bit more than lip service to what he thinks is good for Britain. Which is often the opposite of what actually is."

"You're sounding like a Radical."

"To hear my father and Uncle Hubert tell it, I was one before I disappeared. But as I said, I can't claim to have been driven by conviction."

"I think we're all driven by a complex mix of things." Malcolm watched Julien as the wind shifted the clouds overhead. Despite Mel's and Raoul's warnings, he'd always rather liked St. Juste, but he had at first seemed like an amoral agent for hire with quixotic personal loyalties. Odd to have got to this place where he felt a sense of kinship with the other man over some of the things that mattered most to him. "The League never told you your father was one of their number?" Malcolm asked.

"They've never admitted they know who I am."

"And Carfax? Your uncle Hubert, that is? Have you asked him about your father and the League?"

Julien hesitated. "I own I'm not fond of discussing my father. Especially with Uncle Hubert. But I did ask him once. However much I may try to say my father doesn't matter, his having a connection to the League would be significant. Uncle Hubert wouldn't give me a straight answer. Not surprisingly, as he rarely gives anyone a straight answer about anything. But his evasions can speak volumes."

Malcolm looked at Julien. Twenty-four hours ago he'd have said his personal connection to the other man had begun with his wife. Julien flashed a quick smile. "I know. I don't think much of my father, and Alistair Rannoch wasn't your father at all. But it's odd imagining a connection between them. My father was a natural League member, really. Out for his own gain, not scrupulous about how he got it. Unlike Uncle Hubert, who at least has his beliefs of a flexible sort."

Malcolm thought of Carfax and his comments lately about Julien. And Kitty. "Kitty knows who you are, doesn't she?"

Julien raised a brow. "What makes you think so?"

"I can accept coincidence, but if she doesn't know, her naming her daughter Guenevere strains belief."

A reluctant smile curved Julien's mouth. "I still can't quite believe she did that."

"It says a lot about her feelings for you." Malcolm watched Julien in the shifting light. "Just as your telling her the truth says a lot about your feelings for her."

"Don't romanticize, Rannoch. You don't know under what circumstances I told her."

"I can't imagine your telling her without trust."

"Mmm." Julien looked away. "There are still slaves in Argentina. It was the first place I'd lived where I'd confronted the reality head on. One could say I should have understood it well enough before then."

"There's a difference between understanding intellectually and observing firsthand."

Julien shot a look at him. "Perhaps. Perhaps I'm letting myself off the hook. But in any case, the stark reality struck me, and I was shaken. Shaken enough that I wanted to talk. And I couldn't talk about my mother without talking about myself. Though I wouldn't have talked to almost anyone else." He gave a reluctant grin. "Kitty's important to me. I think you already knew that."

"I had a glimmering."

Julien watched Malcolm for a moment. "She warned me you'd work it out."

"And she probably thought I'd do so sooner as well. How does she feel about being Lady Carfax?"

Julien looked away. "I haven't asked her."

"To marry you, or to become Lady Carfax?"

Julien smoothed a shirt cuff. "Neither, actually. One, at least, seems beyond the realm of possibility."

"Don't underrate yourself, St. Juste."

"With Kitty or with Carfax?"

"Either."

"My uncle is a formidable enemy. And of course there's Kitty's aversion to marriage in general."

"I once had the same aversion."

"I'm not Mélanie."

"Probably a good thing, in this case. Kitty and Mel are better friends than I ever thought possible, but I think Kitty would much prefer you as a romantic partner."

Julien grinned and clapped Malcolm on the shoulder. "You're a good fellow, Rannoch."

"There are those of us who'd back you if you took on Carfax."

"Thank you." Julien drew a breath. "I don't say that as lightly as I usually do. But you're assuming I want to be Lord Carfax."

"I'm not assuming anything. I can understand your being conflicted. I can understand Kitty's being conflicted. But it doesn't change the fact that you could push Carfax out." As he said the words, the reality settled over Malcolm. The easily spoken words could represent an irrevocable shift in their world.

"My dear Malcolm. Do you imagine losing the title would really push Carfax out? Or do anything close to it? He was a force in military intelligence long before he became earl."

"This could destroy him." Somehow for all he was used to thinking of Carfax as a man without limits, this made Malcolm grow cold.

"Nothing's going to destroy my uncle."

"It could save David."

Julien's face went unexpectedly still. "David's situation complicates things. Mind you, he'd make a much better earl than I would."

"He doesn't want it. He never did. I was there when he first learned he was the heir. It was like a physical weight."

"And you think I could wear it more lightly? Aren't you concerned for all the Mallinson tenants?"

"Oddly, I don't think you'd neglect them."

"You always had ridiculous faith in human nature, Malcolm. I suppose it's good it's still intact."

"If you think that's good, it speaks volumes."

Julien swung his head towards Malcolm. His face was in shadow, but Malcolm could feel the pure force of his gaze. "I won't let Carfax destroy David. My word on it. Though for what it's worth, I think David is a deal stronger than anyone credits."

"Yes," Malcolm said. "So do I. It doesn't mean he wouldn't be happier away from the earldom."

"You, of course, could now render any choice I might be said to have in the matter rather superfluous."

Malcolm held the gaze of his boyhood friend. "I wouldn't do that. It's your life. And God knows I know about living undercover. Part of me didn't want to come back from Italy. I hate to think of Carfax's getting away with this, though."

"My dear Malcolm. Surely this is far from the worst thing you've seen Carfax get away with."

"A point. That doesn't make it any better."

"I haven't suffered."

"You've made a remarkable life. But exile isn't easy on anyone."

"Speaking as someone who still loves Britain."

"And you don't?"

Julien adjusted the brim of his hat. "I don't believe I've ever admitted to loving anything or anyone."

"Oh, admitting's a different story. I was prepared to walk away myself."

"But you're glad you didn't."

A hackney rattled by. Two boys ran along the far side of the square, their governess hurrying after them. A chestnut seller pushed a barrow along the pavement. Malcolm breathed in the smell of chestnuts, the soot and grime, the damp air and gray skies, the clatter and energy of London. "I could have been happy abroad. I think I could be happy anywhere with my family. And as I said, a part of me didn't want to leave what we'd found in Italy. But yes, I'm glad we came back." He hesitated. "I don't think it was coincidence that Carfax mentioned your father last night."

Julien's gaze narrowed. "You think he wanted you to put the pieces together? I wouldn't be surprised if he did. It's possible this will come down not to whether or not I can push Carfax out, but whether or not I can keep him from dragging me back in."

"Has he said anything?"

"He's hinted at it. I think he thinks it may be necessary to outplay the League."

Malcolm paused for a moment, more pieces falling together

in his mind. "This is part of why the League have wanted you at least since Italy, isn't it? They want to use you against Carfax. Which means at least someone in the League knows who you are."

"I think so, on both counts. And no, I don't know who in the League knows my identity. Or even which faction it is, though I think it's the group trying to wrest control. The same group that tried to destroy Glenister. I wouldn't be surprised if they turned on Beverston too. Carfax told me at the theatre the night of Mélanie's pantomime that it might be necessary for me to destroy him. A bit dramatic. But I think he's decided that at some point my reemergence might be a way to outwit the League by taking away a weapon they could use against him."

"He has a point. And of course if he could control how you reemerged, it might not destroy him at all."

"Precisely."

"Could he cover up the evidence against you?"

"Oh, yes. He's the one who gathered it in the first place. And once I recovered the papers a year and a half ago, the written proof was gone." Julien frowned at a mud puddle on the gravel. There was something pared back about him, as though external layers had been stripped away.

"I won't do anything with the information until you ask me to," Malcolm said. "Though I don't know that my keeping it secret can contain the secret. But I'll try to make sure it plays out as you wish. I'll try to help you get what you want. Assuming you know what that is."

Julien gave a faint smile. "Funny. Kitty said something similar to me a few months ago."

"Do you know what you want?"

"I didn't then." Julien paused and drew a breath. The wind had whipped up again, bringing a sting of damp that was unmistakably London. "I think now perhaps I do."

CHAPTER 27

Laura refilled her coffee cup and then Raoul's. "Any luck?" she asked, glancing at the sheets of paper before him on the breakfast table. Kitty had sent round a copy of the notes of Carfax's meetings with Spanish and Italian authorities, and Raoul was looking through them for anything that might explain last night's attacks and Thornsby's interest in the matter.

"Nothing so far that would make these more urgent than they seemed from what Kitty and Simon and the others told us last night." Raoul stretched out a hand for the coffee with a grateful smile. They were, unusually, alone in the breakfast parlor. Malcolm had left early to see Beverston and then to update Harry and Cordy (who were going to be very upset at having missed out on the previous night's adventures). Mélanie had just left for the Tavistock, and Blanca had taken the children to the square garden, while Addison was out making inquiries himself. Ben and Nerezza hadn't come down yet. It was still early for everyone, but the tension was making them early risers.

"Do you know the Spaniards and Italians who were at the

meeting?" Laura asked, leaning against the arm of her husband's chair.

"I know the Spaniards by name." Raoul reached up and caught hold of her hand. "I suppose it's possible one of them or one of the Italians could find the release of the notes threatening enough to have taken severe action. Perhaps not on the grounds of what the release would do politically so much as because of what it might do to their careers. The only other named person is an aide Carfax had with him." Raoul looked back down at the papers. "A Toby Wilton."

"Wilton?" Laura set down her coffee cup.

"Yes, does it mean anything to do you?"

"No. That is—Wilton is the name of the family Edith Simmons is governess to. She's the young classical scholar whom Lewis Thornsby's elder brother is in love with. But Wilton's hardly an uncommon name. I don't suppose—"

She broke off as the breakfast parlor door opened to admit Nerezza and Benedict.

"Do come in," Laura said as they hesitated on the threshold. "Valentin just brought fresh coffee."

Nerezza gave a quick, almost shy smile. For all her hardened, brash demeanor at times, she reminded Laura of the teenage girls she had once been governess to, trying out their adult skin and still not quite comfortable in it.

Benedict pulled a chair out for Nerezza while Laura poured coffee for both of them. "I'm trying to convince Ben we needn't run back to the country immediately," Nerezza said. "We met Mr. Rannoch on the stairs earlier this morning, and he said that he didn't think Carfax was a threat."

"It's not Carfax, it's the League." Ben sat beside her. A month ago, he hadn't heard of the League, but now he spoke with the air of one who knew full well what they were capable of.

"If Carfax knew where we were, don't you think the League did too?" Nerezza accepted a cup of coffee from Laura and took a grateful sip. "Rupert and Bertrand have been prepared all month for the League to try something, and they haven't."

"They might be biding their time," Ben said.

"Well, I'm not proposing to go running about London, but I do think we're safe enough here for a bit."

Laura exchanged a quick look with Raoul, because a year ago the Berkeley Square house had proved anything but safe.

"We've had our share of dangers even here," Raoul said. "But I think you're right, it doesn't seem likely the League will try anything immediate, and we'll be prepared if they do."

Nerezza set her coffee down. "Are you worried about the children?" Her gaze went to Clara, who was sleeping in a basket beside the table. "I should have thought—"

"No." Raoul touched her arm with a quick smile. "We're used to protecting the children. Just as Rupert and Bertrand knew they could protect Stephen when they took you to the country. Besides, selfishly, you may have more information to offer. You're the only one who's actually met the person who is apparently trying to wrest away control of the League."

"I wish I could remember something else that might help," Nerezza said. She blew on her coffee, then glanced at Ben. "Just because I can't leave the house doesn't mean you shouldn't. Perhaps you should call on Lady Shroppington?"

Ben grimaced. "To offer my condolences about Lewis, you mean?"

"Yes, and because she might admit something to you."

Ben took a drink of coffee. "I can't help but feel for her. I mean, I think she was as fond of Lewis as she was of anyone. He knew how to talk her round his finger. I always thought she was a bit of a gorgon as a boy. I hadn't seen her much in recent years, what with being at Oxford and going to the Continent. But I did see her in December—just a few days before the pantomime." He smiled at Nerezza in memory of the night they had reunited, but then his brows drew together. "It was a bit odd. I was in Green Park and I saw her across the park with a younger lady. She was wearing a hat with a veil—Lady Shroppington, that is—and I almost didn't recognize her at first, but there's something about the way she holds her shoulders that's unmistakable. I thought I should stop and pay my respects, but she didn't look best pleased when I did. Didn't even present me to her companion."

"What did the companion look like?" Raoul asked.

"Tall. Almost as tall as me, I think. Pretty, but not in a conventional way, if you know what I mean." He flushed. "That is—"

"It's all right, Ben," Nerezza said with a smile. "I don't mind your thinking other girls pretty."

"No, that's not it. I mean—nothing could compare with you and you know it. But there was something arresting about this girl. She had sort of tawny hair that looked as if she couldn't ever keep it pinned up."

Laura set down her coffee, her fingers suddenly numb. "What was she wearing?"

"Wearing? Oh, nothing much. That is, she was wearing clothes, of course. A pelisse, I think. It was dark. Black or gray. Maybe dark blue. Not what you'd call fashionable. In fact—I mean, one doesn't like to stare, but I remember noticing that the hem was quite caked with mud."

Laura pushed her chair back. "You're on child duty for the next hour, sweetheart," she told Raoul. "We can't leave Blanca on her own with all of them."

"Certainly," he replied. "May I ask why?"

Laura bent to tuck the blanket round Clara. "Because the young lady Ben saw with Lady Shroppington sounds very much like Edith Simmons, the woman Lewis's brother Thomas is in love with. Edith told me she'd never met Lady Shroppington. And her employers are named Wilton."

"Very interesting indeed," Raoul said. "You should talk to her at once."

Benedict looked between them. "Are you going alone?"

"Miss Simmons is far more likely to talk to a former fellow governess she already knows than to a Spanish-Irish Radical she's never met before," Raoul pointed out.

"Aren't you worried?" Ben asked.

Raoul settled back in his chair. "No more than Laura would be about me. Have a care, sweetheart."

"WHERE ARE YOU GOING, MUMMY?" Emily asked, as Laura stopped by the square garden.

"To pay a call. I won't be long."

"Is it part of the Investigation?" Colin asked.

Laura tugged on a glove. She'd been in such a hurry she'd left the house without putting them on. "I think so. When the two of you were playing with the Wilton children, did they happen to mention their parents' names?"

Colin and Emily exchanged glances. "The father's starts with a T," Emily said. "Tony or—Toby, that's it. The little boy told us his full name is Winston Eustace Toby Wilton for his grandfather, his uncle, and his father."

"Splendid, darling." Laura pulled on the second glove. "Do you remember anything else in particular the children said about their parents?"

Colin frowned. "Their father was a diplomat, like Daddy. They lived in France for a while, like we did. Oh and—" Colin looked at Emily, frowned again. "I'm not sure about the parents' marriage. Winston told me there was a letter delivered for his father and Miss Simmons moved it, because she said she didn't want their mother to see it. I don't think Winston understood what that might mean." Colin looked up at Laura with grave eyes. "Should I have said that sooner? I told Mummy a lot of things Winston and Sally told us, but I didn't say that."

Because he didn't like talking about trouble between parents. "I understand perfectly," Laura said. "And yes, it may be important, though we wouldn't have understood how until now." She bent to kiss them both. "You're both splendid investigators."

She waved to Blanca, Jessica, and Pedro, and set off to look for Edith Simmons.

CHAPTER 28

Julien came back into their rooms sooner than Kitty had expected. The boys were sprawled on the sitting room carpet, acting out their own version of the Battle of Waterloo with their toy soldiers. Kitty was building a block tower with Genny and attempting to keep her from running into the battlefield. All the while, Kitty kept sorting through the events of the previous night and what they might mean. The attack, the revelations. Who now knew what. And Julien's reaction both to the revelations and to her being attacked. Not to mention what Malcolm might be saying to Julien even now.

She was remembering—probably rather unnecessarily, given how many urgent matters she had to consider—the way he had held her through the night, when light footsteps and the opening of the door signaled her lover's return. Genny crawled over and grabbed his boots.

"Didn't Uncle Malcolm come back with you?" Timothy asked, a British infantryman and a French cavalry officer in one hand and a cannon in the other.

"No, though I'm sure you'll see him soon. He had things to do for the investigation."

"Don't you?" Leo said.

"Not just now." Julien swung Genny up. "What do you say we go to the park? The sky's clearing and there's no sign of rain for a bit."

The boys let out whoops of excitement.

Kitty regarded her lover as the boys ran to snatch up jackets and boots with admirable speed. "Are you going to suggest I stay home and rest?"

"No, I was thinking fresh air would do you good."

She watched him for a moment, as he settled Genny on his shoulders. "It might, at that. I need to clear my head." With everything going on, even a morning in the lodgings felt too confining. But she was still suspicious of Julien's motives. When did he ever do anything without an ulterior motive? Of course, if her suspicions about Malcolm's visit were correct, he could well have reason to talk.

They made their way to Green Park with Genny on Julien's shoulders and the boys running ahead. After throwing a ball with the boys for a quarter hour, Julien retreated to the bench where Kitty was sitting, while Genny took careful steps beside the bench.

Julien leaned back beside her, his arm stretched along the back of the bench, touching her shoulders. "Malcolm worked it out. About me."

A few words that were going to change their lives. "I thought he might have done."

"It was only a matter of time, as you said," Julien said, his gaze on the boys. "Carfax seems to have nudged him along by talking about my father. Which means Carfax wanted him to put the pieces together."

She felt herself stiffen and willed the tension from her shoulders. She'd known from the moment Julien came to London and back into their lives that this was inevitable. That didn't make it any less momentous. "He's pushing you to emerge from the shadows."

"We've known that for a while. But now the pace seems to have accelerated." Julien caught hold of Genny's hand as she worked her way along the bench past them. "Malcolm says he won't reveal anything unless I ask him to. He hasn't even told Mélanie."

"But you're not hidden anymore." She couldn't be quite sure of what his talk with Malcolm had been like, but surely it had let him grasp on to a part of himself that was Arthur. A part she'd never precisely known, for all he had revealed to her. Julien St. Juste, agent for hire, was her comrade and lover. What Arthur Mallinson, rightful Earl Carfax, might be to her was another question entirely.

"No. Or at least I won't be soon, one way or another." Julien put a steadying hand on Genny's shoulder as she moved down the bench. "I talked to Malcolm a bit about my mother."

Kitty watched the fine line of his profile. She could guess what that carefully casual statement had cost him. "I'm glad. He didn't know your mother, did he?"

"No, she died when he was a baby. But he was looking at a portrait of me with her last night when he pieced it together. It hangs in the hall at Carfax House." Julien watched the arc of the ball the boys were throwing. "Malcolm, of course, being Malcolm, was inclined to make excuses for me. More than I made for myself. At least, I think more than I made for myself."

"You never make excuses for yourself, Julien. And speaking as someone who knows Malcolm rather well, while his empathy can make him forgiving to a fault, he also has rather keen insights into other people. Remarkably keen, actually."

Julien's gaze shot to her face. "Talking of insights, he said it said a lot that I told you the truth of my past."

Her throat went tight for reasons she couldn't have

explained. Or didn't want to explain. "You needed to talk to someone. And we were half the world away. That made it easier."

"No." His gaze stayed steady on her own. "That is, I did need to talk and we were half the world away. But I think I'd have talked to you in England or Spain or a jungle in Africa. And I don't think I'd have talked to anyone else anywhere." Julien let his gaze drift over the park. Rolling green lawns beneath a gray English sky. "A few months ago, you asked me what I wanted."

Kitty turned her head to look at him. In the wake of his talk with Malcolm and the revelation of his identity, she'd been ready for warnings, ultimatums, a surprising revelation. Even a farewell. But not this. "I think I actually said surely you didn't want a family."

Julien cast a glance at Genny, walking with one hand on the bench and her gaze fixed on her shiny black shoes with great concentration, then looked at the boys, who were now wrestling with a fine disregard for what the damp grass and mud might do to their coats. "And I said I didn't know what I wanted. Which was true then. And has been for a long time. Since Waterloo, at least. But I think I'm getting a glimmering."

She watched him. "And?"

His gaze shot to her face. "I want you. Not in the obvious ways. Well, of course in the obvious ways. But I want to wake up with you and go to bed with you and spend as much time as I can with you in between."

Genny grabbed hold of Julien's bootleg to steady herself. Julien touched her hair and supported her shoulder as she moved to the next bench. "I want to watch your children grow up and help them however I can." He turned his head back to meet Kitty's gaze again. "I don't want anyone else in my bed. There hasn't been anyone else for some time, by the way. Not since well before we reunited in September. And I find I'm distinctly averse to the idea of anyone else's being in yours."

For a moment Kitty wasn't sure she could breathe. "Darling Julien. Whatever I may have claimed in the abstract, with three children and you, do you really think I have time for anyone else?"

"Well, then." He seemed to release his breath. His arm settled closer round her shoulders. "I don't suppose you'd consider marrying me?"

"Good God, Julien." Perhaps she should have seen it coming, but she hadn't. "Don't get too conventional all at once, there'll be a reaction."

"There are certain advantages. I hate to use the word protection, but I could help you and the children more, should it be needed, in ways I can't as your unacknowledged lover. Besides —" He frowned. "I rather like the idea—"

Kitty raised a brow. "Of my being formally committed to you?"

"No. Of my being formally committed to you."

"Oh." She looked into those brilliant blue eyes that could gleam with mockery or at the oddest times soften with tenderness. "I didn't think you wanted to be committed to anything. Or anyone."

"My dear." He took her hand and lifted it to his lips with the formality of a suitor. "Married or not, I believe I just made a commitment to you. And the children."

His fingers were warm and comforting round her own. And she'd always been afraid of comfort because so often it was an illusion. Possibilities swam before her eyes. For him. For them. For the children. So much determined by what steps they chose now. "You're going to go back, aren't you? To your old life."

"Not if you don't wish it. You're right, I'm going to have to make a decision soon. That's why we had to have this conversation first. Say the word and we'll disappear into the wilds of South America. Not that wilds sound very appealing, but I have quite agreeable memories of the Argentine. Or we can go to

Spain. A bit more challenging to lose ourselves there, but with both our talents I'm sure we can manage to disappear, if that's what you want."

"I thought we were discussing what you want."

"I told you." His gaze stayed open and steady on her face. "I want you. On whatever terms I can get you. I want you to be happy. For someone who's led a remarkably selfish life, I'm not much used to thinking about happiness, but I can't really see being happy if you aren't. But all right—" His gaze shifted across the park as though he were looking through the curtain of trees still damp from yesterday's rain for some vision of what their life might be. "All other things being equal, I suppose I feel a certain impulse to stay and try to repair the damage."

"It's not your damage."

"Some of it is. More than I care to contemplate. From my being gone. From my working for Carfax. From the vacuum I created. I can't leave David with all of it. If I'd made different choices, his own life would be easier."

"I can't see Carfax's letting David go his own way, regardless."

"No, but he wouldn't have been so hard on him. More important, I don't think David would have been so hard on himself." He looked at her. "Would you hate it?"

Kitty looked at the boys, now climbing a tree, at Genny, who had stooped down to pick a blade of grass, at her own and Julien's interlaced fingers. "It's rather a lot to contemplate. A few minutes ago I was convinced I'd never marry again."

"I know. You've said so often enough. You really thought you could get rid of me that easily?"

"Who said anything about getting rid of you?" She'd been more concerned he'd decide to leave for his own reasons. To protect her, to protect himself, because he wanted a life in the shadows. "But marriage is a bit of a leap. You know I'd never be a conventional Lady Carfax."

Julien gave a whoop of laughter that dispersed a cloud of tension hanging over them. "What a ghastly thought. I'd be horrified if you did."

"I think Carfax—your uncle—would be horrified for other reasons."

"I won't deny Carfax is going to be a challenge. But when have either of us not been up to a challenge?"

She found herself smiling. "We've never taken on Carfax directly. Not together."

"I did rather well a year and a half ago. And I didn't have you." He ran a thumb over her knuckles. "I wouldn't insult you with the word 'protect,' my sweet. But given that I'd be dragging you into a situation with Carfax, I trust you'll believe that I'll do everything in my power to protect you from him."

"And yourself?"

"Well, I may need your help protecting myself."

Possibilities danced before her eyes again. She felt like child looking through the window at a sweet shop she knew she wouldn't be allowed to enter. Or at least feared she wouldn't. "I wouldn't give up Spain."

"I'd never expect you to." His voice was singularly free of mockery. "I told you last night I'm perfectly prepared to help while you tilt at whatever windmills you choose."

"As Lord Carfax?"

"As Lord Carfax I could be rather a lot of help to you. I'd sit in Parliament, among other things."

Kitty regarded him. "Are you saying you'd help me in order to indulge me?"

"Since when have I indulged you? I'm saying I'd help you because that's what couples do for each other. At least, that's what I think from observation, not having a lot of experience myself. But also because I think it would be a good idea myself." He drew in and released a breath. "It's just possible I think there are things I could do about some of the things that are rotten in England."

He spoke in the same ironic voice as always. But something had cracked in the studied detachment he wore like armor. "That's rather a staggering statement, Julien."

He returned her gaze, his own unusually free of defenses. "Past time I made myself useful, don't you think?"

"I'd never have called you useless."

"That's because you're kind."

"Don't be silly, Julien." Kitty reached out to steady Genny. "I'm not in the least kind."

"Two can play at defenses, my sweet. At the very least, I haven't paid enough attention to the uses to which I put whatever talents I have." He touched Genny's hair as she picked her way past him, then looked back at Kitty and tightened his fingers round her own. "If it was ever too much for you, we'd leave. My word on it. You know me well enough to know I'd find a way to do it."

"Julien." She reached up without thinking and touched his face. "I'm not your mother. And more to the point, you aren't your father. We can do this."

"So you will?" His gaze rested on her with unwonted tension. "Marry me?"

The clouds shifted in the slate gray of the sky, like pieces of a future still taking shape. Possibilities that had seemed out of reach. Resolves that could reshape themselves. "A woman gives up so much when she marries. Control of any fortune she may have. Of her children. Of her own body. I was lucky, really, that Edward wasn't worse. But I got tired of it. Of having to manipulate him to get the things I wanted. Of not being able to say no. To all sorts of things." She looked down at Genny's clear, determined face, vowing yet again that her daughter's life would be different. "When Edward died, I swore I'd never marry again. Never put myself in circumstances where a man could have that power over me. Not unless it was someone I trusted completely." The future slid into place in her mind. No longer an out-of-reach ideal, but something she could grasp hold of. She pulled their intertwined hands up to her mouth and kissed his knuckles. "I hadn't quite realized until now how very much I trust you. Thank goodness. I want you, Julien. If it takes marriage to get you, I shall have to succumb."

Something sparked in his eyes. "I'd have said no one trusted me."

"Yes, well, it's a good thing we can surprise each other."

His fingers tightened round her own. "My darling—" he said on a note she'd never heard before.

Genny grabbed Julien's leg. The boys, as though aware something had happened, had stopped playing and were looking at Kitty and Julien.

Julien shot Kitty a quick smile, put a hand on Genny's shoulder, and gestured to the boys. The boys ran over. Leo's gaze went from Julien to Kitty. "Is something wrong?"

"On the contrary," Julien said. "At least, I don't think so. How would you feel about your mother's and my getting married?"

"Wizard," Timothy said.

"Are you asking us for her hand in marriage?" Leo asked.

"No," Kitty said. "No one should be asked for a woman's hand except the woman herself."

"Fair enough," Julien said. "On the other hand, as members of the family, your vote on adding me to it definitely counts."

Timothy scratched his head. "You're already part of our family."

"But it would be nice for it to be official," Leo said. He grinned. "Very nice."

"Well, then." Julien shook Leo's hand and then Timothy's. "We have a wedding to plan."

CHAPTER 29

"How long have you been working for them?" Laura asked.

Edith Simmons's fingers closed on the serviceable blue wool of the pelisse that so reminded Laura of her governess days. "Working for whom?" Edith said.

"The Elsinore League."

Edith relaxed her fingers with determination. "That sounds like something out of a novel."

"You needn't pretend," Laura said. "I used to work for them myself."

Edith's gaze shot to her face, her defenses momentarily breached by surprise.

"They didn't tell you?" Laura said. "Or you're surprised I admitted it?" She glanced across Green Park, where she had once again found Edith, and where her two charges were racing over the lawn. "I confess the coincidence startled me at first. And then I realized it wasn't coincidence at all. Why should I have thought I was the only governess the League employed as an agent? Who better to gather undercover information? Nearly every family with pretensions to gentility and children of a certain age employs a governess. We're trained to blend into the background. We observe bits and pieces of family life, parties, social calls, without ever attracting much notice because people are trained not to see us, and we're trained not to attract notice. We move through the public rooms of a house much more than most servants. We overhear things. We can glance through papers. No one raises an eyebrow unless we're caught with the mistress's jewels or in the master's bedchamber. Or in the garden with our charges' elder brother as I once was, but that's another story."

Edith's shoulders straightened. "You've admitted a great deal, Mrs. O'Roarke. I haven't admitted anything. Why on earth do you think I'm working for this League?"

"Toby Wilton has worked for Lord Carfax, whom the League are targeting."

"That scarcely proves anything."

"You were seen here in Green Park talking with Lady Shroppington. Whom you told me you had never met."

"Are you suggesting Lady Shroppington is connected to this League?"

"Her godson Lord Beverston is prominently involved. I suspected she was relaying information for him." Laura glanced at the Wilton children, who were now climbing a tree. "And young Winston told Colin he saw you putting away a letter of his father's and said it might distress his mother. Colin thought it was because it was a love letter, but I suspect in fact you were moving the letter so you could examine it and just making an excuse to the children." Laura regarded Edith for a moment. "They used my daughter to control me. Whom were you protecting?"

Edith gripped her elbows. "Why should anything I did be to protect anyone?"

"Because I've seen enough of you to think you wouldn't work

for people like that without being forced to do so. Or perhaps I've misjudged you. You may have been drawn by the thrill of it. Or the money. Which wouldn't be so shocking. I can't say I'd blame you. It's difficult to be a woman on her own."

"No! I wouldn't." Edith drew a sharp breath. "My younger brother has gaming debts."

"And the League bought them up?"

She gave a quick nod. "He could have ended in debtors' prison. Or my father could have, trying to protect him. Or both. They still could. I never saw myself as the sacrificial sort. But I couldn't stand by—And they made it seem as though I was helping. Working for Britain. It was months before I really understood whom I was working for."

"Yes, it was much the same with me."

Edith's mouth hardened. "I even liked it. Feeling I had a sense of purpose. That I was doing something. Challenging myself. Not that that being a governess isn't a challenge. But it's a prescribed life. There was a freedom in having a secret life. Until I realized working for them was a cage all its own. Is a cage all its own." She looked away, shoulders hunched, then looked back at Laura. "I think that's why I told you. I couldn't bear being in that cage any more. That and that you already believed it, in any case."

"They wanted information on the Wiltons?"

"That was part of it. They said they were enemies of Britain. Hinted they might be foreign spies, which I'm sure now is nonsense. In truth, I still can't figure out why they should be so important to the League." She bit her lip, realizing she had said the name, then shook her head. "Silly, the power a name can have. But they also wanted to use my connections to the Classicists' Society."

For all she'd seen, Laura hadn't anticipated that. "They wanted you to spy on Harry and Cordy."

Edith met Laura's gaze and nodded. "I was already a

member. I knew them. I liked them. But they wanted me to get closer."

"And learn what?"

"Whatever I could. Mostly anything to do with the Rannochs. And your husband. And Lady Frances and Mr. Archibald Davenport. And later, Mrs. Ashford and a man named Julien St. Juste. If they were friends. If they spoke together. I said I'd only seen the Rannochs once or twice when they'd come to lectures, and I hadn't met most of you at all. They wanted me to get closer to the Davenports. I like the Davenports. Which made it harder." She hesitated a moment, fingering a fold of her pelisse. "They also wanted me to get close to Thomas."

"Thomas Thornsby?" Lewis's scholarly elder brother was the last person Laura had expected to hear named.

Edith nodded. "We already—we already were friends. I liked him. Not that I expect him to believe that if—when he learns the truth."

"You'd be surprised at what people can understand. But—Thomas is obviously a brilliant scholar, but the League have little interest in scholarship. Why did they want information about him?"

"I'm not sure. I asked and they wouldn't even give the sort of vague hints they gave me about the Wiltons. But I think it may have been the family connection."

"Family? Edith—" Laura studied the younger woman. "Who recruited you? Was it Beverston?"

"Beverston? Oh, no. It was Lady Shroppington."

For a moment Laura felt she was holding herself upright by sheer willpower. "Lady Shroppington is part of the League?"

"You didn't know? The way they talk, I got the sense the Rannochs knew most of those in the League."

"A great many. But evidently not all. We didn't know they had women as members."

"Not a great many, I think. And not official members. But Lady Shroppington seems to have been involved from the beginning, from what I can make out. She found me because she came to hear Thomas lecture at the Classicists' Society. Wanted to see what he was up to, she said. At first I thought she was worried I had designs on him." Edith gave a rough laugh. "I was quite prepared to get huffy and assure her I had no interest in marrying. When she said she had no desire to discourage my interest in Thomas—though she also made it clear it could never lead to marriage—I wasn't sure what to think. She explained the blackmail over my brother so delicately I wasn't quite sure I understood at first. But in the end it was abundantly clear what she meant. She can be very plainspoken."

Laura was still struggling to assimilate this new image of Lady Shroppington and of the League, seemingly a group of debauched men, having a dowager amongst their number. "Do you think Lord Beverston involved Lady Shroppington in the League? She's his godmother. Perhaps he thought she could more easily talk to a young woman?" Of course the Duke of Trenchard had had no trouble blackmailing Laura into working for him, but then they'd been ex-lovers.

"Lord Beverston came with her to talk to me once," Edith said. "They were definitely working together in the League. But I didn't get the sense Beverston had brought her in. She did most of the talking. Beverston seemed to be taking his cues from her, which was odd because he struck me as a man who is accustomed to leading. The next time I saw her, she was alone. I asked her about Beverston and she said he had to learn his place. That at times he had delusions that he had more power than he did, and they were no longer allies. I was a little surprised she admitted as much to me. I had a sense they'd just had a confrontation and she was still trying to come to terms with it. That day I started to really understand who Lady Shroppington was." Edith met Laura's gaze for a moment. "I don't think Beverston brought her into the League. I think she brought him into it."

CHAPTER 30

"Would you like a cup of tea, Mrs. Rannoch?" Bessie, the Tavistock seamstress, stopped beside Mélanie's chair.

"Thank you, Bessie." Mélanie curled her hands round the steaming cup. In truth, it was welcome. So was the chance to talk to Bessie. "You used to bring Mr. Thornsby tea."

Bessie blushed. She was little more than seventeen, with a freckled face and the sort of warm brown hair that turns golden in summer. "He spent so much time at the theatre. And he was always so kind." Bessie twisted her fingers in her skirt. "Have you and Mr. Rannoch and Inspector Roth learned anything about why he was killed?"

"Not anything that would tell us who killed him," Mélanie said. "Not yet." She gestured to the chair beside her. "Bessie, did Mr. Thornsby ever talk to you about his life?"

"Not really. I mean, he was a gentleman and I was a servant to him, and gentlemen don't really talk to servants, do they?"

"Unfortunately, no. In most cases. But sometimes they let things slip. I've been undercover as a servant."

"Mr. Thornsby wasn't—he never flirted with me. He didn't have eyes for anyone but Miss Blanchard. Sometimes he'd talk about her. How lovely she was. Once—" She hesitated.

"Anything he said might be relevant," Mélanie said in a gentle voice.

"Once he asked if I thought she cared for Mr. Carmarthen."

"What did you say?"

Bessie drew her feet back beneath the chair. "That Miss Blanchard had eyes for no one but him."

"Is that what you believed?"

Bessie frowned. "Miss Blanchard cared for him. I'm sure she did. You can tell how upset she is now. She's not counterfeiting. But—you only have to look at her onstage with Mr. Carmarthen to tell there's something between them."

It was true there was an undefinable magic between Letty and Will onstage. It was on display in today's run-through for all both of them had been through. They were too professional to let emotional chaos interfere onstage. But from her childhood in a theatre company, Mélanie had known onstage chemistry didn't necessarily mean anything between the couple offstage. "Manon and Brandon give that impression onstage too," Mélanie said. "And it's pure theatrical illusion."

"Yes, perhaps. But I've seen Miss Blanchard and Mr. Carmarthen offstage as well. Not holding hands or anything. Just the way they look at each other sometimes." She shook her head. "But I didn't want to hurt Mr. Thornsby. And I didn't want to tell tales on Miss Blanchard. I don't know that Mr. Thornsby believed me, though. I'd see him watching Mr. Carmarthen. As though he was trying to puzzle him out. And then one day last week, he said the oddest thing to me."

Mélanie set her tea cup down. "What?"

"He asked me if I knew Mr. McDevitt. Which I do, of course."

Mélanie nodded. Donald McDevitt, like Thornsby, hung about the theatre. And like Thornsby, she was quite sure he was a Leveller. "Did he say why?" Mélanie asked.

"Oh, yes. He asked me if I thought Mr. McDevitt and Mr. Carmarthen looked alike. I hadn't actually thought about it before, but they do."

Mélanie frowned and considered Will Carmarthen and Donald McDevitt. High cheekbones. Full-lipped mouths. Pointed chins and slanting brows. She wasn't sure she'd ever seen them side-by-side, but comparing them in her mind there was a similarity. "Did Mr. Thornsby say why he'd asked?"

"No, but he did ask if I'd ever seen them together. And the funny thing is, I have. Once after a performance when I'd gone to gather up the costumes that need mending. I heard voices from Mr. Carmarthen's dressing room and then Mr. McDevitt came out. It wasn't my place to wonder what they were talking about, and I think they were both—"

"Part of the Levellers," Mélanie said. "They were."

"So they could have had lots of things to talk about. But in the regular run of things, I never saw them together. So it is a bit odd."

"Yes," Mélanie said. "So it is."

"MÉLANIE." Will looked up as she appeared in the doorway of his dressing room. "Do you have notes on Act I?"

"No, it's going splendidly." Mélanie pushed the door to behind her and stepped into the dressing room. Sometimes the best way to draw out the truth was to confront someone with what one suspected. "Your real name is McDevitt, isn't it?"

Will's gaze locked on her face. "Whom have you been talking to?"

"Bessie. She noticed your resemblance to Donald. But only because Lewis Thornsby asked her about it last week. She also saw you and Donald talking in here late one night."

"That doesn't prove anything,"

"No, but once she mentioned it, I could see the resemblance as well." She watched him for the length of a line of iambic pentameter. "Malcolm's country house is in Forfarshire. We spent quite a bit of time there. I know there's a McDevitt family who are large landowners near Inverness. I could go back to Berkeley Square, pull down Debrett's, look for the names of the children. But for the sake of the play, please don't ask me to do it."

Will gave a faint smile, his gaze not leaving her face. "I grew up in a small village near Inverness. Your family go back and forth from Scotland all the time, but my family didn't. I didn't even go to Edinburgh until I went to university. My mother had died when I was born. My father was happiest when he was fishing or hunting, and my elder brother took after him. I was like a changeling. I liked the outdoors well enough when I could sit down with a book, but I hadn't much interest in fishing and I abhorred hunting. I spent a lot of time on my own."

"It sounds much like the way my husband describes his childhood," Mélanie said.

Will flashed a smile at her. "I liked stories. I liked learning about other parts of the world. But I had no idea what a play was. Not until a group of traveling players came to our village when I was eight. My nurse took me to see the performance in the market square. *St. George and the Dragon*. Funny now to compare that declaiming to what we do at the Tavistock. But I was spellbound from the first. I got her to bring me back to every performance while they were in the village. I read every play I could find in my parents' library." He paused for a moment and pushed his hair back from his forehead. "My father died putting his hunter over a stone wall when I was ten. My brother and I went to live with my uncle and aunt. Our cousins were all mad for horses and fishing too, the girls as well as the boys. My brother fit right in. They all looked at me as though I'd stumbled in from the realm of the fairies. Especially when I tried to organize them to put on theatricals. But occasionally they'd indulge me. We managed a decent version of *Two Gentlemen of Verona* when I was home from school one summer. And of course at school and university I was in every play I could manage."

"So was Malcolm," Mélanie said. "He met Simon and some of his other best friends in a production of *Henry IV Part 1*. But while he knew he'd always love plays, I don't think he ever saw it as his whole life."

"And I couldn't imagine it as anything but my life. My last year at university in Edinburgh my uncle started talking about my taking orders. He had a living he wanted to set me up in. When I balked, he suggested Parliament. Or offered to buy me a commission. All very generous. But when I dragged my feet again and again, he said 'that theatrical nonsense' had addled my brain, and it was time I gave it up. My last holiday at home before I finished up at Edinburgh, he gave me an ultimatum. I had two months after I came down and then I had to decide on a suitable profession. I had an inheritance from my father, but I didn't come into it until I was five-and-twenty, which seemed an eternity at that point. So when I finished up at Edinburgh I didn't go home. I took a stagecoach to London and set up at an inn under the name Will Carmarthen. I'd never been to London before. All I had was the part of my allowance I'd managed to save. I hadn't a clue about earning a living if I couldn't get work as an actor. I tried to get auditions at Drury Lane and Covent Garden, but I couldn't get past the doormen. By the time I showed up at the Tavistock I was starting to wonder if I had enough left to get a coach to a provincial town with a theatre. I remember being a bit lightheaded when I went to the Tavistock, because all I'd had to eat was an apple and a cup of coffee from a Covent Garden stall. That and desperation may have made me bold. Bold enough to get past the doorman and to launch into the St. Crispin's Day speech before Simon could politely say no. I knew that speech by heart by the time I was ten. Even with that and the hunger and desperation, I was shocked when he hired me."

"Were you really?" Mélanie asked.

Will gave a faint grin. "I know I'm good. I was probably more arrogant then, untrained, than I am now. Still, to have a man I admired so much take me seriously and be ready to put me on the stage of one of London's major theatres—yes, that was a shock. Followed by relief at the promise of earning some money. When I asked him how soon we got paid, he gave me an advance on my salary. I went to the White Rose and had my first hot meal in weeks. And along with the relief, I was deluged by the terror of my London debut as Benvolio. Terror and exhilaration. I was happy as I'd never been before."

"Surely you worried you'd be recognized?"

"Constantly, for the first few months. I dyed my hair—it's not much darker than Letty's naturally. My family tended to stay in Scotland. My uncle and aunt hadn't been to London since their wedding journey and my brother and cousins had never been."

"Did you communicate with them?"

"I sent a letter three months after I got my position at the Tavistock. When I was sure it wasn't all a dream. I said I'd gone on the London stage. I was over one-and-twenty and my own master, so they couldn't try to stop me. But I said I'd use a different name and avoid letting anyone know who I was, to avoid sullying the family name. And that I wouldn't attempt to access any of my inheritance. So long as they left me in peace. I sent it off with some trepidation, though I told myself they couldn't drag me off like an eighteen-year-old at Gretna Green."

"What did they reply?"

"They didn't. I never heard from them. After a few months I stopped expecting to."

"That must have been hard."

Will shrugged. All these years later, the gesture was still a bit defensive. "Easier this way. A clean break. No need to wonder if I should try to go home, no need to fear a confrontation. No need to feel torn. None of my family were likely to come to London. But some of my school and university fellows might. Some were English, some were from Scots families who traveled south more than ours did. Someone who knew me could stumble across my path. I remember the first time I saw someone I'd gone to university with in a Covent Garden coffeehouse. I was sitting with a group of actors, he walked in with two other young blades. He looked right at me with no hint of recognition. Funny how much context does. We see what we expect to see."

"Yes," Mélanie said. "We do. Sometimes even when we're trained to look beyond the obvious."

"I'd stopped worrying about it," Will said. "Occasionally I'd see a familiar face in a coffeehouse, in the green room, passing on the street. But no one seemed to recognize me. One time a chap from school stared at me for a bit. I just looked back and after a moment he shrugged and said, 'Sorry, you reminded me of someone I used to know.' I started not to be sure if I recognized people because I'd known them in my old life or because I'd seen them at the theatre or elsewhere in London. Being William McDevitt started to seem not much more real than being Benvolio or Mercutio or Prince Hal or any of the other roles I'd lived deeply while I portrayed them onstage."

"I know the feeling," Mélanie said. "In a sense. From being under deep cover." There were so many times, before Malcolm learned the truth, when her life as Suzanne Rannoch had seemed more real than her life as Mélanie Lescaut.

Will nodded. "When you're an actor, what happens onstage often seems more real than the real world, in any case. I belonged in the theatre as I'd never belonged at home." He hesitated a moment. "I know it must seem odd, my turning my back on my family. Especially my brother."

"Not necessarily," Mélanie said. "My husband's relationship with his brother was complicated. They were very different. I could never quite make sense of it when I first married Malcolm. It wasn't as complete a break, but they didn't see each other much for years, though they'd been close as boys."

"Ted and I weren't," Will said. "We lived in a sort of mutual toleration. I didn't dislike him. But I confess I found him deadly dull. I don't think he disliked me. But I think I completely baffled him. I was glad to hear he'd married—our cousin Jane, as it happens—glad to hear they had children. But I felt no desire to see either of them. As I said, I'd come to believe I'd left William McDevitt behind completely. Until one night I walked offstage as Laertes, went into the green room, and saw my cousin Donald sitting with John Stanhope and Lewis Thornsby."

"He was with Thornsby?"

Will nodded. "Though that wasn't what struck me at the time. For a moment I thought I'd been found out. But Donald gave no sign of recognizing me. I walked over to some of the other actors and gave no sign of recognizing him. I thought perhaps he, like my school friends, really didn't recognize me. But the next night, he showed up at a Levellers meeting with Stanhope. Even then he gave no sign of knowing me. I told myself it really might be coincidence. Until later that night when Donald caught me by the arm in the alley behind the Tavistock. He gave me a bear hug, actually, which was a bit of a surprise. He said he was glad to know I was well and he had no desire to disrupt the life I'd made. That was why he hadn't said anything to me sooner. We repaired to a table at the back of the White Rose. He said he hadn't come looking for me. He hadn't had any notion I was Will Carmarthen until he went to the theatre with his friend Stanhope and saw me onstage. Stanhope had already told him about the Levellers and offered to bring him to a meeting. That surprised me because none of the family had ever shown much interest in politics, and what interest they had shown had been staunchly Tory. Donald said that had changed when he went to university. He's three years younger than I, so he'd been quite young when I'd last seen him. He said he could understand wanting to make a new life, and he wouldn't disrupt mine. But he wanted to be part of the Levellers. He wanted to make a difference. He sounded a bit of a starry-eyed idealist, but then I suppose we all started out that way."

"You didn't let anyone know you knew each other?" Mélanie asked.

Will shook head. "Donald asked me if I missed home. I told him what the theatre meant to me, and he seemed to understand. He said my uncle and aunt had been very concerned when I first disappeared, which made me feel a bit of a rotter. Then after three months, he said, they told everyone they'd had a letter from me saying I was taking ship for America. And another one saying I'd found employment in New York about six months later. So I knew they'd got my letter. And they'd spun a story to explain why I'd disappeared and wouldn't be back. I suppose I should be grateful they hadn't told my brother and cousins I was dead."

"I'm sorry." Mélanie reached out to squeeze Will's hand.

"Don't be. As I said, it was easier in a lot of ways. I had the life I wanted, with no encumbrances and no guilt about those I'd left behind. Donald wanted to tell my brother he'd found me. I told him that would do little good. Ted knew I'd gone off to make a new life. I was as distant from him and my old life as if I'd been in New York. What was the point of an awkward reunion where we'd have little to say to each other, and have to awkwardly face the fact that we were both going back to our separate lives? When I pressed Donald, he admitted Ted hadn't talked about me in some time. He said it wouldn't hurt anything for the Tavistock company and the Levellers to know we were cousins. I said I'd made a promise to my uncle. Donald said, given his father's cutting me off, that promise was meaningless. I said I felt bound to stick to it, even so. And I wasn't really William McDevitt any more. Finally, Donald said it would feel damned odd, but he'd try to pretend he only knew me through the Levellers. He's kept his word, as far as I know. When I got in trouble in Lancaster, he said he almost wrote to his father. I implored him not to, even if I came a cropper again. It could bring down my uncle's wrath on the Levellers and make things worse. He did seem to understand that."

"You said you first saw him talking with Lewis Thornsby," Mélanie said.

"Yes." Will frowned. "I scarcely thought of it at the time, but in retrospect, I've been wondering. Supposedly Donald met Thornsby through Stanhope. They all had supper together one night, and Donald got to talking about his newfound sense of injustice. It all made sense at the time. Now I'm questioning anything to do with Thornsby. And anyone. As you must be."

"Did they seem to be particular friends after your cousin joined the Levellers?"

Will's frown deepened. "They moved in the same circles. There's always been a bit of a divide in the Levellers between those of us from the Tavistock company and the young men about town. For all Tanner and Kit try to smooth the divisions over. The actors and stagehands are all too well aware we can't dine at the places our fashionable friends like to frequent. And at the same time, we pride ourselves that we're real artists, unlike the sprigs who hang about the green room and enjoy associating with us. Which is supposed to make up for the fact that we can't dine at Rules three times a week and have our coats tailored on Bond Street and order new boots every year. At least, that's what we tell ourselves. And yes, I have those thoughts, even though I gave up that life. I should be ashamed of it. I sometimes am. In any case, Donald naturally hung about with the men-about-town in the Levellers. I more or less encouraged that by telling him not to acknowledge we were cousins. And he was one of the newer, younger Levellers, not in the inner circle like Kit and Roger Smythe. But I don't know that I'd have said he and Thornsby were particular friends." Will's frowned deepened. "The truth is I haven't spent that much time with Donald. And I rather set it up that way."

"Are you going to tell Letty the truth about who you are?" Mélanie asked.

"Don't you see?" The face Will turned towards her was set with a torment that was at once youthful and old beyond his years. "I've wanted Letty to take me seriously as a suitor for months. And that might actually make her do so. But that would be worse than anything."

"You've more or less given that life up."

"She might not believe it would last. My giving it up, I mean."

"Do you? Believe it will last?"

Will frowned. "I can't imagine going back. I want a life in the theatre. I can't see that changing. And I can't see my family's accepting my life in the theatre. I used to think I could run forever. But I'm realizing one can't simply hide from the past or the truth of who one is. So I suppose I'll have to face my heritage at some point, in some fashion. Even if it's to renounce it. I thought I'd already done that. But it seems now more as though I've been hiding."

"I wouldn't call it hiding. Does Donald know how you feel about Letty?"

Will's mouth twisted. "The whole company and all those about it seem to know, to some degree. Donald once asked me why I didn't tell her the truth. He actually said if I had my inheritance I'd be a better match than Thornsby." Will shook his head. "As if somehow that would make me happy."

CHAPTER 31

Roth turned his tankard on the scarred table at the Brown Bear Tavern. "Could the two sets of attackers you met with last night have been working for two different people?"

"They could," Malcolm said. "That occurred to me. Which makes the question of who wants those particular papers, and why, even more interesting."

Roth cast a quick glance round the tavern. It adjoined the Bow Street Public Office, but the cacophony of sound made for good cover. "Thornsby wanted them. And he's working for the Levellers."

Malcolm took a drink from his own tankard and hunched his shoulders forwards so he could speak in a low voice. "According to Beverston, Thornsby was working for the man who's trying to take control of the League. Alexander Radford, as he calls himself. And Thornsby was recruited by my brother. Which makes sense, because Edgar was working for the faction trying to wrest control of the League."

"So, could the papers somehow betray who this Alexander Radford really is?"

Malcolm considered for a moment. "It doesn't seem likely, based on what's in the papers, but it's possible, I suppose. Kitty sent a copy of some of them round this morning. Raoul's going through them."

"And I don't suppose you're going to tell me what's in them. No, never mind. I'm impressed you've told me as much as you have."

Malcolm started to speak, then checked himself as he saw a gleam of pale hair in the shadows, caught by the hazy sunshine as the door opened. Julien made his way between the tables with his usual habit of acting as though he belonged anywhere, but when he reached Malcolm and Roth's table, he hesitated. "I'm sorry to interrupt."

"You're not." Malcolm grabbed an empty chair from an adjoining table and pulled it over.

"I trust Mrs. Ashford is doing well," Roth said, as Julien seated himself.

"To hear her tell it, she wasn't attacked at all." Julien's drawl was slightly more pronounced than usual. "I think this may be the first time in my life I've been accused of fussing. I'm not even sure precisely what it means, save that Kitty has accused me of doing it at least five times since we got home last night." Julien motioned to a waiter to bring him a pint. "However, from the detached perspective of one who would never fuss but knows how to change a dressing and watch over a comrade, I can say there's no sign of infection, and she's well enough to complain about being sidelined. The last probably isn't much comfort, as Kitty would complain about being sidelined with a raging fever, broken legs, and half her blood gone." Julien sat back in his chair. "Is there news? Or oughtn't I to ask that?"

"Only updating Roth on last night's events," Malcolm said. "He wonders if the two sets of attackers could have been working for two different people."

The pot boy deposited a pint of stout in front of Julien. He took a measured sip. "An interesting thought. Carfax and the League being obvious suspects."

"Quite," Malcolm said.

"And all the more reason to regret that Kitty isn't content to stay home for so much as a morning." Julien returned his tankard to the table.

Roth pushed back his chair. "I should look in at Bow Street. And I suspect you came here to speak with Rannoch."

"You're a good fellow, Roth."

"Not perhaps the best talent in an investigation. But thank you, Mr. St. Juste."

Julien watched Roth leave the tavern, then took another sip from his tankard. "Thank you for giving me the time to sort matters out."

Malcolm studied Julien across the table in the dusty light of the tavern. Still hard to believe he was Arthur Mallinson. And at the same time, hard to believe it hadn't been obvious that he was long since. "I'm only sorry you can't have as much I suspect you need."

"I sorted a lot today." Julien set the tankard down carefully so the pewter precisely covered the damp ring on the dark wood. "I asked Kitty to marry me this afternoon." He looked up at Malcolm. There was a light in his eyes Malcolm had never seen before. "She said, as she's said before, that after Ashford she'd made up her mind never to marry again. Never to give a man the ability to have power over her. Unless she found a man she trusted. So I thought I was done for. Then, to my amazement, she accepted."

Malcolm found himself grinning. "That's wonderful."

"You don't sound surprised."

"That you asked her to marry you? No. That she accepted? Not that either."

"That she trusts me?" Julien shook his head. "I didn't think anyone trusted me."

"I rather think Kitty may know you as few people do."

"That's not necessarily an argument in favor of trust, Rannoch." Julien's fingers curled round the handle of his tankard. "Until she agreed, I didn't realize how nervous I was."

"I remember feeling distinctly ill when I proposed to Mel. And yes, I didn't know who she was. But I knew I wanted to marry her. That never changed. Still, probably easier to be going into it with rather more knowledge of each other."

"I don't know that there's going to be anything easy about this." Julien grinned. "Not that I'd want there to be. That wouldn't be Kitty." He wiped a trace of liquid from the side of his tankard. "I was hoping you could assist us."

"Of course. In what way?"

Julien took a drink of stout. "Are you acquainted with the Archbishop of Canterbury?"

Malcolm set down his own tankard. "You want a special license."

"In the circumstances, it seems prudent. I could quite easily come up with a forgery. Probably one no one could detect. But for a number of reasons, I'd rather have the real thing."

"I've met the archbishop, but Aunt Frances knows him better. She got a special license from him for Raoul and Laura. I can talk to her—just let me know when you want me to do so."

"This afternoon, if possible."

Malcolm's fingers stilled on the handle of his tankard. "What else has happened?"

"Nothing definitive." Julien's gaze drifted round the tavern as he spoke, the gaze of one used to keeping all the terrain in view. "But I want us to be married as quickly as we can. Tonight, if possible. No, not so that Kitkat won't change her mind—I actually don't think she will. But the night of the pantomime last month, Carfax was making noises about my knowing what my duty to Britain was. The sort of rot he can talk when he's made up his mind to something. He said it wouldn't be a bad thing for me to put down roots. Then he came right out and said Kitty wasn't the wife he had in mind for me."

"No. I don't imagine she would be."

"Quite. Which is a problem. Given that, at least in David's case, Carfax has shown himself like a dog with a bone when it comes to the question of establishing a suitable heir. " Julien frowned at a dent in his tankard. "Carfax may have been behind the attack on Kitty last night. You said it yourself."

"You think he wanted to get rid of her because of her relationship to you?"

Julien swung his gaze to Malcolm. "Would you put it past him?"

"I don't know that there's anything I'd put past Carfax now. But it wasn't just Kitty who was attacked."

"No. Whoever was behind the attacks last night probably didn't want the papers printed. But Carfax could have seen getting rid of Kitty as a side benefit." Julien took a meditative sip of stout. "There was a time when my first instinct would have been to kill Carfax for that. I can't swear that I wouldn't, if something really did happen to Kitty." For a moment, Julien's face hardened and Malcolm caught a glimpse of the man Raoul had seen stick a knife in a target's ribs without breaking stride. "But I'm not sure his knowing quite what Kitty means to me would improve the situation."

"On the contrary."

"The trouble being that for a man who's so seemingly lacking in emotions, he's damnably good at detecting them in others. For all I've worked for him at times, for all I've struggled to break free of him, I haven't had to actually see him that much these past years. That will change if I stay in Britain and try to resume my identity. Carfax was starting to talk to me like an heir that night at the Tavistock, and I can imagine few things from my uncle that are as frightening."

Malcolm thought of the many things Carfax had done to

David. "Nor can I, actually. I was always grateful Alistair had little interest in me. I think he was vaguely surprised I'd found someone who'd marry me at all. Of course, Raoul pulled plenty of strings when it came to my marriage." He could say that now in a calm voice. And Julien St. Juste was one of the few people he could say it to. "But on the whole, I'm glad he did."

Julien looked at Malcolm for a moment, started to speak, hesitated, then said, "I was in and out of Lisbon in those days. The days when you met Mélanie. Usually in disguise. Enough so that I'm not sure even O'Roarke or Mélanie would have recognized me. Not that they necessarily would have done anything if they had, except be on their guard. I was working for the French more often than not. I went to a party at Charles Stuart's. I saw you dancing with Mélanie. That wasn't a surprise —I'd got wind of her mission. I saw the way you were looking at each other. That wasn't such a surprise either—at least, not the way you were looking at Mélanie. You're a unique man in a lot of ways, Rannoch, but a lot of men would look at Mélanie that way. The way she was looking at you was a bit more surprising."

"She was playing a role." Malcolm's voice was thick.

"Some things are hard to manufacture. Perhaps I'm too arrogant in thinking I can see through artifice, but I've always been rather good at it. One reason I couldn't abide life in the beau monde, as it happens. But in any case, after I saw you and Mélanie dancing, I saw O'Roarke watching you dance. I'll never forget the look on his face. Wonder and loss at the same time. Even I felt for him, and I didn't feel much in those days. Seeing his son falling in love with the woman he loved. And seeing her falling in love back." Julien paused and drew a breath that might almost have been awkward. "I don't think he'll ever tell you this, not in so many words at least, but he knew."

Malcolm nodded. He didn't trust himself to speak.

"But perhaps you already knew that," Julien said.

"In a way. Not entirely." Malcolm hesitated a moment. "Thank you."

Julien nodded. "I don't think I quite appreciated the ramifications then. I didn't acknowledge the existence of the emotions involved. Or at least, that they could lead to anything lasting. That anything approaching domesticity could ever make a former agent happy."

"I don't think you need to worry about being too domestic, St. Juste."

"You aren't precisely domestic yourselves. But I'd say you were always better suited for it than I am. So is Mélanie, though I'm not sure I realized it at the time. Even O'Roarke has more of a talent for it, though I wouldn't have admitted to that either."

"Considering your life—even what I knew of it before today—I wouldn't underestimate your talent for anything."

Julien gave a twisted, half-abashed smile. "There are different types of talents. But I confess I'm quite intrigued to try. And while I have no doubt we could outwit Carfax, I see no particular need to put it to the test."

Scenes from the past shot through Malcolm's mind. "Fair enough," he said. "And prudent."

"Yes, I'm a man of forty sneaking about behind my uncle's back. But better to outflank Carfax. Besides—" Julien hesitated a moment. His gaze fixed out the tavern window, his face in profile against the thick glass. "We're running a number of risks just now, all of us. Kitty was almost killed last night. I'm going to make damned sure it doesn't happen again. But I also know I'd be a fool to be certain of anything, and as her lover I have no official connection to the children. And should anything happen to me, it might help Kitty to have the Mallinson name. Whatever happens, I'd like to ensure she has that."

"St. Juste—"

Julien swung his head round and met Malcolm's gaze with a quick smile. "Don't worry. I have no intention of getting myself killed. I'm rather happy just now, as it happens. Life has a clarity I never thought to find. But that doesn't mean I can't be prudent."

Julien St. Juste, talking quite like a husband and father. Malcolm hid a smile, though oddly it wasn't nearly as surprising as it once would have been. A thought occurred to him. Julien had said he wanted to give Kitty the protection of the Mallinson name—"You're going to get married as Arthur Mallinson."

Julien's gaze slid away again, fixed on the flickering shadows of the tavern's blackened fireplace. Then he looked back at Malcolm. "I want to make sure the marriage is legal. And—it's folly to think I can hide forever. Especially as Kitty doesn't seem keen to disappear."

"And you?"

Julien took a long drink from his tankard. "I can't run from it forever. And I seem to have developed a rather tiresome need to do something useful with myself. If I'm not quite determined to solve the world's ills like you and Mélanie and O'Roarke, I at least feel compelled to attempt to solve some of the problems that are of my own making."

"So you've decided it's time to pull the sword from the stone."

"Oh, for God's sake. And people wonder why I changed my name." Julien set down the tankard. "You're much more likely to do good for England than I am. But it seems there may be more for me to do here than I once thought."

"You're a good fellow, St. Juste."

"Perish the thought."

Malcolm watched him a moment longer. "It's challenging, coming home after life in exile. I found that, and my exile was self-imposed and not as complete as yours. I still had a lot of ghosts to face. I'm not sure I could have done it without Mel. And without her encouragement, I don't think I'd have even tried."

Julien gave a faint smile. "I'm damned sure I couldn't do this without Kitty. But don't tell her. I don't want her to be burdened."

"Fair enough," Malcolm said. "Though I don't think she'd find it a burden. I think she'd probably be inestimably glad to know what she means to you."

"Always the optimist, Rannoch."

"Sometimes optimism is clear-sighted."

Julien gave a faint smile. "Sometimes." He hesitated a moment. "I realize how fortunate I am. I shall endeavor not to make a mull of it."

"My dear fellow. I think everyone thinks that when they marry. Well, everyone who isn't a hopeless, pompous idiot."

"I'm relieved not to be in that category."

"You're a lot of things, St. Juste. But not that." Malcolm leaned forwards, arms on the table. "Knowing Aunt Frances, she'll have no trouble getting you the license today. But I'm going to have to give her the names for the license. I'm going to have to tell her about you."

"I know." The truth settled in St. Juste's eyes. A truth discussed, acknowledged, but perhaps not really faced until now. "I always liked your aunt. She had the good taste never to show any interest in my father. Despite his making some rather heavy-handed attempts at flirtation. I think she'll keep it to herself."

"I have no doubt she will. I think she can also keep the archbishop silent for a few hours. But the Archbishop of Canterbury is inherently political. Manners Sutton, the current archbishop, is the brother of the Chancellor of Ireland, who could be called a friend of Carfax."

"Yes, I know." Julien's gaze was focused. "This is all going to unravel very quickly. All those damnable jokes about a wedding ending a man's peace are going to come true, and in this case it has nothing to do with actually being married. All the more reason to make sure Kitty and I are legally married first."

"I couldn't agree with you more."

"We were hoping—if you and Mélanie are willing, we'd like to have the wedding in Berkeley Square."

"My dear fellow. We'd be more than happy."

"So of course you'll have to tell Mélanie. And O'Roarke and Laura. And since Frances will know and we can't ask her to keep it from Archie, you should tell the younger Davenports as well. I don't think you have many secrets from them. And I need to tell David. All things considered, I'd like to have him there. And Tanner."

Malcolm nodded. "I wish Gelly could be there."

"So do I." Julien reached for his tankard. "She's probably the first person I let myself consider family."

CHAPTER 32

Lady Frances Davenport stared at Malcolm. "My word. I confess I thought that I was far too jaded to be shocked, long before I stumbled into your world of agents and double agents. And then I thought I'd become quite accustomed to everyone's having a secret identity. Even those closest to me. But I never expected to find the dead coming back to life. Or to realize that I could still be shocked by Carfax."

"Nor did I," Malcolm said. "On either count."

"Arthur was an engaging little boy," Frances said. "And a quite charming young man. I can't believe I didn't—"

"Believe me, I'm asking myself the same thing. Of course, part of a good disguise is playing off expectations. Very useful to have everyone think one is dead."

"It was such a tragedy. His death. His supposed death. He seemed to have such promise. His cleverness was quite apparent, though I don't think he had an easy childhood." Frances glanced towards the door to the drawing room where Archie could be heard playing with their nine-month-old twins and Frances's ten-year-old daughter, Chloe. "The late Lord Carfax was hardly the warmest of fathers, even by beau monde standards. I don't think his wife had a very easy time of it. I was thinking of her actually, that night at Vauxhall when we saw Josefina perform last September, and then again when you had Josefina and her family to dine. Josefina seems to have built quite a happy life for herself in London. I don't think Pamela Carfax ever did. I fear at the time I didn't appreciate enough how hard it must have been for her, being an outsider. Sometimes one is so on the inside oneself one can't see it."

"I've certainly been guilty of that." Malcolm thought of Mélanie and then, unexpectedly, of Oliver Lydgate, visiting Carfax Court in their Oxford days. If Oliver hadn't been an outsider, Malcolm doubted Carfax would ever have been able to recruit him.

"However little I think of the current Lord Carfax, Arthur's father was worse," Frances said. "Well, perhaps I shouldn't say that, for the present Carfax has so much more power and is a much cleverer man, which allows him to accomplish so much more. But his elder brother was a wretched human being."

"Julien said you had the good taste to refuse his advances."

"Good heavens, I should think so. Even in my youth I had some discrimination. And they were singularly crude advances. I remember one night at Vauxhall being distinctly unnerved. Hubert Mallinson actually came to my rescue."

"Julien thinks his father may have been an Elsinore League member."

Frances's brows rose. "That would explain a great deal about Carfax's attitude towards the League."

"Yes, that's what Julien and I both thought."

"We'll have to ask Archie. It's possible he even knows. There's seemed no need to discuss the late Lord Carfax. Suddenly this makes him quite relevant."

"Yes," Malcolm said, "it does. And casts an interesting light on the games the League have been trying to play with his son."

"I like him," Frances said. "That is, I like Mr. St. Juste and I liked Arthur Mallinson. And he's been treated quite appallingly."

"You think you can get the license?"

"Oh, yes." Frances tucked a pale blonde curl into its pins. "I'll say the Arthur Mallinson in question is a country cousin who got a young woman with child and is eager to have the wedding handled quickly, without it coming to Carfax's attention. That should buy Julien and Kitty a bit of time. But once the archbishop lets out the name Arthur Mallinson to someone, Carfax will know to be on his guard."

"I can't imagine Carfax isn't already on his guard where Julien is concerned. This should at least give Kitty and Julien enough time to get married without Carfax's trying to stop the wedding."

Frances's carefully plucked brows drew together. "Do you really think he would?"

"Julien does, and he arguably knows Carfax better than any of us."

"But surely Julien is a threat to him, married or not."

"I think Carfax may have moved beyond that. He may have decided that to outwit the League he has to resurrect Julien. I can see his thinking that, and Julien says he's been hinting at it. That in a sense makes Julien his heir. And we know how Carfax is about his heir's marital prospects."

Frances took a sip from the cup of tea on her escritoire. "Actually, Carfax is Julien's heir." She set the cup down, sloshing tea, which was unlike her. "You don't think—"

"That Carfax would have Julien killed? No, not on moral grounds, but because if he thought it a viable course of action, he'd have done it long ago. But judging by his attitude towards David, he's likely to have very definite ideas about the sort of earl he wants Julien to be."

Frances snorted. "I would think even Carfax would realize he can't control Julien St. Juste."

"Have you ever known Carfax to believe he can't control

anything?"

Frances tugged her handkerchief from the gathered cuff of her long sleeve and blotted the spilled tea. "Kitty would make an admirable countess."

"Kitty's a revolutionary, in her way. And you know what Carfax thinks of those. I suspect he'd prefer a more settled alliance."

"Whatever else Carfax is, he's no fool. I can't imagine his thinking Julien would be happy with anyone remotely settled."

"Who said anything about Carfax's thinking marriage equated to happiness?"

"You have a point there. Although he found happiness in his own marriage. At least, he did until Amelia learned about Gelly." Frances folded the handkerchief and smoothed her violet-striped taffeta skirt. "If you ask me, Amelia may be more of a threat than Carfax. Not to Julien's marrying Kitty, but to Julien's becoming Arthur again."

"She married Carfax when he was Hubert Mallinson."

"And she was quite besotted with him and content to be an army wife. But she's had over two decades of being a countess. More to the point of thinking of her children as an earl's children. And she's rather less besotted with Carfax after the revelations about Gisèle."

"You're a very astute woman, Aunt Frances."

"I understand ambition and what it can mean to give something up. Especially in the beau monde." She reached for the paisley shawl draped over the back of her chair. "I should get to the archbishop without further delay. I trust you have a clergyman to perform the ceremony?"

"Already working on it."

"My word." She wrapped the shawl round her shoulders and pushed another pin into her hair. "I feel as though I were assisting with an elopement. It makes me feel quite schoolgirlish."

She got to her feet, but turned back at the door. "You realize we're on the verge of a scandal that is going to shake Mayfair—not to mention Westminster."

"Oh, yes."

"I used to love a good scandal. Now all I can think of is what it will do to those I care about."

MÉLANIE STARED AT HER HUSBAND. She had come back to Berkeley Square from the Tavistock during the midday break. Laura was out and might have something interesting to report when she returned, Raoul said. But before she could ask more questions or share her discoveries about Will, Malcolm had come in with news that dwarfed all other revelations.

Her shoulders shook with laughter. She put her head in her hands.

"Darling?" Malcolm said. He was sitting beside her on the library sofa.

"I'm not sure what other response is possible." She looked up at him, then at Raoul, who was sitting on a chair beside them, apparently equally amazed. "On my first mission I tried to steal a paper from Carfax's nephew."

"Technically, you tried to steal it from Carfax," Malcolm said, "given that Hubert Mallinson has never had any legitimate right to the title."

"Which makes the whole thing all the more absurd." Moments from the past shot through her memory. The night she had met Julien. The night she had spent with him. The journey to protect Hortense Bonaparte. His mockery, his flirtation, his unexpected moments of caring for Hortense and perhaps for her. Her panic when she'd seen him again in London a year and a half ago, a panic which seemed rather laughable now. Telling Malcolm about him for the first time.

"All this time. I thought Julien was someone from my past we were entangled with. And it turns out you knew him years before I ever did."

"I knew Arthur Mallinson," Malcolm said. "You could say I didn't know Julien St. Juste at all."

"But they're the same person, on some level." Mélanie met Malcolm's gaze. "Perhaps more so than any of us realized."

She looked at Raoul. So did Malcolm. Raoul was watching in silence, his face bemused.

"You really didn't know?" Malcolm said.

Raoul shook his head. "No suspicion. Arabella didn't tell me, but then there were a number of things she didn't tell me. And this certainly explains a lot about St. Juste."

"He's David's cousin," Mélanie said. "And Gisèle's." She looked at Malcolm. "You grew up with him."

"I knew him," Malcolm said. "Until he seemingly died when I was seven. He was kind to David and me. Kinder than a lot of boys his age were. He drove Carfax and his father mad. You can imagine the sort of tongue he had on him as a teenager."

Mélanie smiled. "And this means Carfax—Hubert Mallinson—"

"Is a fraud." Malcolm's voice was iron cold. "Hard as it is to believe, I don't seem to have appreciated the depth of his crimes."

"I told St. Juste only yesterday that half of being a strategist is improvising," Raoul said. "Carfax seems to have done that brilliantly when his brother discovered Arthur's crimes, and Arthur staged his assumed death. Brilliantly or diabolically. Or perhaps both."

"But the risk—" Mélanie said.

"Carfax is a man who lives with risk. Calculated risk, but sometimes extreme risk. He had papers to keep St. Juste from reappearing for a long time."

"And I suspect he thought it likely Julien—Arthur—would get himself killed," Malcolm said.

Mélanie looked at Raoul and then back at Malcolm. "This means Napoleon Bonaparte's wife was the lover of one of Carfax's agents."

"I don't think so, precisely," Malcolm said. "That is, I don't think St. Juste was Carfax's agent, precisely. He made it clear he was going his own way and choosing his own jobs from the first, and I think he was telling the truth. I can't imagine he told Carfax a number of Josephine's secrets. It certainly doesn't sound as though he told her about Queen Hortense and her child. For one thing, Carfax would almost certainly have used the information. For another, St. Juste's loyalty to Josephine and Hortense has always been apparent."

"That's true," Raoul said. "Even when I thought him far more ruthless than I do now. Still, learning he was Carfax's nephew would shake a number of those who have employed him through the years. I can imagine the shock waves through intelligence circles."

"It's rather remarkable he told Kitty the truth of who he is," Mélanie said. "One might say it proves how he feels about her. Though that's been apparent for some time."

"Speaking of which," Malcolm said, "I hope you don't mind hosting a wedding."

Mélanie felt an unbidden smile break across her face. "I've been thinking they'd get round to it. And yet—" She shook her head. "Even a few months ago, if you'd have told me Julien would ever be married—"

"A lot's changed." Malcolm's face grew serious. "Julien wants the wedding quickly. Aunt Frances is getting a special license from the Archbishop of Canterbury. They'd like to be married tonight. To make sure Carfax doesn't interfere."

Mélanie met her husband's gaze. Somehow, for all she thought she'd accepted the truth of Julien's past, the implications really hadn't hit her until now. "It's not going to be easy for them."

"No," Malcolm said. "A lot will have to do with what Carfax wants and how he decides to play things. I think he's accepted that Julien has to emerge as Lord Carfax. I'm not sure he's accepted the idea of Kitty as Lady Carfax."

"You think he'd try to stop the wedding?" Mélanie asked.

"Given how he's tried to manipulate David, you think Carfax would cavil at that?"

The thought of Carfax's bursting into their drawing room just as the minister asked if anyone knew of any impediment would have been funny if it hadn't seemed quite so real a possibility. "It seems clear Carfax wouldn't cavil at much of anything," she said.

"Though given his determination to have an heir for the earldom, you'd think he might be pragmatist enough to realize he should settle for having Julien married," Raoul said.

"You're assuming Carfax can be pragmatic when it comes to his goals," Malcolm said.

"He can," Raoul said. "On occasion."

"Then there's the League," Malcolm said. "They're not going to like this at all."

"Julien's marrying Kitty, or Julien's emerging as Carfax?" Mélanie asked.

"Both. They wanted to use the truth of who Julien is against Carfax. I think that's why they've been so lenient with him. They've been hoping to win him for their side in their battle with Carfax. He's going to be openly declaring himself their enemy. I think that's another reason he wants himself officially tied to Kitty. So their bond is legal whatever happens to either of them. He admitted as much to me. He and Kitty are going to come round in a bit with the children. Julien wants to talk to David, and I said I'd go with him."

Mélanie squeezed her husband's hand. That talk was not

going to be easy for David, and she was glad Malcolm could be there for it. "I'll talk to Mrs. Erksine about putting together a wedding supper. I need to go back to the theatre in a bit. It's actually a bit of an echo of the revelations about Julien, though nothing like so shattering. Still, it's interesting. I know where Will came from." She told them, quickly, along with the information that Donald McDevitt was his cousin.

"It doesn't prove Will isn't undercover," she said. "And it doesn't relate directly to Thornsby, though Donald was with Thornsby the first time Will saw him in London. I need to talk to Donald. Perhaps—"

She broke off at the sound of the front door and voices. They went into the hall to find Laura as well as Cordelia, Harry, Livia, Drusilla, and Archie Davenport, Harry's uncle and Frances's husband. "I have some interesting discoveries to report," Laura said. "I thought we should all gather together. Frances is out, but Archie left word for her to come here. Perhaps you want to get Ben and Nerezza. Their perspective could be helpful, especially Ben's."

Mélanie and Cordelia took Livia and Drusilla up to the drawing room, where Ben and Nerezza and Blanca were playing with the other children. Blanca assured Mélanie she could watch all the children, though with a look that said she wanted an explanation later. By the time Mélanie and Cordelia came back downstairs with Ben and Nerezza, Kitty and Julien had arrived with Kitty's children. Leo and Timothy happily ran upstairs to join the other children, Leo carrying Genny. The adults moved into the library. The news of Kitty and Julien's imminent wedding provided a brief distraction from whatever Laura had to relate.

"Please," Kitty said, with a smile and quick look at Julien, "no ghastly chorus of best wishes. We're hardly love's young dream and we're doing this for practical reasons."

"Among other things." Julien reached for her hand.

Kitty squeezed his fingers, but said, "Yes, but Laura has news far more important than our own."

Frances arrived with the promised special license as they were settling themselves. Which was a good thing, Mélanie realized, as Laura launched into her account of her morning and her talk with Edith Simmons.

"Good God," Cordelia said. "I thought we'd at least come to terms with who the League were and what they were capable of. Even if we didn't know quite all the names, we've known from the first that they were a group of men who plotted their own advancement under cover of being a hellfire club. Or at least we thought we did."

"The original hellfire clubs included ladies," Frances observed. She looked at her husband. "Archie, did you know any ladies were Elsinore League members?"

Archie had been a League member for over three decades, giving information to Malcolm's mother, Arabella, and to Raoul. Though since his marriage to Frances, he was certainly not trusted by the League. "My darling." Archie was frowning, but he gave his wife a faint smile. "Surely I'd have told not only you but everyone in this room."

"My dear, I think at this point it's a given that any of us—all of us—may have reasons for keeping certain pieces of information secret."

Archie's gaze settled on Frances's own, at once hard and tender. "Possibly. But at this point I can't think of anything about the League I'd keep secret. The stakes are too high, the fight too serious."

"Ben?" Mélanie looked at Benedict, who was staring at a medallion on the library carpet as though it were a portal to another world he'd stumbled into.

"I hadn't even heard of the League until a month ago," he said. "I was shocked my father was involved. The idea of Lady Shroppington—" He shook his head in amazement.

"St. Juste?" Malcolm looked at Julien.

"I've never been a League member," Julien said.

"No, but they've tried to recruit you. You've been on the fringe of their councils at times. Gelly has, even more so, and she talks to you more than to any of us."

Julien shifted in his chair. "From all my interactions, they've seemed the sort of hellfire-club-with-an-ulterior-motive that you all assume them to be. The only people I've dealt with are men. Although—" He crossed his legs and dragged the toe of his boot over the carpet. "Gelly's been trusted and accepted more than one might expect. Given the usual—and quite deplorable—lack of appreciation for women's intellect." He glanced at Kitty, then his brows drew together. "I hadn't thought of it, but that might support the idea that at least some of them aren't unaccustomed to having women in their councils."

"Edith is under the impression Lady Shroppington was involved with the League before Lord Beverston was," Laura said. "Which implies back to its founding. Could she have been a mistress of Alistair Rannoch's?" She looked at Frances.

It was Frances's turn to frown. "She's at least a generation older than Alistair, but that's hardly a bar to anything."

"I should think not," Julien said. "I was sixteen years younger than Josephine." He glanced at Kitty, who was seated beside him. "Sorry."

"It's hardly a secret, sweetheart," Kitty said. "And hardly anything to do with us."

He drew her hand to his lips and kissed her knuckles. "That's my Kitkat."

"It's not her age that surprises me," Frances said. "Henrietta Shroppington was already considered a high stickler when I made my debut. She'd have been about the age that I am now, but she looked distinctly matronly." Frances frowned. "Of course, that's the view of my seventeen-year-old self, to whom I am sure I would now seem positively decrepit. Still, she doesn't strike me as the sort to catch Alistair's attention." She glanced at Raoul.

"Don't look at me," Raoul said. "I can claim no insights into Alistair, and I certainly wasn't aware of the women he dallied with."

"I was wondering more if Bella said anything to you," Frances said. "If she guessed there were women—or a woman—connected to the League."

"No," Raoul said. "At least, she never said anything to me about it. But then, there was a great deal she didn't tell me about."

"You were partners in fighting the League," Archie said.

"I'm not sure Bella and I were ever partners in anything," Raoul said in a quiet voice. He looked at Julien.

"She never said anything about it to me," Julien's voice was unusually direct. "She certainly didn't tell me everything either. But I can't recall her expressing any particular interest in Lady Shroppington."

"Nor can I," said Frances. "My guess is she didn't know."

"Lady Shroppington pulled her great-nephew into it," Harry said. "Though she set Edith to spy on her other great-nephew. And on Cordy and me."

Cordelia met her husband's gaze. "I was so surprised by the revelations about Lady Shroppington I hadn't really had a chance to think about Edith. It's odd, with all the spying we live amongst, we haven't been spied on ourselves until now."

"At least not that we know of," Harry said.

Cordelia drew her pink-and-cream Norwich shawl about her. "I expect I'll start going over every conversation I've had with Edith. But I can't help thinking it's beastly what Lady Shroppington did to her. Whereas what she did to us—"

"Is the same thing I did to Mélanie and Malcolm," Laura said. "Only what I did was worse. Edith wasn't actually living in your house and watching your children."

"Nothing you did for the League made you anything but exemplary with the children," Mélanie said. "In a way, we should be grateful to them for bringing you to us."

"Put like that, I should be exceptionally grateful to them." Raoul reached for Laura's hand.

"Yes, it's very sweet of all of you to say it, and in that sense I'm grateful to them too." Laura squeezed her husband's hand. "But it doesn't change the fact that I was living in Mélanie and Malcolm's house and spying on them while I took care of Colin and Jessica."

"It makes one wonder." Harry contemplated the toes of his boots. "How many governesses in London are working for the League. I should have thought of it sooner."

"So should I," said Raoul. "I was too horrified at how Trenchard took advantage of Laura's personal situation to see it could be part of a larger pattern."

"We all were," Malcolm said.

"I can understand the League's wanting to spy on us," Cordelia said. "I mean, we're involved in working against them. But though Thomas is an excellent scholar, I confess I'm baffled as to why they'd want information on him."

"You aren't the only one," Harry said. "I can't imagine why the League would have an interest in a classicist."

"The League collect art," Mélanie pointed out.

Harry's brows drew together. "An interesting point. I don't know of any work Thomas has done that could relate to classical art, but it's possible."

"Perhaps they wanted him to authenticate something," Kitty said. "Or spot a forgery."

"Or they were worried he might spot a forgery," Julien said. "They seem to use art as a sort of currency in their efforts to gain influence. And also as a mark of status. My father certainly used it as both. Some of the art they deal was certainly acquired illegally. I wouldn't be surprised if some of it was inauthentic."

Laura was frowning. "So Lady Shroppington wanted to spy on her elder nephew. But she brought Lewis into the League?"

"Not according to Beverston," Malcolm said. "He said Edgar did." He flashed a brief look at Kitty. Kitty sent a look back meant to indicate he shouldn't be silly and avoid talking about it on her account. "And I have an odd feeling he was telling the truth."

"Did Lady Shroppington have any connection to Edgar?" Laura asked.

"Even before I learned my brother was the Goshawk, working for the Elsinore League, and pretending to work for Carfax, I can hardly claim to have known him well," Malcolm said. "But I know of no connection he had to Lady Shroppington. I'm not even sure they were acquainted." He looked at Frances.

"She was hardly in Arabella and Alistair's circles," Frances said. "She'd have looked askance at the Glenister House set. I suppose all of that could have been a pose—the sort of thing you call 'deep cover'—but I have no memory of her ever even being at the same party as Edgar."

"So Edgar just happened to recruit her nephew when they both have a connection to the League?" Cordelia asked. "Or the League set him to recruit Lewis Thornsby rather than having Lewis's aunt do so?"

"They might have thought he'd be more likely to listen to a soldier and agent than to his aunt," Harry pointed out. "Just because he was her heir doesn't mean he'd listen to her. And it's possible she kept her connection to the League secret even from Thornsby."

"And yet she recruited Edith," Laura said. "And went to a meeting with her with Beverston. So Beverston certainly knows about Lady Shroppington's role."

"Nerezza saw Thornsby talking to this man calling himself Alexander Radford," Kitty pointed out. "Who seems to be the man trying to take over the League. Which rather raises the question of what Lady Shroppington knows about Alexander Radford and his efforts."

"It does indeed," Raoul said. "According to Beverston, he's opposed to the faction Alexander Radford represents."

"Edith said she was under the impression that Lady Shroppington and Beverston had fallen out a few months ago," Laura said. "That could fit with the time frame in which the factions in the League became clearer."

Nerezza was frowning. "So Alexander Radford is an outsider trying to take control of the League, and Lady Shroppington is helping him. Even though she's been involved with the League from the first?"

"It looks that way," Malcolm said. "But whoever Alexander Radford is, he's obviously at some pains to keep his identity secret. Which raises the question of why."

"Not to mention why Lady Shroppington would ally herself with an outsider," Cordelia said.

Malcolm nodded. "It's funny, when we called on her yesterday, there was a moment when she put me in mind of a spymaster. I had no idea how spot on I was."

Benedict looked up from the carpet again. "Surely she's not a spy!"

"Not for a country, perhaps," Malcolm said. "But she's certainly running agents and dealing in information."

"None of which explains why Lewis Thornsby was killed," Harry said.

"No," Malcolm agreed, "it doesn't. Save that he was caught in some very complicated games." He looked at Julien. "We should go to see David before it gets much later. And I know Mel needs to get back to the theatre. Perhaps the rest of you can puzzle out some more answers before we all get back."

CHAPTER 33

David stared across his library at Julien. Arthur. The cousin he had last seen as a boy of eight. "You—"

"I know it's a shock," Julien said. "I'll understand if you'd rather not speak to me."

"Not speak to you?" David crossed the library carpet in five steps and embraced Julien. "How could I not be glad to have my cousin back?"

"You always were much too decent for your own good, David." Julien's back was to Malcolm but his voice was suspiciously husky.

David drew back and regarded his cousin. "I still can't believe this. You—"

"Did some things that could have got me killed. So I ran away."

"Father made you run away."

"No, I did that on my own. He could have dragged me back to face the consequences."

"Don't tell me Father couldn't have hushed it up if he'd wanted to."

"I'm not sure. He wasn't quite as powerful as he is now. If

he'd done anything else, my father would have insisted on turning me over to the authorities. Which, Uncle Hubert once had the goodness to tell me, would have been a sad waste. I must say he had a point there. Mind you, it might have been easier for all of you, but personally I far prefer being alive. Of course, Uncle Hubert might have left me to go my own way instead of compelling me to work for him. So one can't precisely claim he was altruistic."

"Your father died a long time ago," David said.

"Yes, that's true," Julien agreed.

"And I don't think my father for a minute considered bringing you back to Britain and giving up the title."

"Oh, no, I'm sure he didn't," Julien said. "He had power before he was Lord Carfax, but I have no doubt he enjoys his power as Lord Carfax and finds it useful. And Uncle Hubert can justify almost anything on the grounds it's useful in his work and therefore good for Britain."

"Including betraying my mother," David said. "Sorry, Malcolm."

"No apology necessary," Malcolm said. "Though I should point out that my mother was equally willing to go to great lengths in pursuit of her cause. And to justify those lengths."

David's hands curled into fists. "All his talk about the earldom and the future of it. He tried to destroy my relationship with Simon. And with Malcolm and Mélanie. All to get me to produce an heir to a title that was never mine to begin with."

Julien braced his hands on the library table behind him. "Do you want it? Because I think one could say you've been through enough it should be yours if you do. I can disappear."

David gave an unexpected whoop of laughter. "*Want* it? I've been dreading the idea of being Earl Carfax ever since I got word that you were dead. Ask Malcolm. I was horrified." He swallowed. "That isn't the only reason I was upset."

Julien clapped a hand on his shoulder. "That's because you

took—take—it seriously. Most boys—and most men— wouldn't. Still, having forced yourself to come to terms with the prospect—"

"I'd like nothing better than to be rid of it. Truly."

Julien's hand tightened on David's shoulder. "I'm sorry, David. I'm sorry I left you with this mess for so long. Whatever games Uncle Hubert and I were playing, you shouldn't have had that burden."

"It doesn't sound as though you had a lot of choice," David said.

"I could have tried to come back sooner."

"Father might have turned you over to the authorities. He still might."

"It would be harder now I have the written evidence. His word against mine. It's true taking on Carfax is always a challenge. It's also true I've been known to relish a challenge. Indeed, since Waterloo I've rather keenly felt the lack of one, much of the time. But I also enjoyed my freedom."

David watched his cousin closely. "Are you saying you don't want it back?"

"Want? That's an odd word." Julien was silent for a moment. "I'd wouldn't have said so. I'd made up my mind I *should* reclaim it. That I might even be able to do some good. I never used the word 'want.' Kitty asked me what I wanted, and it wasn't to be Carfax. It was her, and the children. But I suppose—I can't deny it has a certain appeal. Not the earldom, per se. Home. Britain, I suppose. God, don't let your father hear me say that. But I said as much to Mélanie years ago, on that journey with Hortense. I can be in Britain as Carfax. I can come home. I can see a life I can carve out for myself. So yes, I suppose you could say I do want it."

David nodded. "You'll be better at it than I would have been."

"I highly doubt that. But I think I may be effective. Assuming we can pull this off."

"If you and I choose to make the truth public, I don't see what Father can do about it."

"Trust me, you don't want to find out," Julien said.

"We may have to."

"Possibly. But given that the League, or at least some in the League, know the truth, your father seems to have decided revealing the truth ourselves may be a way to outflank them. He's made a lot of noises about my assuming my rightful position. And he's shown an interest in my taking a wife."

"Oh, God."

"Precisely. You should appreciate the risks more than anyone. Kitty apparently doesn't suit his idea of a Countess Carfax. Which is why we're going to be married tonight before he can try to intercede."

David grinned. "I wish you both very happy. And I applaud your good sense."

"I'd like you to be there. And Tanner and the children."

David smiled. "We'd be honored."

SIMON LET the silence linger after the end of the scene and gave a nod. "That works. Perhaps even better than the original. Good delivery, Brandon."

Brandon gave a somewhat abashed smile.

"Don't let it go to your head," Manon said, "but that was quite convincing. If I weren't a happily married woman, you could sweep me off my feet. Onstage, that is."

Brandon grinned at her. "Praise of the highest order."

Simon glanced at his watch. "Right, we still need to work on the bows, but I think we can break for tea." He looked at Mélanie. "It's good."

"Don't jinx it."

He grinned. "It's not opening night yet. Everything all right in Berkeley Square?"

"Yes, but there've been some developments. I can't explain here, but we're hoping you and David and the children can come to Berkeley Square tonight." Hard to look Simon in the eye knowing that even now David was learning he wasn't rightful heir to the Carfax title, but she couldn't tell Simon. He had to hear it from David.

Simon nodded. "We shouldn't be late here."

Mélanie went into the green room, where most of the actors had been joined by several of the Tavistock's supporters of various ages. Manon was talking with Jennifer Mansfield. Manon's daughters, Roxane and Clarisse, who played Fiona's daughters in the play, were chattering with Jennifer and Sir Horace's elder daughter. Sir Horace, their younger daughter in his lap, was expanding on parallels between *Past Imperfect* and Shakespeare's comedies, particularly *Much Ado About Nothing* and *Love's Labour's Lost*. At another time Mélanie might have been diverted. Both plays had been an influence on her. The comparisons were flattering, and self-styled expert though he might be, Sir Horace was not without insights. But she had a more pressing conversation she needed to engage in. She moved to the other end of the room, where Donald McDevitt was talking with Letty. Letty met Mélanie's gaze for a moment and then excused herself shortly after. Mélanie took her place on the frayed chintz sofa.

"It's difficult for Miss Blanchard," McDevitt said. He shifted on the sofa. "Difficult to know precisely what to say to her."

Now she had thought to look for a connection to Will, the resemblance was obvious, yet Will and Donald were quite different. The Levellers were a diverse group, but Donald stood out. He looked as though he'd be more at home sparring at Jackson's, or shooting at Manton's, or putting his hunter over a fence. As though he'd be more likely to go to a coffeehouse to play dice than to debate ideas. Of course, it was possible to do all of those things. Even those among the Levellers who were more romantic than revolutionary tended to be intellectuals. In fact, more than anyone, Donald put her in mind of Thornsby.

"Sometimes, the most one can do is listen." Mélanie studied Donald for a long moment. "You look like him. More than most cousins do."

Donald cast a quick glance about. "I don't know—"

"You needn't worry about being overheard in this racket. Or about denying it. Will told me."

"Will *told*—"

"After I guessed. So he didn't have much choice."

Donald stared at her. "He wanted it kept secret."

"Yes, I quite understand that. I honor you for acceding to his wishes. But is it really true that you just stumbled upon him at the Tavistock?"

"Why should it be anything else?"

"It's quite a coincidence. Of course, they do happen. But, like my husband, I'm wary of them."

"Why on earth would I have gone looking for Will?"

"Because you suspected he wasn't in New York?"

"Well, if I'd known that, I might have gone looking for him, but I didn't know, and if I had known and I'd found him, why would I have kept it secret and hung about the theatre?"

Donald's blue eyes were guileless. Too guileless? Perhaps the revelations about Thornsby were making her jump at shadows. "You were in Lancaster when Will was arrested."

"Yes. Terrible time."

"I heard Thornsby and Letty and Tim Scott were very involved in trying to get him free."

"So they were. Did what I could, as well. Will didn't want me to write to my father. I would have done if it had gone on longer, though. Though I don't know that Father could have got him out. Doesn't have Worsley's pull."

"Will said you were with Thornsby the first time he saw you in London."

"Was I? I don't remember that. But I may well have been. Thornsby was a friend of my friend Stanhope who brought me to the Tavistock and to the Levellers. So I met him before I met Will. That is, before I met Will again."

"What did you think of Thornsby?"

"Er—not much. That is, he was a regular fellow. Very decent chap, but never seemed serious about much. Except Letty."

"Yes, that seems to be the general opinion. When did you see him last?"

"The night before he died." Donald dashed a hand across his eyes. "I didn't come to the Tavistock the day he—the day of the murder. But the night before, a group of us dined at Rules. None of the actors. Thornsby and Stanhope and Longworth and me. Thornsby was a bit abstracted. Stared into his wine glass most of the evening. Quite unlike him. He was a cheerful fellow, usually. But by the end of dinner, he looked a bit better. As we were going out the door, he looked at me and said he'd finally made up his mind to what he had to do." Donald scanned her face. "Do you know what he meant?"

"No," Mélanie said.

"Nor do I. But I can't help worrying that whatever it was got him killed."

CHAPTER 34

Malcolm and Julien returned to the Berkeley Square house to find enticing smells floating into the hall from the kitchen. The children's excited voices sounded from the first floor. Nerezza came running down the stairs. "We need more ribbon," she called over her shoulder to Ben, who was hanging over the first-floor stair rail with Livia and Emily beside him.

Nerezza stopped at the base of the stairs and smiled at Malcolm and Julien. "We're arranging flowers in the drawing room. Lady Frances and Lady Cordelia got the most amazing assortment of hothouse flowers delivered quickly. I don't know how they did it."

"I don't know how my aunt does a number of things," Malcolm said.

"It's very thoughtful," Julien said. "I only hope the bridal preparations don't send Kitty fleeing."

"It's keeping the children occupied," Malcolm pointed out.

"A good point," Julien conceded. He reached into his waistcoat pocket and pulled out a delicate gold ring set with a quite magnificent emerald surrounded by tiny pearls. "My mother's," he said. "The only thing I took with me when I ran off that I didn't sell." He held it out to Malcolm. "Be a good fellow and hold on to it until it's needed."

Malcolm took the ring and smiled. If anyone had suggested a few months ago that he'd be standing up with Julien at his wedding, let alone his wedding to Kitty...

The afternoon passed in the bustle of preparations and further discussions of the evidence in the Thornsby case, none of which got them very far. Mélanie returned from the Tavistock again as the sky was darkening, with the news that the run-through had gone better than expected in the circumstances and Simon and David and the children would follow shortly. Soon after, everyone scattered to change into evening clothes. Malcolm carried Jessica upstairs on his shoulders and then took a spare shaving kit to Julien. He returned to his and Mélanie's bedchamber to find his wife half into a gauzy black evening gown embroidered with gold stars.

"Thank goodness," she said. "I'm struggling with the strings."

"St. Juste brought a complete change of clothes, but managed to forget his shaving things," Malcolm said as he went to her side. "Rather nice to know even he can be flustered."

"You think he and Kitty will be happy?" Mélanie asked, as Malcolm did up the tiny strings that fastened the gown where it wrapped closed on one side.

"Yes, I do," Malcolm said. "I think they're desperately in love, for one thing."

He was looking at the strings, but he knew Mélanie smiled at his phrasing. "They'd neither of them thank you for using those words."

"I'm quite sure they wouldn't. That doesn't make them less true. You saw St. Juste when Kitty was wounded. You've seen them the past few months."

"Yes. It's not a Julien I ever thought to see, but it's undeniable. Being Lady Carfax won't be easy on Kitty, though."

Malcolm did up the last of the strings and smoothed the shoulders of her gown. "St. Juste won't expect her to be anything she doesn't want to be. And he'll know how to wear the mantle of Carfax."

Mélanie turned to face him. "I think Julien will be good at it."

"So do I. But he won't let it define him the way David has. He'll make it into what he wants."

Mélanie turned to her dressing table and picked up her diamond earrings. "He's not going to be able to live in the shadows." She threaded an earring through her ear. "Of course, he really hasn't ever since he moved in with Kitty and the children."

"No, I don't think there's been any going back for Julien for some time." Malcolm stripped off his coat and started on his waistcoat buttons. Addison, he saw, had left evening clothes out on the bed for him. "And I don't think he'd want there to be."

Mélanie cast a glance at him over her shoulder. "I love it when you talk like a romantic, darling."

"I'm a realist." Malcolm tossed his waistcoat after the coat and decided he'd better redo his neckcloth. It was a special occasion, after all. "And I think they have a realistic chance of being happy."

Malcolm dressed quickly and went down to the drawing room to find the only other person present so far was the bride. For all her insistence on the wedding's being pragmatic, Kitty had put on a gauzy claret-colored gown and a citrine necklace and earrings. She'd also redone her hair, in a loose knot that wouldn't have taken a great deal of time but showed attention to the importance of the occasion.

She turned at Malcolm's entrance and gave a quick, slightly awkward smile. "I wore white muslin when I married Edward. I couldn't bear to wear anything similar. And I don't think Julien would appreciate anything too maidenly."

"I can't imagine St. Juste not appreciating what you chose," Malcolm said. "You look beautiful." He could say that now, without worrying that either of them would take it the wrong way.

Kitty smiled again, less awkwardly. "The room looks so lovely."

"Frances and Cordelia both love parties," Malcolm said, closing the door. "And it's good to celebrate moments that mean something."

"Thank you." Kitty's voice was a bit husky. "I know this wouldn't be happening without you."

Malcolm smiled at the woman he had once thought the center of his life. "I did little enough. If you thank anyone, it should be Aunt Frances."

"To whom I am also inestimably grateful." Kitty drew the folds of her shawl, gold embroidered with claret, about her shoulders. "Julien was very eager to have the wedding as quickly as possible. Which might seem like youthful ardor in another bridegroom, but I suspect is because he's afraid one of us won't survive. I have to admit he has a point. Danger has a way of clarifying the mind. Last night was particularly clarifying."

A number of options he wouldn't quite let himself consider raced across Malcolm's mind. "He's being prudent."

Kitty wrapped the folds of the shawl with a quick twist. "Not something I tend to associate with Julien."

"He's not used to having a family." Malcolm hesitated. "He's also afraid Carfax will try to intervene."

"There, I agree, he also has a point." Kitty glanced in the mirror and tucked a strand of hair into its pins. "It's hard to imagine."

"Being married?"

"No, being Lady Carfax."

Amelia Carfax's elegant face shot into Malcolm's mind. She hadn't yet been Lady Carfax when Malcolm first met her, but she was the only Lady Carfax Malcolm had known. "I've seen you play any number of roles."

"But I always knew I could leave."

Malcolm found himself smiling. "That's what Mel said about marrying me. That is, she admits she thought she could leave at first, but she knew she wouldn't be able to do so for a long time."

Kitty's gaze settled on his face for a moment. "You sound very matter-of-fact."

"I am. Now. She decided she couldn't leave. And I don't think she wants to."

Kitty echoed his smile though her gaze remained steady. "I'm quite sure she doesn't."

"Which makes the way it started all the more remarkable. And something to be grateful for. Of course, Mel was playing a role. With me. With society, certainly. You don't have to."

"We all have to play roles in life. It's part of what keeps it interesting."

"But I don't think St. Juste will ever expect you to play one you don't wish to play."

"Nor do I, actually." Kitty turned to the mirror and adjusted the draped neckline of her gown. Her fingers stilled for a moment on the twists of fabric. "This must seem odd."

"On the contrary. I couldn't be happier."

She gave a faint smile and twisted the citrine and gold links of her necklace into place as though to prove she could do so with steady hands. "Even you enjoy winning. And it does rather prove your point in our quarrel over what I might have done with Lewis Thornsby. That is—I could hold my ground and say marriage doesn't make a bit of difference, and it's quite true, in many cases marriage wouldn't. But married or not, you're quite right. I wouldn't have betrayed Julien. Not like that."

Malcolm watched her, leaning against the door. "No. I know you wouldn't."

She shot a look at him over her shoulder. "Don't go about having too much faith in me, Malcolm. You're liable to be disappointed."

"Now you sound like my father."

"Ha." She turned back to the mirror. "Raoul could give lessons on the art of looking far worse than he is. While being impossibly noble."

"Quite." He hesitated a moment. "I truly am happy for you. For both of you. And it doesn't matter a whit—"

Kitty met his gaze in the looking glass. "That we never got here?"

He smiled without rancor. "You said it would have been a disaster if we had. I don't entirely agree with you, but I do agree we're happier as we are. Besides, we were different people then." He hesitated again. "I like St. Juste. I have from the first, actually, for all Mel's and Raoul's warnings. But that doesn't matter a bit. What matters is that you love him."

Kitty made one last, seemingly unnecessary adjustment to the necklace and turned from the mirror. "I do. Quite ridiculously. Dear God, I don't believe I said that. I don't know what's come over me, but it's true."

"And I trust him," Malcolm said.

"Trust him to do what?"

"Well, any number of things, as it happens. But in this case, to make you happy."

"I'm not sure Julien trusts himself to do that."

"No, I suspect he doesn't. He's as hard on himself as the rest of us. Perhaps more so. Domesticity has a way of mellowing one. Not that I'm suggesting you're in for anything of the sort."

"It doesn't sound as disagreeable as it once would have done. Besides, the one thing I can't imagine being with Julien is bored. And I trust him. As I've trusted few people in my life. He makes me happy."

"Well then," Malcolm said. "That's everything."

CHAPTER 35

Laughter rippled across the drawing room. A champagne cork popped as Raoul opened another bottle by the drinks trolley. It might, Malcolm thought, have been any of a score of other parties they had given, most of them frequented by much the same circle now gathered in the room. At this moment an outside observer would never have guessed they were in the midst of a dangerous investigation. Or that they had just witnessed the wedding of two people who were close to the last people in their circle anyone would have expected to get married. And that the implications of that marriage would ripple across personal and intelligence circles far beyond their own group.

Julien and Kitty were standing by the fireplace. Julien was talking to Archie, and Kitty to Simon, but their fingers were intertwined.

"Hard to believe we got here, not just from four months ago, but from yesterday." Harry brought Malcolm a fresh glass of champagne. He watched as Julien bent down to scoop up Genny, who had toddled over to him. "I seem to remember we were once all afraid of him."

"In the right circumstances, I'd still be afraid of him." Malcolm accepted the glass and lifted it to Harry's own. "Of course, in the right circumstances, I'd be afraid of my wife."

Kitty was laughing at something Simon had said. For a moment, she looked carefree in a way Malcolm had never seen. "I wonder—"

He broke off as the door opened and a new arrival slipped into the room.

"Roth." Malcolm went forwards quickly to greet Jeremy Roth. "We're in the midst of an unexpected celebration. St. Juste and Kitty just got married."

Roth's face was intent, but at that, his gaze widened slightly. He cast a quick look at Julien and Kitty, who were now being tugged across the room by Timothy. "That's splendid."

"It happened very quickly," Harry said. "Cordy and I are only here rather by chance."

"And we're keeping it secret for the moment," Malcolm said. "Especially from Carfax."

"Understood." Roth hesitated, as though seeking words for something he didn't want to say. "I'm sorry to intrude."

"Nonsense." Mélanie had come over to join them. "Let me get you a glass of champagne. I take it there's news?"

"Yes. Thank you, no champagne. I need to speak with Tanner. Perhaps you could bring him into the small salon?"

Malcolm exchanged a quick look with Mélanie. "You get Simon," she said. "I'll stay with the guests. Harry, I was going to go down for more champagne. May I send you instead?"

Harry, being Harry, didn't ask any of the multitude of questions he no doubt had. Simon, who was laughing with Cordy and Bertrand, raised his brows but followed Malcolm without question.

Roth had preceded them into the small salon. He was standing in front of the fire, hands jammed into the pockets of his greatcoat, which he had not removed as he usually would do on a visit.

"I'm sorry to do this," Roth said, when Malcolm closed the door. Roth's face was set. Malcolm hadn't seen him look so uncomfortable in Berkeley Square since his very first visit. "But I have a warrant for your arrest, Tanner."

Simon stared at Roth, seemingly rooted to the ground.

Malcolm, who had thought himself prepared for most eventualities, felt similarly rooted to the floor. "On what grounds?" he asked.

"Bow Street received a report that Tanner was heard threatening Mr. Thornsby two days before his death."

"From whom?" Simon demanded.

Roth's gaze fastened on Simon's own, dark with compassion. "Officially, I'm not permitted to say. Unofficially, I can say that the source was apparently someone within the Tavistock. And I wasn't told the person's name."

"I'm not sure what this person claims to have heard," Simon said. "I did tell Lewis to have a care what he said in the green room, that not everyone who congregated there supported us. That was two or three days before his murder. I've said as much to other young Levellers. It was so inconsequential I didn't tell Malcolm or you. Not because I was hiding anything, but because it didn't occur to me it could have anything to do with his death."

Roth nodded. "I can understand that. The person in question also claims to have seen you depositing a knife in a rubbish pile at the corner of Southhampton Street the night of the murder." Roth hesitated, gaze steady on Simon's own. "A search of the rubbish pile did recover a bloody knife."

Simon's hand closed, white-knuckled, on a chair back. "So the source may be the killer."

"Or in league with the killer. I'm doing my best to learn the source's name."

"But meanwhile, you're under orders."

"As you say." Roth's gaze continued steady. "Of course I understand you'll need to say goodbye to Worsley and make your excuses to Mélanie. I have some things to discuss with Malcolm. I left a patrol in front of the house but there's no one guarding the mews."

Simon returned Roth's gaze. "That's good of you, Roth. But it's not fair to you. And I need to keep this above board to clear my name and get home to my family. I suggest we leave quietly. Malcolm, tell David. Once we're gone. There's no point in disrupting the celebration. I don't want to make a scene in front of the children, and there's nothing he could do just now."

"Where are you taking him?" Malcolm asked Roth.

"Newgate, most likely. I'll send word as soon as I know."

Simon clapped Malcolm on the shoulder. "Don't waste time on farewells. That makes this into more than it is. Tell Mélanie if I'm not out by morning, I'll send instructions for rehearsal."

CHAPTER 36

David cast a quick glance round the cell, then crossed to Simon and took his hands. For a moment, Malcolm knew how much he wanted to do more. Malcolm had a keen memory of Mélanie's visiting him in prison in Vienna. Their relationship had been a tangle, and he'd been far from certain he could escape prison and still raw from his sister's murder. But he'd been able to embrace his wife without fear of who might see them. He'd clung to her with rare abandon and never thought that simply the ability to take her in his arms was something to be thankful for.

Simon's fingers tightened on David's hands with an equal impulse for more. "How are the children?"

"Worried," David said. "They're in Berkeley Square. We told them you'd had to go answer some questions. Teddy asked me if you'd been arrested, when George and Amy and Jamie couldn't hear. I admitted you had."

"Good for you," Simon said. "Always best to tell them as much of the truth as possible."

"I said it was a misunderstanding and we'd get you out soon. Which is also the truth."

"It's certainly a misunderstanding," Simon said.

"We'll get you a solicitor in the morning," David said. "Mélanie sent a hamper of food"—he gestured to the hamper Malcolm had placed on the one table in the cell—"and I've given the turnkey funds so you'll have more decent food. Assuming this goes on, which it shouldn't." He placed his hands on Simon's shoulders. "We're not sure yet where the accusation came from. My first instinct was to go to Carfax House and accuse Father, but St. Juste pointed out that if Father was behind it, that would only tip him off to our knowing." He cast a glance over his shoulder at Julien, who was tactfully hanging back beside Malcolm.

"I'm not sure Carfax *was* behind it," Simon said. "He's gone a long time without trying to interfere between us. And it sounds as though he's resigned himself to St. Juste's taking over the title." He looked at Julien. "Arthur's taking over the title."

"I don't think I'll ever be Arthur again," Julien said.

"It wouldn't be the first time Father's seized on chance and improvised," David said. "And he's always found you a threat."

"I can't believe he thinks me that much of a threat," Simon said.

"He thought we were all a threat at Oxford." Malcolm took a step forwards. They had moved from intimacy to investigation.

"You think he's behind this?" Simon asked.

"I'm not sure. Someone obviously is pulling strings. Carfax is a likely suspect, but I agree this is an unusual time for him to attack you."

"He's bided his time before." David dropped his hands from Simon's shoulders. He moved to the side to let Malcolm and Julien into the conversation, but remained close to Simon. "For all we know, his telling St. Juste he wants him to take over the earldom is a feint in some plot to get rid of St. Juste."

"That's actually a good point," Julien said. "Don't think I

haven't considered it. It's part of the reason Kitty and I got married tonight."

"I'm sorry," Simon said. "Sorry to have ruined your celebration."

"Don't be an idiot, Tanner. It's hardly your fault you were arrested, and it didn't ruin anything. And it was a practical ceremony, in any case."

"I don't for a minute believe that last," Simon said.

Julien gave a reluctant smile. "Well, perhaps not. I'll even go so far as to admit the evening meant a lot to me. And while I couldn't be sorrier for the way it ended, it doesn't lessen the rather unsettling amount of—er—joy"—he coughed—"it brought, in the least."

"*Bravo,*" Simon said.

Julien's smile deepened slightly. "I'm learning."

"Someone wants the papers you're trying to publish," Malcolm said.

"You think the same person who was behind the attacks last night is behind this?" Simon said. "But locking me up doesn't get them the papers. It doesn't even stop publication. Hapgood started distributing the pamphlets this afternoon."

"We still aren't sure what the point was of the attack last night either," Julien said. "Or if your arrest is connected."

"My arrest may not be an attack on me at all," Simon said. "It may be an attempt to divert suspicion from whoever did kill Thornsby."

"The League have tried to get to Carfax through you and David in the past," Malcolm said. "They had tried to blackmail Percy Shelley into getting Simon to write indiscreet details about his relationship with David."

David swung his gaze to Malcolm. "But this plays into Father's hands."

"Does it?" Malcolm said. "That depends on what your father wants, which is always difficult to tell with Carfax. If you defend Simon and that gets you in trouble, they could think that gives them a wedge against Carfax."

"That seems roundabout, even for the League," David said. "But I agree, if either Father or the League are behind this, any predictable action we take potentially plays into their hands." He turned back to Simon. "If Father comes and tries to make you some sort of offer—"

"My freedom in exchange for giving you up and disappearing into the wilds of Canada? Don't worry, I'll laugh in his face."

"It's not funny, Simon."

Simon reached for David's hand. "The idea that anyone thinks I'd even contemplate such an offer is distinctly funny."

"It would be interesting, though," Malcolm said. "If anyone tries to use your imprisonment as leverage to get you to do anything, it might give us a clue into what's behind your arrest."

"So I should play them along?"

"You're an excellent actor. This might be a good time to put those skills to use."

"I've always been fairly good at improvisation. In truth, I'd relish the chance to help."

"Don't take unnecessary chances," David said.

"The operative word being 'unnecessary,'" Simon said. "I think we're all going to have to take chances to resolve this."

"We'll both disappear if we have to," David said. "It wouldn't be the first time we've broken someone out of prison."

"It won't come to that," Simon said.

"You can't know that," David said. "The thing is, we're prepared if it does."

Simon put a hand on David's shoulder. "From one of the most law-abiding people I know, that's quite a statement of affection. And don't think I don't appreciate it. Are you going to stay in Berkeley Square tonight?"

"I think it will be easier on the children. Mélanie said they'd try to settle them in the night nursery with the others, if she could."

"If anyone outside of us can settle Jamie down, Mélanie and Kitty, not to mention Laura and O'Roarke and Addison and Blanca, may be able to do the trick."

"You've never been away from Jamie overnight," David said.

"No, I know," Simon said. "I've come back late, but I haven't gone without tucking him in or looking in on him. I hope he'll understand."

"My dear fellow." David glanced at the door, then leaned in and kissed Simon. "When you're back home with us, they'll understand everything."

SIMON TOOK a sip from the flask of coffee Mélanie had sent. She'd sent a bottle of wine too, but for the moment he needed his wits about him. And far too much tension was roiling through him for the bread, Stilton, apples, and other delicacies in her hamper to tempt him. He crossed from the table with the hamper to the narrow bed, mostly because it felt better to pace. Laura had gone through this, with more evidence against her, and without the confidence that the Rannochs, on whom she had been spying, would support her. She'd been missing Emily then too, with no assurance she'd ever see the daughter who'd been taken from her at birth. His case was not nearly so bad. He could get through this. There was no reason to want to claw at the walls of his cage. No reason for the gnawing fear that Carfax had perhaps at last won and he wouldn't see David and the children again.

He clunked the flask down on the headboard and debated opening the wine—if nothing else, in hopes it would still the tumult raging through him.

The key scraped in the lock. Simon spun towards the door,

hoping to see David, braced for something more alarming. The door grated open. The turnkey stepped aside, and the man who entered the cell was not David, but David's father.

Simon pushed himself away from the bed, grateful he had not touched the wine. "I've been expecting to see you, sir."

"I didn't know you were here until just now, as it happens," Carfax said. "David didn't send word to me. Nor did Malcolm. Probably afraid of what I would do."

"Does that surprise you?"

"Very little surprises me. But no, there's a certain logic to their fear."

Simon studied his lover's father, the man who had been the greatest threat to his relationship with David for over a decade. From the moment he and David had met. The cell was lit only by a single lamp, leaving Carfax in shadow, as he so often was. "I don't suppose you know who is behind the accusations against me?"

Carfax adjusted one of the earpieces on his spectacles. "I do, actually, but this isn't the place to talk of it. Better in Berkeley Square, for a number of reasons. Assuming you're willing to take me there with you. Assuming Malcolm lets me in the door."

Simon stared at Carfax. It could be hard to keep up with him, but this was unusually fast. "In case you haven't noticed, I'm imprisoned."

"You were imprisoned. You're free to go."

Simon continued to watch Carfax. He'd have told one of his actors the pause dragged on too long for dramatic tension.

"It's not a ploy." Carfax adjusted the other earpiece. "They have it on my authority that you're under my protection. You won't be disturbed again about this or about anything else, unless you take actions so extreme, I flatter myself even you wouldn't attempt them."

Simon took a drink from the coffee flask, braced for what Carfax was going to ask of him next. "Good of you."

"I'm not asking you to change, Tanner. I think Britain can survive you."

Simon raised a brow. "I'm not sure whether to be flattered or insulted."

Carfax gave a faint smile that flashed in the shadows. "I don't discount you, Tanner. But I think Britain's institutions can withstand you."

"You're coming round to Malcolm's way of thinking."

"Don't let him get a glimmering." Carfax crossed the cell in two strides and touched Simon on the arm. "You'd better get back to David before he worries himself sick. Whether or not you take me with you to Berkeley Square—where I have no doubt David and the others are waiting—is entirely your own affair. But I'd advise you to do so."

Simon met Carfax's gaze. "That's probably for the best, for a number of reasons. Among other things, I imagine you'd like to see your grandchildren?"

"You're a generous man, Tanner."

"I didn't say it to be generous. And I only hope I'm not a fool."

CHAPTER 37

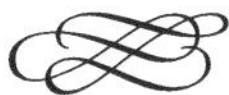

Malcolm looked round at the opening of the drawing room door, expecting Valentin with more coffee. Instead he saw Simon, followed by Carfax.

David sprang to his feet, took three steps across the room, and went still, seeing his father.

"Uncle Simon!" Jamie hurtled forwards with no such qualms.

Simon ran to meet him and knelt down to catch the boy in his arms.

The older three Craven children ran forwards and hurled themselves on Simon as well, but Teddy drew back after a moment to study Carfax, who had stopped just inside the door. "Grandpapa?"

"Your grandfather was a great help in getting me released," Simon said.

David stared at his father, as though he were trying to strip away layers to uncover an elusive truth. "You never fail to surprise me, sir."

Simon got to his feet, holding Jamie. "Carfax has some information to share with us. It seemed best to bring him here." He met Julien's gaze for a moment, as though in apology for bringing Carfax into the scene of the wedding.

"Quite right," Julien said. "I suspect we'd all like to hear what he has to say."

"I imagine we could all do with a drink as well," Simon said. "Perhaps some lemonade for the children. I suspect Carfax would like a whisky. I know I would."

Impatient as Malcolm was, and as concerned as he was about Carfax's presence in their house with Julien and Kitty, he knew the children needed time to reassure themselves that Simon was indeed back and safe. It was some minutes before the children finished their lemonade and returned to their game with Blanca and Addison keeping them company, and the other adults could settle themselves beside the fire.

Simon, who had been rolling on the carpet a few minutes before with children gleefully knocking him over, looked at Carfax with a hard face. "You said you know who was behind the accusations against me."

"Yes." Carfax settled back in his chair. He had chosen a simple straight-backed one. "It wasn't me, though I suspect that was your first thought."

"Tempered by the fact that you might have tried it a score of times in the past," Malcolm said.

"Quite. In fact, by the time I heard about it, Tanner was already in Newgate or I'd have acted sooner. Pressure was apparently placed on the home secretary directly. I had quite a confrontation with Sidmouth to reverse matters." Carfax said it easily, but Malcolm was quite sure Carfax had relished the confrontation.

"Amazing what use information from years past can be put to, isn't it?" Julien said.

"As you well know." Carfax took a drink of whisky. "Sidmouth does like to bluster, but there was never really any question that he would listen to me. And in the end, he confessed who had insisted on Simon's arrest. I must say, the answer surprised me. It was Lady Shroppington."

Silence rippled across the drawing room.

"You don't look as surprised as I expected," Carfax said. "May I take it you know something about her?"

Malcolm glanced at Mélanie, then at Raoul, then at the others. "She's apparently connected to the Elsinore League."

"She's—" Carfax set his glass down. "That *is* interesting. I had no notion they had women members.

"Nor did I," Archie said. "And I was a member myself."

"Lewis Thornsby was working for the League," Malcolm said. "Edgar recruited him. Apparently Thornsby and Lady Shroppington were both connected to the faction in the League that is trying to put Alexander Radford in power."

"And I assume they have their reasons for wanting to remove Tanner from the field of play." Carfax looked at Simon. "My compliments on the release of the pamphlets, by the way."

"You don't happen to have been behind the attacks in Hyde Park last night, do you?" Julien asked in an even voice.

Carfax met his nephew's gaze across the room. "I rather think I'd be taking my life in my hands if I said yes. But as it happens, I truly wasn't. The first I heard about the attacks was a report early this morning, and even now I don't have all the details of what happened. Malcolm didn't mention them when he came to see me last night."

"I couldn't without tipping you off about the pamphlets before they were released," Malcolm said.

Carfax gave a faint smile. "I confess that while I suspected Tanner and Kitty were behind some of the recent news out of Spain that's been printed, I didn't even realize you had this latest information until a source kindly sent one of the pamphlets round to me this evening. If I had known, I'd have made an effort to stop you. It will cause some difficulties, to say the least. But it hardly rises to the level of murder."

Malcolm stared at him. Carfax raised a brow. "Not convinced?"

"No," Malcolm conceded. "We actually were saying much the same last night. But someone hired two groups of ruffians to attack those involved in printing the pamphlets last night and gave them specific orders to kill Kitty."

Carfax's gaze shot to Kitty. She was sitting by quietly, watching him. The emerald ring Julien had given her had vanished from her hand moments after Carfax had come into the room. "I'd have quite understood," she said. "You wouldn't have done it for personal reasons."

"But the papers hardly would have warranted it, as I said. Quite aside from the fact that I'd have known it would bring Julien down on my head. And that I am fond of you, Kitty."

"That's never stopped you," David said.

"It's given me second thoughts," Carfax said.

"So the papers bothered someone else," Malcolm said. "Who?"

"An interesting question." Carfax settled back in his chair and took a drink of whisky. "I don't have my printed copy on me at present, but I'm sure you're all familiar with the notes by now. There were only two meetings, one in Spain, one in Italy. The only people present at both were myself and an assistant I brought, who actually took the notes."

"Toby Wilkins," Laura said.

"Yes." Carfax inclined his head.

"Lady Shroppington planted an agent in his home."

Carfax raised his brows. "That is an interesting development."

"So what might Wilkins know that Lady Shroppington might be interested in?" Malcolm asked.

Carfax tented his fingers below his chin. "Any knowledge he had of the meetings was contained in those notes. Difficult to see how Wilton would be of interest beyond the notes. He's able enough, but for better or worse he doesn't have your flexibility of thinking."

"I recognized most of the names of those present," Raoul said. "Even those I hadn't actually met in person. Save for one man at the meeting in Naples. An Antonio Barosa."

"Yes." Carfax met Raoul's gaze for a moment. "The minister of police fell ill and sent him along instead."

"The minister of police of Naples?" Nerezza asked.

Carfax turned his gaze to her. "Yes. The same gentleman with whom you were entangled, my dear. Whose secrets you gave to the Carbonari. I've known him since we were both just out of university. I attempted to detain you as a favor to him when you first arrived here. But it was more a debt of friendship than any particular concern for what you might do, as I told Malcolm."

"But the Elsinore League wanted her dead." Ben shifted closer to Nerezza on the settee where they were sitting.

"Seemingly because of this man who calls himself Alexander Radford, not because of the minister of police," Carfax said.

"What was Antonio Barosa like?" Raoul asked.

"About our age, I'd say. Closer to mine than yours, perhaps. On the portly side. From Sicily originally, judging by his accent. Didn't say a great deal, but drove a hard bargain about what Naples was willing to give up."

"Could the stomach have been padded?" Raoul asked.

Carfax's eyes narrowed. "I didn't see the man stripped down, so it's possible. I had no suspicion of it. But then, I wasn't looking for a disguise."

"No, you wouldn't have been. What color were his eyes?"

Carfax frowned in a seemingly genuine effort of recall. "Green in some lights, blue in others. At times they looked almost brown."

Raoul looked at Nerezza. "You said Alexander Radford had hazel eyes."

Nerezza's eyes widened. "You think this Antonio Barosa was Alexander Radford in disguise?"

"There's nothing to suggest that," Carfax said.

"Nothing save the fact that the same people who want to get rid of Nerezza because of her connection to Alexander Radford want to get hold of the notes of that meeting Antonio Barosa attended," Raoul said.

"Lewis Thornsby took lodgings where the papers were being printed," Kitty said. "He seems to have searched for the papers. And he tried to get both Kit Montagu and me to tell him what we were doing."

"And Lady Shroppington planted a spy on the Wiltons," Laura said.

"And Beverston as good as confirmed that Alexander Radford is the man trying to take control of the League," Malcolm said.

"Thornsby couldn't have known about the meeting notes when he first took lodgings with Hapgood," Simon pointed out.

"No," Malcolm agreed. "I suspect at that point he was trying to learn what you were all doing with the papers from Spain. He told Roger he'd heard you and Kit talking about something that might be treasonous."

Simon's eyes narrowed. "Kit brought up the lines were crossing. I didn't know Thornsby had overheard us. Or that he'd told Roger."

"I think at that point Thornsby was trying to sow dissension among the Levellers. But recently he tried very hard to get both Kit and Kitty to take him into their confidence. I think that was because he'd learned about the notes of the meetings in Spain and Italy. And they may have interested him because Antonio Barosa is Alexander Radford."

Carfax unclasped his hands and pushed up his spectacles. "It's possible. I don't see the point of such a deception. Nor do I like to think I might have been taken in by it—but I can't swear I wasn't."

"The League have shown an interest in you," Julien said in a quiet voice. "Particularly Alexander Radford's faction in the League."

"Yes, they evidently think I pose some threat."

"False modesty doesn't become you, sir. Of course you pose a threat, and you've made it your business to try to take them down. But I wonder if there's more to it. It's almost as if they've been going after certain enemies. O'Roarke. You. Lord Glenister."

Carfax frowned. "You're making leaps like O'Roarke, Julien."

"O'Roarke's leaps are bloody brilliant. And in this case, I think, spot on."

For a moment, Carfax and Julien weren't antagonists, they were spymaster and spy. Or just possibly uncle and nephew. "It doesn't prove Barosa is Radford," Carfax said. "Or that he isn't. And in any case, the papers don't reveal Barosa's identity."

"I don't know who Alexander Radford really is, but they want to get rid of me," Nerezza pointed out. "There seems to be a lot of concern about keeping his secrets, for whatever reason."

"So there does," Carfax agreed.

Malcolm regarded his former spymaster. "Thornsby was trying to barter the list of Radical disturbances I showed you for information about the notes of that meeting. So I think the Radical disturbances are something he uncovered, not something he was behind."

Carfax took another drink of whisky. "All right. We seem to be at the point where secrets are doing more harm than good. I'll admit to being behind those incidents. Shocked, Malcolm? Let me guess. Now you think I'm lying and I wasn't behind them at all."

"No, I'm inclined to believe you. I think the sketch of the rifle trajectory aimed at the royal box was something else Thornsby had uncovered. That's why you haven't been more worried about it, because it was your plot all along. Were you actually planning a foiled assassination attempt, or was the evidence supposed to be uncovered in advance?"

"My dear Malcolm. You can't imagine I would really orchestrate shooting at the royal box."

"My dear sir. Under the right circumstances, I wouldn't put actually assassinating a member of the royal family past you."

"That's treason."

"It's also murder, which I'm even more inclined to cavil at."

Carfax set his glass down. "The drawing was supposed to be uncovered before any plot could be attempted. There'd be no direct proof to convict anyone."

"You relieve me," Simon said in a dry voice. "So you weren't planning to hang any of us?"

"I have no interest in hanging any of your group, Tanner. That would turn you into martyrs, among other things. And while I freely admit to having far fewer scruples than just about anyone in this room—including Julien, I now think—I really do try to stay away from needless killing. The whole point of agent provocateur operations is to create discord and uncertainty."

"And ruin lives," Malcolm said.

"I'm prepared to share information, Malcolm, not to have a moral debate."

"Who orchestrated the activities?" Malcolm asked.

"Various agents of mine."

"Including your agents among the Levellers."

"Given that a number of the activities involved the Levellers, that's a fair assumption."

David's gaze was fastened on his father. "By God—"

"No," Malcolm said, "your father's right. Right now we all need to share information. Which is why your father is going to tell us who his agent among the Levellers is."

Carfax regarded Malcolm for a long moment. "That's asking a lot."

"You're asking us to work with you."

Carfax gave a faint inclination of his head. "For all your tiresome scruples, you've always been a good negotiator, Malcolm. Fair enough. It's Donald McDevitt."

Mélanie released her breath.

Carfax's gaze shot to her. "You suspected?"

"Not precisely. I talked to him this afternoon. He didn't strike me as a typical Leveller. When did he start working for you?"

"About six months ago. He came to me himself, as it happens. He said he thought he had an interesting way into the Levellers."

"So he told you about Will?" Mélanie asked. "Had he already met Will at the Tavistock?"

"No, but he'd seen Carmarthen onstage and realized it was his cousin."

"So, everything he said to Will, their whole reunion, it was all part of his work for you."

"I don't think any of us are strangers to the jealousies between brothers," Carfax said. "And Donald and Will had grown up rather as brothers."

"Donald set up Will's arrest in Lancaster?" Simon said.

"Yes, that went further than I meant it to," Carfax said. "Donald's directive was simply to cause some unrest. Framing anyone, let alone a Leveller, let alone his own cousin, wasn't part of it."

"Did you tell him to watch Thornsby?" Malcolm asked, keeping his voice steady. Throttling Carfax would get them nowhere, and while he hadn't known the mole's identity, none of this was anything he hadn't already known or suspected. "Or did Donald tumble to Thornsby's working for the League?"

"Donald had a university friend who knew Thornsby.

Donald was the one who first let me know he thought there was more to Thornsby than met the eye."

"Thornsby stole the list of disturbances from Donald," Malcolm said.

"I suspect so. And the drawing of the rifle trajectory. Though in the end, its being found on him served more or less the intended purpose."

"When did you last talk to Donald?" Malcolm asked Carfax.

"He came to see me yesterday. He told me the last time he'd seen Thornsby was the night before the murder."

"Do you believe him?" Malcolm asked.

Carfax took a drink of whisky. "Are you suggesting Donald killed Thornsby?"

"Someone did. And unfortunately, for all we've learned, we're no closer to determining who."

"I'll arrange a meeting with Donald and see what more I can learn," Carfax said.

"I'll talk to Beverston again and see what I can get him to admit about Lady Shroppington," Malcolm said. "At least knowing the assassination plot was a fabrication of yours takes away some of the urgency."

"Yes." Carfax looked from Mélanie to Simon. "No need to worry about your opening. I'm quite looking forward to it."

David pushed back his chair. "If we've said what needs to be said for the moment, we need a word with you in private, Father. Perhaps Mélanie would give us the use of the small salon."

"We?" Carfax asked.

"Julien and I."

CHAPTER 38

David regarded his father in the delicate sea-green precincts of the small salon. This room, with its airy walls and spindle-legged furniture, seemed an odd setting for what had to be said. But David had wanted the nearest room available. "What's the catch, sir?"

"The catch?"

"In your getting Simon out of Newgate."

Carfax moved to a delicate chair upholstered in ivory silk. "There isn't one."

"You're good, Father. But I've learned to see round you."

"In this case, you're jumping at shadows." Carfax set his glass down on a satinwood end table and lowered himself into the chair. "I thought we'd all decided to be allies for the moment. Even Malcolm seems to see it that way."

"Why should Arthur and I believe a word you say?" David asked.

Carfax met his gaze, then looked at Julien. "Ah. Well, I assumed you knew the truth. Especially when the two of you wanted to talk to me together."

"But you weren't going to admit it until we did," David said.

"It seemed prudent."

David nearly strode across the room and pulled his father from the chair. "You manipulated me. You tried to force me into a life I didn't want. To destroy the man I love. For the sake of a title that isn't even rightfully mine."

"Oh, for God's sake, David. You're a revolutionary. You don't believe in bloodlines anyway."

"But you do. You kept telling me it was important to preserve them. You did everything you could to get me to have a son. All so he could grow up and live a lie. Did you think about what might happen to this hypothetical child in ten, or twenty, or fifty years if the truth came out?"

"Naturally, I assumed it wouldn't. As I assume O'Roarke did, with the truth about Mélanie."

David was not going to be diverted by Mélanie's past, this time. "You assume that, knowing St. Juste? Arthur." David looked at his new-found cousin, then looked back at Carfax. "Damn it, Father, you couldn't control him now. How could you possibly think you could in the future? Which doesn't even really matter considering that it was *wrong*."

"David, I'd have thought your view of the world had grown nuanced enough not to talk about simple rights and wrongs."

"Some things are clearly wrong, sir. If you chose to commit fraud, that's your own affair. But you dragged me into it. Along with Mother and the girls, but you made it your excuse for trying to control my life."

Carfax curved his hands round the fluted arms of his chair. "If you're done with your principled rant, David, perhaps you'll permit me to address some of the issues?"

"What could you possibly say to—"

"Your uncle was determined to hand Arthur over to the authorities. Which would have been a sad waste."

"Thank you," Julien said. "I tend to agree."

"My uncle died over two decades ago," David said.

"We were in the midst of a war, and it was no time to try to resurrect Julien's reputation."

"And you didn't trust me," Julien said. "Not that you trust me now, but I think your view of me was rather worse then."

"True enough," Carfax said. "Besides, it was helpful for me to have the title and the power that went with it. No sense in denying it."

"My God," David said.

"I'll say this for you, Uncle Hubert," Julien said. "You're refreshingly honest."

"Don't pretend you even considered doing the right thing until recently," David said. "Otherwise you wouldn't have been so intent on my marrying and producing an heir."

"You'd have been a good earl, David," Carfax said.

David stared at this father. "Your rescuing Simon. It was all because you'd given up on me, wasn't it?"

"David." Carfax's voice cut with unwonted force. He pushed himself out of his chair, then dropped back into it. "You can't possibly think my concern for your future was only because you were the Carfax heir. If anything, this makes your ability to look after your family even more vital. You won't have a title to protect you. And we're going to find ourselves at open war with the League." He flicked a glance at Julien, then looked back at David. "Part of my willingness to risk turning the title over to Julien is my confidence that you'll be all right."

David held his father's gaze.

"Yes, I know," Carfax said. "I might say that anyway, if I wanted you to go along with it. But it happens to be the truth."

David folded his arms across his chest. "Why should Arthur and I listen to anything you say?"

"Among other reasons, because this will be a great deal easier if we all work together."

"Leave it to you to fall back on the idea of working together."

"I hate to admit it, but he has a point," Julien said. "On the other hand, I won't blame you if you want nothing whatsoever to do with him."

"I don't think I have that luxury." David folded his arms over his chest. "Why did you save Simon, Father?"

"Because I don't like to see the League win. Because my grandchildren are attached to him. Because I'm not indifferent to him myself. Because you love him."

Leave it to Carfax to speak words David had never imagined hearing on his lips. For the length of several heartbeats, David could simply stare at his father. "If you're counting on my gratitude, it will get you nowhere."

"No, I don't believe it will. I don't believe anything will. And I mean that as a compliment." Carfax regarded David with a faint smile. "You've set a dangerous path for yourself. I had hoped you could have the life you want without running so many obvious risks. But you've shown you can take care of yourself and the family you've built. In the future, you'll find me an ally in your efforts, not an opponent."

David sucked in his breath. "You can't expect me to believe that."

"No? I suppose I wouldn't, in your shoes. This could be a gambit. Win you over, get you to relax your guard. But no matter what I do, I don't think you're ever going to marry."

"No," David said. "I'm not."

"Well, then. Whatever you think of me, you might ask yourself if I'm the sort to keep hitting my head against a brick wall."

"What do you call the past two years?"

"A point," Carfax conceded.

"My God, sir. When I think of the damage—"

"None of it's irreversible."

"Speak for yourself."

"You and Tanner look stronger than ever."

"I suppose we are, in a way. None of that excuses what you did."

"I'm not asking you to excuse it." Carfax took a drink of whisky. "But I hope you'll stop wasting time worrying about me, and focus on our common enemies."

"Father—" David's gaze narrowed. "Are you asking me to be an ally?"

"I'm hoping you are one. At least, in certain things. I should have realized long since how effective you could be." Carfax settled back in his chair. "I meant what I said at the start, David. Your ability to take care of your family impresses me. I'm not sure what the future holds for me. That's something we need to discuss with Julien. But I trust you and Simon to look after the children and yourselves. You've certainly done so through some very trying times."

David stared at him, stretched out a hand, let it fall. "Father—"

"Don't start worrying too much, lad. I'm not precisely in desperate circumstances. When it comes to taking care of oneself, I've always done rather well."

"Truer words were never spoken, Father." David searched for words to express a sentiment he wouldn't have been able to imagine feeling a quarter hour since. "Thank you."

"For letting you live the life you want?"

"No. You should have done that a long time since. For believing in me."

"I should have done that a long time since as well." Carfax watched him for a moment, then looked at Julien. "The next few months may be particularly trying for all of us. Amelia may cause difficulties."

"Mama?" David asked.

"She warned me she'd choose you and your sisters over me. Arguably, not a bad stance. But I believe she meant that she wouldn't let me trade away what she sees as your birthright."

"She knows it's not my birthright. At least, I assume from your words she knows about Arthur."

"She does. She recognized him at the O'Roarkes' wedding."

"So she knows the Carfax title isn't even my rightful inheritance."

"She may believe you've come to deserve it."

"Oh, well," Julien said. "If we're talking about deserving—"

"I'll talk to Mama," David said.

"Thank you," Carfax said. "She's rather more in charity with you than with me at the moment." He looked between David and Julien. "We have a number of decisions to make."

"Not until the Thornsby business is settled," Julien said.

"We have a bit of time to plan," Carfax conceded. "I imagine you want to get back to Tanner and the children, David."

"You want to talk to Julien."

"It might be a good idea."

David glanced at Julien. Julien inclined his head and gave a faint smile. David looked between his father and cousin, and left the room, wondering how he had come to be so in charity with his father.

JULIEN REGARDED his uncle for several seconds after the door closed behind David. "Kitty and I were married this evening." He tossed the words down like a gauntlet.

Carfax raised his brows. To Julien's surprise, a faint smile crossed his face. "I was wondering when you'd get round to it."

Julien never trusted Carfax, and particularly not when he was smiling. "You don't look as though you mind."

"On the contrary. I've wanted to see you married, and though, as I once said, Kitty Ashford isn't the partner I'd have chosen for you, it's become apparent she's the one you want. I've learned to control my interference."

"Ha."

"I've always liked Kitty."

"Oh, for God's sake. Since when have you liked anyone?"

"It's not that I don't like people, I just don't let my liking them interfere with what needs to be done. The two of you will look after each other."

Carfax's sounding benevolent was even less trustworthy than Carfax's smiling. "You've been warning me off marrying Kitty for weeks. You told Mélanie you were worried about our relationship. You told Malcolm."

"So I did."

"You'd think you'd have realized such vehement opposition was likely to make us do quite the opposite."

Carfax leaned back in his chair. "Yes, you'd think I would."

Julien stared at his uncle. "Oh, my God."

Carfax adjusted his cuff. "I bungled things badly with David. I'm fully capable of bungling again, but I rarely make the same mistake twice. I do realize separating two people determined to be together is likely to have all sorts of adverse consequences. Much better to try to make the relationship work."

"I was so sure you'd object, that we got a special license to get it done at once."

"You'd have wanted a special license anyway. I hope you're not saying you're sorry to be married?"

"Of course not. I was rather stunned she accepted me."

"Well, then. Just as well you didn't let things drag out because you were afraid to put it to the touch."

Julien folded his arms over his chest. "One more thing. I don't know that we'll have any more children. We haven't decided yet." Actually, they hadn't talked about it at all, but he wasn't going into that with Carfax. "We're quite happy with the three we have, and they need a lot of attention just now. If we decide to have more, and we have a daughter or two, we aren't going to keep going just in hopes of having a son."

"Fair enough."

Julien leaned against a console table, arms folded across his chest. "You're sounding entirely too equable, sir."

"Say I'm mellowing in my old age."

Julien gave a hoot of laughter.

"Or that I'm too relieved to see you settled to cavil at details."

Julien watched his uncle for a moment in the lamplight. Mostly, Carfax looked little different from the way Julien remembered when he had disappeared from Britain twenty-five years ago. But there were lines in the weathered skin on that sharp-featured face that Julien didn't remember, or that were more deeply scored. An unfamiliar warmth tugged at Julien's brain. Carfax normally sat with the light at his back. Had he positioned himself with the light falling across his face precisely to play on Julien's sympathies?

"Of course, as long as I'm living in the shadows, none of that matters," Julien said.

"No." Carfax turned his glass in his hand. "But you're not going to remain in the shadows, are you?"

Julien met his uncle's gaze. "It's settled, then?" For all his decisions, for all his talks with Kitty and Malcolm, for all the talk they had just had with David, it was still difficult to believe it had come to this.

"My dear boy, was it ever really anything else? You don't seriously think we can go on this way, do you? Malcolm knows. David knows, and he'll never put up with the secret. Once you decided to show yourself in Britain, it was only a matter of time. Surely you knew that."

Had he? Or had he been fooling himself? Had he really believed he could go on as he was, or could disappear whenever he wanted? The night he'd killed Edgar Rannoch, the night he'd stayed with Kitty, the night he'd learned he had a daughter. Surely at that point, he'd known there was no turning back. Not unless Kitty wanted to disappear with him, and he couldn't ask that of her unless she chose it for herself.

The truth was, for weeks now, he'd been on a sort of holiday, enjoying the time when he could still play at being an agent who could sink into the shadows. Shadows could be comforting. They'd been his home for nearly a quarter century. And however much he'd emerged from the shadows recently, the prospect of leaving them behind permanently still made him grow cold.

"How long have you known?" he asked Carfax.

"Since a year ago, when I found out you were working with Gisèle, and it was clear you were staying in Britain. I saw the risks six months before that, when we exchanged information the night of the Waterloo banquet. My misguided attempt to control David was my last effort at building a bulwark against what I should have seen as inevitable."

Julien leaned back and rested his weight on his hands. "You had other options, surely. You could have had me killed. I haven't been much use to you as an agent since Waterloo. You must have considered it."

Carfax crossed his legs. "Obviously, I examined every move available to me. That didn't seem the right one, for a number of reasons. Your re-emerging actually solves a number of problems. David's managing well, but this will make things easier for him. You saw how he reacted just now. He never really wanted the earldom. And it will take the wind out of the Elsinore League's sails nicely."

"You sound very sanguine."

"You'll make a good earl, Julien. Arthur."

"My father didn't think so."

"No, but though you tend to lump us together, your father and I didn't see eye to eye on a number of things."

"I can't imagine it will be easy for Aunt Amelia."

Carfax frowned slightly. "She knows you're back. As I said, she recognized you at the O'Roarkes' wedding."

"Yes, I thought she probably would."

"She's glad you're alive and well. But she has concerns about the children, as I mentioned to David. I hope David can make her see it's better for him. The girls are settled, except for Lucinda, and it shouldn't damage her prospects. I know it won't be the life Amelia expected, but then, that's been true in other ways."

"She married you when you were Hubert Mallinson. And seemed quite happy about it."

"I like to think so. But I've disappointed her in a number of ways."

"Isn't disappointment inevitable at some point, in any relationship?" Julien said without consciously formulating the words, which was unusual for him. "We're none of us perfect. But the alternative is to eschew relationships entirely. Take it from one who's tried. It's not particularly comfortable."

Carfax gave a wintry smile. "You and Kitty understand each other, at least. That's good to have, going in. In fact, I may have been wrong when I said she wasn't the bride I'd choose for you."

"Admitting you're wrong, uncle? Don't strain things. I'm not sure we can sustain the reaction."

Carfax leaned back in his chair. "It's a long time since you've called me uncle."

He hadn't been consciously aware of that just now either. Not that he was about to admit it. "I couldn't have, without breaking cover. Now it seems I'm going to have to." The reality settled over him, like a mantle that didn't quite fit yet. "As I said, we should wait at least until the investigation is concluded." He still couldn't quite believe they were talking about it.

Carfax tented his fingers together. "Assuming you're willing to cooperate with me, we should be able to concoct a reasonable story to explain your reappearance. The Rannochs got away with saying Laura Dudley—Laura O'Roarke now—had had amnesia."

"Then we definitely can't use that."

"You were young, you quarreled with your father, and he disowned you. You ran away. We can use a lot of the truth. During the war you were busy serving your country undercover—"

"Ha."

"There's some truth in that, if we don't talk about whom else you served."

"There are going to be a number of uncomfortable questions for both of us."

"Which is why we need to work together. Your past actions can be explained. And mine—"

"If you really believed I was dead, yours don't enter into it."

Carfax's smile deepened. "Precisely. If we time it correctly, we can surprise the League."

Julien shared his uncle's appreciation of the prospect. But —"It's all very well, sir, but the League know the truth. They're likely to try to use it, as a spoiler if nothing else, because they can't use me and my past to control you."

"Leave that to me." Carfax settled his elbows on the chair arms. "Truthfully, Julien, you're less of a challenging case to rehabilitate than Mélanie Rannoch and O'Roarke."

"You didn't make Mélanie and Raoul safe."

"No, Fanny did, quite brilliantly. But I can learn from her example."

Julien cast a glance round the room and thought of his uncle's house. "We don't need—I have no particular desire to live in Carfax House."

"Let Kitty redo it the way Mélanie redid the Berkeley Square house. It's yours. Make it your own. We'll be quite comfortable back at the Grange. In many ways, we had the happiest years of our marriage there. I doubt this will be quite the same, but it won't be due to where we're living."

Julien pushed himself away from the table, then hesitated. "I'm not proud of all the things I've done, but I'm not sorry, on the whole, that I had the chance to disappear. I wouldn't have the life I have now without it."

"My dear Julien. I didn't send you off for your own benefit."

"I know. You did it for your own. Or Britain's. I think you have a damnable time telling the two—or your own version of the two—apart. I expect you thought I'd most likely get myself killed, and then you'd be Carfax anyway and the title would be David's safely. Still, I've learned one can find oneself lying awake at night second-guessing all sorts of past actions. Should you ever find yourself doing that over our shared past, at least know I'm very grateful I didn't remain in the beau monde all these years. I imagine I'd be insufferable now, if I had."

"Who says you aren't insufferable?" Carfax returned. But he smiled as he said it. "Give my felicitations to your bride."

A few hours ago, even at the start of this interview, Julien would have shied away from doing anything of the sort. But now he nodded. "I will. But you'd much better come back upstairs and do so yourself. And you haven't been properly introduced to our children."

Carfax got to his feet, a little stiffly.

Julien waited for him and then opened the door. But before they left the room, he said, "Uncle Hubert? Thank you."

After a surprisingly long interval talking with the children, Carfax got to his feet and walked over to Malcolm, who was opening a bottle of champagne by the drinks trolley. "I was wondering how long it would take you to work it out," he told Malcolm.

"Your nephew said much the same thing."

"I imagine that isn't all he said."

Malcolm wrapped a towel over the champagne cork. He wasn't about to be drawn into confidences about Arthur

Mallinson with his uncle. "You almost destroyed David's life in your quest for an heir and the earldom wasn't even yours to begin with."

"I would think this would make you understand my concern for a stable line of succession."

Malcolm thought back to the moments he'd seen Carfax confront Julien in Hyde Park a year and a half ago. That was just before Carfax had used Mel's past to try to drive a wedge between David and Simon. Not that whatever had motivated him excused anything. "How could it be stable? It wasn't even yours."

"My dear Malcolm. As I've freely admitted to you, it isn't bloodlines themselves that matter, it's the appearance of continuity they provide."

"And that excuses what you've done?"

"I've improvised. You've improvised yourself on more than one occasion. Quite brilliantly."

Malcolm twisted the champagne cork under the towel. "Forget bloodlines. Forget inherited privilege. You've spent years worrying about an heir. And you're quite ignoring the fact that you have a remarkably capable candidate right in front of you. Who also has the advantage of being the actual possessor of the title."

Carfax twisted his signet ring round his finger. "It didn't seem that way twenty-five years ago."

"No, I can imagine a lot of things seemed different twenty-five years ago."

"Among other things my brother was determined to throw Arthur to the wolves. Which would have been a sad waste."

"And was a good excuse to keep quiet about the fact that he was alive." The champagne cork popped free. Malcolm refilled Carfax's glass. "Of course if he'd have got himself killed you'd have been earl anyway. Which I imagine seemed likely."

"Julien was too useful for me to want him to get himself

killed. Though I admit at that point the thought of him as Carfax filled me with horror."

"And now?"

Carfax took a sip of champagne. "You make some good points."

"He's very like you. Only I think he has rather more scruples."

"Oh, undoubtedly."

Malcolm refilled his own glass. "He he isn't your heir, of course. You're his."

"Quite." As often with difficult issues, Carfax made no attempt to deny it. "Until he has a son of his own."

Malcolm's gaze jerked to the Ashford children. Julien was on the carpet helping Timothy guide Colin's toy carriage. Leo had Genny in his lap. Kitty was bent over both of them, laughing. "Kitty's a very good mother. She's very protective of her children. And she's decided Julien's good for them."

"And you think he's good for them."

"He is. It's a talent I wouldn't have thought he had. Or perhaps I should have done, seeing him with Gelly."

Carfax's brows drew together

"Gelly knows," Malcolm said. "Apparently she's known Julien is Arthur Mallinson for some time. Since long before she learned you were her father." He watched Carfax for a moment. Even behind the spectacle lens, he could see Carfax's struggling to digest the information. "And yes, that does mean Julien places a rather extraordinary amount of trust in Gisèle. Even more than I realized. It also means you really can't keep this contained."

"That's been apparent for the some time." Carfax pushed his spectacles up on his nose. "I have many faults, Malcom, but never let it be said I don't know how to adapt."

"David will be happier," Malcolm said. "He'd have made a good earl. But it's never really been what he wanted."

Carfax grunted. "I don't know that it was ever what Julien wanted either."

"Julien knows how to wear power. He won't let it own him. Though I think he'll be conscientious."

"Yes, so do I," Carfax said. "He's shown of late that he takes his responsibilities seriously. We saw that with Gerald Lumley."

Leave it to Carfax to bring up the example of Julien's protecting someone he himself had been trying to have killed. Malcolm lifted his champagne glass Carfax's own. "Thank you, sir."

"For what?"

Malcolm clinked his glass to Carfax's. "For being flexible when you most needed to be."

CHAPTER 39

Kitty closed the door of the boys' room and looked at Julien. Her husband. Was she ever going to get used to that? And why did the words squeeze her chest and bring a betraying prickle to her eyes?

Julien was looking down at Genny, asleep in her cradle. As though aware of her regard, he looked up and gave a crooked smile.

Oddly, Kitty found herself unsure what to say. Almost as though they were a typical couple on their wedding night and not two people so intimately acquainted in so many ways. "Carfax sounded surprisingly genuine in his congratulations."

"Yes." Julien coughed. "It seems his negativity about our relationship was an attempt to get us to do the opposite."

Kitty stared at him for a moment, then burst into laughter.

"Yes, I know," Julien said. "I should have seen it. I might have done, if I hadn't been so bloody terrified of what he might do to separate us." His gaze settled on her face for a long moment. "I was watching David with Tanner tonight when we went to see Tanner in Newgate. The sheer terror of losing the person he loves. And I realized that while tonight was much worse, he's lived with that terror for every moment they've been together. The fear that someone—that his father—would try to pull them apart. The fear that they could be hanged if there were public proof of their relationship. And yet he let himself love Simon." Julien smoothed Genny's blankets. "He let himself make a family with Simon. He was ready to give up everything he knew and the country he loved —and he loves Britain in a way I've never been able to comprehend—to preserve that family. He's a much braver man than I am."

"It's always a risk in caring for someone," Kitty said. "Knowing one could lose them. It can play merry hell with one's nerves." Several moments danced in her memory. The day Julien had left Buenos Aires. The night he'd been shot in the alley behind the Tavistock, only a month since. Dozens of moments when she'd wondered if he'd leave. "But there are compensations."

Julien crossed to her side and took her in his arms. "I'm sorry. This isn't the wedding night I wanted to give you."

Kitty choked. "Julien, darling. Aside from the fact that that's the fault of Lady Shroppington, and that it was all resolved more quickly than we could hope, it's not as though we're stepping tentatively into matrimony. This is no different from last night. Well, aside from the fact that my wound is a bit more healed. I'm very happy to be married to you, but there's no need to dress it up in romance."

"That's my Kitkat. I'd never dare dress anything up in romance with you. And you're right, it doesn't change what we are to each other. But—" Julien hesitated, gaze shifting over her face. "I was so focused on getting through today without any disruption. I didn't quite realize—" He drew a breath that had the scrape of thoughts that cannot quite be put into words. "Today meant a great deal to me."

Kitty put a hand up to touch his face. "All right. I'll confess it did to me as well. And to own the truth, I didn't think marriage meant anything to me."

He put his hand over her own. "I haven't had a home since I was sixteen. I'm not sure I properly had one then. But I have no doubt I have one now."

She swallowed. For a moment, she wasn't sure she could speak. "That's rather remarkable, Julien."

"Not so remarkable as your saying you trust me."

"For heaven's sake, sweetheart. I leave my children with you. What greater sign of trust is there?"

His gaze stilled on her face.

She remembered the first time she'd left the children with him. An urgent message from a Spanish contact on her maid Dolores's day off. Julien's easy offer to stay. And she hadn't even thought twice about it. "You've never failed us, Julien."

"Kitkat—"

"I know. We can never tell what will happen. But I don't think you ever will, if it's in your power to do otherwise."

"Trust is a rather amazing gift."

"You gave it first. You told me who you are."

His gaze scoured her face. "I never consciously decided to, you know. It just seemed obvious to me that you needed to know."

"Well, then."

"I love you, Kitkat. I think I've said those words more in the last four-and-twenty hours than I have in my entire life."

She reached up to kiss him. "I love you ridiculously, Julien. I'm not sure what's come over me, but I don't even feel foolish saying it. Well, not very."

He settled into the kiss and held her to him. "I expect we'll go back to something like normal. I can't imagine either of us continuing long in this sea of sensibility. But I'm never quite going to be the person I was before I met you."

"I think you were becoming the person you are now long

before you I met, my darling. But I'm glad I was there at the right time."

He caught her hand and kissed it. "My loving you has nothing to do with timing and everything to do with who you are, sweetheart. Though it's probably just as well I didn't meet you at the age of twenty. I'd have been sure to make a mull of it."

"And I'd only have been fourteen."

"Mmm." He rested his cheek against her hair. "There is that. All things considered, it's a good thing I went abroad."

"Julien." She put her hand up and turned his face back towards her own. "You were forced abroad. You were little more than a child."

"I'd done some very adult things." He frowned. "I seem to have discovered at some point in the last year that I have a conscience. Or perhaps I grew one."

"Stop being provoking. You've always had quite a fine-tuned conscience."

He laughed. "Like the pianoforte at Carfax Court that's been ignored since my mother died. A good instrument, but sadly out of use."

She put her hands on his chest. "Will you stop and let me finish, you provoking man? I'm trying to be serious for once, and tell you what you mean to me, which is difficult enough for me without your complicating it. I may never manage to say this again. I think about my own boys, and I can't forgive Carfax, and especially your father, for what you went through. But I'm inestimably grateful things worked out so that we met."

He turned her hand over in his and kissed her palm. "As am I. And my darling girl, what I'd gone through at sixteen is nothing compared to what you'd gone through."

She shrugged. "Folly to compare wounds. We've both been cut rather deeply. No sense in feeling sorry for ourselves. But if ever we're going to do so, this does seem a night to give way to sentiment. Kiss me again, Julien. It's still our wedding night, and I don't think it's been ruined in the least."

MALCOLM STRIPPED OFF HIS CRAVAT. "Julien and Kitty are married. Simon and David seem more secure than they have in a decade. The papers are published. Carfax came into our house without my throttling him. And soon he won't be Carfax anymore. Not a bad day."

Mélanie unfastened her second earring. "We still don't know who killed Thornsby."

"No." Malcolm tossed the cravat onto the green velvet chair. "But we know the assassination plot isn't a real threat. There's nothing to hang over your opening."

Mélanie watched her husband in the light of the Argand lamp. It picked out strands of bronze in his hair, warmed his skin, shot through the fabric of his shirt. "You can't think that matters beside the investigation."

Malcolm crossed to her side and cupped a hand round her cheek. "I think the opening is in two days now, and it's your priority, as it should be. We have time to investigate what happened to Thornsby. We don't face an immediate threat."

Mélanie scanned his face. "You're saying that because you don't want to disrupt the play."

"I'm saying that because the play is important. And I'd never forgive myself if this interfered with it."

"You're going to go on with the investigation, and you want me to focus on the play."

"I'm going to poke a bit round the edges. If I discover anything significant, I'll tell you. But there's no urgency, as I said."

"The League—"

"The League have always been a threat, and still are. The

information about Lady Shroppington is interesting. But it doesn't change anything immediately. If I had a bill up for vote you'd tell me to get through that while you looked into things. This is no different."

She held his gaze. "Darling—"

He put his hands on her shoulders. "We're partners, sweetheart. Nothing's changed."

She pulled him close and held him to her. Because she couldn't bear it if it had.

CHAPTER 40

Malcolm found Beverston in Hyde Park again. The morning after Julien and Kitty's wedding and Simon's arrest dawned fine, but with a sharp chill that made Malcolm grateful for his greatcoat and the thick scarf Addison had tossed to him on his way from the house.

"Rannoch." Beverston reined in to allow Malcolm to pull up beside him. "Two days in a row. I take it you have fresh news?" His gaze flickered over Malcolm's face with a trace of concern. "Is Benedict all right?"

"Ben's fine and proving quite insightful. Though he's a bit shocked, as we all are, to have learned your godmother is working with the Elsinore League."

Beverston's hands jerked on the reins.

"I must say I'm impressed," Malcolm said. "With all we thought we knew about the League, we had no notion women were involved."

'They aren't, in general," Beverston said.

"So Lady Shroppington was an exception? Was she Alistair's mistress?"

"Was she his what? No."

"I'm particularly intrigued that you fell out with her. I assume you had your reasons, because she doesn't strike me as an easy enemy to make. Just as I assume she had her reasons for casting her lot with Alexander Radford, rather than you."

Beverston put up a hand to tug the brim of his hat lower on his head. "You don't know what you're dealing with, Rannoch."

"I know that Alexander Radford and Lady Shroppington's faction are, or at least were, trying to kill the woman your son loves, because she could identify Radford."

"Which should tell you how dangerous the situation is. And also, possibly, why I put myself on the other side."

"Because you were so horrified they were trying to kill Nerezza?"

"Among other things."

"Did you try to persuade Lewis to turn on them?"

Beverston's mouth hardened. "Lewis was very set on the course he'd taken. After one or two attempts, I knew there was no dissuading him. Until—"

"What?" Malcolm said, as Beverston stared at the leafless tangle of branches ahead.

"I don't know that this will help you, Rannoch, but I suppose there's no harm in telling you. I saw Lewis in White's the day before he was killed. He interrupted me in the midst of a rather good beefsteak and a particularly fine claret. He wanted to know about Horace Smytheton's role in the League."

"Smytheton?" Sometimes Malcolm almost forgot that the Tavistock's patron had ever been a League member.

"Yes, that was rather my reaction," Beverston said. "I told him Smytheton had worked with Alistair and Dewhurst in France but that he hadn't had much to do with the League in years. And he'd never really been a significant member. That's hardly a secret."

"Did Thornsby say why he was asking about Horace?"

"No. And I didn't think much of it, because it was hard for

me to imagine anything to do with Horace Smytheton being of much interest. But as he turned to go, he looked back at me and said he was changing his mind about what was important. At the time, I thought he was talking about that actress he was besotted with. But now I think it may have been something else entirely."

~

"LEWIS THORNSBY?" Sir Horace Smytheton regarded Mélanie over the tea table in the green room. "I'm sorry the young man is dead, but I can't say I ever spoke more than a half-dozen words to him. Agreeable enough chap, but very little actual knowledge of the theatre, you know. The one time I tried to talk to him, he kept muddling Ophelia and Cordelia."

Mélanie added milk to her tea. They were in a break in the dress rehearsal. "He asked Lord Beverston about you the day before he was killed."

Sir Horace's brows drew together. "That's right, forgot Beverston was a friend of the Thornsby family. We're actually distantly connected, you know—Beverston and I, that is. Smythe and Smytheton. Both branches of the same family, if one goes back to the Civil War. But even when I was involved with the—er—League"—he cast a quick glance round the green room, where various of the company were relaxing with tea and studying scripts—"I didn't have much to do with Beverston."

Mélanie took a drink of tea. She was going on five hours sleep, with little more than twenty-four hours until the opening. "Did Thornsby ask you any questions?"

Horace added some sugar to his own tea. "One of the few times we talked, he asked me how it had worked when I'd married Jenny. What my family had thought. I told him all the family I cared about had come round, and I was happier in the theatre than in society. Said I'd never regretted following my heart. That my only regret was keeping the marriage secret for so many years. Not hard to tell the boy was asking about it because of Letty Blanchard. Of course, I had the benefit of a comfortable fortune, which Thornsby didn't. Don't think I steered him wrong, do you?"

"I think Lewis Thornsby was very set on what he wanted, when it came to Letty Blanchard." In fact, it seemed the one clear thing about Thornsby. "And I don't see how it could be wrong to tell the truth about how happy you are with Jennifer."

"Perhaps Thornsby was asking Beverston what he knew about my marriage to Jennifer."

"I don't think so. Beverston told Malcolm that Thornsby very clearly asked about your role in the League."

Sir Horace clunked down the sugar bowl. "Thornsby was involved with the League?"

"Apparently."

"He must have been following up on old gossip, then. I haven't had anything to do with the League in years." He patted Mélanie's arm. "It's a tragedy, my dear. But you can't let it dim the opening. You've written a splendid play. You need to focus on that." He put some almond cakes on a plate. "Promised these to the girls. Can't keep them waiting."

Mélanie watched Sir Horace cross the room and settle himself on the sofa, where his ten-year-old daughter was entertaining her baby sister. Mélanie had always liked him. And she certainly believed he'd left the League behind. And yet—

"What is it?" Simon came over to the tea table, a pencil stuck behind his ear, blue shadows of fatigue pulling at his face, eyes alight with intensity.

Mélanie took another drink of tea. "Did you ever see Thornsby talking to Horace?"

"Sir Horace? Not that I can recall. You know what little use Smytheton has for anyone who can't dissect the finer points of Shakespeare. Why?"

"Thornsby asked Beverston about Horace the day before he was killed. Horace can't imagine why. According to Malcolm, Beverston couldn't either. Something doesn't quite add up."

Simon glanced at Sir Horace and his daughters. Jennifer had joined them, and seemed to be remonstrating with Horace not to give the baby so many bites of almond cake, though she was smiling as she said it. "Whatever his past, Smytheton isn't a man who seems to have secrets these days. Though I suppose we've learned not to say that about anyone."

"No." Mélanie swallowed the last of her tea. "Sir Horace told me to focus on the play. And he was right in that."

"We're as ready as we're ever going to be." Simon poured himself a cup of tea and took a grateful swallow. "Or at least, more ready than I've felt before a score of openings. With just enough still to work on for no one to get too complacent."

Mélanie smiled at him. "That's because you didn't write this one."

"Yes, which allows me to be confident in just how splendid it is. And ticket sales are excellent."

"Thanks to the gossip." Horrible to think they were benefiting from Lewis Thornsby's murder.

"Partly thanks to the gossip. Partly thanks to your being a leading light of the beau monde. The point is, whyever they bought tickets, we'll have a full house to appreciate a brilliant play." He scanned her face. "It's quite normal to be nervous. I'm nervous before every opening."

"Yes, I'd have been nervous, no matter what. But you have to admit these past few days have been particularly fraught."

"A massive understatement, my sweet." He took another swallow of tea. "At least Carfax is less of a threat. Less than he's been in all the time David and I have been together."

"That's a lot to be thankful for. It's just that—"

She broke off as Letty Blanchard slipped into the green room, cast a quick glance about, and then walked straight over to them. "I'm sorry." She looked between Mélanie and Simon. "I thought I could keep quiet about this. I thought that was the best thing to do. But I'm sick to my stomach, and I don't think I can go on tomorrow if I don't tell you."

Simon set down his tea cup. "Then we'd best find somewhere quiet to talk." He put a hand on Letty's arm and led the way to a rehearsal room close to the green room.

Letty drew a breath as Simon closed the door. She didn't sit in any of the straight-backed chairs scattered round the room, but stood twisting her hands together. For all her rouged cheeks and blackened lashes and fashionably cropped hair, Mélanie was reminded of nothing so much as her children when they were owning up to something.

"Lewis told me he knew who the mole in the Levellers was. When he proposed to me. The night he was killed. I'm not sure why he said it. He seemed to realize he shouldn't have, the moment he did. I think perhaps he wanted to impress me. To get me to take him seriously. But I think he was going to meet the mole that night. I think that's why he went back to the Tavistock."

"Why didn't you say so sooner?" Mélanie asked.

"I couldn't. I—"

"Letty—" Will opened the door and froze on the threshold, still in his shirtsleeves from rehearsal. "Oh, sorry. I wanted to talk to Letty about our last scene."

Letty turned to him, her gaze stricken. "Oh, God, Will, I'm sorry."

"Why? It's going quite well. I just thought—"

"Not the scene. I told them. That Lewis told me he knew who the mole was."

"Good God. But what's that to do with me?" Will asked.

Letty stared at him, while Mélanie and Simon both went still. "Because I thought—"

"You thought I was the mole?" Will stepped into the rehearsal room and slammed the door shut behind him. "You thought I'd do that to my friends? To all the things I believe in?" He turned away. "My God, Letty, what a bastard you must think me."

"No! I just—I'd never have suspected you on my own. But Lewis said he'd started to suspect in Lancaster. That the attack wasn't what it seemed, and that if I knew what had really happened, I'd feel very differently about those I cared about. I couldn't make sense of it, but you were attacked in Lancaster and you're someone I— " She bit back the words and looked away. "I had a horrible feeling it meant you were behind it." She forced her gaze back to his face. "I knew if that was true, you'd have reasons. Even then, I wasn't sure. But I couldn't take the chance and betray you—"

Will stared at her, his face a taut study in conflict. Mélanie cast a quick glance at Simon but knew better than to speak. If they weren't in the middle of an investigation, they'd have both slipped from the room.

"You thought I'd have sold secrets," Will said. "Hurt my friends. Your friends. Why on earth would you want to protect me?"

"Will, you provoking idiot." Letty crossed to him with a swish of her sarcenet skirts and seized the front of his waistcoat. "Don't you realize that my instinct was to protect you, no matter what? Don't you realize what you mean to me?"

Will stared down at her, face still as ice over a roiling river. "You made what I mean to you perfectly clear when you set your cap at Lewis Thornsby."

"Will." Letty's gaze clung to his face. "You know I wasn't—"

"You weren't in love with Thornsby? No, I didn't think you were. But you can't deny you were ready to marry him."

"I didn't accept his proposal."

Will drew a rough breath. Her face was inches from his own and it was clear how much that cost him. "You didn't turn him down either, did you?"

"No, not right away. I wasn't sure—"

"He could keep his fortune?"

Letty didn't flinch. "I deserved that. And no, I wasn't. But I also wasn't sure I was ready to give up the theatre." She drew a breath, gaze still trained on his face. "And even more, I wasn't sure I was ready to give up you."

Will's hands came up to grip her arms. For a moment, he seemed one thought away from pulling her to him. Instead he said, "You already gave me up."

"But I'd have lost the chance of getting you back."

"You could have married Thornsby and taken a lover."

"You're assuming I'd have done that to Lewis. I'm not quite so cold as you think me. And even if I'd been willing to play Lewis false, I know you. You wouldn't have lived a lie."

Words Mélanie had heard David use about Simon. She didn't risk a glance at Simon, but she knew instinctively he recognized it too.

"No," Will said. "I wouldn't. No matter how much I wanted it."

It was Letty's turn to go still, as his words sank in. "You—"

"I confronted Thornsby the day before he was killed. Because I was worried he was leading you on. At least, that was my excuse. The truth is I was more than half driven by jealousy. The truth is I couldn't get you out of my thoughts, Letty. Even if you thought I was worth less than a handsome fortune. Even if, apparently, you thought I was a conscienceless traitor who would turn on his own friends."

"I never said—"

"You thought I'd be capable of the action. I don't see how such a betrayal could be justified. If I had done it. Which I didn't." He looked at Mélanie and Simon. "I have no way to prove I'm not the mole, but I hope to God at least you believe me, because they have to go on searching for the actual mole."

Letty let out a breath like one who'd been pulled from

drowning. "Thank God. I've been so terrified ever since Lewis told me."

"So, you do believe me?"

She nodded. "I look at you and I'm certain. And you're never going to forgive me now for doubting you, are you?"

"I don't think what's between us is what's crucial, at the moment." Will gripped her hands where they clung to his waistcoat then detached himself and turned to Mélanie and Simon. "Do you think the mole killed Thornsby?"

"It's certainly something we have to consider," Mélanie said. She hesitated, because Will didn't yet know the mole was his cousin.

"But—" Letty was hugging her arms round herself, digging her fingers into the folds of her shawl, as though Will's moving away had left her physically bereft. "Why did Lewis say I'd feel differently about those I cared about when I knew the truth? Was he trying to mislead me and make me think it was Will?"

"It's possible he was," Mélanie said. "I suspect he sensed what Will meant to you and was jealous."

"But when the truth came out, I'd have known. Of course, just about everyone in the Tavistock company is a friend. But I'm not sure I'd call them the people I'm closest to. Although—" She met Will's gaze for a moment in a look that had nothing to do with the romantic tangle between them.

"We share everything," Will said. "We create characters and worlds together. We speak our own language. What else is a company of players?"

Letty nodded. "Yes, precisely. Perhaps that's what Lewis meant. Perhaps he was even jealous—not of an individual person, but of what I share with the company."

"That's very insightful," Mélanie said. "I suspect he may well have been. But as it happens, we know who the mole is. And it isn't Will or any member of the Tavistock company."

Letty looked at her, at once hopeful and wary. Will raised a brow. "Who?"

Suddenly Will was the one Mélanie longed to comfort. "It was Donald."

While Will went white, she told him quickly what Carfax had told her.

Will scraped a hand over his hair. "Christ. I should have known his coming to see me in London was suspect."

"You couldn't possibly have done."

"After a childhood in which we were strikingly lacking in sympathy, I'm a fool that I didn't. I suppose that's why he hasn't been about the theatre the last day or so. I can't believe I didn't see it, never suspected—"

Letty reached for his hand. "Perhaps you wanted a reminder of your home. You couldn't talk to any of us about it."

Will looked at her. "You aren't surprised?"

"About who you are? I mean, I knew you had a family somewhere, and I've wondered, but with everything else going on, that scarcely seems the thing to focus on."

Will gave a faint smile. "Quite right." He squeezed her hand and looked back at Mélanie and Simon. "Why was Thornsby planning to confront Donald? Why not simply tell Simon? Or Kit or Roger?"

"Probably because Thornsby had his own loyalties outside the Levellers," Malcolm said. "He appears to have been working for a group called the Elsinore League. Who were also opposed to the Levellers' activities."

"So Lewis was a mole?" Letty said.

"We don't know quite what he was reporting, but yes, he seems to have been," Mélanie said.

"Oh, my God," Letty said. "All my suspicions of Will, and Lewis was doing the exact same thing. I should be shocked and sickened and say I can't believe it of him. But—I liked Lewis. I wasn't in love with him, but I truly did like him. But the thing is,

I *can* believe it of him. Because he didn't believe in what he was doing, the way Will did. The way you do," she added, looking at Simon. "And Kit and Roger and even Brandon. Lewis was playing at it. I'm an actor. I can tell acting. Especially acting that doesn't have conviction behind it."

"You're an astute woman, Letty," Simon said.

"Did Thornsby know Donald was my cousin?" Will asked.

"I don't know," Mélanie said, "but perhaps that's what he meant when he told Letty it would impact those she cared about."

"There's more," Letty said. "Lewis told me he'd uncovered something dangerous. That he couldn't be sure what would happen, but that he wanted me to believe he was trying to do the right thing. He said that, when he proposed. Do you know what he meant?"

Mélanie cast a quick look at Simon. "No. It's possible he was trying to say he was doing the right thing in betraying the Levellers. But it's also possible he was betraying the people he was working for."

Letty shook her head. "I didn't know him at all. I suppose that makes it all the worse that I actually contemplated marrying him."

"Choices in life are complicated," Will said. "One makes them for different reasons. I shouldn't have blamed you for what you wanted. You shouldn't blame yourself."

Letty met his gaze. "The problem was I didn't know what I wanted. And now, of course, I can never be sure if I'd have gone through with it."

"We can never know what any of us might have done in different circumstances," Will said. "It's not a play where we can write alternate endings."

"No," Letty said. "We're just left to wonder."

Will touched her cheek. "No sense in dwelling on what

didn't happen. We have enough to do to take care of the future. We have a villain to catch. And a show to open."

"MALCOLM." Amelia Carfax spoke from the stairs as the footman admitted Malcolm to Carfax House. She was midway down the stairs, gowned in bronze-green silk, her hair immaculately curled. She had been greeting ball guests at the head of those stairs for over twenty years. "It's too long since we've seen you. And Mélanie. I imagine she's busy with her play."

"She's at the theatre now." Malcolm gave his hat and gloves to the footman.

"We're looking forward to the opening." Lady Carfax descended the stairs. "I understand Mr. St. Juste married Mrs. Ashford at your house last night."

Macolm met the gaze of his childhood friend's mother. "Yes. We're very happy for them."

"David told me." Lady Carfax smoothed a crease from her full sleeve. "He said he was happy for them as well. He said he was happy about a number of things. I am endeavoring to emulate him."

Malcolm met her gaze. Even when he'd been a child, she hadn't been the sort to invite hugs, but he had a sudden impulse to give her one. "This must have been a great shock."

"In some ways. In others, I've been preparing for it for a long time." Lady Carfax smiled and touched his arm. "You can't get in the middle of this, Malcolm. The Mallinson family will have to sort it out." She stepped back and glanced down the hall. "You'll find Hubert in his study. I think he's expecting you."

On his way to the study, Malcolm paused to glance at the painting of Arthur and Pamela. Arthur had been about the same age Leo was now. It would be good for Julien and Kitty to be in this house with the children. It should be theirs. But it was very odd to imagine Carfax House without the present Lord and Lady Carfax.

"Glad you're here, Malcolm." Carfax looked up from his desk and for once actually pushed his papers aside and gestured Malcolm to a chair. "I've seen Donald McDevitt," he said, when Malciolm was seated. "When I confronted him with Miss Blanchard's story, he admitted he met Thornsby at the Tavistock the evening Thornsby was killed. He says Thornsby claimed to know he—McDevitt—was a mole working for me and that he'd been setting up agent provocateur operations. McDevitt says he denied it and stalked out of the theatre. He said he didn't tell me because he didn't want to admit he'd been found out. Also I suspect because he didn't want to put himself at the scene of the murder. He claims Thornsby was alive when he left. That he had the sense Thorsnby was waiting to see someone else."

"Do you believe him?"

Carfax twirled his pen between his fingers. "He certainly has a motive. But I'm inclined to think he's telling the truth. For one thing, according to Julien, Thornsby's murder looks like the work of a professional. Which McDevitt isn't."

Malcolm nodded. "So we're still looking for Thornsby's killer."

"Most likely. I can't be sure about McDevitt, of course. I'm having him watched, and we may learn more. But I doubt he'll go back to the theatre."

"Do you know anything that would make Horace Smytheton of interest recently?"

"Smytheton?" Carfax's brows rose. "The last time I was him was in the grand salon at the Tavistock during the interval for *Twelfth Night*, telling Tanner how he'd have staged the production. I must say Simon was very patient. What's Smytheton got to do with this?"

"The day before Thornsby was killed, he asked Beverston about Smytheton's role in the League."

Carfax set his pen on the blotter. "Smytheton was quite a capable agent in France, for all bumbling façade. I watched him and Jennifer Mansfield for quite a while after they settled in Britain. But there's nothing I know of that he's been involved in lately."

"That you know of," Malcolm said.

"Quite," Carfax said.

CHAPTER 41

"Lewis Thornsby seems to have changed in the last days of his life." Malcolm adjusted the last fold in his cravat and glanced in the looking glass on the chest of drawers beside his shaving kit. After all, tonight was the opening of his wife's play. His appearance warranted a bit more care than usual.

"Yes." Mélanie was at her dressing table, fastening her earrings. "He told Beverston he was changing his mind about what was important. He told Letty he wanted her to think well of him. And Donald McDevitt said Lewis told him he'd finally made up his mind about what he had to do. Oddly, for all Donald's lies, I'm inclined to think that was the truth."

"So am I." Malcolm reached for his black cassimere coat and pulled it on. "I thought at first it was that Lewis had decided to propose to Letty. Now I'm wondering if there was more to it. If he was turning on the League."

Mélanie fastened her second earring. "If that was the case, something must have changed in the past few days. Or he learned something new. But what?"

"What indeed?" Malcolm said. "He knew about the papers. He was obviously more than willing to go along with that."

"Perhaps he drew the line when they decided to have Kitty killed. No, that doesn't work. Kitty's meeting with Simon and Kit and Hapgood wasn't set up until after Lewis was murdered, so they couldn't have set the attack in motion before."

Mélanie turned from her dressing table. She was wearing a new gown of rose-violet silk with lavender lace overlaid on the bodice. Her hair was pinned back and threaded with a slender pearl bandeau, but loose curls still tumbled down her neck.

"You look beautiful," he said.

Mélanie smiled. "I'll admit I'm not averse to flattery. I need all the confidence I can muster tonight. But how I look is hardly the chief concern."

Malcolm turned to the dressing table and picked up a black velvet jewel box he'd fetched from Asprey's that morning. "Something to commemorate the occasion," he said, holding it out to her.

He watched closely as she opened the box, wondering if he'd chosen right. He usually chose delicate jewelry, and not always the most expensive stones. But this wasn't a jewel at all, but a simple circular gold medallion inscribed with *F & G,* the initials of her two main characters.

A smile broke across Mélanie's face. "It's perfect."

He crossed to her side and kissed her. "Happy opening, sweetheart."

"I'M glad you could be here, Jeremy."

Roth grinned. He was in unaccustomedly formal attire, a dark evening coat and trousers, and a gray silk waistcoat. "I wouldn't want to miss it."

Malcolm cast a gaze round the passage behind the boxes at the Tavistock. It seemed as though everyone he'd known in his life in the beau monde and the diplomatic corps was in the theatre now. "There's no reason to expect anything to go wrong. The assassination plot was a fabrication never meant to become reality. Thornsby's murder doesn't seem to have had anything to do with the play."

Roth put up a hand to his neckcloth, tied tighter than the loose style he usually affected. "But you're worried."

"Difficult not to be."

"For what it's worth," Roth said, "I'll own to being a bit so myself. And also to realizing there's no reason we should be. Let's try to enjoy the evening for Mélanie. And then tomorrow we can return to the puzzle of Thornsby's death."

Malcolm smiled and went into their box, while Roth went off to join his sister and his sons. Laura, Raoul, Kitty, and Julien were already in the Rannoch box with the children. Harry and Cordy and Frances and Archie and their children were to the right, and Rupert and Bertrand to the left with Rupert's wife, Gabrielle, and her lover, Nick Gordon, and Gaby and Rupert's son, Stephen, who had just come up to London from their country house, as well as Blanca and Addison. Nerezza and Ben had remained in Berkeley Square, as they still couldn't be sure how safe Nerezza was in public. Aline and Geoffrey were supposed to be in the Davenports' box, but hadn't yet arrived. Paul and Juliette and their children were sitting with Manon's husband, Crispin. Malcolm saw Kit with his mother and his younger sister, Selena, further along the line of boxes with Roger and his wife, Dorinda, though Sofia wasn't with them. And Carfax and Lady Carfax with two of their daughters and sons-in-law, Mary and Gui, and Isobel and Oliver. David was in the next box with the children and his youngest sister, Lucinda. Amy and Teddy were waving at Colin and Emily, while David tried to subdue Jamie. Malcolm waved to his friend and wondered if Lady Carfax's gaze had drifted to Julien and Kitty and, if so, what she thought.

Malcolm waved to his young friends, Sandy Trenor and Bet Simcox, then glanced across the theatre and caught sight of Lady Shroppington. Not surprising, perhaps. Everyone who wielded any sort of influence in Mayfair seemed to be there. There was a ripple through the crowd as the prince regent took his place in the royal box with a large party. Including Sir Horace Smytheton, Malcolm noted. Perhaps not surprising. Sir Horace had been a crony of the prince in his younger days, and he was the Tavistock's patron.

"I understand he made a considerable effort to get Prinny here," Frances said, leaning over the rail from her own box. "Horace is very excited about Mélanie's play."

"Sir Horace has always been a good judge of literature," Malcolm said with a grin. "I wonder—"

He broke off as the curtains at the back of the box stirred and Aline's husband, Geoffrey, stepped into the box. Claudia was tugging at his hand, but there was no sign of Aline.

"Allie sends her apologies," Geoffrey said, as Claudia ran to sit by Chloe at the rail. "She and Sofia were making crucial progress on the coded papers and didn't want to leave it. She insisted we come. In truth, I think she wanted us out of the way so they could focus. Sofia sent me with a message for Kit."

Mélanie slipped into the Rannoch box just before the curtain. Her face was taut, but also alight with excitement. She pulled Jessica onto her lap. Jessica, who even at three found the theatre magical, went still as the play began, caught by its spell. As was Malcolm. For all the worries he had confided to Roth, he felt himself escape into the world his wife had created.

The intervals passed in a whirl of visits to the box, getting ices for the children, ordering and opening champagne. One could feel the excitement in the air. It was going splendidly, but he didn't dare say that to Mélanie. All he could do was smile and press her hand and press his champagne glass to hers.

They were partway through the third act when the curtains stirred at the back of the box. Malcolm looked over his shoulder to see Aline and Sofia. He pushed himself to his feet and went to meet them at the back of the box. "I was afraid you wouldn't make it."

Aline gripped his hand and nearly crushed his bones. As she turned her face into the light, he saw the tension in her gaze. Behind her Sofia was pale as bleached linen. "We decoded the papers," Aline said. "You should see them at once."

Malcolm followed them into the anteroom without a word.

Aline opened her reticule and pulled out three sheets of closely written paper. She held them out wordlessly.

I don't know where this will go. But I want to leave a record. I'm afraid that the League want to make use of the assassination plot that was only ever meant to be pretend. Not to assassinate the regent. To get rid of one of his party. Sir Horace Smytheton.

CHAPTER 42

Malcolm looked from Aline to Sofia. "Allie, get Harry and Archie and Rupert and Bertrand and Addison. Sofia, get Roth."

He looked back into the box and gestured to Mélanie. She came at once, as did Raoul and Laura and Kitty and Julien. Malcolm held out the paper. "We have to move the regent's party," he said. "As quickly as possible, without a full panic. Take Frances, Mel. The two of you should be able to do it."

Mélanie ran into the passage without further speech.

Malcolm looked at Julien. "Which box would they shoot from?"

Julien pulled back the curtain to the box, glanced round the theatre. "Third from the end would be best."

Malcolm studied the box. It was full, as were all the boxes. In fact, Emily Cowper and Lord Palmerston were in it with her brother, William Lamb, and his wife, Caroline.

"How they devil would they manage it?" Kitty asked, standing beside Julien and Malcolm. "I think everyone in the boxes with the right angle is someone Malcolm knows."

Malcolm was scanning the boxes with his opera glasses. "Yes.

Of course, I can't swear none of them is working for the League, but I can't see someone known to society taking this risk."

"No, it would take a marksman," Julien said. "They'll have hired a professional. My guess is the assassin has the rifle already hidden in the antechamber. He—or possibly she—will slip through the curtains while people are looking at the stage. Probably disguised as a footman. Take the shot, drop the rifle, run, shedding the footman's costume as he goes. At least, that's the way I'd do it."

"Right." Malcolm turned to the others. "So, while Mélanie's clearing out the royal box, we fan out in the passage behind every box that has a possible angle. Stop anyone we don't know from going in. And hope there aren't a lot of orders for champagne. Oh, Archie, good," he added as Archie and Harry came into the anteroom, closely followed by Rupert and Bertrand. "I need you to get the regent's carriage to meet him at the side entrance. Mélanie and Frances will bring him there."

"And the rifle?" Kitty asked.

Malcolm looked at Julien. "Your husband and I are going to find it."

"MRS. RANNOCH." The prince regent looked round as Mélanie and Frances came through the curtains into the royal box. The equerry in the antechamber had recognized Frances and let them past without questions. "It's a splendid play. Didn't expect to laugh so much."

"I'm flattered, sir." Mélanie curtsied and then dropped down beside the regent's chair, her skirts pooling round her. Her head was below the rail and the regent had to bend down to speak with her, which put him at a safer angle. "But I fear I need to ask you to leave. And everyone in your party." She glanced round the box.

"Good lord! But surely—"

"There's no time to waste, sir." Frances put a hand on his shoulder, an intimacy that seemed to break through to him.

The prince's attendants were already helping him to stand and moving towards the door.

"Surely I can stay," Sir Horace said.

"No." Mélanie caught his arm in a firm grip. "On no account, Sir Horace, I beg you."

He raised his brows but let her hustle him from the box.

"Damned shame," the regent said in the antechamber. "Wanted to see how the play ended."

"We'll bring the company to the palace and give you a special performance, if you like," Mélanie said.

"Would you really, my dear? That's splendid. Do hope Gideon and that charming Fiona can patch it up. I quite like them."

"There's a side way I can take you out of the theatre. Archie Davenport has arranged to have your carriage brought round. I promise we will explain more later, but now I beg you will go quickly. We can't afford to have a panic in the theatre. I know you may be relied upon to do what is best."

The prince nodded and patted her hand as though he had been entrusted with a commission of the greatest importance. "You may depend upon me, my dear."

MALCOLM AND JULIEN examined the damask-hung walls of the antechamber to the box occupied by Emily Cowper, Palmerston, and the Lambs. Malcolm could hear the clash of blades from the stage. They must be at the scene in which Brandon, as Gideon, fought with Will, who played the young man who ran off with Gideon's sister, played by Letty.

"That pedestal with the vase has been moved," Malcolm said. "You can see the indentations in the carpet."

They shifted the pedestal with the vase of roses to the side, and the bulge in the gold damask wall hanging behind was obvious. Julien tugged at the fabric, which had been loosely tacked. He reached beneath and pulled out a very serviceable looking rifle.

"Good thing the assassin thinks like you," Malcolm said.

While Julien disarmed the rifle, Malcolm went through the curtains into the box.

"Malcolm." Emily Cowper looked over her shoulder in surprise. "What on earth are you—"

Malcolm knelt down and looked among his friends. "Has anyone unexpected been in here? Anyone you don't know?"

"A score of people at the interval," Palmerston said, eyes narrowed, "but all friends, or at least acquaintances."

"Good. Have you ordered champagne?"

"No," Emily said. "We were debating it."

"Do me a favor and don't. I'll make sure you get plenty afterwards. And I'll explain then. I promise."

"Do you need help?" William asked.

"The best help you can all be is to stay here and act normal."

"Malcolm." Caroline caught at the sleeve of his coat as he got to his feet, eyes even wider than usual. "Should we be frightened?"

Malcolm smiled at the woman he'd known since childhood. Caro could be fanciful at the best of times. "No. Just watchful."

Brandon and Will were shaking hands on stage. Letty ran into Will's arms, her brother's opposition to their marriage ended. Brandon as Gideon turned to Manon as Fiona, who had gone with him to stop the elopement.

Malcolm went back out into the passage. Julien was lolling against the wall across from the box. Kitty was a little further down the passage to the left, pretending to be fixing her hair in a pier glass, though Malcolm knew she was watching every flicker of movement in the reflection. Raoul was to Julien's right, seemingly examining the program. Harry was sipping a glass of champagne still further to the right while Rupert and Bertrand and Roth and Addison were further to the left.

Malcolm exchanged a quick look with Julien and took up a position between him and Raoul.

Even with the excitement of a new play by one of Mayfair's most dashing political hostesses, the passage was far from empty while the performance went on. People passed by, bent on flirtation or in search of liquid refreshment, and in one or two cases, MPs or diplomats seeking a quiet place for a colloquy. Malcolm had done the same, at times, for all his love of theatre. Harry stopped one footman with a tray of champagne and carried the champagne into the designated box just to be safe.

They should be approaching the last scene of the play, if Malcolm's memory was right. And with any luck, by now Mélanie, Frances, and Archie had the regent and his party, including Sir Horace, safely away.

And then, suddenly, there he was. A footman in a blue-and-silver coat and a powdered wig like all the others, making for the door of Emily and Palmerston and the Lambs' box, a tray of champagne expertly balanced.

Kitty was suddenly in front of him. She snatched up the bottle and filled a glass with champagne. "Oh, how lovely, I'm so parched."

"Here now, those are spoken for." The footman tried to tug the tray away.

"I'm sure they won't mind." Kitty added more to her glass. The footman tugged again. The tray and bottle went flying, sending a fountain of champagne into the air and scattering a hail of broken crystal on the floor. Kitty tripped and fell into the footman, who tumbled to the floor. Probably because she'd kneed him in the groin when she bumped into him. Malcolm lurched across the passage and sprang on top of the footman, only to feel a sharp jab in his arm. The assassin had a knife.

Malcolm's recoil was enough for the assassin to push himself to his feet. Julien grabbed him. The assassin jabbed the knife into Julien's hand. Malcolm caught the assassin's leg before he could run. Julien had hold of the assassin's knife arm, and was struggling for control of the knife. Kitty brought the silver champagne tray down on the assassin's shoulder. Raoul ran up and dealt the assassin a blow to the jaw that sent him tumbling to the floor again.

By the time Harry, Bertrand, Rupert, and Roth ran up, they had him under control. Raoul was lashing the assassin's hands with his cravat when Palmerston and William Lamb came out of the box.

"Sorry," Palmerston said. "There was a limit to how long we could act normal—good God, do you need help?"

"All under control." Malcolm pushed himself to his feet, avoiding the litter of broken crystal.

"Your arm's bleeding," William said.

"A scratch. St. Juste has one too."

Palmerston surveyed the group. "Is this anything to do with those pamphlets about Carfax's secret meetings that have been the talk of Whitehall and Wesminster the past few days?"

"In a roundabout way. I promise I'll explain. As much as I can." Malcolm looked down at the bound assassin who remained completely silent. "Meanwhile, I hate to say this, but we need Carfax."

CHAPTER 43

"Oh, good," Cordelia murmured, leaning over the rail that separated her box from the Rannoch box, where Laura sat with the children. "They're all out of the royal box."

Laura watched as Mélanie, the last to leave, slipped from the box, her rose-violet skirts disappearing from view. Curious glances were directed to the royal box from those on either side, but in general, attention in the theatre still seemed to be on the stage. The duel was over and the younger lovers reunited, and Fiona and Gideon were finding their way back to each other. The performance was going splendidly, but it took all of Laura's willpower not to run after her husband and Cordelia's, and Malcolm and the others. If it weren't for the children—

"I know," Cordelia said. "It's beastly waiting."

Laura gripped her friend's hand on the rail between the boxes. "Beastly."

"If—"

Cordelia broke off as the curtains stirred at the back of the box. Edith Simmons ran in, in a plain gray gown, hair slipping from its pins about her face. "Mrs. O'Roarke. Cordy." She dropped into an empty chair behind Laura, next to the rail, where she could speak to both of them. "Lady Shroppington came to see me this afternoon."

"Does she know?" Laura asked. The guilt about the situation she might have put Edith in had hovered over her ever since their talk.

"She knows you both talked to me and that I spoke with you again, but she just thinks you were trying to get information. She actually said she was confident I wouldn't betray her trust, not only because of my brother but because I wouldn't be able to bear the thought of Thomas's knowing what I'd done." Edith locked her hands together. "Little does she know. Of course, I'm eaten away by what I've done to Thomas. But in the end, what does his thinking well of me matter if I don't think well of myself?"

Cordelia touched her arm. "I don't think Lady Shroppington is the sort to think to that way."

"No. Thank goodness. She wanted to see me about Thomas. She wants me to find out if Lewis left any papers for his brother."

"What sort of papers?" Laura asked.

"She didn't give details. She rarely does. She said if there were any papers, I had to retrieve them. She said she knew I could get Thomas to confide in me, because she knew how he felt about me and how I felt about him. But she also said that she knew I wasn't so foolish as to think our relationship could go anywhere, as Lewis had done with Miss Blanchard. She said she knew she could count on me to find the truth and retrieve any papers, because I'd want Thomas to be safe. I couldn't make sense of the whole thing. But there was something about her expression—I've never seen it so hard. It doesn't matter. I made up my mind to stop working for Lady Shroppington when I talked to you, but I thought I could get more information. I talked to Elsie. She's the Wiltons' under housemaid, and her cousin Molly works for Lady Shroppington, though I doubt Lady Shroppington even knows the connection. She doesn't miss a lot, but her concern doesn't tend to extend below stairs. It was Elsie's evening off tonight. She had a word with Molly. Elsie just came home and reported to me." Edith looked from Laura to Cordelia. "Lewis Thornsby called on his aunt the night before he was killed. They quarreled."

"We knew she didn't want him to marry Letty Blanchard," Cordelia said.

"Yes, but Molly heard him say, 'I can bring this whole thing down about your ears, and don't you forget it.'"

Laura had already scraped back her chair by the time Edith finished speaking.

"Go," Cordelia said. "Edith and I will watch the children."

Laura ran.

LAURA FOUND her husband tying a napkin round Malcolm's arm in the passage behind Emily Cowper's box. Kitty was performing a similar office for Julien. Two footmen who appeared to really be footmen were cleaning up a wreckage of broken glass on the damp carpet. The smell of spilled champagne filled the air.

"He had a knife," Malcolm said. "He managed to get both Julien and me."

"But he didn't get away." Kitty knotted off the handkerchief round Julien's hand.

"Where is he?" Laura asked.

"Roth's taken him to Bow Street. So far, he's refusing to talk. Bertrand and Rupert went with him. Addison's making sure Archie got the regent away. Harry's getting Carfax. Because, much as I never thought I'd say this, we're going to need Carfax to make sure the assassin isn't set free or murdered before we can get his story. I said I'd go to Bow Street as soon as I get bandaged up. But first I need to talk to Mel."

"There's someone else you need to talk to." Laura looked round the group, then back at Malcolm. "You need to find Lady Shroppington."

MÉLANIE WENT backstage after seeing the regent's carriage off. Sir Horace had refused to leave the theatre, but Frances and Archie had him in charge. She could hear Manon and Brandon speaking the lines of the last scene as she neared the stage. Simon was standing in the wings, the glow from the footlights slanting over him. He gave her a quick smile, but raised his brows in inquiry. Mélanie mouthed, "I'll tell you later," and went to stand beside him. Manon looked at Brandon and delivered the last line Mélanie had worked so hard to craft.

The curtain tumbled down on Gideon and Fiona's fragile rapprochement, and applause broke from the audience.

"Listen." Simon turned her towards the audience and put his hands on her shoulders. "You did that."

"Not me alone."

"No. But we couldn't have built this world without your words. Remember. For all the times in the future you'll struggle to get the words right." He pressed a kiss to the top of her head. "It's your moment. Drink it in."

"OH, RANNOCH." Lady Shroppington met Malcolm's gaze without apparent alarm, and with only mild surprise, as he stepped into her box. Half the occupants had left. The others, Lord and Lady Sheffield, a couple of Lady Shroppington's generation with whom Malcolm was slightly acquainted, were gathering up their things. "Should have thought you'd be busy congratulating your wife," Lady Shroppington continued. "I have to admit it was quite a diverting play. I don't agree with the points she was trying to make, but I'll concede she made them well, and it's a good story. She certainly writes as someone conversant with secrets in a marriage."

"I need to have a word with you. In private."

Lady Shroppington opened her mouth as though to protest, then looked at the Sheffields. "I'll see you in the lobby. There's sure to be a dreadful crush waiting for carriages, in any case."

Lady Sheffield drew her swansdown-edged cloak about her shoulders. "You're sure, Henrietta?"

"Yes, if I don't, Rannoch will be pestering me in the morning before I've finished my chocolate."

Lord Sheffield cast a hard glance at Malcolm, then gave his wife his arm and led her from the box.

Lady Shroppington regarded Malcolm. "With your beautiful wife to congratulate, why on earth are you wasting time on me?"

"I might say, to let you know your plot didn't work. But then, you know that, don't you? You probably knew it the moment the regent and his party left the royal box. I expect you're hoping your man realized his target was gone, and called the whole thing off. But he didn't have a view of the inside of the theatre. We caught him going into Emily Cowper's box."

Lady Shroppington's face gave nothing away. She was a match for Carfax and Raoul when it came to self-command. "My dear Mr. Rannoch, this story sounds more fanciful than your wife's play, and rather less coherent. I was a bit surprised Prinny left, as he seemed to be enjoying himself. But then, he's always been fickle. In any number of ways. But I can't imagine why you think it should be any concern of mine."

"Because you'd hired a marksman—probably a former rifleman—to shoot someone in the royal box."

Her brows shot up towards her elaborate waves of hair. "I beg your pardon? Mr. Rannoch, I don't know how many glasses of champagne you've consumed, but you seem to have me confused with your Leveller friends."

"It was clever." Malcolm leaned against the wall of the box, legs crossed at the ankle. "Carfax and his agent had fabricated a Radical assassination plot that was never meant to go further than some suspicious papers. You learned about it from Lewis—who had set himself to uncover Carfax's agent provocateur plots as a way to ingratiate himself with the Leveller leadership—and you decided it was an ideal way to get rid of Sir Horace Smytheton. It would be put down to an assassination plot gone awry, and discredit the Levellers into the bargain."

"Good lord, Mr. Rannoch." Her gaze showed a perfect combination of amazement, amusement, and beneath it, a touch of frustration. "I scarcely know where to begin. Why on earth should I wish to get rid of Horace Smytheton, of all people? Save for his questionable taste in marrying an actress, he's entirely blameless."

"An excellent question. Save that he's also a member of the Elsinore League and worked with Alistair Rannoch and Lord Dewhurst in France."

For the first time he thought he caught the faintest crack in her gaze. It revealed not fear, but a glint of implacable hardness. "What on earth is the Elsinore League? A theatrical society?"

"You undoubtedly know more about them than we do. We had no idea women had positions in the League until we learned about you. We also know Lewis was working for the League."

"Are you claiming I embroiled him in this society?"

"No, apparently my brother did that."

"Captain Rannoch? My dear Mr. Rannoch, I begin to fear for your mental state."

"But I think Lewis was reporting directly to you after Edgar died," Malcolm said. "He was trying to recover papers that may betray Alexander Radford's identity."

"Who the devil is Alexander Radford?"

"I only wish you would tell me. We still don't know. Save that he is trying to wrest away control of the Elsinore League from the founders and you are evidently working with him. But Lewis balked at killing Horace Smytheton. Or he decided to use what he knew to threaten you, so you'd agree to his marrying Letty Blanchard. In any case, you realized he was a liability." Malcolm studied her across the box. "I'll do you the credit of saying I think it cost you something to get rid of him."

Lady Shroppington's gaze settled on his own. The mask was gone, leaving only the hardness. "You can't prove a word of that, Mr. Rannoch."

"No," Malcolm agreed, "I can't. But I wanted you to know what I knew. For one thing, so you realize how any further action against Horace Smytheton will be met."

Lady Shroppington's gaze remained on his, steady as a sword's point. "I always knew you were a threat. From the time you were quite small."

"My dear Lady Shroppington. You didn't meet me until a few days ago."

"Officially. I have been aware of you for a very long time indeed, Rannoch."

A dozen questions race through Macolm's mimd as he met that steely gaze, but he merely said, "Good evening, Lady Shroppington. I imagine this is far from the last time we will speak."

"I DON'T UNDERSTAND," Sir Horace said. "Why on earth should they have wanted to kill me?"

"You're a member of the Elsinore League," Mélanie said.

"Yes, but I haven't had much to do with them in years, as I

said to you. Nothing at all, recently. Surely there's some mistake."

They were back in the green room, where they'd had their earlier conversation, and many of the same people were present, but now it smelled of fresh hothouse flowers, champagne, and delicacies sent over from Rules for the opening night party. Sir Horace had a glass of champagne in his hand, but he was frowning. Jennifer, sitting beside him on the sofa, looked like a lioness protecting her mate.

"There's a split in the League." Archie took a drink of champagne and stretched his bad leg out in front of him. He and Horace had known each other for years, and had once been members of the League together, though Archie had secretly been gathering information against them. "Someone is trying to take over. And that seems to involve getting rid of a number of the original members, one way or another. They targeted Glenister a few months ago."

Sir Horace looked up from contemplation of his champagne glass. "But I'm hardly on a par with Glenister. He was one of the founders."

"You worked with Alistair Rannoch in France," Mélanie said. "And he founded the League."

Horace frowned. Jennifer put a hand on his arm. She too had been in Paris in the eighties and nineties, and she had worked with Horace and Dewhurst and Alistair Rannoch in their activities supporting the Royalists. Save that Jennifer had actually been a spy for the revolutionary government. Which Horace now knew. "There were a number of secrets from those days, Horace."

"But why should those secrets matter now? I've never even heard of this Alexander Radford. Who the devil is he?"

Mélanie looked from Raoul and Laura to Julien and Kitty to Cordy. Malcolm, Harry, Bertrand, and Rupert were still at Bow Street. "We'd all very much like to know."

"Well, I don't see how I could be a threat to some man I've never met and don't know anything about." Sir Horace downed his champagne as though to punctuate his point.

"Do you think they'll try again?" Crispin Harleton asked. He was sitting by quietly, his arm round Manon.

"They haven't persisted in trying to kill me," Raoul said.

"So far," Laura pointed out.

"So far. And they seem to have left Glenister alone since their plans in September fell through. Perhaps—"

He broke off as the door opened and Malcolm and Harry came into the room, followed by Carfax, Rupert, and Bertrand.

"He's giving us his story," Carfax said. "Roth is taking it all down and getting him to sign it."

"And in exchange?" David asked.

"He's going to be transported. Not to Botany Bay, to Canada. Before the League can arrange a convenient accident for him."

"Who is he?" Simon asked.

"Rhys Tunstall," Harry said. "A former rifleman. I'd never met him before, but I'd heard him mentioned as a particularly deadly shot."

"I actually met him," Rupert said. "At a regimental dinner. Seemed perfectly innocuous. But then the best agents often do."

"He says Edgar recruited him and that they knew each other in the Peninsula." Malcolm moved to Mélanie's side and squeezed her shoulder. "And that with Edgar gone he's been taking orders from Lady Shroppington. He also became Lewis Thornsby's main contact with the League when Edgar died. Apparently Lady Shroppington wished to remain somewhat removed from League business when it came to her great-nephew. Though she doesn't seem to have caviled at it with Miss Simmons." He turned to Edith.

"But then I wasn't related to her," Edith said. "We had no outside relationship to muddy up. In fact, she was very concerned to keep me in my place when it came to Thomas."

Malcolm nodded. "A good point. In any case, Tunstall admits to meeting Lewis Thornsby at the theatre several times, including about a week ago when Lewis complained that his work among the Levellers was starting to feel like treason because he was betraying people he liked."

"That must be the conversation I overheard," Letty said.

"I think so, yes," Malcolm said. "Tunstall says a few days later Lady Shroppington gave directions that the papers Kitty and Simon and Kit were trying to have printed must be recovered at all costs. Despite Thornsby's qualms, apparently he set about that readily enough. Then he discovered the League were planning to make use of the rifle trajectory drawing he'd stolen from Donald McDevitt and use the plot to get rid of Sir Horace. Tunstall says Lady Shroppington summoned him the night before the murder, probably just after she had the confrontation with Thornsby that Miss Simmons heard about from her friend. Lady Shroppington told Tunstall that Thornsby had become too dangerous and had to be got rid of."

Silence settled over the green room, weighted with the stark horror of premeditated murder. Mélanie gripped the bare skin of her arms, between her ivory silk gloves and her lace sleeves. They all had known Thornsby had been murdered. They were most of them hardened agents. And yet hearing it put like that—

"So Tunstall killed Lewis?" Letty said in a small voice.

Malcolm nodded again. "He says he arranged to meet Thornsby at the theatre, supposedly to negotiate. Thornsby apparently didn't have a clue how ruthless his great-aunt could be and wasn't on his guard. Tunstall says he left the rifle trajectory sketch on Thornsby because it would cast suspicion on the Levellers and muddy the waters about who might be behind Lewis's death. Because Carfax knew there wasn't an actual plot, they weren't worried about precautions tonight. And then once Sir Horace was killed, it would look like a failed assassination attempt on the regent and the Levellers would be blamed. And

Carfax couldn't very well say otherwise without implicating himself."

"I confess it never occurred to me how the sketch might be used," Carfax said. "An error."

David shot a look at his father.

"I've never claimed not to make them," Carfax said.

"There's more," Bertrand said. "Tunstall says Lady Shroppington tried to task him with killing Kitty and the others involved in printing the pamphlets. Apparently she'd bribed one of the messengers carrying notes between all of you and got wind of the meeting. But Tunstall says he drew the line at killing a woman."

Kitty snorted. "The man draw odd lines. But I'm very glad he drew this one. I suspect he'd have been much more successful than the attackers we did face."

"Quite." Malcolm's face was grim. "She had to scramble to hire those ruffians, which accounts for their less than spectacular level of skill. Tunstall also said he refused because—"

"What?" Kitty said.

"That it would be as good as his life to kill Julien St. Juste's woman."

"I'm not anyone's woman," Kitty said, "but he had a point."

"He did indeed," Julien said in a quiet voice that was somehow lethal.

"Did he say why Lady Shroppington and the League wanted Horace dead?" Jennifer asked.

"He claims not to know," Malcolm said. "Just as he claims not to know who Alexander Radford is. And I'm inclined to think he's telling the truth. He was a hired agent, not a League member."

"Is there anything more in the papers Thornsby left?" Cordelia asked.

"Unfortunately no," Aline said. "Most of the rest sum up what we already knew. And there's a long personal message for Miss

Blanchard." She looked at Letty. "I've saved a copy of that just for you."

Letty swallowed. "Thank you."

"We won't be able to act against Lady Shroppingon," Carfax said in a crisp voice. "But I'll make sure she knows what we have from Tunstall in writing." He looked at Sir Horace. "It should be enough to keep you safe. But you'll have to be on your guard."

"We're always on our guard, Lord Carfax," Jennifer said.

Carfax nodded. "Roth will assign a patrol to keep watch on your house."

"And Lewis?" Letty asked.

"There's no way to convict Lady Shroppington for his murder any more than for the attack on Sir Horace," Carfax said.

"You mean you don't want the messiness of trying to convict her," Will said. He was perched on the arm of the settee where Letty sat.

"That too," Carfax said. "But practically, it would be extremely difficult."

"We'll make sure Thomas knows the truth, at least." Harry turned to Edith, who was sitting beside Cordelia. "He can decide what to say to his parents."

Carfax frowned as though he was not best pleased with this, but did not attempt to argue.

"Thank you," Edith said. "I need to talk to Thomas too. He needs to know the truth. The full truth."

"You can't go back to the Wiltons'," Cordelia said. "It's not safe. Lady Shroppington may put things together about you, now that she knows Malcolm's worked out the truth. You can come home with us, at least until you decide what you want to do."

"Perhaps you'd be willing to help me with the children's lessons," Laura said. "We've been looking into starting a school for disadvantaged children on one of the Rannochs' country properties, and I'd very much welcome your thoughts."

Edith started to protest, then shook her head. "I'm not so selfless as to cavil at good fortune. But the Wiltons—"

"I'll warn Wilton about Lady Shroppington and the League," Carfax said. "And get his opinion of Antonio Barosa." He glanced at Malcolm. "You should probably talk to him as well in case I've missed something."

Malcolm nodded. "Thank you."

Carfax gave a grunt of acknowledgment.

"We can call on the Wiltons as well," Cordelia said to Edith. "I know you'll want to see the children."

"I can come with you to see Thomas if you want," Harry said.

Edith met his gaze. "Thank you, Colonel, Davenport. I can't tell you how much that means to me. But I need to do this on my own."

Harry nodded, quiet appreciation in his gaze.

"I meant to come see you tomorrow, in any case, Miss Simmons," Malcolm said. "To tell you your brother's debts have been discharged. The League have no hold on him anymore."

Edith stared at him. "Why are you being so kind to me? I was working for your enemy."

"Among other things, because I don't like to see the League win," Malcolm said. "But more than that, because I have sympathy for anyone who's been in their clutches."

"And Lady Shroppington?" Sofia asked. She was sharing an overstuffed armchair with Kit. "Who's going to stop her?"

"We are." Malcolm's gaze swept the company. "But we're going to have to learn what she's after first."

CHAPTER 44

Julien looked down at the boys in their nursery beds and pulled the door to, then glanced at Genny in her cradle. Sound asleep, a spit bubble on her lip, her arm round the stuffed unicorn he'd bought at a stall in Covent Garden Market the morning after he realized she was his daughter. He'd spent the night before holding Kitty, both of them fully clothed, and slipped out early in the morning to find Gisèle and tell her he had killed her brother Edgar before Edgar could kill Malcolm. And somehow, on the way he'd found himself clutching a mug of coffee, staring at white fabric and gold yarn and embroidered eyes and nose and mouth, while the reality that he was a father washed over him. He'd fished out his purse and tucked the toy into his coat, and for all the pain the day held, he'd felt strangely new born. Genny had been asleep that night when he'd tucked the unicorn into the crook of her arm. The boys had been asleep too, but looking at them, realizing what he might be to Genny, he'd begun to have a sense of what he might be to them too.

Kitty had come up beside him as he'd looked down at Genny that night and slid her hand into his own. It had been a moment of dreadful sentiment, the sort they both shied away from, the sort neither of them would put into words. But they'd stood there for what might have been minutes, drinking in the sight of Genny sleeping, before Kitty turned and stepped into his arms.

Now, four months later, Julien turned to look at the woman who had become his wife. Nothing was really different. Oh, it was different from that night, when everything had been tentative and new. But they'd been putting the children to bed, and walking or stumbling to—or tumbling into—their own bed (even if it was only to fall into exhausted slumber in each other's arms) for weeks now. The fact that they were legally bound to each other didn't change what was between them. He wouldn't want it to. And yet—

"I know," Kitty said. "We're married."

"And Lord and Lady Carfax, apparently."

"Don't remind me. I was just getting used to the first." She went up to him and slid her arms round him. "It's odd," she said, leaning back to look up at him. "It doesn't seem strange to be married to you. I thought it would, but it feels oddly as though I couldn't be anything else. I'm going to stare round in confusion, wondering who is being addressed, the first time someone calls me Lady Carfax, though."

Julien grimaced. "Carfax wants us to move into Carfax House. I told him he was welcome to keep it, but he insists. We needn't live there if you prefer not to, though."

Kitty glanced round the bedchamber, the door to the nursery, the other door to the sitting room. "We can't very well stay here."

Julien looked from door to door at the space that had shaped their lives. "No, I suppose not. Pity, though. I'm quite fond of it." It was the only home he had shared properly with anyone in his forty years.

"Carfax House must have been your home as a boy."

"It was never really a home. But yes, I lived there."

"*We* needn't live there. Just because Malcolm and Mélanie made Berkeley Square their own doesn't mean we need to follow suit."

"No, we don't need to. But Carfax House can be a powerful symbol. And we're going to need a base for what we want to accomplish."

"I don't want to raise the children in a symbol."

"Of course not. If we don't think we can make it work for us, we'll let it or sell it and find somewhere else. Berkeley Square is a beautiful house, but I don't think either of us has the time that Mélanie spent on it to spend on Carfax House. It has a decent garden though, and the gates can be useful. And there are plenty of rooms."

Kitty watched him for a moment. "Julien—"

"Only if you want to," he said. "I told Carfax that. And also that if we did, we wouldn't go on until we had a son."

"It's funny." Kitty drew the folds of her dressing gown about her throat. "I didn't think I wanted children at all, particularly. Or more accurately, I didn't think about it much at all. I love Leo—you know how much—but it would be folly to say I was anything but unhappy about my pregnancy. But once he was there—his own person, not a reminder of his father—it meant something else entirely. I wanted him to have a sibling. And I wasn't unhappy when I realized I was carrying Genny. Partly because it was a reminder of you."

"You might have told me."

"You were an ocean away. I was married to Edward, and I didn't think you had any interest in having a family."

He had a keen memory of the boat from Buenos Aires. Looking back at the harbor, wondering if he would see Kitty again. He was used to saying goodbye to lovers. Sometimes with more qualms than others. But he couldn't deny he'd felt a pang as the city receded into the distance. He wouldn't have admitted he had perhaps said goodbye to the love of his life. But he had been keenly aware that he'd said farewell to the person who understood him better than anyone else. "I didn't particularly," he said. "Not then. But if I'd known I had a child—"

"Whom you couldn't acknowledge."

"I'm not entirely free of feeling an obligation. And I'd have wanted to know her. Even if she couldn't know who I was."

Kitty put her hands on his chest. "I wasn't trying to keep her from you."

"Sweetheart, you had a right to navigate matters however you could. And I'll freely confess to having attempted to give even more of an illusion of not wanting ties than I in fact did."

She watched him for a moment, her wonderful green eyes very steady. "If I'd stayed in Argentina—"

He put his hands over her own. "Yes, well, we needn't confront that now. But I think I'd have found a way to go back." He looked down at their fingers, interlaced against the blue velvet of his dressing gown. "Mélanie asked me once if Josephine was my first love."

Kitty's gaze flickered over his face. "What did you say?"

"That I was young enough that she might have been. But as it happens, she wasn't."

"Who was?"

"I'm looking at her."

Kitty drew in her breath slightly.

"Falling in love is difficult enough. You can't imagine I'd do it more than I had to."

Laughter convulsed her. "Darling Julien. You make romantic declarations like no one else."

There were other things he'd never told her and probably never would. At least, not in so many words. That he found a peace with her he'd never known in his life before. That the thought of being without her sent him spiraling into terror. That he knew what happiness was now, when he'd never really even considered it a possibility.

Her gaze settled on his own. "I never answered you. I'd have said I was happy with three children. But I think I want one with you."

Feelings he couldn't quite articulate tumbled within him. "You have a child with me. One could say you have three. You certainly have one."

"I know. And I'd say three too. But I want one where we can do it together from the start."

He felt his fingers tighten involuntarily over her own. "You don't need to do that for me."

"I'm not. I'm doing it because it's what I want. Though I suppose you could say I'm doing it for us. Funny." She shook her head. "Not a word I'm used to."

"Nor I."

"Not for a bit, though. The children have a lot to adjust to."

"Probably a good idea for you to see what sort of a father I make first."

"Darling Julien, I've watched you be an excellent father for months now. I know I accused you of playing at domesticity, but the truth is you were uncannily good at it from the start. I only worried you might decide you wanted something else. Not other than the children. Other than me."

Julien pressed a kiss to the tip of her nose. "For a sensible woman, you can take some surprising ideas into your head, Kitkat."

"You've been free for a long time, Julien. You valued your freedom so much you stayed away from home for a quarter century."

"That was a bit more because I valued my life."

"If you really wanted to come back, you could have found a way to do it. Especially of late."

"Perhaps. I think you may be overrating my abilities. But it's true I was quite convinced I preferred not to have ties. No risk of anyone's getting hurt. But I wouldn't say I was a martyr. I couldn't see what all the fuss was about."

"My point precisely."

"I was already weakening by Argentina, my love. I'd seen enough real moments between people—even Hortense and Flahaut, who didn't last—to have a sense of what it might be worth. When something seems to make so many people happy, one has to wonder."

"It also makes people unhappy."

"A fair point." Julien scanned his wife's face. So familiar, yet it would always challenge him, he thought. "I have doubts, Kitkat. About the sort of father and husband I'll make. About managing the Carfax heritage without letting it consume me. About not letting Uncle Hubert control me. But I don't doubt my feelings for you. And I don't worry I'll want to go back into the shadows. I know too well how happy I am to have escaped them." He hesitated a moment, gaze locked on her own. "Of course, you could be pardoned for having all manner of doubts."

"Oh, I do. About being Lady Carfax. About trying to navigate that world. About what on earth we're going to do with Carfax House. About your Uncle Hubert, and perhaps even more about your Aunt Amelia. About my own abilities to be a partner in a relationship. Two words which sound rather laughable, given my history—well, relationship more than partner. A fellow agent can be partner, and I've managed that well enough. But my romantic history is undoubtedly a sad tangle. But I don't have doubts about you, Julien. I don't have doubts about my feelings for you. Which is why I'm willing to risk this. And absurdly happy to have the chance to try." She shook her head. "We sound rather solemn, don't we?"

"We sound like two people rather confounded by our good fortune. Which is entirely logical in my case, and quite inexplicable in yours."

She slid her hands up his chest and linked them behind his

neck. "I meant it, Julien. I trust you. And I'm not worried you'll change your mind anymore."

"I should hope not. The truth is, my darling, anything less than what we have sounds hopelessly drab and lacking in excitement." He gave her a crooked smile, then kissed her. The kiss of a partner to a partner, a parent to a parent. Of someone coming home.

AFTER UPDATING Nerezza and Ben on the events of the evening, Malcolm and Mélanie, Raoul and Laura looked in on the children, whom Blanca and Addison had brought home long since, and then said goodnight outside the night nursery door. Given that she couldn't remember when she'd last slept more than five hours, Mélanie knew she should be exhausted, but between the play and the investigation, every nerve in her body thrummed with energy.

"Tonight leaves a lot of interesting avenues to explore," Raoul said.

"So it does." Malcolm met his father's gaze, then looked at Laura. "With everything else, have I thanked you for working out Edith Simmons' past and at the same time gaining her confidence?"

"I simply followed the facts to a logical conclusion," Laura said. "But I confess it was quite satisfying to turn what I learned about the League against them. And I think Edith Simmons may prove an interesting ally."

"So do I," Mélanie said. "I quite like her."

Laura nodded. "I was so relieved she turned on the League, and then so worried I'd put her in danger."

"The life of a spymaster," Raoul said.

Laura turned to him. "I'm not—"

"You turned an agent and had her reporting to you sweetheart." Raoul kissed her hand. "And you managed it far more ably than I did at the start."

They turned to go, but Raoul looked back, hand on the door. "It was a memorable night for a number of reasons, but not least because of the play. I don't think you've ever impressed me more, Mélanie. Which is saying a lot."

Mélanie looked at her former spymaster and felt a smile break across her face. "I'm glad you were all there."

In their bedchamber, Malcolm stripped off his cravat and stared at the crumpled linen. "I can't believe I missed half the last act."

Mélanie unfastened the pendant he'd given her before they left for the theatre—it seemed so much longer ago than the few hours it in fact was. "You've seen plenty of rehearsals. And there'll be another performance tomorrow night."

"I know. But tonight was special." Malcolm walked to her side and took her in his arms. "Raoul was right. There was magic in the air."

"Is that what they're calling assassination plots these days?"

"The magic was there long before we knew about the plot." He touched her face. "You created something. A world that seemed more real than our own. Despite everything else we were going through."

She scanned his face, scarcely able to articulate how much his words meant to her. "Darling—thank you."

He nodded and pressed a kiss to her forehead.

"What are we going to do next?" she asked. "About Lady Shroppington?"

"Gather information. Fortunately, as spies we're all quite well suited to that. We've learned a great deal in the past few days. But in many ways, it's just pointed up how much we don't yet know."

"I asked Harry and Cordy and Frances and Archie and Julien and Kitty to come round in the morning," she said. "I'll ask

Rupert and Bertrand as well. And I think we should include David and Simon."

"So do I," Malcolm said without hesitation. She didn't remark on it, but she took note of how much his relationship with David had shifted.

"And Carfax?" she asked.

"Not until the rest of us have made a plan of action."

Mélanie rested her hands on his chest. "I don't think any of us need fear being bored."

He looked at her for a moment. "I don't want to delay your starting on your next play."

She smiled at him, the different parts of her world shifting in her brain. It was a juggling act. But then, when had her life ever been anything else? "I think I can do both, dearest."

Malcolm grinned and pulled her closer. "Yes," he said. "So do I."

A READING GROUP GUIDE

The Tavistock Plot

About This Guide

The suggested questions are included to enhance your group's reading of Tracy Grant's *The Tavistock Plot*.

1. How do you think Mélanie managed balancing being a playwright and an investigator?
2. Who do you think has changed more in the eight years between the Prologue and Chapter 1, Julien or Mélanie?
3. Malcolm is concerned that the investigation will put Mélanie and him and Raoul and him on opposite sides because they will disagree about which tactics to support to bring about change. Do you think this is a dilemma they will face in the future?
4. Do you feel differently about Lord Carfax by the end of the book?
5. How you think Mélanie's becoming a playwright has impacted the Rannochs' marriage? How was this

investigation different from others they have undertaken?

6. Malcolm wonders if he'd be happier fighting outside the system as a Leveller than inside it as an MP. What do you think?
7. What do the choices faced by Lewis and Letty and Thomas and Edith say about the role economics played in marriage in the Regency era?
8. What do you think of Julien's actions in the *Unicorn* rebellion? How do they relate to Malcolm's debate with Will about what steps to take to bring about political change?
9. What do you think lies ahead for Kitty and Julien? Do you think Kitty will be happier with Julien than she would have been with Malcolm? Why?
10. Compare and contrast Will and Julien.
11. What do you think lies ahead for Letty and Will?
12. What do you think lies ahead for Edith and Thomas?
13. How do you think Alexander Radford is connected to Lady Shroppington?

ALSO BY TRACY GRANT

Traditional Regencies

WIDOW'S GAMBIT

FRIVOLOUS PRETENCE

THE COURTING OF PHILIPPA

Lescaut Quartet

DARK ANGEL

SHORES OF DESIRE

SHADOWS OF THE HEART

RIGHTFULLY HIS

The Rannoch Fraser Mysteries

HIS SPANISH BRIDE

LONDON INTERLUDE

VIENNA WALTZ

IMPERIAL SCANDAL

THE PARIS AFFAIR

THE PARIS PLOT

BENEATH A SILENT MOON

THE BERKELEY SQUARE AFFAIR

THE MAYFAIR AFFAIR

INCIDENT IN BERKELEY SQUARE

LONDON GAMBIT

MISSION FOR A QUEEN

GILDED DECEIT

MIDWINTER INTRIGUE

THE DUKE'S GAMBIT

SECRETS OF A LADY

THE MASK OF NIGHT

THE DARLINGTON LETTERS

THE GLENISTER PAPERS

A MIDWINTER'S MASQUERADE

THE TAVISTOCK PLOT

ABOUT THE AUTHOR

Tracy Grant studied British history at Stanford University and received the Firestone Award for Excellence in Research for her honors thesis on shifting conceptions of honor in late-fifteenth-century England. She lives in the San Francisco Bay Area with her young daughter and three cats. In addition to writing, Tracy works for the Merola Opera Program, a professional training program for opera singers, pianists, and stage directors. Her real life heroine is her daughter Mélanie, who is very cooperative about Mummy's writing time. She is currently at work on her next book chronicling the adventures of Malcolm and Mélanie Suzanne Rannoch. Visit her on the Web at www.tracygrant.org

Cover photo by Kristen Loken.

ABOUT THE AUTHOR

Tracy Grant studied British history at Stanford University and received the Firestone Award for Excellence in Research for her honors thesis on shifting conceptions of honor in late-fifteenth-century England. She lives in the San Francisco Bay Area with her young daughter and three cats. In addition to writing, Tracy works for the Merola Opera Program, a professional training program for opera singers, pianists, and stage directors. Her real life heroine is her daughter Mélanie, who is very cooperative about Mummy's writing time. She is currently at work on her next book chronicling the adventures of Malcolm and Mélanie Rannoch. Visit her on the Web at www.tracygrant.org

Photo Credit: Kristen Loken

facebook.com/tracygrant
twitter.com/tracygrant
amazon.com/Tracy-Grant

Printed in Poland
by Amazon Fulfillment
Poland Sp. z o.o., Wrocław

58334160R00271